PULP

Also by Robin Talley

LIES WE TELL OURSELVES
WHAT WE LEFT BEHIND
AS I DESCENDED
OUR OWN PRIVATE UNIVERSE

PULP

ROBIN TALLEY

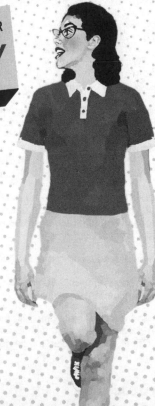

HARLEQUIN® TEEN

ISBN-13: 978-1-335-01290-6

Pulp

Copyright © 2018 by Robin Talley

Printed in U.S.A.

To the rich community of queer writers, editors and publishers
who changed the world so many times over and are still changing it today.

Friday, September 15, 2017

It took all of Abby's willpower not to kiss her.

She'd gotten pretty good lately at staring at Linh without making it obvious. Most of the time, at least. Some days were harder than others, though, and today might be the hardest yet.

They'd just gotten back from a Starbucks run, and Abby kept darting looks at Linh out of the corner of her eye. They were sitting only inches apart on the lumpy old couch in the senior lounge, and as Linh sipped her drink and scribbled in her notebook, Abby couldn't shake the memory of precisely how the echo of iced coffee tasted on Linh's lips.

She knew she should stop thinking about this. Or at the very least, she should *pretend* to stop. She and Linh were officially "just friends" now, for reasons Abby was still trying to forget, and she was supposed to be doing her very best to act like that arrangement was perfectly fine with her.

So as she sat next to Linh, her feet tucked under her, Abby really did try to focus on the laptop screen balanced on her knees. Even though it was basically impossible to tear her eyes away from the spot where Linh's soft brown hair curled into the nape of her perfectly sloped neck.

The senior lounge was nothing special—just a tiny room in a far-off corner of the fourth floor, with a few couches and a dusty TV that had probably last worked in the nineties—and everyone at school except Abby and Linh seemed to have forgotten it existed. Which made it the perfect place for Abby to secretly pine after her ex-girlfriend, since no one else was around to notice and make fun of her for it.

"I can't believe Mr. Knight already wants my first lab done by Monday." Linh wrinkled her nose down at her notes. Abby didn't know if it was good or bad that Linh was so oblivious to her silent yearning. "Don't the teachers know fall of senior year is supposed to be about college applications? We shouldn't have to start our projects until next semester."

Abby didn't want to talk about college applications or senior projects, but she *did* like it when Linh made that cute wrinkly-nose face. "Yeah, you're totally right."

"Do you have something due next week, too? What did you pick for your topic anyway?"

Abby scooted over to peer down at what Linh was writing. It was a blatant and probably pathetic attempt to get close to her, but Linh didn't seem to mind. She glanced up at Abby with a smile and went back to jotting notes about molecular techniques.

When they were this close, it was so easy to remember how it used to feel. Kissing her. Being encircled in a pair of arms that had no intention of letting her go.

Kissing was Abby's favorite activity in the entire world.

It was pure sensation. When you were kissing someone, all you had to do was follow your instincts. There was no point stopping to worry about what came next.

That was the best part of being in love. The way it set the rest of the world on mute.

"So for real, what are you going to write? Poetry?" Linh finally met her eyes, and Abby blushed. Ugh, as if she wasn't transparent enough already.

Not that Linh seemed to mind that, either.

"Nah, I've decided my poetry sucks." Abby tried to arrange her face into a casual smile. They were halfway through their free period, and she was determined to get through the rest without giving herself away. "In eighth grade I had to write a love poem for French, and the best I could do was *Je t'aime, ma puce, je t'aime tellement.*"

Linh took Chinese, not French, so she asked, "What does *puce* mean?"

"Flea." They both laughed.

It would be so easy to close the space between them. Last year, that was exactly what Abby would've done. Linh would've leaned in, too, and they would've kissed, and everything would've been perfect. No need for pining or pretending.

But this wasn't last year, so Abby forced herself to keep talking instead. "No, but in France calling someone your *flea* is the same as calling them, like, *sweetie* or something."

"You wrote a poem about how much you adore your sweet pet flea?" Linh grinned.

"Basically."

Their faces were still only inches apart, but Linh had made no effort to move away. Was Abby imagining it, or was there some decidedly nonplatonic tension in the air this afternoon?

When they'd broken up, back in June, Abby had been sure it was temporary. They were both going out of town for the summer, Linh to visit family in Vietnam and Abby to creative writing camp in Massachusetts, but once they were back home in DC she was positive they'd put their summer-of-breakup behind them.

So far, though, there had been no definitive progress in that direction. Sometimes the two of them still acted mildly flirty with each other, and sometimes they acted like friends. But since Linh never gave any clear signals of what she wanted, they seemed stuck in this constant awkward limbo.

And so, once again, Abby kept talking.

"It was the only term of endearment I could find that was always female." Abby tried to sound breezy. "You know how I was back then—all about the gay."

"Oh, as opposed to now." Linh smiled again.

Okay, this really, *really* felt like flirting. And more than just the mild kind.

Abby loved flirting almost as much as she loved kissing. She loved all the trappings of romance. Sending flowers on Valentine's Day. Picking each other up for dances. Posing for couple-y selfies and going for long walks in the park hand in hand on sunny afternoons.

And being held. Abby loved being held most of all.

She should know better than to get her hopes up. It had been months since there was anything romantic between her and Linh. Still...

"Well, I have a more nuanced understanding of gendered nouns these days." Abby held her gaze. She remembered how to flirt, too. "I'm still all about the gay, though."

"Obviously." Linh laughed again. "So when's your project plan due anyway?"

Oh, who *cared* about the stupid project plan?

Abby broke eye contact. She flopped back against the couch, and the moment between them evaporated in an instant.

Everything had been going so well. Why did Linh have to keep asking about her project? Sometimes Abby wished she went to one of those schools you saw in shows, where everyone cut class and no one cared about homework.

"I keep forgetting." Abby turned away. "I just need to pick my genre."

"What? You don't even know when it's *due?*" Linh's tone shifted from flirty to concerned. "Do you seriously not have any ideas at all?"

Abby squirmed, but this time she didn't laugh.

Fawcett was a magnet school, and all the seniors had to do a yearlong thesis project. Linh was doing a big, complicated experiment Abby didn't understand for her Molecular Techniques and Neuroscience Research class, and Abby had chosen to do hers in Advanced Creative Writing. She was supposed to write a novel, or a collection of short stories or poems that was long enough to be a novel.

Usually, for Abby, coming up with creative writing ideas meant choosing from the dozens of possibilities that had already been circling through her mind. This time, though, she was at a loss. The creative part of her brain had fizzled sometime around the day she and Linh broke up.

Or maybe her *entire* brain had fizzled. That would explain a lot, come to think of it. Lately, Abby seemed incapable of remembering anything she was supposed to do except obsess over her ex.

"This is a big deal, Abby." Linh sat up, putting way too much space between them. "I turned in my plan two weeks ago. If you don't get started soon, how will you have time left for your college applications?"

"I know, I know." Abby tried to think of some explanation that would get Linh off her back. "My brother's been sucking up all my time lately. I keep having to take him to dance class since my parents are always out of town."

The truth was, just *thinking* about college applications made her shudder. She hated how competitive everyone got over that stuff. As though they were all suddenly reduced to SATs and GPAs and other quantitative acronyms that had nothing to do with who they really were. And the essays weren't any better. How could anyone seriously sum up their view on the world in five hundred words?

Senior projects were the same way. Everyone at Fawcett obsessed over them as if they were curing cancer or painting the Sistine Chapel instead of doing glorified science fair projects and book reports.

"Hey, maybe I could get credit for writing *Broken Dreams* fanfic." Abby grinned. "Do you think I could just write a bunch of short stories about Velma being a lesbian and change the names?"

That did the trick. Linh laughed and pulled off Abby's cat-eye glasses, balancing them on the tip of her own nose.

Okay, this couldn't only be happening in Abby's head. They were *definitely* flirting.

"You and your fifties obsession." Linh flipped the glasses up at Abby, giggling. "That show's been canceled for, what, a year?"

"Two years. Anyway, *Broken Dreams* wasn't the fifties, it was the early sixties." Abby smiled and grabbed her glasses back. As much as she wanted to keep up the playful vibe, she couldn't let Linh have her glasses. Abby loved how they looked, but she could also barely see without them.

"Is *Broken Dreams* fanfic even a thing?" Linh asked.

"Definitely." Abby slid her glasses back on and reached for her laptop. "Want to read about Walter and Earl getting it on in the back of the accounting office?"

"Ew. Although kind of, now that you mention it." Linh pulled the computer onto her lap and started a search.

Abby laughed. In ninth grade, she and Linh used to read fanfic together every day. They were obsessed with a dumb show called *The Flighted Ones*. Their favorite pairing was Owen/Jack, or "Ojack," as the true fans called them. Abby had stayed up late at night writing long, overwrought stories describing Ojack's first date, or their first kiss, or their First Time. (This was back before Abby had had a First Time of her own, so writing fictional versions felt deliciously scandalous.)

"Ha, look at this." Linh turned the screen so Abby could see it. "Someone made a list of all the gay stuff that ever happened on this show. Do you remember a woman trying to lick Velma's neck?"

"What? No!" As Abby leaned in to see the screen, an ad off to the side of the main article caught her eye.

In the image, a woman in a tight red dress with a gorgeous flipped hairstyle stood behind a bed. In front of her another woman, wearing an old-fashioned skirt and blouse, was lying down. The words *I PREFER GIRLS* loomed beside them in giant red font.

Abby pointed. "What's that?"

"Huh, I don't know." Linh clicked on the image. "Are those characters from *Broken Dreams*?"

"I don't think so. Those look like fifties outfits to me."

If there was one thing Abby knew, it was fifties fashion.

She'd been a devotee since middle school. She used to make her own fifties-inspired outfits, starting with simple wrap tops and pencil skirts, until the year her grandparents gave her a sewing machine for Hanukkah and she upgraded to sailor suits and cocktail dresses.

Finding the old patterns and sewing them was fun, but it took forever. After she'd spent months making her prom dress sophomore year, Abby decided she'd had enough of ironing musty old fabrics and sorting through tangled piles of thread. Now her sewing machine sat in the attic and she ordered retro-style clothes online.

Which meant the outfits were the first thing Abby noticed when Linh clicked through to the page with a bigger version of the same image. The women under the *I Prefer Girls* label were dressed simply—a clingy sleeveless dress on one, a pink blouse and black skirt on the other. The blouse was unbuttoned nearly down to the woman's waist, so you could see her slip beneath. Or maybe that was her bra.

The page's headline read "The Best of 1950s Lesbian Pulp Fiction."

"Wait a second. Is this *seriously* from the fifties?" Abby pulled the computer onto her own lap. "Is that a *book* cover?"

"I didn't know they had lesbian porn back then." Linh leaned in to see. "Oh, wait. There's another one— Wow. Scroll down."

Abby scrolled. Below the picture of *I Prefer Girls* was another cover. This one was called *Warped Women*, and it also featured a woman in a red dress. She was holding a whip and leaning threateningly over another woman who was crouched on the floor. The crouching woman's blouse was unbuttoned, and underneath she was wearing a black lace bra. Her left boob was basically hanging out of it.

"What kind of books *are* these?" Linh's mouth was agape.

Abby kept scrolling. Image after image, with more of the same. The covers showed women in varying states of undress, and they had titles like *When Lesbians Strike* and *My Wife the Dyke* and *Twilight Girl*. The captions beside each cover listed publication dates—1963, 1955, 1959, 1965...

"Fifties lesbian porn." Linh laughed harder than ever. "Hey, I think we've found your genre!"

"Can you even imagine?" Abby kept scrolling. The images got sexier the farther she went. "I can't believe they got away with this. I mean, there aren't even books like this *today*, as far as I know. Plus, they had censors in the fifties. That's why all the movies sucked."

"Here, let's make a new one. For your senior project." Linh leaped to her feet and grabbed the cement column that stood next to the couch. She pulled down the neckline of her T-shirt, stuck out her chest, lifted one knee onto a cushion and tilted her head forward, imitating the woman on the cover of the last book on the page, *Dormitory Women*. "Did I get it right?"

All Abby could think was that there should be a law banning your ex-girlfriend from doing sexy poses in front of you before you'd officially gotten back together. Seriously, this had to be a legitimate form of torture.

But she did her best to keep acting nonchalant as she held up the computer screen to compare. Linh *did* look kind of like the woman on the painted cover, with her dark hair and thick eyebrows, even though Linh's warm eyes and inviting smile were a thousand times prettier than the cover model's. Not to mention that Linh was wearing a T-shirt and cutoffs, and the *Dormitory Women* model was in a tight white blouse and severely belted skirt.

"Hmm—I think your hand needs to be lower down…" Abby carefully adjusted the position of Linh's hand on her thigh and brushed her hair forward over one shoulder, trying to act as if her intentions were solely artistic. As if touching Linh didn't activate any still-in-love-with-her segments of Abby's brain, or other body parts. "Pout your lips more. There, that's perfect." Abby lifted her phone and snapped a photo.

"You do one next." Linh pointed her chin toward the laptop screen.

"Okay!" Abby scrolled until she found a cover she liked. The book was called *Woman Doctor*, and the cover showed a woman, a psychiatrist apparently, sitting in a chair taking notes on a pad while a younger woman with curly blond hair lay on a couch behind her. The whole design seemed to be some bizarre male fantasy, because the patient appeared to have gone to her therapy appointment wearing an old-fashioned slip and nothing else.

Abby's hair was brown, straight and boringly plain instead of blond, thick and curly like the woman on the cover's, and she was wearing a green shirtdress instead of a tight-fitting slip. Still, she tried to imitate the patient's pose, throwing herself facedown on the couch and twisting so that her butt and her boobs were angled toward Linh at the same time. "Ow. This is not a natural position. *Ow.*"

"That's awesome, though. You've almost got it, but you need to pull your hair over your face more."

Abby pulled. "How's that?"

"Better." Linh laughed and reached for her phone. Abby laughed, too, lifting her head from the cushion. "Hey! You're breaking the pose. I didn't get a photo yet."

"I can't help it. I'm a warped woman!"

Linh was still laughing, but when she sat back down she

moved to the other couch, putting two armrests between them. Abby sat up, trying not to let her disappointment show, and tugged the hem of her dress back down.

"I want to read one of those books." Linh pointed to Abby's computer. "I bet they're hilarious. Plus, those covers are pretty hot."

"The covers are basically just ads for cleavage."

"There are worse things to advertise."

"True." Abby flushed. "Let's find an ebook."

She balanced her computer on her knees and turned so Linh could see the screen, then ran a search for *lesbian pulp fiction*. While the results loaded, Abby drummed her fingers on the edge of her laptop and tried to think of a good excuse for her to move to the other couch, too.

"Huh, okay, so there's like five million results." Linh pointed to the screen. "Here, that one has a list."

Abby clicked through and skimmed the article. "I was right about the censors. This says the books basically always ended with someone either turning straight or dying. Otherwise the publishers could've gone to jail."

"Whatever, I don't care. I just want to read the sex scenes."

Abby laughed, delighted, and scrolled down. The article had a list of books at the bottom, with more of those ridiculous covers. "These titles are so weird. *Strange Sisters. In the Shadows. Voluptuous Vixens.*"

"*Voluptuous Vixens?*" There was so much glee in Linh's voice that Abby giggled, too.

"*Edge of Twilight. The Third Sex. A Love So Strange.*"

"Boring. See if you can find that *Warped Women* one."

"Hey, wait, the article says this other one's good. And it's free to download." Abby cleared her throat and read.

"The classic and enduringly popular novel of two young girls coming of age in Greenwich Village. The story's heroines, Paula and Elaine, stand alongside such classic lesbian pulp characters as Beebo Brinker and Leda Taylor."

Linh cracked up. *"Beebo?* What kind of names are these?"

"Fifties names. Here, get this—the author's name is 'Marian Love.' So cheesy. Her book came out in 1956. It's called *Women of the Twilight Realm.*"

"Why do so many of these books have *Twilight* in their name? Is there lesbian vampire subtext?"

"Well, I'm downloading it, so I guess we'll find out. Wow, check it out, this cover is cheese-tastic, too."

The image on the screen had rips running through it, as though someone had taken a photo of an old, beaten-up copy of the book and uploaded it as the official cover. The picture didn't have as much cleavage as some of the other books, but Abby could tell it would still have been shocking by fifties standards. It showed two women sitting on a bed together, one with short brown hair and one with long blond waves. The blond one, dressed in a filmy nightgown, was crying onto the brown-haired woman's shoulder. The brown-haired woman was smoking, wearing a necktie, patting the other woman's shoulder and staring at her boobs. Above the title a tiny line of type read "They were women only a strange love could satisfy. A daring novel of the third sex."

"I didn't know people were allowed to smoke on book covers," Linh said, studying the screen.

"Everyone smoked everywhere in the fifties. They didn't know it was gross yet."

"Whatever. Turn to the beginning. I want to read about the strange love these two ladies get up to."

Abby clicked into the text and read the first line out loud.

"Elaine had already had her heart broken once. From now on, she was keeping it wrapped up in cellophane."

Abby stopped reading. "What's cellophane?"

"You don't remember that song from *Chicago*? 'Mr. Cellophane'?"

"Oh, right." Abby and Linh had both done theater in middle school, before their schedules got so packed. "Well, is cellophane bulletproof or something? Why would you wrap your heart in it?"

"How would I know? Come on, find the sexy parts."

"Here, you can look." Abby passed her the computer.

"Okay..." Linh clicked through the pages. After a minute, she frowned at the screen. "This is all just talking so far. Everyone's sitting around in a bar with all their clothes on." She clicked again and again, still peering down. "And...that's the end of chapter one already. What kind of porn *is* this? These covers are false advertising."

"Keep going. Maybe the porn's in chapter two."

While Linh clicked, Abby turned to her phone to look up *cellophane.*

The characters on the cover of *Women of the Twilight Realm* didn't look that much older than Abby. She wondered who'd broken Elaine's heart so badly that she needed to protect it.

And would that even work? Wrapping your heart in metaphorical armor? Maybe you could keep yourself whole just by concentrating hard enough.

Before she could find anything, her class-reminder chime popped onto the screen.

"Shit!" Abby's panic bubbled, wiping away all thoughts of vintage lesbians. She snatched the computer from Linh and shoved it into her backpack. "I forgot. I'm supposed to meet with Ms. Sloane in three minutes. Shit, *shit!*"

"Ms. Sloane?" Linh didn't get up, but there was alarm in her eyes. "Isn't she your project advisor?"

"Yes. Shit, shit!"

"Wait—is this your meeting about the project proposal? The one you still don't have a topic for?"

Abby pinched the bridge of her nose. "Yes."

"Abby, this is serious! You could get in real trouble!"

"I know, I *know*. I'll figure something out on my way there."

Abby threw open the door without waiting for Linh to say anything more and charged down the hall, ignoring the sophomores who turned to stare from the doorway of the art room.

She tried, desperately, to come up with an idea. *Any* idea.

Maybe she could write fanfic after all. She'd posted a *Flighted Ones* story back in middle school that had ninety-seven chapters, and some of them had even been good. Maybe she could pull out some of the chapters, change the names and rework them into something Ms. Sloane would find acceptable.

It wasn't a great idea, but it was all Abby had. She raced across the hall and down the stairs to the third floor, her platform Mary Janes thundering on the tiles. She'd probably have to take the story offline before she turned in her project, in case Ms. Sloane ran one of those plagiarism searches. It would suck to lose all those reader comments, though.

"Abby?" Ms. Sloane stepped through her classroom door. Abby came to an abrupt halt. "Are you all right?"

"I'm great." Abby tried to smile, but she could barely catch her breath.

"What were you doing? Did you go for a run during your free period?"

"Um, yes." Abby cursed inwardly as Ms. Sloane peered

down at her Mary Janes. Her creative writing teacher was an old-school lesbian, and Abby should've known she'd have strong opinions about sports attire.

Ms. Sloane was Indian-American, and in the wedding photo she kept on her desk, her dark curly hair was striking next to her wife's sleek blond chignon. The effect made their matching cream-colored wedding dresses look that much more practical-lesbian-chic. It was obvious they'd planned every last detail to maximize the striking visuals while also making sure there would be no long trains to trip over or bobby pins poking their ears. The two of them probably shared a whole closet full of affordable yet top-quality and carefully coordinated running shoes.

"All right, well, come on in." Ms. Sloane held the door open. At least she wasn't dwelling on Abby's feet. "I'm excited to see what you've got for me. The rest of the seniors have already started their projects, so we'll have to play some catch-up. I was surprised you signed up for the last advising slot. Last year during our workshops you always tried to be ahead of the game."

Abby tried to breathe evenly as she followed Ms. Sloane inside. This classroom was her favorite place in the whole school. It was narrow and cozy, with a long, oval-shaped table where everyone sat for their discussions. Abby used to relax the second she entered this room, but today it was having the opposite effect.

"Um, well." She tried to think of what to say. Teachers never understood that homework couldn't always be priority number one every second of every day. When you were deep in postbreakup withdrawal, were you seriously supposed to work ahead in every single class? "Nothing to fire up the creative muse like tight deadlines, right?"

"Wrong, in my experience. Nonetheless…" Ms. Sloane smiled and sat at the head of the long table, gesturing for Abby to sit beside her. She'd always been easy to talk to, and she was the main reason Abby had stuck with creative writing, even when the boys in last year's workshop had made her roll her eyes into the back of her skull when she was forced to critique their pretentious wish-fulfillment hetero foreplay scenes. "So, let's see your proposal."

Ms. Sloane held out her hand. Abby stared at the outstretched brown palm.

Riiiiiight. She'd somehow forgotten she was supposed to turn in a written proposal.

Shit.

"Um, well…" Abby tried to act as if this was all going exactly as she'd planned. "I wanted to ask if I could have until Monday for the written portion. My computer had a meltdown last night when I was going to hit Print."

"Oh, that's too bad." Ms. Sloane didn't blink, but she glanced down at Abby's backpack. A corner of her laptop poked up through the zipper. *Shit, shit.* "You know, I've been told I'm talented with computers. Why don't you let me take a look. I'll see if I can get the file to load, and then we can review it together here on your screen."

Shit shit shit shit shit.

Abby tried to think rationally. What was the adult thing to do in this situation? Whatever it was, she should do that instead of freaking out.

But Ms. Sloane was wearing her you-won't-fool-me expression. No matter what she said, Abby was going to disappoint her.

Abby gave up on being an adult and just focused on not crying. "I… I'm sorry, Ms. Sloane."

"You're sorry," her teacher repeated. After a moment of pained silence, she sighed. "Abby, this isn't like you. Last year, you turned in all your assignments early. You always came to class prepared, even eager, to join the discussions. Is anything wrong? Maybe something going on at home?"

"It's nothing. I'm sorry. It's senioritis, that's all."

"Senioritis comes in May, not September." Ms. Sloane's expression was so serious it was making Abby's head hurt. "You can talk to me, Abby. If there's a problem, I want to help."

Ugh. Adults could seriously be the *worst*. If they weren't ignoring the fact that you existed, they were falling all over themselves acting like they knew better than you.

As if Abby couldn't be just plain heartbroken. Of *course*, in Ms. Sloane's mind, there had to be "something going on at home."

When, in reality, *nothing* was going on at home. That was kind of the definition of Abby's home, in fact. She could barely remember the last time anyone in her family had voluntarily interacted with anyone else.

"No. There's nothing." Abby shook her head forcefully. "Can you please just take points off my grade, or whatever?"

"That's not how senior projects work. It isn't about earning points, it's about creating something worthwhile. It's about coming out of the year with a concrete result that's meaningful to you on a personal level."

"I know." Abby wished desperately that she were somewhere else. Anywhere else. Words like *worthwhile* and *meaningful* always made her want to hurl.

"All right, well." Ms. Sloane leaned back in her chair and frowned. "We'll talk through your plan today and you can email me your formal proposal over the weekend."

"Okay." Abby began to frantically rework her *Flighted Ones* story in her head.

"I must say, I'm already looking forward to reading your new work," Ms. Sloane went on. "I know you've been struggling to break away from the fanfiction you used to write and create something wholly yours. Not that there's anything wrong with fanfiction, of course—I always tell my younger students that it can be a lot of fun, and a great way to develop your writing skills—but this new project is a real opportunity for you to force yourself out of your comfort zone so you can mature as a writer. You've been on the verge for quite some time, and I hope that with this project you'll truly allow your creativity to take hold."

Shit. Ms. Sloane had seen through her *again*.

Abby tried to think fast, but the only story on her mind just then was *Women of the Twilight Realm*.

"I—um, well. I've been thinking lately about lesbian pulp fiction," Abby heard herself say. "You know, those books from back in the fifties."

"Have you?" Ms. Sloane's eyebrows shot up. As though Abby had genuinely surprised her for the first time today.

"Yes." Abby tried to figure out where to go from here. She'd always been good at bullshitting. "I've been researching the genre, and I thought it might be interesting to try to reclaim it from a modern queer perspective. I mean, apart from the gorgeous clothes the fifties were basically awful, especially for marginalized communities, so I thought it would be *worthwhile* to examine the books from a contemporary point of view."

"Well, the genre's already been reclaimed, of course." Ms. Sloane's usual I'm-an-expert-in-everything tone had already returned. "Although surely you came across that in your research. Lesbian-owned publishers have been rereleasing the pulp classics specifically for queer audiences since the eighties."

"Of course." Abby hoped she didn't look as thrown as she felt. If that was true, she had to switch tactics fast. "Well… what I want to do is write one of these books that's genuinely, you know—good. I want to break away from the gay tragedy trope."

Ms. Sloane nodded. "Some would argue that many of the books from that era are already *good*, if that kind of value judgment is possible with literature, but I understand your perspective. It's an unusual proposal, but I think it has a lot of potential. My concern, though, is that this could wind up simply being another fanfiction exercise for you. It's important that your senior project be written entirely in *your* voice. That it be unique, not simply following a formula or imitating an existing style."

"Oh, I agree. Ah…" Abby tried to think of what else Ms. Sloane might want to hear. "I was thinking I'd invert the formula. Take a critical look at the conventions of the genre and turn them on their heads. Examine the notions of romance and oppression and come up with something unique. Particularly in light of the election, and how so many people's opinions on social justice seem to have started regressing in the past year or so."

Abby only had a vague idea of what she was talking about, but it must have sounded as if she did, because Ms. Sloane raised her eyebrows again.

"All right, you've sold me." Her teacher held up her fingers and began ticking things off. Abby took the hint and reached for her pencil. "You'll still need to submit your formal proposal, and since you're writing historical fiction, you'll need to research the period as well as the genre. Which of the pulp books have you read so far?"

"*Women of the Twilight Realm*, by Marian Love." She'd read a few sentences, at least.

"Only one? Okay, then you'll need to read at least three more before the end of the semester. Aim for a wide range— no two books by the same author. One of the books you read should be *The Price of Salt*, but you can get that from the public library. Patricia Highsmith had a lot of terrible beliefs, but the writing itself is unparalleled. You're familiar with the conventions of the genre already?"

"Totally." Abby tried to remember what the article had said as she jotted Ms. Sloane's instructions into her binder. "Lesbian romance novels that ended with the characters dying or turning straight."

"Of a sort. Still, a lot of them, whether intentionally or not, also touched on the bigger issues facing the LGBTQ community in the fifties and sixties. That means you'll need to spend even more time at the library. Read up on the bar raids, the Lavender Scare here in DC, all of it. Start a research journal to keep track of what you learn. Remember, this was pre-Stonewall and pre-second-wave feminism, so there's a reason all the pulp authors wrote under pseudonyms—it might as well have been the Dark Ages for queer women. It was also the Jim Crow era, so you'll need to read about racial segregation, too. The pulps were overwhelmingly white, but you'll need to know about the real world of that time regardless. And you should study up on the overall postwar American economy while you're at it."

"Uh." That was a lot of research. It was a good thing Abby liked the library.

"After you've made some headway, let me know and I can

set up a meeting for you with a friend of mine," Ms. Sloane
went on. "He's a historian focusing on LGBTQ political
movements. He can point you to more resources."

"All right," Abby said, though she had no intention of
meeting Ms. Sloane's historian friend. She hated going up to
strangers and asking them for stuff.

"You can work on the research over the next few weeks,
but I'll expect your proposal by email tomorrow, and an out-
line for the novel and at least twenty hard copy pages from
your first draft a week from Monday." Ms. Sloane stood up.
"Don't worry. We won't critique them in the workshop until
I've given you notes and you've had a chance to revise."

"Okay." Sensing the meeting was over, Abby climbed to
her feet. Ms. Sloane held up a finger.

"And…" Ms. Sloane watched her pick up her backpack, her
fingers fumbling as she wound the straps over her shoulders.
"I'm here. If you ever need to talk."

Abby nodded briskly and left the room.

There were still five minutes left in her free period, so Abby
found an empty spot in the courtyard and took out her laptop. *Women of the Twilight Realm* was still open on the screen.

*Elaine had already had her heart broken once. From now on,
she was keeping it wrapped up in cellophane.*

Abby wanted to know who had broken Elaine's heart. But
most of all, she wanted to know if the cellophane had worked,
and where she could get some of her own.

She clicked through to the next page.

2

Monday, June 27, 1955

Janet had made a terrible mistake.

Two weeks ago, when she'd written the letter, she'd still been flush with her discovery. She hadn't been thinking clearly.

But her mother was always telling her she was rash and reckless, and Janet had finally proven her right: it was only *after* the postman had already whisked her letter away that she'd realized a reply could come at any time. That it would be dropped into the family mailbox alongside her father's Senate mail, her mother's housekeeping magazines and her grandmother's postcards from faraway cousins. That anyone in the family could reach into the mailbox, open that letter and discover the truth about Janet in an instant. And that they could realize precisely what that meant.

So Janet had spent every afternoon since perched by the

living room window, listening for the postman's footsteps on the walk.

Each day, when she heard him coming, she leaped to her feet and tore out the front door. Sometimes she beat him there and burst outside while he was still plodding up the steps to their tiny front porch. On those days, she forced a smile and held out trembling fingers to take the pile of letters from his hand.

Other days she was slower, and stepped outside just as he'd departed. Those days she pounced on the stuffed mailbox, flinging back the lid where JONES RESIDENCE was written in her mother's neat hand.

Then there were afternoons like this one. When Janet was too late.

She'd made the mistake of getting absorbed in her reading, and when she heard the slap of brown leather filtering through the window glass she'd told herself it was only the next-door neighbor, a tall Commerce Department man who left his office early in the evenings and never looked up from polishing his black-rimmed glasses.

And so Janet's eyes were still on the page in front of her—it was one of her father's leather-bound Dickens novels; Janet's parents had been after her to read as many classics as she could before she started college in September—when the mailbox lid clattered. Before she realized what had happened, her mother's high heels were already clacking toward the front door. "Oh, there you are, Janet. Was that the postman I heard?"

Janet bolted upright, the Dickens spilling from her lap. She bit back a curse as she knelt to pick it up, smoothing back the bent pages as her mother frowned at her. "Really, Janet, you must take more care with your father's things. And what *is* that getup you have on? You know better than to wear jeans in the front room, where anyone walking by could see you."

"Sorry, ma'am." Janet tucked the volume under her arm and stepped past her mother, narrowly beating her to the door. Janet was an inch taller than Mom now, and her legs were still muscled from cheerleading in the spring.

She jerked open the front door and slid her hand into the mailbox before Mom could intervene. Three letters today. Janet tried to angle her shoulders to shield the mail from view.

The first two letters were for her father, in official government envelopes with his address neatly typed on by their senders' secretaries. The third letter bore Janet's name.

It had come.

A short, sharp thrill ran through her as her fingers reached for the seal. Would this be the day everything changed?

Two weeks ago, she'd discovered that slim paperback in the bus station. That night, she'd read every page and found herself so enraptured, so overwhelmed, that she couldn't help writing to its author. Now here it was—a reply. The author of that incredible book had written a letter just for Janet.

But Mom was still standing right behind her. Could Janet slip the letter into her blouse without her seeing?

"What's gotten into you today?" Mom reached over Janet's shoulder and plucked all three letters from her hand. Simple as that. "What's this one with your name?"

"It's nothing." Janet ached to snatch the letter back, but forced herself to breathe instead as Mom tucked her finger behind the seal. Everyone in the family had always felt free to open Janet's mail. She was eighteen years old, but still a child in their eyes. She'd have to think of a lie quickly.

The letter had been addressed to Janet by mistake. That

was what she'd say. Whoever had sent it must have found her
name on some list of recent high school graduates.

No, of course Janet couldn't possibly imagine what the letter might refer to. She'd never heard of any "Dolores Wood"
or "Bannon Press." As a matter of fact, the letter could be a
cleverly disguised Communist recruitment tool. For safety's
sake, they really ought to burn it before the neighbors saw.

Though the idea of burning that letter, before she'd even
had a chance to read it, made tears prick at Janet's eyes.

"Oh, it's from the college." Mom withdrew a single sheet
of paper from the envelope and scanned it. "It isn't important. Only a packing list."

"The college?" Janet hadn't even glanced at the return address on the letter, but there it was. The letter was from Holy
Divinity.

Janet couldn't believe she'd been so foolish.

"Well, you won't be needing this." Mom tucked the letter into the pocket of her apron. "They must send it out to
all the new girls, without regard for which will be moving
into the dorms."

Janet nodded, hoping her mother couldn't hear her heart
still thundering in the silence.

"Are you all right?" Mom frowned again. "You look
flushed. Your father and I had planned to go to the club for
dinner, but if you need us to stay home—"

"It's nothing, ma'am." Janet shook her head, but she could
feel blood rushing to her cheeks under her mother's scrutiny.
"I, ah—I have to get ready for work or I'll be late."

Mom's frown deepened. "I didn't realize you were working tonight."

"I am." Janet wasn't. Another stupid, rash thing to say. Now
what could she do? Put on her uniform and show up at the

Soda Shoppe, ready to trot milkshakes out to station wagons on her night off?

To put off that decision, Janet dashed past Mom into the row house and ran up the narrow wooden stairs, her footfalls echoing behind her. Dad was always after her not to run in the house, saying it would disturb her grandmother's rest, but Dad wasn't home. Besides, Grandma always said it did her heart good to hear a child scurrying about the house and that Dad should shut his cake hole.

Janet reached the second-floor landing and threw open the door of her small bedroom, the hot air hitting her like a steaming kettle. The room was the same as always—the bed neatly made with its delicate pink spread, the flowered wallpaper that was starting to peel around the edges after a decade of Washington summers, the round mirror over her dresser with photos tucked into the frame. They were school portraits of her friends, mostly, plus an old yearbook photo of Janet and Marie in their cheerleading uniforms with pom-poms at their hips, their bent elbows lightly touching.

That photo was Janet's favorite.

Marie, her shiny hair framing her dark-rimmed glasses and always-gleaming smile, had been Janet's best friend all through school. For years they'd done everything together, sitting side by side in every assembly and every lunch period. In junior high they'd been the only two girls to enter the science fair at the boys' school, growing mold in carefully labeled jars and winning a red ribbon for their trouble. In high school they'd practiced their cartwheels and splits on the football field, giggling every time they fell onto the grass and making up silly variations to the official St. Paul's cheers. Janet had never been happier than when one of the chants she made up provoked a fresh bout of laughter from Marie.

Marie was a year ahead of Janet, though, and after she graduated Janet's senior year had been lonely indeed. Marie had spent the year at secretarial school, learning to type and take stenography and do other important things while Janet sat in Latin class again, wearing her childish uniform blazer and holding out her palm for the nun to strike when she forgot a conjugation.

That morning, eager to hear her voice again, Janet had tried to call Marie, but she was out, as usual. Janet had been forced to leave a terribly awkward message with her mother instead. Mrs. Eastwood had always seemed to think Janet was somewhat odd, and she could only have made that impression worse with the way she'd stumbled through the quick call.

She'd tried to explain that she was only calling to ask about Marie's job search. Now that she'd finished her business classes, Marie had been so busy with applications and interviews they hadn't seen each other in weeks. Janet was desperate to talk to her again.

Most of all, she longed to tell Marie about the book she'd found. Janet couldn't wait to hear what she thought of it— even though she could probably guess. Despite their shared memories, Janet knew it was unlikely Marie would want to remain her friend once she knew her secret. No normal person would.

Still, Janet was determined to tell her. There was no one else she could talk with about this. Certainly no one in her family. If her parents ever found out… Janet didn't dare to think of it. Marie was the only one who might be willing to listen.

Janet broke her gaze from the glossy photo and knelt on the floor next to her bed. She lifted the pink spread and in a single, practiced move, slid her hand between the mattress and bedframe until her fingers reached the cracked paper spine. She checked again to make sure the bedroom door was fully closed before carefully withdrawing the book from its hiding place.

She needed to find a better spot for it. The weight of the mattress had not been kind to the binding. The cheap glue had already started to come undone, and a few pages were loose, but Janet tucked them back into their proper place. She sank onto the rug between her bed and the wall, where she'd be out of view of anyone barging in, and gazed down at the book's cover.

Its background was a deep, glaring shade of red. That color was what had first caught Janet's eye when she'd spotted the wire rack full of books at the Ocean City bus station. It had been surrounded by similarly glaring paperbacks—detective fiction, gangster stories, the sorts of books you saw certain men reading on the streetcar. The sorts of books her father dismissed with a sniff as trash.

But it was the drawing, the strange image that stood out starkly from that palette of red, that had held Janet's eye for far longer than it should've.

It showed two girls, neither much older than Janet herself. One girl had blond hair and one brown. Both had long, dark eyelashes and full, red lips. The dark-haired girl perched on a bed in the foreground, her legs long and slim, her skirt pulled up above her knees. Her green blouse was unbuttoned far enough to show a hint of pale slip beneath and a curve of bosom above. The blond girl stood farther back, dressed in nothing but a white nightgown that clung to her curves and a pair of deep brown stockings, the hems at the thighs fully visible below her shockingly short gown.

The dark-haired girl sat twisted around on the bed, so

that the two girls' eyes met. The blond's lips were parted, as though to speak to the other girl.

Or, perhaps, to kiss her.

Janet blushed at the thought, as she did every time. Though she knew well enough that within the book's pages the girls *did* kiss, and even more besides.

Janet had only glanced around the bus station for a tiny moment before she slipped the book under her blouse. It still mortified her to remember. The price on the cover was thirty-five cents, and Janet had had two dollars in her purse, but she couldn't imagine showing her purchase to that smirking boy behind the cash register.

That novel was the only thing Janet had ever stolen in her life. She'd read it straight through that first night, and she'd stared at the cover in secret every day since.

Yellow letters above the drawing screamed the book's title, *A Love So Strange*. Smaller black text below read, "A world spoken of only in whispers, where women enjoy twisted passions. Betty knew it was wrong…but she was powerless against her unnatural attractions."

At the bottom, in the smallest type on the cover, was the author's name, Dolores Wood.

Janet had read each of those words more times than she could count. Still, whenever she gazed at that cover, her eyes were pulled to the illustration. To the girls' eyes where they met across the room. To the shapes of their bodies in their skimpy clothes.

Janet pressed one finger into the dip in her lower lip. Her breathing had grown heavier.

She'd never imagined there was a word for the strange feelings she'd had so many nights, alone in her bed, in the dark silence of her room.

Lesbian.

The word made her shudder. But it sent a tiny shiver down her spine, too.

Janet had never understood, not until she turned the thin brown pages of Dolores Wood's novel, that other girls might feel the way she did. That a world existed outside the one she'd always known.

It had never occurred to her that life could be different from what had already been set out for her. Ill-fitting uniforms and nickel-sized tips at the Soda Shoppe. Her parents pausing in the dining room to listen as Janet made phone calls in the kitchen. Solemn history and mathematics lessons taught by stern-faced nuns. Then, someday, an equally solemn wedding to a faceless man, and a future spent baking solemn casseroles for solemn, faceless children.

Janet had never thought books like *A Love So Strange* could be written, let alone published and sold—and right in the middle of a public bus station, too. She'd never imagined some girls might actually *do* the sorts of things Janet had only furtively imagined in those brief, solitary moments between waking and sleeping.

Reading *A Love So Strange* had made Janet remember some things differently, too.

The way she and Marie had talked and laughed while they'd practiced their cheers. The way they'd touched, lying side by side on Marie's back porch while her parents were out on warm summer afternoons.

The way Janet would trail her fingers along Marie's bare arm after she'd pointed out some item in a magazine. The way Marie would smile and wait several moments before she drew her hand away.

When Janet thought of kissing a girl, the way girls kissed

other girls in the pages of Dolores Wood's book, she always thought of kissing Marie. When she thought back to Marie's smiles on those lazy afternoons, she wondered if Marie might feel the same way, too.

If Janet could only show that book to Marie, it could change everything.

Still, she should never have sent the letter.

She'd been so foolish, to dream of writing a book of her own. To scrawl out that letter with all her silly, immature questions for Mrs. Wood. To address it to the publisher listed on the book's cover and drop the envelope into the mailbox, as though it were as simple a matter as sending in for a catalog.

Downstairs, she heard the front door open, then close again. "Janet! Come back down!"

At the sound of her mother's voice Janet scrambled to her feet, shoving the book back into its hiding place. She winced as she felt the cover bend. "Coming, ma'am!"

Only then did Janet remember she'd said she had to work tonight. Mom would wonder why she hadn't already changed into her uniform. She tried to think of another lie—she'd checked her schedule upstairs and realized she wasn't working that night after all; there, that one was simple enough—but all thoughts of lies and excuses left Janet's mind when she reached the bottom of the staircase and saw Marie in the foyer, smiling at her now-apronless mother and fiddling with the strap of her purse.

A delicious thrill ran through Janet all the way to her toes. She wished she'd thought to reapply her lipstick.

Marie looked as she always had, with each dark curl in place, her glasses polished to a gleam. Yet she looked older than usual, too, somehow. Her suit was neat, the skirt perfectly tailored where its hem fell around her calves. The jacket was a matching blue flannel, and the string of pearls her parents had given her for her eighteenth birthday was wound around her neck.

Janet had never seen her friend look so much like a real grown-up. A lovely grown-up, at that.

"There you are, Janet." Mom turned from Marie with a lingering smile of her own. Janet's mother had always been fond of Marie. She talked about her using words like *stable* and *settled*. Especially when she sought to admonish Janet.

Janet ignored her and bounced toward Marie. "I'm so glad you came! I have so much to tell you."

"It's been ages, hasn't it?" Marie's smile was wide enough to match Janet's own. "I'm terribly sorry I missed your call this morning. I was at an interview."

"An interview." Janet's eyes drifted down to Marie's neat suit. She flushed. "Of course."

"I've been so nervous." Marie smiled, and fumbled again with her purse. "It's wonderful to see you, though."

"Marie has the most exciting news." Mom held out a hand, ushering them into the living room. She didn't approve of dawdling in the foyer. "I'll bring you girls some refreshments."

Mom left for the kitchen, where she could still overhear every word they said. Even so, as Janet and Marie took seats on the sofa, Janet leaned in close and said, "I was just looking at our photo from the cheerleading squad last year. I remember that as if it was yesterday."

"Do you?" Marie smiled. She looked even more sophisticated from this distance. "It seems like a hundred years ago to me."

Janet's smile began to fade.

"There we are." Mom set down a tray of chocolate chip cookies and two glasses of milk, sitting primly in the armchair opposite the cold brick fireplace. "Now, Marie, I simply can't wait one moment longer to hear what Janet thinks of your news."

"Well, then, what's your news, Marie?" Janet wished Dad were here, so they could smile together at this ostentatious etiquette. Mom treated every visitor like President Eisenhower.

Laughter sparkled behind Marie's eyes, too, but, ever demure, she didn't let it reach her lips. "I've been offered a job, just today. I'm going to be a typist at the Department of State!"

"Marie!" Janet clapped her hands. "That's marvelous! That's the kind of job we all dreamed of having, do you remember?"

"Of course."

Any sort of government work had seemed glamorous to the girls of St. Paul's Academy. Their mothers had all gone to work as "government girls" during the war, of course, but they'd retired once the men came home. These days only the most elite girls, those capable of passing stringent tests and maintaining the highest personal decorum, were hired to work as government secretaries and typists. Janet's own distant ambition, of studying journalism in college and working for a newspaper or magazine someday, was far less exciting.

Working for the State Department was perhaps the most prestigious government position of all, surpassed only by working in the White House itself. At the State Department, a girl might meet a famous ambassador or foreign film star. Perhaps there might be a need to travel overseas, to take dictation for an important summit in Paris or Rome, or even some far-flung country like China.

It was all temporary, of course. The true goal, spoken of only through happy whispers over cafeteria lunches, was to meet a government man with an impressive job of his own, perhaps one with a title like *director* or even *undersecretary*. Once you were married, you'd leave your job to set up housekeeping so you'd be ready when the children came along.

Of course, though, it was far too early for Marie and Janet to think about any of *that*.

"Well, I'm not surprised," Janet said, still beaming. "Didn't you have the highest marks of all the girls coming out of school?"

Marie cast down her eyes. "Thank you, Janet. I was hoping we could go out tonight to celebrate, but your mother said you're working."

"Oh, no, I'm not. Let's go celebrate!" When Mom raised her eyebrows, Janet hastily added, "Sorry, ma'am, I was confused about my schedule. May I please have permission to go out with Marie?"

"Certainly."

"Wonderful! If we leave now we can catch the streetcar pulling in."

Marie rose instantly, nodding toward the untouched milk glasses. "Thank you for the refreshments, Mrs. Jones."

"Of course." Mom's plastered-on smile stayed firm as she eyed Janet's plain blouse and jeans. "Janet, Marie and I will wait here while you change."

Janet longed to be out the door, but her mother was right. Janet rarely wore much makeup, and most days she preferred Bermudas and button-downs to frills and fashion, but no restaurant in Georgetown would let her in for dinner wearing pants. "I'll be fast, I promise."

She ran upstairs, exchanged her jeans for a simple plaid skirt and stockings, and ran back down. Mom eyed her again, probably wishing Janet had at least taken the time to run a comb through her short blond curls, but all she said was,

"You girls have a lovely evening. Marie, please do send your mother my regards."

"I will, ma'am, thank you."

Janet grabbed her purse, took Marie by the arm and pulled her out the door before her mother could launch into a new round of pleasantries. The streetcar was already clanging as it approached the end of their block, and the girls had to run. Marie's high heels made her stumble, and Janet, in her ballet flats, was faster. She stepped onto the wide streetcar platform and held out her hand to help Marie aboard as the car pulled out, both girls laughing so hard the driver admonished them with a glare as they started north up Wisconsin Avenue.

It was exhilarating to be going out without her parents on the spur of the moment this way. Janet was certain Mom wouldn't have allowed it if she'd been with anyone but Marie, and she flushed with pleasure at the thought.

"I thought we'd go to Meaker's for dinner." Marie squirmed through the crush of after-work passengers, struggling to keep her footing as the car lurched forward. A man in a fedora reached for her elbow to steady her, nearly dropping his cigarette.

"That sounds perfect." Janet smiled at the man until he released Marie's arm.

The two of them made their way to the back of the car. Janet couldn't stop herself from staring down at Marie's clothes. The perfect fit of her suit. The way she stood gripping the ceiling strap, with one heel turned out to steady herself as the streetcar rocked over bumps. The shape of her legs, so pretty in her stockings. It reminded Janet of—

The book. It reminded Janet of the picture on the cover of *A Love So Strange*.

She swallowed and tried, again, to make herself breathe.

"Are you all right?" Marie peered at Janet tremulously as the streetcar swung beneath them.

"I'm fine." Janet had never felt finer, in fact.

"You're sure? Meaker's is just another block, but we can catch the car going the opposite way if you need to go home."

"I don't want to go home." As they reached their stop, Janet hopped past Marie down to the sidewalk, glad to feel earth beneath her feet once more. She wasn't quite sure what type of place Meaker's might be, but she didn't care. "We have to celebrate, don't we?"

Marie smiled and took Janet's arm. "We certainly do."

The restaurant turned out to be a small, quiet place on a side street off Wisconsin, with worn white tablecloths and dim lamps overhead. The girls were seated right away, and Marie ordered for both of them, smiling up at the waiter with a poised nonchalance Janet envied.

Marie was so strong and composed. She showed none of the clumsy awkwardness Janet always felt. It was a lucky thing Marie had wanted to celebrate with her.

Janet smiled fondly across the table as two drinks appeared in front of them. She recognized the glasses from her parents' cocktail parties. "What are these?"

"Martinis." Marie smiled and lifted her glass. Janet imitated her, trying to look equally refined. The waiter hadn't said a word about identification, so he must've thought the girls looked older than their eighteen and nineteen years. No one here at Meaker's, it seemed, had realized Janet was nothing but a plain schoolgirl. "My father always orders them on special occasions."

Janet took a swallow. The drink was cool, with a hint of spice. It tasted very adult. She could picture the girls in *A*

Love So Strange sipping drinks like these alone in their apartment one evening.

Marie asked about a friend from high school she hadn't seen lately, and soon they were caught up reminiscing about their high school days. Before long, Janet's glass was empty and a fresh drink had taken its place. She wasn't sure exactly how much time had passed, and she couldn't quite remember what had just been said that had made her laugh so hard. All she knew was that Marie was laughing, too, and that was all that seemed to matter.

Their food had arrived, but Janet had barely eaten. Marie's pot roast and potatoes were in a similar state.

"So this fellow Mom wanted me to go out with tonight," Marie was saying, as she took another sip, "he's a college man in town for the summer. Dartmouth. His uncle works with Dad at Treasury, and he's a dreadful bore—"

"How do you know he's a bore?" Janet interrupted. "Have you met him already?"

"No, no, but you know how these college men are."

Did she? This was the first time Janet had heard Marie talk about college men that way. Or was it merely the first time Janet had noticed it? Had Dolores Wood's book changed the way she saw everything, all at once?

"In any case," Marie went on, "Dad's up for a promotion— that's why they've been going to the club so often—and so Mom thinks I ought to go out with this Harold Smith fellow, since his uncle would be Dad's boss if he gets the new job. But I told Mom I didn't want to go out with some strange college man. I said I wanted to go celebrate with my best friend. Mom huffed and puffed, but what could she say in the end? Soon I'll be earning my very own paychecks, and she and Dad won't have any say over what I do."

"Really?" Janet hadn't thought of that. "Won't you go on living with them, though?"

"Well, sure—unless I were to move in with some of the other State Department girls, I suppose. A few of my business school classmates invited me to share an apartment, but I didn't have a job yet so I had to tell them no. Wouldn't that be magnificent, though? Not to have to follow anyone else's rules? To be able to go out whenever you chose, with whomever you wanted?"

Janet nodded, but in truth she couldn't imagine such freedom. Until she'd read *A Love So Strange*, her dreams had only extended so far as a college dorm. It seemed a lovely idea, though, to be away from her family's watching eyes.

But in a dorm, of course, there were still strict rules and curfews. Living at Holy Divinity, only a mile or so up Wisconsin Avenue, might be even more restrictive than living at home. At least in the house Janet was allowed to use the phone when she chose, provided Mom, Dad and Grandma didn't need to make a call.

"I must admit, I'm a bit nervous." Marie bit her lip, and Janet forgot all her musings about college and apartments.

In their place, her hope flared bright. Could Marie be nervous for the same reason as Janet?

"What will everyone in the office think of me?" Marie gazed down into her drink. "What if I don't keep up with the other girls? What if my boss expects more of me than I can do?"

Janet tamped down her disappointment. "Oh, you don't need to worry about that. They'll all adore you. How could they not?"

Marie smiled up at her, yet she still looked bashful. "That's kind of you to say."

"I'm not being kind. I'm being honest. You're perfect, Marie."

The words were out of her mouth before Janet could think about how they sounded. Now she felt bashful, too.

Yet Marie didn't look embarrassed as she held her gaze across the table.

Neither of them spoke, but something passed in that shared look that Janet couldn't have named. It buzzed through her with an energy she'd never known.

Unless that, too, was solely in Janet's imagination.

The waiter came to take their empty glasses, inquiring if they needed anything else. His eyes were on Marie and she answered for them both, in a voice so grown-up Janet couldn't believe she'd ever found cause to be nervous about anything. "No, thank you. I suppose it's getting late."

The waiter left, and Marie withdrew a few bills from her purse and tucked them under the glass. Her every movement was mesmerizing. "We ought to catch the streetcar. Your mother will be worried."

"Oh, forget my mother." Janet laughed and climbed awkwardly to her feet, holding the table to right herself.

Marie laughed, too, and followed. On the way out of the restaurant, she took a matchbook from the front desk and slipped it into her purse with a smile. Janet grabbed one, too, giggling.

The sidewalk was dark under the burned-out streetlight as the girls stumbled outside, the pavement grit caking under their heels. Up ahead, on Wisconsin, people were walking quickly along the sidewalk, but out here there was no one out but the two of them.

"I'm glad you didn't have to work tonight after all." Marie tucked her arm into Janet's as they began to walk. "This afternoon, the very instant the man at State told me I'd gotten the job, I knew the only person I wanted to celebrate with in all the world was you."

Janet closed her eyes, tasting the words.

If she were Sam, the main character from *A Love So Strange*—if she'd had Sam's courage, her knowledge of girls, her understanding of the world—she would kiss Marie. Right where they stood.

Sam didn't bother with waiting. She went after what she wanted.

Of course, even Sam wouldn't dare kiss a girl out in the open darkness, where anyone might see them. But maybe they could move somewhere out of sight. Duck beneath the awning of the shuttered corner shop, perhaps.

Sam would've said a clever line, too. Something witty and alluring.

Janet opened her eyes.

She meant to think of something clever. Truly, she did. In the end, though, the words that came out were, "Um…let's go over there."

Marie didn't seem to mind her abruptness. Her eyes were bright, her answer quick. "Yes, let's."

They hurried around the corner and stood, silent, their eyes locked on one another's. Janet could no longer think about books or jobs. She couldn't think about anything but Marie and that look they'd shared across the table.

She closed her eyes. And all at once, there in the darkness, it was happening. It was real.

Janet was kissing her.

It was madness. She knew it was madness, because in that moment Janet could not have prevented herself from kissing Marie if all the world had tried to stop her. And so it was some time before she began to understand that Marie was kissing her back.

She could scarcely breathe. In all the world, there existed nothing but Marie's lips on hers. Marie's hair, soft under her hand. Marie's body, pressed so close Janet could feel the seams in her flannel suit.

"Hey!"

The girls sprang apart, four feet of space materializing between them in an instant. There was no way to tell where the shout had come from.

Who'd seen them? Would her parents find out? Already, before Janet had even truly found out for herself?

"Is it the police?" Marie whispered. Janet hadn't even thought of that.

"Hey!" The shout came again. This time, it was punctuated by a round of laughter from high above. A girl's laughter.

Whoever had shouted, it wasn't the police.

Janet tilted her head back, looking for the source of the sound. Next to her, Marie did the same.

They both saw it at the same time. A girl, framed in an open window. An apartment two stories above the darkened store.

A man leaned toward her, and the girl ducked out of his way, still laughing, holding a bottle of beer. The girl's eyes were locked on his.

She hadn't seen Janet and Marie.

Only then did Janet feel the full weight of relief crashing down around her.

She lowered her gaze, locking eyes with Marie. Marie's breathing was rapid, but a smile danced behind her glasses. The madness of their kiss had touched her, too.

The sound of the streetcar made Janet's heart beat faster.

It was late, and the next car may not come for some time. They'd have to dash for it.

She longed to take Marie's hand—that was what Sam would've done—but she didn't dare. Instead, they turned and ran in a single movement.

This time, Janet didn't beat Marie to the curb. This time, they stayed together.

They climbed onto the sparsely populated car and took seats side by side. They didn't dare to touch, but they watched each other carefully. After another moment, they began to laugh.

Janet waited for her heart to slow, for normalcy to retake her mind. Yet as long as she waited, it never came.

3

Monday, September 18, 2017

It was decided, then. Elaine would go to New York.

The prospect gave her a special pleasure. When she told others her plans, though, they gave her sympathetic looks.

"You know what they say." Aunt Fay wagged her finger at Elaine. "Absence makes the heart grow fonder. The day after you get there, that fellow of yours will see what he's been missing out on. We'll be dancing at your wedding by spring."

"I'm not going to New York so Wayne will propose," Elaine tried to tell her. "I'm going to start a new life of my own."

"Of course you are, honey." Her aunt winked. Elaine didn't bother arguing further.

Wayne was a nice enough boy, she supposed. He was polite to her parents, and he called Elaine "sugar." When he drove her home after their dates, he kissed her quickly and pleasantly in the front seat of his car, and he didn't try to fight her when she pushed his sweaty hands away from the front of her dress.

Even so, Elaine wasn't disappointed that, after a year of going steady, he hadn't yet offered her a ring. Elaine wanted more from her future than Wayne Ellis. She wanted more than her aunt or her parents or anyone in Hanover could ever understand.

Abby rolled her eyes and switched off her phone screen. So far, this *Women of the Twilight Realm* book was thoroughly predictable.

"You won't believe how over-the-top these books are." Her breath was coming out in pants. The fourteen-story escalator at the Tenleytown metro station had stopped running and Abby, Linh and their friends were climbing it with their rally posters over their heads. "This one is so corny."

The health care protest they'd gone to downtown with the rest of the Genders & Sexualities Alliance had been awesome, with lots of quality chanting and creative homemade signs. It wasn't actually over yet, but they'd had to leave early. Linh and Savannah had practice, Ben had a Black Student Union officers' meeting at Panera, and Vanessa was supposed to go straight home to work on college applications.

"Is it the same book we started reading on Friday?" Linh shouted over her shoulder. She was ahead of Abby, even though she was carrying three signs and a leftover six-pack of bottled water.

Linh was on the cross-country team, and sometimes she ran up and down the stalled metro escalators to clear her head. It was pretty adorable. Last year Abby used to come to the station to watch sometimes, leaning against the pillar at the top of the tunnel with a fond smile. When Linh finished her workout she'd come up to meet her, looking all disheveled and glowy. They'd grin at each other for a few happy, wordless moments, until Linh's stomach started growling audibly, and then they'd go off hand in hand to get smoothies.

Breaking up was the worst idea they'd ever had.

"Yeah, *Women of the* stupid *Twilight Realm*," Abby called up to her. "So far it's all about how this woman has to move to New York because her boyfriend—and pretty much every male character we've seen so far in her little town in the boonies—is a giant tool."

"Was that the fifties version of feminism?" Ben asked from behind Abby. He was panting, too. Ben shared Abby's aversion to extracurricular activities that involved getting unnecessarily sweaty. "Leaving town to find a less tool-ish dude to go out with?"

"Probably," Linh called back. "As if fifties New York was full of enlightened, eligible guys."

"Well, it's a lesbian book, right?" Savannah shouted from the top. She ran cross-country, too, and she was the only one in their group who could keep up with Linh. "So soon she'll find some enlightened, eligible ladies."

"Dude." Vanessa poked Ben in the back with their I Am Not a Preexisting Condition poster. "You can't just pause halfway up the escalator. If I'm not home in fifteen minutes my mom'll be waiting for me at the door with a stopwatch and the Common Application."

They all groaned, Abby loudest of all.

"My dad's worse," Linh called back. "I'm supposed to write an essay every single night, and he makes me print out every draft before I go to bed. Then he slides them back under my door the next morning with notes in the margins."

"Did you decide how many schools you're applying to?" Vanessa asked. "My mom keeps saying I need to do all the

Ivies. I tried to tell her everyone says that's a bad strategy but she won't listen."

"What? That's a bad strategy?" Savannah sounded alarmed. "That's what my cousin's doing. He said if you can get into all eight you get to meet Anderson Cooper."

Abby sped up until she was behind Linh, her breath heaving and her wedge sandals thumping on each step. If she intervened fast enough, sometimes she could get her friends to stop with the college talk before they remembered they were competing for slots and started eyeing each other warily.

"I don't want to apply to *any* Ivies," Linh was saying. "My dad thinks I should, but I just want to go to MIT. I'm starting to think about Hopkins, too, though."

"So anyway, I guess all these books are like that," Abby interrupted. She tried to raise her voice so they'd all hear, but that wasn't easy given how hard she was panting. "I read a bunch of plot summaries over the weekend, and they're all ridiculous and tragic. Plus, lots of them are about these really young characters, some even younger than us, who get seduced by way older women. Like in their thirties."

"Ew." Linh wrinkled her nose. "That's so gross. Not to mention illegal. Why would they even *want* to?"

"Because they don't seem to realize it's gross? I don't know, it's weird. I skipped ahead, and at least this *Twilight Realm* book isn't that way—the characters are twenty-one and twenty-five, which I guess isn't *that* sketchy. But all the stories are such clichés. The characters go to these lesbian bars in Greenwich Village and have melodramatic conversations about how terrible it is to be a lesbian, and then they go home and have melodramatic lesbian sex. Then by the end they either check themselves into an asylum or die in botched abortions or cult rituals or whatever. And if they *do* survive, most of them wind up forgetting they're gay."

"What, do they turn out to be bi?" Linh tilted her head hopefully. She was bi, and she was always talking about how impossible it was to find bi characters anywhere. Abby agreed with her—she used to identify as bi, too, before she realized that whenever she started to imagine kissing a guy, she usually got too bored to finish—but it wasn't exactly easy to find lesbian characters most of the time, either.

"That would seem logical, right?" Abby threw up her hands. "I thought that was where they were going with it at first, but I guess maybe they didn't realize being bi was a thing yet? Because all these women seem to suddenly discover that they were totally straight all along. Even though two chapters earlier they were getting it on with their thirtysomething lady friends and very obviously into it. I was thinking that maybe in *my* book, though, I'd have one of the characters have sex with her boyfriend and actually enjoy it, and realize that she *is* bi. Then she'll have to stress over how to tell her girlfriend. That never happens in these books, so I think Ms. Sloane would like it. I'd be inverting genre tropes."

Abby was completely out of breath by that point, so she stopped talking and turned around to help Ben as they emerged into the open air of Wisconsin Avenue. Savannah and Linh stood waiting at the top, watching as a pair of Secret Service police cars sped through the intersection ahead of them. Abby wiggled her eyebrows at Linh in what she hoped was a flirty way, but Savannah, to her chagrin, had already changed the subject back to college.

"You won't have to miss the Maryland meet when you go visit Penn, will you?" Savannah's tone made it clear that missing the meet would be a ridiculous thing to do. She was only a junior, so she was slightly less obsessed with college than the rest of them.

"No, I can do both. The meet's not until that Sunday." Linh turned back to Abby. "By the way, I meant to ask you. I'm trying to get my parents to let me go visit Penn on the fourteenth. It's a one-day trip, up and back on Amtrak. Do you want to come? They won't let me go by myself but they said if you went, too, we could go together. They already said they'd buy our tickets, and it'll be fun. Your parents will let you, right?"

Linh was asking her to come on a trip? Just the two of them?

Abby wanted to say *yes* right away, but everyone had climbed off the escalator by then, and they were all watching. She didn't want to look desperate. "Um." She reached for her phone. "Let me check my calendar."

"I hope you can." Linh had that overeager look she got sometimes when they talked about college. Uh-oh. Maybe this wasn't about wanting to spend time alone with Abby after all. "It's time you started visiting schools. I know Columbia's your first choice, but you should probably come up with a list of ten or so, don't you think?"

Abby unlocked her phone and did her best not to react. Sometimes Linh came on kind of strong when there was something she thought Abby should do. Still, any time with her was better than none. "Let's see, it looks as though—okay, yeah, I guess I'm free the fourteenth."

"Uh, Abby, your calendar isn't even up." Ben had come up out of nowhere and swiped Abby's phone from her hand, glancing up at Linh with a smirk. "Also, just FYI, you two aren't nearly as subtle as you think you are. You might as well— Hey, wait a second, what *is* that?"

Abby grabbed the phone back. Ben had somehow switched her phone screen to her collection of pulp book covers. She seized the chance to change the subject.

"It's one of those bizarro novels," she told Ben, pulling up the *Satan Was a Lesbian* cover and holding it out for them to see. "They were all like this."

One by one, her friends started laughing as they got a look at it, exactly as Abby had expected.

"That can't be real." Ben squinted down. "It's got to be Photoshop."

"Nope! It was an actual book." *Satan Was a Lesbian* was the weirdest cover, and title, Abby had found so far. It showed a woman in mom jeans brandishing a whip at another woman in lingerie while the titular Satan watched gleefully from above. "But in *my* book, I'm going to invert the usual boring gay tragedy story. My main characters will wind up getting sent to a mental hospital that they think will beat away their gay, but it'll turn out to be this secret lesbian commune in Vermont, and they'll live happily ever after and adopt a bunch of cats. Except it can't be totally conflict-free, so I'm also going to have one of their queer friends die a really gruesome death. She'll get decapitated by her girlfriend's ex or something."

"You should have her get killed by Satan himself." Ben pantomimed stabbing someone. "*Herself*, I mean. She can whack your protagonist with a magic Lesbian Satan death blade. Hey, the school's calling you."

He passed the buzzing phone back to Abby. The caller ID read Fawcett School. Weird. "Hello?"

"Hello, this is Ms. Jackson in the middle school office calling. I'm trying to reach Abby Zimet?"

"Yes, this is Abby."

"Oh, good, I'm glad we found you. If you're still on campus, could you come to the office, please?"

That was even weirder.

Something didn't feel right about this, but there was no real reason to say no. Abby wasn't exactly on campus, but she was only a block away. And at least this would get her out of having to go home and interact with whichever of her parents was in town today. "Uh, okay. I'll be there in a few minutes."

Abby told her friends what was going on, and they all got ready to leave. Linh tried to catch her eye, but Abby pretended not to notice. Flirting was one thing, but she'd learned the hard way that it was best to stay quiet when it came to stuff that may or may not turn out to be actual problems.

Everyone split up and waved goodbye, tucking their signs under their arms. Abby tried to maneuver her sign without bending it. It said Women Deserve Health Care! If You Don't Believe Me, Ask the Woman Who Gave Birth to You, and she wanted to save it for the next protest.

As she turned to start up Wisconsin, squinting in the bright sun, a groaning 96 bus rolled past her. Abby adjusted her backpack, took out her phone and pulled up the website she'd found.

She was already behind on her research for Ms. Sloane, so she'd Googled *gayness in the fifties* earlier that afternoon and landed on some ancient government report. It was a faded, scanned PDF, dated December 15, 1950, and titled Employment of Homosexuals and Other Sex Perverts in Government. Abby had put off reading it, since it didn't exactly sound cheery, but now she picked a page at random and zoomed in.

There are no outward characteristics or physical traits that are positive as identifying marks of sex perversion.

Undoubtedly, the authors of this report had thought themselves brilliant to have made this point. Also they were apparently using "sex perversion" as a synonym for not being straight, so that was…interesting.

Abby glanced up as she crossed the alley in front of the Whole Foods, then turned back to her phone.

Sex perverts, like all other persons who by their overt acts violate moral codes and laws and the accepted standards of conduct, must be treated as transgressors and dealt with accordingly.

Well, that sucked.

Abby scrolled, looking for something more relevant to what Ms. Sloane wanted from her, but this document read like a parody of an old textbook. There was no way people in the fifties, or any other time for that matter, seriously sat around worrying this much about each other's "moral codes."

One homosexual can pollute a Government office. This sub-committee is convinced that it is in the public interest to get sex perverts out of Government and keep them out.

Abby sighed and closed out of the PDF while she waited for the light to change. She was almost back on campus, and this document had nothing to do with lesbian pulp novels. The characters in *Women of the Twilight Realm* didn't exactly sit around reading government reports.

Besides, Abby had spent her entire life in DC. She knew how much the people in Congress loved to hear themselves talk. Some guy was running for Senate who'd said homosexuality was evil and should be against the law, but him saying that didn't change the fact that gay marriage had been legal for years. *That* guy might believe Abby was going to hell for being in love with Linh, but that didn't make it true. Abby didn't even *believe* in hell.

She crossed the parking lot and reached the bottom of the short hill that separated Fawcett Middle School from Fawcett High. Abby had barely been inside the middle school building since she'd finished eighth grade. Walking down the green-tiled front hall felt like going back in time.

She was startled out of her nostalgia when she pushed open the office door and saw her eleven-year-old brother, Ethan. He was sitting alone in the waiting area in his dance class uniform—a white T-shirt and embarrassingly tight black leggings. His arms were folded across his chest, and when he saw Abby, he groaned.

"What are *you* doing here?" Abby's mouth fell open. "Why did they call *me*?"

"Abby. Good, you're here." Ms. Jackson, the office assistant, gestured to her from behind a desk. "We've been trying to reach your parents. Do you have another number for either of them?"

She'd come all the way here for this? Abby tried not to let her frustration show. "Probably. Which numbers have you tried?"

They compared phone lists, and Abby read out the numbers for Mom's work cell and Dad's assistant. Ms. Jackson thanked her, then vanished into an inner office and shut the door. Abby carefully laid her protest sign by the desk, but she kept her backpack strapped to her shoulders so she could get out of here fast when this was over.

Meanwhile, her brother was staring at the ceiling as though Abby wasn't even there. Ethan was in that weird stage halfway between looking like a little kid and an almost-teenager. All he cared about was dancing—he took regular classes with the rest of the sixth graders during the school day, plus extra advanced classes in the afternoons—and he didn't bother to change clothes afterward, which didn't do much to offset his overall awkwardness. It was as if puberty was being intentionally mean to him, and he hadn't noticed yet.

Abby and Ethan had been pretty close when they were younger. They used to have a running joke about how they were a two-person superhero team. Their parents were the villains, especially when Dad was trying to limit their screen time or Mom was making them eat vegetables.

Once, when Abby was in fifth grade and Ethan was in kindergarten, he'd fallen from the climbing gym on the temple playground and his nose turned into a bloody mess. Abby had wiped off his face and hugged him until he stopped crying. When their mom got there, Abby didn't really want to let him go. It had been kind of nice, feeling needed.

Lately, though, she'd been avoiding her parents and Ethan altogether. Mom and Dad were just insufferable—on the rare occasions when one of them tried to relate to her, they only made it that much more obvious that they had no idea what it was like being a teenager, much less a queer one, in 2017—and as for Ethan, he'd basically turned into a different person than the kid she remembered.

"Okay, so." Abby put her hands on her hips, the stiff fabric of her vintage dress rustling. "What's going on?"

Ethan shrugged and tilted his head back, avoiding her gaze.

"Don't be a dick, Ethan." At that, his head shot up. She'd never called her brother a dick before, but if he was going to *act* like a dick... "Did you get in trouble?"

"I didn't *do* anything." His eyes trailed down to his sneakers. "Mr. Salem started it."

"Mr. Salem?" Abby didn't hide her surprise. "What did he do?"

Ethan *loved* his dance teacher. When they used to have family dinners he'd always go on and on about what Mr. Salem had said in class that day, or what funny twist he'd added to the choreography, or how he'd told Ethan he was the most promising student he'd had in years.

Abby had seen Ethan dance. He wasn't bad or anything, but she was still dubious about the authenticity of that last comment.

"He was being a jerk." Ethan shrugged. "He kicked me out of class for being, like, two minutes late."

"Well, yeah." Abby remembered that from her own dance-class years. "You know you aren't allowed to be late to the studio. Besides, I thought you always tried to be there five minutes early, since you're a dance dork and everything."

"I'm not a dance dork." Ethan leaned forward and pinched the bridge of his nose. His face was red and blotchy. Shit— had her goofy kid brother been *crying*? "Anyway, it was only two minutes."

"Okay, but what's the big deal? School's over. Why didn't you just go home?"

Ethan looked away.

"So you *are* in trouble." Abby tried to sound stern. "What did you do?"

"It isn't some huge deal." Ethan rolled his eyes. "I only told him it was a dumb rule. Then I kind of, um—" Ethan's voice fell. "Threw my water bottle at his head."

"What?" Abby's jaw dropped. This was so unlike Ethan

she might as well have fallen into an alternate universe. "Did
you *hit* him?"

"Um. Kinda." Ethan pinched the bridge of his nose again.
"He moved, and it kind of—bounced off his shoulder."

"That's horrible!" Abby kept expecting him to say he was
joking. Ethan was always thirsty, and he carried one of those
huge metal water bottles everywhere he went. Getting hit
with it would be *incredibly* painful. "You could've really hurt
him!"

"Yeah. I know."

"What the hell?" She couldn't believe he was just *sitting*
there, impassive. "Did you *want* to hurt him?"

"I only..." Ethan bent down so far all Abby could see was
the back of his head. His thick brown hair pointed into a
tiny V at the base of his neck. "I only wanted him to leave
me alone."

Abby didn't understand. The Ethan she'd grown up with
would've at least been *sorry* for doing something like this.

"Do you think Mom and Dad will both come?" Ethan
didn't look up. "They did that time I got sick in gym."

"Yeah, well, your appendix ruptured. You had to be hos-
pitalized. Water-bottle throwing probably isn't on the same
level."

Ethan let out a noisy breath. "It's like you *want* me to almost die again."

"You didn't almost die." Abby rolled her eyes, but she was
thinking, *If you want to see Mom and Dad voluntarily in the same
place at the same time again, almost dying is probably your best bet.*

"Anyway." Ethan wouldn't meet her eyes. "They're calling them both, right?"

"I don't know. They'll probably see who they can get to
come. Dad was supposed to get back into town this morning,

but he's only staying one night before he has to leave again. Maybe they'll call Mom, but she's in—"

"Pennsylvania. I know."

Abby sat down beside him on the bench, her backpack thumping heavily behind her. "She'll be back tomorrow."

"Yeah. Because Dad'll be gone by then."

Abby pretended not to hear the resentment in his voice. "They have to travel for work, Ethan."

He shrugged and didn't answer, even though he had to know it was the truth. Their mom was the president of a think tank, and Dad was a lawyer for the National Institutes of Health. They both worked long hours, and they were always having to leave DC for conferences and meetings and other stuff Abby had given up trying to keep track of.

"Everyone's parents travel for work." Abby fixed her eyes on her sandals. "It isn't a big deal."

"I don't know anybody whose parents travel as much as Mom and Dad do."

And a memory swam into Abby's mind before she could stop it.

It was a week after the fight—the big fight, the one Linh saw—and everyone at home was being even quieter than usual. Well, Ethan and Abby were, at least. Mom and Dad, whichever one of them was home at any given time, were trying to act normal. Except they kept smiling too hard or sighing too loud, and making it that much more obvious that they were faking.

But their Tudor-style row house was a hundred years old, and the walls were thin. When you were upstairs, it was nearly impossible to have a conversation without everybody else on the second floor hearing you. Most of the time there was nothing *to* hear, since no one in the family spoke to each other anymore, but that night was different.

Mom was on the phone in her room. Abby could tell she was trying to keep her voice down, but it wasn't working.

"No, no. Fine. Stay in New York if that's what you want. I'll be here, doing everything. Again." There was a thin, pained note in her voice Abby had never heard before. As though she was actively trying to sound like she was suffering. "No, he's fine, but I already told you she's upset. You don't remember? I think she had a fight with her girlfriend, and—*yes*, it was about that. What did *you* think? No, no, she didn't say anything, you know she never tells me anything, but if you paid attention to anything other than yourself, maybe you'd start to realize—"

Abby didn't hear any more after that. She shoved a pillow over her head, dug out her headphones and turned the music up loud enough to drown it all out.

Now, though, she kind of wished she'd kept listening. As far as she knew, that phone call was the last time her parents had actually spoken to each other.

"They're never both home at the same time," Ethan was muttering. "You're hardly ever home, either."

"I have a lot of work to do. I'm a senior, dude." Abby tried to sound playful. She'd called him *dude* when he was a kid, and it always used to make him smile.

"But don't you think—"

"All right, Ethan, it shouldn't be much longer." The principal's voice boomed above them. "Abby Zimet! So good to see you."

"Hi, Mr. Geis." Abby stood up. Mr. Geis had been the assistant principal when she was in middle school. "How are you?"

"Very well, Abby. You must be a senior? I'm sorry, you're

probably missing a meeting or practice this afternoon, aren't you?"

"I just got back from the health care protest at the White House."

"Of course you did." Mr. Geis smiled at her, but from the way his eyes kept darting down, she could tell he wanted to focus on Ethan. "You always were passionate about the causes you believed in. Are you taking Contemporary Politics this semester?"

"No, I'm doing the Women's and Gender Studies seminar instead." Come to think of it, didn't she have a paper due for WGS sometime this week? On that campaign down in Virginia—the transgender candidate who was running against the homophobe?

Abby remembered talking to Vanessa about it, but she couldn't remember when she was supposed to turn it in. It couldn't have been due today, could it?

Shit...

"Well, don't let us keep you, Abby." Mr. Geis was still smiling at her brightly. "It was good seeing you. Now, young man, come into my office, please."

Abby watched her brother climb to his feet without lifting his head and follow the no-longer-smiling Mr. Geis into the inner office. He didn't look back.

"Your dad should be here any minute," Mr. Geis was telling him as Abby turned to leave.

"What about my mom?" she heard Ethan say.

Mr. Geis paused. "Your father said she was out of town."

"She isn't coming?" Suddenly, Ethan sounded frantic. He couldn't actually be surprised Mom wasn't coming all the way from Pittsburgh to pick him up from school, could he?

"I'm sure you'll talk to her when she's back home." Mr.

Geis had barely gotten the words out before Ethan started moaning. Footsteps squeaked in the hall outside. "Is something wrong, Ethan?"

"I don't feel good," Ethan croaked, in the fakest voice imaginable.

"What's going on?" It was Dad, frowning in the doorway. Of course he'd show up right as Ethan was laying on the drama. "Abby? What are you doing here?"

His suit jacket was rumpled. He'd probably been wearing it since he got up that morning in New York. He would've worn it the entire train ride back to Union Station, and the cab ride to his office after that, and then through all his meetings or lunches or whatever it was he did all day. Neither of their parents ever went home until it was absolutely unavoidable.

Behind them, Ethan moaned again.

"Is Ethan sick?" Dad's face shifted from confusion to worry. For a second, Abby was jealous *she'd* never thought to try fake moaning. "I thought they said he got in trouble with his teacher."

"You can go on in, Mr. Zimet," Ms. Jackson said, emerging from the back room. She didn't seem particularly worried. She'd probably heard plenty of fake moans in her time. "Your son's in with Mr. Geis. He was feeling fine before."

"All right." Dad turned back to Abby, as though waiting for her to solve this puzzle for him.

"He wants Mom," she whispered, as patiently as she could manage. "He thinks if he's sick you'll both come, the way you did when he had that appendix thing. You should probably get Mom on the phone. If he hears both your voices he might calm down."

"Abby, it isn't as simple as…" Dad glanced toward the office. "Wait for us out here and we'll all go home together, all right?"

"Oh, um…" Her eyes darted up, down, anywhere but at him. As much as she wanted her parents to act like parents again, the thought of actually being alone with her dad and her brother for any amount of time was excruciating. "I've gotta go. I have a big project for, uh, French…"

But Abby couldn't think of anything more to say about her fictional French project, so she darted under Dad's arm and out of the office.

She was halfway down the hall before she realized she was running. Dad wouldn't come after her, though, not with Ethan and Mr. Geis waiting.

She swung around a corner into the huge, vacant main stairwell, listening out for footsteps in the hall behind her. Nothing came.

Abby climbed up one floor, and then another. The third floor looked empty. Surely Dad wouldn't think to look for her up here. When they got out of their meeting he'd assume she'd already gone home, and he'd take Ethan somewhere to give him a talking-to.

She opened her laptop with shaky hands, though she wasn't sure why—it wasn't as if she could focus enough to do homework right now.

That was when Abby noticed the ebook sitting on her desktop, staring at her. *Women of the Twilight Realm.* Without pausing to think, she clicked it open. She was still on the third chapter, and the point of view had switched from Elaine to another character.

The new girl was magnificent.

She was young, certainly—no more than twenty or so. Her

hand-stitched clothes marked her as a stranger to New York. She was a stranger to bars like Mitch's Corner, too, Paula was sure of it. She'd seen enough first-timers to know the mix of apprehension and anticipation they always carried, even when they were doing their best to look tough. Before tonight, the pretty, little blond girl hovering by the jukebox with an unlit cigarette clamped between her fingers had never set foot in a queer bar.

She'd thought about it, though—Paula was certain of that much, too. There was something about the steely set of the new girl's hips, and the way every so often she cast her eyes from side to side, watching the bar's patrons as they danced and drank and talked. Yes, the girl might be new, but she wasn't a total innocent.

Paula ordered a beer and a martini, and then, holding the drinks tight, sauntered over beside the new girl to peer down at the jukebox. The blond didn't look up.

"The songs in that thing are no good," Paula said, lifting the martini glass. "Old Max is so stingy he probably hasn't bought a new record since the Hoover years."

The blond met Paula's eyes for a moment, then shifted her gaze back to her own white schoolgirl blouse.

Paula smiled. The new girl's nerves only made her look prettier.

"I suppose I wasn't really looking for a good song." The girl took the offered martini and drained half of it in one gulp. "I only hoped that if I waited long enough, someone interesting might come over and talk to me."

Paula didn't bother trying to conceal her reaction. She laughed, long and loud, and let herself relax a little. "I hope I fit the bill."

The girl appraised Paula, taking in her height, her faded brown slacks, the full glass of beer sweating in her hand.

"Interesting, yes." The girl nodded. "So far. But if I'm going to make a full assessment, I think we'll need to dance."

Paula smiled. If she was going to keep up with this one, she'd need to be quick. She took both drinks and set them on the little table next to the jukebox, then looped her arm around the girl's back and steered her toward the dance floor.

"You got a name, new girl?" she asked, teasing, as they started to dance.

"Elaine."

"It's a pleasure, Elaine. I'm Paula."

"Well, Paula, what do the girls do for fun in this city when they're not sipping martinis and dancing to old records here in Mitch's Corner?"

Paula smiled again, winding her arm around Elaine's back to pull her in close. "I can only speak for myself, Elaine, but I like to hit the movies."

"Alone?"

"If I have to. But I've found everything looks better when there's a pretty girl by your side."

Abby tilted her chin to the ceiling. In spite of herself, a grin crept onto her face.

Meet-cutes were overdone, but Abby had always loved those old-fashioned romance novels the library had on spinner racks. The formulaic romantic comedies you could get on Netflix, too. They were all so predictable. Maybe that was why it was so delightful to lose herself in them.

She could recite the plot template by heart. A woman and (usually) a man met, traded witty banter and fell in love. There was always some stupid obstacle to them living happily ever after—one of them was a cattle rancher and the other one was a vegetarian, or one was a workaholic and the other was a manic pixie dream girl, or whatever—but they figured out how to overcome it and learned important lessons along the way. Then they *did* live happily ever after, without ever encountering a single problem for the rest of their lives.

It was all ridiculous and silly and unrealistic. Abby knew that. She'd only ever been in love with one person, but she still knew fantasy when she saw it.

Love didn't conquer all. Whatever else was going on in the lives of Paula and Elaine outside that smoky bar in 1956 wasn't going to stop just because the two of them had danced and bantered.

But God, it would be fucking wonderful if it did.

Abby settled down with her back against the wall and clicked through to the next page. She put in her headphones so she wouldn't hear anything from downstairs and focused on the screen in front of her.

It wouldn't be so bad to lose herself again.

4

Tuesday, June 28, 1955

"Welcome to the Soda Shoppe, your top spot for a refreshing drink and a bite to eat. I'll be your carhop this afternoon."

"Hi there, honey. Could I get a cheese sandwich and a Summer Freeze?"

"Righty-o." Janet suppressed a yawn as she scribbled down the order from the bald man in the station wagon.

Someone whispered loudly over her shoulder. "Janet? Janet! Over here!"

Janet didn't let her smile slip as she delivered the next line in her script—"Back in a jiff!"—and trotted away from the station wagon to see Shirley, one of her fellow carhops, looking anxious.

"Could you cover car nine for me?" Shirley shifted from one foot to the other. "I haven't had my break yet and I'm about to burst."

Janet glanced over her shoulder. "Sure. You'd better hurry or Mr. Pritchard will see."

"Thanks, Janet. You're a star."

Janet waved her on and trotted to space nine. Carhops were permitted to trot across the parking lot, but never to run. Mr. Pritchard, who watched over the staff with an unyielding expression and a blue vinyl apron tied snugly around his middle, was even stricter about running on shift than he was about break schedules.

Janet took down car nine's order and trotted inside to the food counter. The Soda Shoppe had started out as a regular restaurant, with tables inside and waitresses to serve them, before Mr. Pritchard realized he could make a lot more money sending high school girls out to the parking lot while the customers sat in their Oldsmobiles and Chevrolets. Now the shiny lunch counter inside sat empty while Janet, Shirley and the other girls wore out their saddle shoes trotting from car to car in their too-hot-for-summer-in-Washington cotton uniforms.

As she lifted her tray, Janet gazed at the empty phone booth that sat at the edge of the parking lot, the cars on M Street whizzing past.

Soon. Janet's shift would end soon, and then she could call her. That prospect was the only thing getting her through the afternoon's endless script recitations and grease drips.

So an hour later, when the last car of her long lunch shift finally pulled away, Janet rushed to finish her side work, folding napkins and marrying ketchup bottles faster than she ever had before. She tapped her fingers on her apron while Mr. Pritchard inspected her station, and when he finally cleared her to go Janet trotted as fast as she could to the phone booth and shoved a dime into the slot.

She picked up on the second ring.

"I'd hoped it was you." The smile was clear in Marie's voice before Janet had even finished saying hello.

Janet wound the phone cord around her fingers and turned her back on the still-busy restaurant. She was smiling, too, even though Marie couldn't see her.

"I haven't been able to stop thinking about last night." Marie's voice was a low, warm whisper.

"Neither have I." Janet closed her eyes. If she tried hard enough, perhaps she could pretend they were still on that dark street outside Meaker's.

"I want to see you again, soon, but I start work tomorrow. I'll probably be busy for the next few days."

"I understand," Janet replied, though her stomach sank. "Maybe we could meet this weekend."

"I'd like that. I should be free Saturday."

"Saturday it is, then."

They fell silent. Janet traced the tips of her fingers along the curve of the phone cord, wishing she were tracing the delicate skin of Marie's shoulder instead.

"Could you wait a moment, please?" Marie's tone suddenly grew a tad too polite. This must've been how they taught girls to talk on the phone in secretarial school.

"Certainly." Janet giggled and waited, wondering what Marie's teachers would've thought of the moment she and Marie had shared the night before.

"There, that's better." Marie's voice came muffled after a pause. "I've brought the phone into the pantry. The cord may be about to snap, but at least we can talk in private. Though I'm supposed to be helping my mother with the ironing."

"Oh." Janet opened her eyes. "Well, if you have to…"

"But I don't *want* to help her. I'd rather talk to you." Marie paused, drawing in a sharp breath. "I'd rather talk to you always."

"Oh." Janet's knees felt unsteady. "Oh, Marie—it's the same for me."

"Where are you? I can hear cars going by."

Janet smiled again. "I'm in the phone booth at the Soda Shoppe. I keep worrying Mr. Pritchard will come yell at me for forgetting to fold a set of napkins."

"Tell him you have more important things to do. Like talk to me."

Janet's smile stretched from one end of the phone booth to the other. Marie sounded exactly like Sam in *A Love So Strange* when she and Betty first fell in love.

Was that what was happening to Janet and Marie, too?

"Marie?" Mrs. Eastwood's voice was unmistakable, even through the pantry door. "What are you doing in there? I need your help. Besides, you shouldn't stretch out the phone cord."

Marie sighed into the phone. Janet sighed, too. "I suppose I'll see you Saturday. Good luck at the new job."

"Thank you." Marie's smooth phone manners were back, probably for her mother's benefit. "Please give your family my best."

Janet smoothed out her uniform before she left the phone booth, but her smile stayed wide.

The walk home was no more than fifteen minutes along M Street and up Wisconsin. Nothing in Georgetown was terribly far from anything else. Janet's and Marie's houses were close enough that their parents had often driven them to school together when they were still too young to ride the streetcar unaccompanied. Marie's job, though, would be in the next neighborhood over. The State Department had been in Foggy Bottom since the war.

It was hot out, and Janet, already warm from her shift, grew sweaty as she walked under the hot sun in her silly blue cap, smiling at the shoppers who nodded as they passed. Everyone recognized her Soda Shoppe uniform. Employees were never allowed to be in "partial uniform," even when their shifts were over.

Janet wished she had a proper job like Marie. Neither of the girls in *A Love So Strange* had to trot around with steaming piles of cheeseburgers for hours each day. They worked in sensible offices with spiteful coworkers.

Janet had reread half the book after she'd gotten home from Meaker's the night before, and she'd reread the other half that morning before her shift. She couldn't stop thinking about the moment when Betty first told Sam she was falling in love with her. Sam had replied that she'd known she loved Betty since the first time they danced.

Were there truly girls—*other* girls, girls Janet had never even met—who thought things like that? Who *said* things like that?

Janet and Marie didn't much resemble the girls on the cover of *A Love So Strange*. Janet was blond and Marie was brown-haired, so they matched on that count, but neither of them wore as much makeup as those girls, and Janet certainly didn't own any clothes that tight.

She supposed the girls' looks weren't what mattered in the end. What mattered was that, like Janet, the girls in Dolores Wood's book didn't seem to have much interest in men.

Until the book's odd ending. In the final chapter, Betty had suddenly become interested in a fellow she worked with, and Sam was fired from her job and threw herself in front of a speeding taxi.

Janet always skipped that chapter now. It felt as if it had been glued on to the *real* book by mistake. *A Love So Strange* was meant to be about two girls living in New York, going out in Greenwich Village, kissing and dancing and drinking with other girls like them. *That* was the book that mattered.

It still seemed impossible that such lives, such places, could be real—and yet they had to be. Why would Dolores Wood write about them otherwise?

In *A Love So Strange*, Sam never spoke to her parents. She'd been forced to leave the family because of how she was. Betty was on good terms with her parents, but only because she kept up the pretense that she was normal. When Betty's parents came to visit, Sam slept in the small bed in their spare room as though she were no more than a roommate, and the two girls were careful to make sure that room looked truly lived in, too, hanging pictures on the walls and storing knick-knacks on the shelves. They intended to look innocent, even if someone were to report them to the police.

What would happen to Janet if her family discovered she'd kissed Marie? Or, for that matter, if they found the book tucked under her mattress?

Her parents would be devastated. Grandma, too.

Janet would never be able to live a regular life. She'd never get married. Unless she were to move far away, leaving behind everything she'd known, and somehow found a husband for herself in a strange new city.

Janet wasn't entirely sure she wanted a husband anymore, though.

She'd never thought much about that particular question before. It had never seemed a question in the first place. *Everyone* got married. It was either that, or become a nun like the sisters at St. Paul's.

Well, at least there was no need to worry about her family calling the police. Her father's career was on shaky ground as it was, now that the Democrats had retaken Congress. If they found out about Janet, it would mean disaster for him. Besides, nowadays everyone knew these things were for doctors to handle. If Janet's parents found out, they'd want her cured and quickly.

Perhaps they'd send her to St. Elizabeths. That was the new name for the local asylum, though some still called it the Government Hospital for the Insane. What if news of Janet's admission got into the papers, though? The man who wrote the Washington Watch column was all too eager to write about the wrongdoings of Republicans, and a Senate committee attorney's daughter entering an asylum would be news for at least a day or two, even if her specific illness wasn't revealed. That day or two of news could be enough to ruin her father's prospects forever.

No—most likely, her parents would confine her to the house. They might find a discreet doctor to make house calls until she was properly cured.

Janet wondered what such a cure entailed. All she knew about psychiatry was that the patients lay on couches and closed their eyes. That didn't seem *so* terrible—but could it really change the way she felt about Marie?

Though the real problem was, Janet didn't *want* to stop feeling the way she did.

Perhaps resistance to treatment was part of the sickness. Yet she didn't feel sick. She felt healthier than she ever had before.

As Janet's squat two-story row house came into view, she squared her shoulders and pulled off her cap. She ought to simply put all these worries aside for the time being. It was going to be a very busy summer.

The house was quiet as she approached. Her parents had gone to dinner at the club again, leaving Janet and Grandma to an evening on their own. On nights like this one, Janet usually warmed up a casserole and chatted with Grandma while they ate. After dinner they might listen to the radio awhile, then read in comfortable silence until bedtime.

The heat indoors was nearly unbearable on summer nights, so Mom and Dad usually slept on the screened porch at the back of the first floor, with Janet and Grandma on the separate porch just above. It had been their pattern ever since Grandma moved in. She'd declared as soon as she'd unpacked that, although she'd consented to live with them, she would not be forced to tolerate Janet's father's snores. It had been bad enough when he was a boy, she'd said, but now that he was grown she was no longer obliged to suffer.

Janet climbed the steps to the front porch, taking care to avoid the rickety old railing, and unlocked the front door, slipping off her shoes in the foyer in case Grandma was resting. In the evenings, every sound in the house was magnified.

A bright shape on the entry table caught Janet's eye as she shrugged off her uniform jacket. A white envelope, solitary and stark against the shining black wood.

Janet snatched up the letter, her jacket falling to the floor. Panic rose in her throat at the sight of the typed letters across the front, spelling out her name in neat black ink. As her eyes flicked to the return address, she half prayed it was merely another letter from Holy Divinity.

Not this time. *Bannon Press*, the envelope proclaimed, followed by an address in New York City.

It had come.

Janet hugged the letter to her chest, her shoulders trembling under her thin white blouse. The envelope felt warm against her skin.

The seal was still in place. This letter was hers and hers alone.

Janet would take it straight to her room. She wanted to read the letter over and over, the way she'd done with *A Love So Strange*. She ran up the steps, her heart pounding, and didn't slow when she reached the second-floor landing. Her hand was on the door to her bedroom when the voice came behind her.

"Why are you in such a hurry there, girl?"

"Grandma." Janet tried in vain to steady herself before she turned. Her grandmother stood in the bathroom doorway, a fresh smile on her wrinkled face. Janet lowered her hand, wishing she were wearing a skirt so she could hide the letter in its folds. "Did you have a nice day?"

"Oh, your father came home for lunch and it was wretched, as always." Grandma tsked. "When you're not here to make it interesting, that is. I don't know why they need you at that restaurant so much of the time."

"Oh?" Janet racked her brain for a way to slip into her room without her grandmother following.

"Yes, yes. You know your father, always on about something." Grandma folded her arms, and Janet steeled herself for a rant. "These days he'll talk about nothing but that new bill. This ridiculous measure by the people who want to blaspheme the Lord's holy name."

"The In God We Trust bill?"

"That's the one. The fools think if we put that on all our money, it'll keep the Communists from blowing us into the sky. As if any one of those men down in Congress truly understands the first thing about Scripture. Or about Communists, for that matter."

"Oh, Grandma." Janet bent down to turn on the fan so it would cover the sound of their voices. The houses on either side of them were separated by no more than a narrow wall of bricks, and conversations carried so easily Janet sometimes felt she knew the neighbors' problems as well as her own. Dad never liked it when Grandma talked about Communists, but he especially didn't like it when the neighbors might hear.

Grandma had been a Socialist as a girl. She'd even been arrested once, for demonstrating against the draft during the first World War. She'd wanted to go on living in New York after Grandpa died, but Dad insisted she move in with them, telling the neighbors he wanted to look after her health. When they were alone, though, he said he'd made her leave because Grandma couldn't be trusted not to walk into the United Nations one morning and tell Churchill himself to go fly a kite.

"Oh, don't you worry about me, girl." Grandma laughed as Janet switched on the fan. "Your father may act as though he's in charge of what I do and don't say, but trust me, he knows better! Now, enough political talk. You be a helpful child and tell me a happy story about your day."

Janet tried to think, but her whole focus was on the letter tucked against her leg.

She hated having secrets from her grandmother. When she was younger, Janet had always gone to Grandma with her problems first. She'd poured her heart out to her time and again, sharing all the worries about school and friends that Mom and Dad never seemed to understand. Janet's parents believed all problems stemmed from rule breaking, and so any troubles she encountered were of her own creation, but Grandma didn't hold with that philosophy. She always knew exactly what to say to make Janet feel all right again.

This new problem was altogether different from the sort Janet used to bring her, though.

"My friend Marie starts her new job tomorrow," Janet finally said. "She'll be a typist at the State Department. A much better job than delivering cheeseburgers, if you ask me."

Grandma laughed. "One of these days I need to borrow your father's car and you can bring me one of those burgers. I'm a good tipper."

Janet laughed. "You don't have to tip me, Grandma."

"Well, what if I want to? I'm sure I have a nickel somewhere in these pockets." Grandma pretended to search her housedress.

Janet laughed again. "Shall I go ahead and heat up the casserole?"

"No, don't you worry about that on my account. Don't tell your mother, but I ate while I was out shopping this afternoon. I couldn't take another night of casserole."

"I won't tell her if you promise not to tell her I ate at work, too. She's always after me not to eat the Soda Shoppe food. She says it'll make my skin greasy."

"She doesn't need to worry about that." Grandma patted Janet's cheek. "No girl for miles around has a complexion as fresh as yours."

"Thanks, Grandma." Janet smiled and reached for her door-knob. "I hope you have a good night, then."

"A good night?" Grandma tilted her head to one side, her shrewd eyes drifting down to the letter in Janet's hand. "Aren't you coming downstairs to listen to *Dr. Sixgun* with me? Don't make your poor grandma listen to those cowboys shoot up that desert all by my lonesome."

"Yes, of course I'll come." Janet was getting desperate.

"I just need to change out of my uniform first. I'm awfully sweaty."

"All right, well. You do it quickly."

Janet nodded, trying to look demure, the way Marie always did around adults. Grandma only laughed and waved before padding off in her slippers.

Janet waited until she was certain her grandmother was downstairs. Then, nearly tripping in her haste, she rushed into her own room, ignoring the swell of heat that smacked her in the face, and shut the door behind her. She threw herself down on the bed and ripped open the envelope. She made the sign of the cross, praying she wouldn't be interrupted again before she'd read what the envelope contained.

Her hands were shaking so hard it took her a moment to realize four pieces of paper had fluttered out onto the pink bedspread. One was covered in neat black handwriting. Janet scooped up that one first.

It was a letter from Dolores Wood.

Dear Miss Jones,

(First, allow me to congratulate you on selecting such a cleverly simple pseudonym! "Janet Jones." Much more appropriate than something long and strange, like "Dolores Wood.")

Miss Jones, as you can imagine, I receive a great many letters from readers. I wish I had time to reply to them all, but it wouldn't be possible or I'd never have time left to write books. However, your letter stood out to me when I received it from my publisher, as you sound not unlike myself when I was a younger girl. In fact, I will admit that your letter affected me a great deal. At such a young age, *to have the nerves required to obtain a book like mine must have taken a great deal of fortitude. Your courage bodes well for your future.*

You requested my advice on how to become a writer yourself. My advice is simple: the only way to become a writer is to write. Every young writer has a story inside, usually countless stories. You must put yours onto paper.

Your letter didn't specify what kind of writing you mean to undertake, but should you have an interest in paperback fiction, I've taken the liberty of asking my editor to include his specifications alongside my letter.

Should you wish, I would also be happy to read your writing and offer my thoughts on it. When I first began to write, the perspective of older writers on my work was invaluable to me.

Finally, because I remember, too, being young, and having no money to call my own, I've enclosed bus tickets so that you may visit when your manuscript is ready. You can find me most evenings at the Sheldon Lounge on West Fourth and Charles Streets.

Wishing you well,
Dolores Wood

Janet had to read the letter twice, then three times, before she was certain she understood its contents.

Dolores Wood had written to her.

Dolores Wood wanted Janet to visit her in New York. At a place called the Sheldon Lounge.

Was the Sheldon Lounge like the places she'd written about in *A Love So Strange*? Was it a—a *lesbian* bar?

Janet couldn't wait to show this letter to Marie. She'd be astonished.

She reached for the other slips of paper. Sure enough, two of them were bus tickets, from Washington to New York and back again.

Janet had never taken a bus by herself. She and a few friends had traveled to Ocean City after graduation, but that had simply been for a day at the beach, and with one of the girls' older sisters as a chaperone. Janet's parents would never allow her to travel so far as New York on her own.

She tucked the tickets away in the drawer of her dressing table. The fourth piece of paper in the envelope was typewritten, from the Bannon Press office.

Dear Miss Jones,

Per the suggestion of Miss Wood, you are hereby invited to submit a manuscript for consideration by Nathan Levy, editor of Bannon Press. We have found success in publishing the novels of Miss Wood and similar works of Lesbiana by other authors, as interest in this topic has recently increased among paperback readers.

Our books, both fiction and otherwise, must speak honestly and candidly about the true nature of this topic, revealing its dangers and immoral associations (such as with other forms of criminality, witchcraft, et cetera). Our stories must end with appropriate resolutions for characters who engage in these practices. All manuscripts must be typewritten with one-inch margins.

Please send a whole or partial (100 pages or more) manuscript to the address below for review. Be sure to preserve a carbon copy of your original manuscript. Should your manuscript be accepted for publication, you would be granted an advance payment of $2,000. Bannon Press maintains all control regarding book titles, covers, advertising and the like.

Yours truly,
Sally Johnson,
assistant to Nathan Levy, editor-in-chief

Bannon Press
54 W 23rd St., 17th floor
New York, NY 10011

This letter was even harder for Janet to understand than Dolores Wood's. Her eyes kept skipping from word to word.

Lesbiana.

$2,000.

Witchcraft.

Witchcraft? Did it really say *witchcraft?*

Janet checked again. It did.

Her eyes drifted back to Dolores Wood's letter, and the drawer that held her bus tickets. Miss Wood must have thought Janet was older than she was. Eighteen-year-old girls didn't accept bus tickets from people they'd never met, or venture off by themselves to faraway cities.

Besides, it was beyond her wildest imaginings that she might actually go to New York and meet Dolores Wood herself. That she might enter a bar and see other girls like Janet and Marie. Girls who "engaged" in "practices" like the ones the Bannon Press letter had mentioned.

Janet's mind spun. She closed her eyes, and all at once she saw a story unfolding.

A nondescript bar with no windows on a quiet Greenwich Village street. The type of place workingmen hurried past without looking up. Those men wouldn't notice the girls who walked in and out of the bar with their eyes trained down, their hands tucked discreetly into their coat pockets.

Janet could see it all perfectly. As though she'd visited this bar already, where girls danced with other girls, as though that were a perfectly normal thing to do.

Behind her closed eyelids, Janet pictured two girls sitting at a small, grimy table, slightly removed from the other patrons. One of the girls had dark, curly hair and glasses. The other had blond hair and reminded Janet of a girl she'd once seen on television—the daughter of a contestant on some quiz show. The girl on the program had worn bright lipstick and a lovely dress, and as she'd smiled and twirled before the cheering audience her skirt had billowed out, offering the briefest glimpse of her knees.

Something about that girl had captivated Janet in a way she hadn't quite understood, but now she saw that she was *exactly* right for the story forming in her mind.

The blond girl in the bar had met the brunette that very night, Janet decided. It was the first time either of them had dared to enter the place. Which was called... Penny's Corner. And the two girls were... Paula. And Elaine.

Their story was only just beginning.

Janet opened her desk and reached in blindly, grabbing her old home economics notebook and a pencil. She turned to an empty page. A strange, tingling feeling flowed into her fingers as she wrote the first words.

> I'd never come to an establishment like this one before. At first, I was so nervous I could barely see straight, but when I spotted the blond sitting in the back, looking lost and lovely at the same time, I knew I'd made the right choice.

As Janet's pencil scratched across the paper, the tingling sensation crawled up to her chest. It was just like the night before, when she'd climbed onto that streetcar with Marie.

Janet lowered the notebook, gazing down at the pencil marks on the page. She'd just written the first sentences of her first novel. From here, the story could only grow.

A new set of lines began to take form in her mind. They were for later in the story, so Janet skipped her pencil down the page.

> "There's something I have to tell you, Elaine. Something I've longed to tell you."
> I was so breathless I could barely speak. "What is it, Paula?"
> "I love you. I've loved you from the moment I first saw you."
> I closed my eyes and tasted each word.

Elaine and Paula would fall in love. Janet could see it as clearly as she saw her own reflection in the mirror. The tenderness the two girls shared would be deep, true and undeniable. Until, tragically, society came between them, as it always must.

A title drifted into her mind, too. *Alone No Longer.* Janet wrote it across the top of the page.

She kept writing, the words coming to mind faster than she could scrawl them out. She jotted down notes for later, too. Scenes she would write soon, about love and loss and heartbreak.

Sometime later, her grandmother knocked on the door, but Janet claimed a headache and wrote on. She wrote all through the evening and the night that followed, until her eyes refused to stay open and the pencil fell from her limp fingers. Yet even as she finally felt herself passing into sleep, that tingling sensation never went away.

5

Tuesday, September 19, 2017

"It's for the best." Paula shrugged. She'd told this story to other girls before Elaine, enough times that she could say the words without them hurting much anymore. "They wanted me gone as much as I wanted out. They'd just as soon have nothing to do with me, and I feel the same way."

"Even so." The night's chill had crept in through the dark window. Elaine shivered in her thin blouse. She tapped out her cigarette, the ashes pooling in the tin with those they'd already smoked that evening. "It must've been hard, leaving. Knowing you were never coming back."

"Plenty of people have it worse." Paula shrugged again, but the movement took more effort this time. She suspected Elaine could tell she was putting up a front. Elaine, it seemed, could always tell what she was really thinking.

"I don't know what I'd do if my parents ever found out." Elaine shivered again. "Or the others back home. I suppose

*you're right—that's how it is for everyone—but that doesn't
make it any easier. What did your parents say when they found
out? How did you tell them?"*

"I didn't tell them." Paula let out a long, heavy sigh. "They
found out. I'd gotten a letter, from a…a friend. I should've
thrown it away, but I was careless. It was a sweet letter, the
first sweet letter I'd ever gotten from a girl, and though I hadn't
seen her again after that, I saved the letter so I could remember. I was young, and, well—that letter was the thing I loved
most in all the world."

Elaine nodded. Paula took in a deep breath.

"Well." Paula dropped her eyes, studying the tin of ashes.
She'd never told anyone this part of the story before, but she
wanted Elaine to know the truth. "What happened was, my
mother found it in my dressing table. She was prowling around
my things, probably looking for evidence I was up to no good—
she was always sure I was bad news. That afternoon, she came
down to the living room where I was doing my homework by
the fireplace and shoved the letter in my face, asking why a
girl was writing those sorts of things to me. Before I could even
think of what to say, she threw it in the flames."

"She burned your letter?" Elaine reached out to take Paula's
hand. Suddenly her touch was the only thing holding Paula to
the ground. "The letter you loved so much?"

"Like I said, it was my own fault." Paula drew a cigarette
from the pack with a shaky hand. "I should've known better
than to save it in the first place."

"I don't think it was your fault at all." Elaine stroked Paula's
hand, leaned across the table and kissed her lips. Her mouth was
warm and soft. "Someday, I'm going to write you a new letter.
One nobody can burn."

Abby closed her computer, the scene still echoing in her mind.

She traced her fingers over the stickers on the laptop's protective case. It was old stuff, mostly—a rainbow flag, a Bernie logo from the primaries and a Hillary one from the general, the "Feminism Is the Radical Notion That Women Are People" illustrated quote Ms. Sloane had given her last year after she told off one of the guys in their workshop for submitting his third story about a superhot robot babe.

It all dated back to when she and Linh were still together. Maybe that was why none of it felt right anymore. Abby wasn't the same person she'd been then.

She should probably peel off all her stickers with some Goo-Be-Gone. Start fresh. The way Paula had started over when she moved to New York.

Except...the past always followed you. Right? That was what Paula had learned, and Elaine, too. It was a miracle that Paula and Elaine had even made it out of the places they'd come from in the first place.

Or, well, it would've been a miracle if any of it had been true. Elaine and Paula were fictional, obviously. Even though they felt so incredibly real.

Abby wondered, not for the first time, if the characters were *entirely* imaginary. Marian Love could've drawn inspiration from people she knew, or even from her own life. Authors did that sometimes, right? Wrote carefully disguised stories about things that had really happened? Paula and Elaine felt too solid, too three-dimensional, to have come from nowhere.

Abby had finished the last page of *Women of the Twilight Realm* late the night before. At first she'd sat on the bed in a daze, overwhelmed by all the hours she'd spent in Elaine and Paula's world. Then she'd realized it was the perfect moment to start writing her own story, when her mind was still totally immersed. She'd opened a blank doc and tried to write a meet-cute for her two main characters, but none of the words she wrote sounded remotely cute compared to Marian Love's.

So she'd searched for more information about the book instead. She'd been hoping to find a sequel, but apparently Marian Love had never written another book, even though *Women of the Twilight Realm* sold millions of copies. In fact, she seemed to have straight-up disappeared off the face of the earth. And just like the other pulp authors, she hadn't been writing under her real name anyway.

Abby didn't understand it. How could anyone write a book that had such a huge impact, then vanish without ever writing more? How could Marian Love have resisted the lure of all those fans? Abby had kept writing fanfic for years, mostly because of the comments people left begging for more chapters, but the highest number of comments she'd ever gotten on one story was a hundred or so. She couldn't imagine having *millions* of people read something she'd written.

She opened her laptop again. She'd skipped her lit mag meeting—Abby was the editor, but it wasn't as though she had to be at every single meeting or the world would end—and come straight home from school. Her plan had been to spend the whole afternoon writing, so she'd have at least some chance of meeting Ms. Sloane's deadline, but she kept going back to *Women of the Twilight Realm* and rereading her favorite scenes instead.

She kept staring at the cover, too. Now that she'd finished the book, it made more sense. Paula was the one in the tie, and Elaine was the one with the fabulous boobs. Though if the sex scenes inside were accurate, Paula's boobs were pretty fabulous, too.

Plus, it had turned out to be so much more than a romance

novel. The story definitely started out with what Abby's fandom friends would've called "insta-love"—Paula and Elaine had sex and declared passionate love for each other the first night they met, and moved in together a few days later—but the obstacles they were up against were a lot more intense than in the romantic comedies Abby had seen. When Elaine tried to break up with her flaky boyfriend from back home, he arranged to get Paula fired from her job *and* basically outed Elaine to her parents, which led directly to Elaine's father committing suicide.

Probably. That last part was kind of unclear. It could've been an accident.

Strangely enough, though, the book didn't wind up being a downer in the end. Plus, it was honestly pretty fun just to read a novel that was all about lesbians. Abby hadn't realized how neat it would be to see characters like her front and center in a story. Sure, she spent plenty of time with queer people in real life—all her friends were somewhere on the queer spectrum, since Linh and Ben were both bi, Savannah was questioning, and Vanessa didn't use labels for sexual orientation but definitely didn't identify as straight—but it still sent happy shivers down Abby's spine to see the word *lesbian* used nonchalantly so many times in one novel.

Most of all, though, it was the romance that had swept her away. Sure, the book had its sappy, melodramatic moments, but there was just something about the way Paula and Elaine loved each other so *deeply*, even though they knew the outside world would never understand. True love, the kind they had, was strong enough to withstand absolutely anything.

And the ending—wow. Even with all the terrible things that had happened to Paula and Elaine, the end of their story still managed to be a perfect fantasy. The kind Abby loved most in the world. Despite all the challenges they'd faced, despite living in a world that would never understand them, the ending made clear that it was all going to be okay, because they had each other.

Maybe that wasn't realistic, but who cared? Abby had already had enough reality to last her a lifetime.

Footsteps rang out on the stairs, and Abby groaned silently. Every board in their house creaked in anticipation before you even touched it. It always annoyed her on shows when teenagers snuck out of their houses. If Abby had ever tried that her parents would've caught her before she'd even made it to the landing.

She hoped it was only Ethan. He'd go straight to his room without bothering her. But as the creaking got closer, it was clearly too heavy to be her brother.

Abby closed her eyes, bracing herself.

A knock on the door. "Abby? Can I come in?" It was Mom.

"Okay." Abby opened her eyes and arranged her face into a carefully bored expression.

"It's good to see you." Mom stepped inside slowly. She didn't hold out her arms for a hug, the way she always used to do when she got home from trips. Abby had told her parents she was too old for hugs a while ago, but it still felt kind of weird that nonhugging was their new default. "I missed you while I was away."

Abby hated it when her parents did their fakey-fake forced-affection talk. If they genuinely missed her, they wouldn't leave so often. "What did you guys wind up doing to Ethan? Is he grounded?"

"He had to apologize to Mr. Salem, and he lost his phone and his computer for a week."

"What, that's it? He basically attacked someone!"

Mom sighed. "Punishments are for adults to decide, Abby. So, how's school?"

"Okay." Abby struggled to think of something to say about school. Mom always tried to act as if she was interested in her life, which meant she never gave up until Abby told her at least one story about her day. "We went to Starbucks during free period and Ben got into this big involved debate with the barista about *Game of Thrones*. Then Vanessa told them both to quit it unless they were ready to talk about the inherent sexism in the writing, and we all started fighting about Daenerys, and Linh and I were almost late for stats."

Mom laughed and settled down into the desk chair, opposite Abby on the bed. "How's it going with you and Linh being friends now that you've been back in school for a few weeks? I know it can be difficult after a big change."

"It's fine." Abby wished she hadn't told her parents about her and Linh breaking up. She doubted they would've noticed if she hadn't spelled it out for them. Back in June, when it first happened, they hadn't seemed to realize she was crying in her room every night. Of course, the whole thing had been their fault in the first place, but they never seemed to grasp that, either.

But Abby had gone over and over it in her head, and it was the only explanation. The weirdness between her and Linh had started that day in May, when Linh and Abby had sat motionless on the stairs watching Mom and Dad's mutual meltdown.

Right after that whole thing happened Abby had been pretty messed up, so they'd gone to Linh's house. There was nowhere else to go. It was a long walk, all uphill, and they'd left Abby's house so fast to get away from the parent drama that they'd wound up leaving Linh's backpack on the floor of

Abby's room. The backpack had probably had stuff in it Linh needed for school the next day, but they didn't talk about that. They didn't talk about anything, in fact.

Instead, when they got inside Linh's house and saw that it was cool and dark and empty—deserted except for the two of them, the tasteful linen furniture and the cat purring in front of the restored brick fireplace—they'd started kissing. Then they went up to Linh's room.

If Abby had known that was going to be the last time they had sex, she probably would've paid more attention to the details. She'd be able to remember exactly how it started, exactly what they were wearing, exactly who said what and when. Though she wasn't sure either of them had said much of anything, come to think of it.

There was another fanfiction term—*hurt/comfort*. It used to be one of Abby's favorite fic genres, back before she knew what actual hurting felt like.

In hurt/comfort stories, something bad happened to one character, and then another character comforted them. Usually with lots of soft words and making out. Or more than making out, depending on the story's rating.

That evening, as she gazed into the sunset during the slow walk back from Linh's house, Abby had reflected, *This is my very own real-life hurt/comfort story.*

She'd thought putting a label on it might help. She was wrong.

Abby and Linh had never spoken about anything that happened that afternoon. But a few days afterward, Linh started talking about breaking up.

She was casual about it at first. So casual Abby got away with pretending not to understand, for a while. The problem was, Linh kept bringing it up. They were going to be apart for the summer anyway, she'd pointed out, with Linh off in Hanoi and Abby in Massachusetts—and *everyone* knew long-distance relationships were basically impossible. Maybe, she'd finally said one afternoon, casting a sideways glance at Abby, they were only delaying the inevitable.

Abby didn't let on how much that hurt. *She* hadn't stopped caring about Linh just because her family was slowly imploding.

But she didn't want to fight about it, because the very idea of fighting made her think about her parents. When Abby's mom and dad were fighting, they didn't even seem to care if they were hurting each other. Sometimes, they almost seemed to *want* to hurt each other.

So the night before Linh's flight, when she oh-so-casually mentioned breaking up again, Abby closed her eyes and nodded. She was tired, and so she agreed, because agreeing was easy.

She'd told herself it was temporary. That by the time the summer ended, Linh would realize how wrong she'd been, and they could pick up where they'd left off. For now, though, they'd agreed to be "just friends." Abby figured that was better than nothing at all.

They emailed every day that summer. At first, they kept it light. Linh told Abby about all the mistakes she was making as she struggled to learn Vietnamese, and about how every time she tried to cross the street she was positive she was going to get hit by a speeding motorcycle. She told funny stories, too, about how it was so oppressively humid that standing on the riverbanks watching the dragon boat races felt like standing in the middle of a thick wet cloud, and how she'd feared for her life the first time she climbed onto the back of her cousin's motorized scooter, but once they started moving the adrenaline rush was so addictive she was thinking about borrowing the scooter and venturing out on her own.

As the summer went on, though, Linh's emails changed. She started writing Abby long messages late at night about how complicated her feelings were becoming the longer she stayed in Hanoi. She wrote about how frustrating it was when strangers greeted her in Vietnamese, then started politely treating her like an out-of-touch foreigner when they realized she didn't understand. The language barrier put a constant strain on things at home, too, since Linh was spending all her time with her cousins. She was having a great time getting to know them, but communicating was still a big challenge. And as the end of the summer got closer, it was upsetting her more and more to think that this could be one of the last chances she'd have to spend time with all the relatives she'd grown close to.

Abby read all of Linh's emails closely. She spent hours looking up college cultural exchange programs and internships in Vietnam that Linh might be able to apply to next year, and she sent her long, detailed replies full of links and bullet points.

She tried to read between the lines of what Linh was saying, too. Sometimes, sprinkled throughout the stories about her trip, there would be occasional less-specific comments. Comments like, *It's just so hard to know if you're making the right decisions until it's already too late.* And, *Lately I've been changing my mind so often I can barely think in a straight line.*

Those comments gave Abby hope. Maybe too much hope.

But she knew better than to ask about that over email. That conversation should wait until they were in the same country, at least. So instead she told Linh funny stories of her own, like the one about the poetry reading her creative writing camp had gone to, and how all the boys had giggled and made inappropriate gestures during the poems about sex, and how it made her feel bad for all the straight and otherwise non-gay girls who had to put up with that kind of thing on the regular.

Abby didn't usually say much about her *real* life in those emails. There never seemed to be anything worth saying. She mentioned once or twice that her parents seemed to carefully coordinate their phone calls so that she never wound up talking to them both on the same day, and that she and Ethan only texted each other in emojis now. But she always tried to make those stories funny, too, using plenty of emojis of her own.

Either way, all that emailing had brought her and Linh closer—or so Abby thought. She was sure that when the school year started up again, Linh would realize she'd been wrong to freak out about what happened, and things could go back to the way they'd been. Or at least some approximation.

Abby wasn't that concerned about the details of exactly *how* they'd get back together. Not as long as the end result involved being held again. Being held, and feeling like she mattered to someone.

But that still hadn't happened, and Abby was still trying to act like that was perfectly fine. In the meantime, her family was slowly, slowly, *slowly* falling apart—but she was supposed to pretend everything was fine there, too.

And if Abby herself was also in the middle of a very gradual collapse, then hey, at least no one else seemed particularly bothered by it.

Mom cleared her throat, but she was still giving Abby that expectant half smile. As though she genuinely thought they'd now launch straight into old-fashioned girl talk about Abby's postbreakup social life.

"Hey, so, um…" Abby tried hard to think of something to say. She had to throw her mom off track before she suggested they dig into low-calorie ice cream and pop in a *Little Women* DVD or something. "I think I've decided. Is it okay if I make my donation this year to the ACLU?"

"Of course." Mom smiled. She was always up for talking about charitable giving. Everyone in the Zimet-Cohen family chose a charity to give to out of their savings every year. "I might do the same thing, after I figure out how much to give to the Northam campaign. So, Abby, I wanted to let you know—"

"Also, I meant to tell you." Abby cut her off before she could launch into some other topic Abby didn't want to talk about. "I finally have an idea for my senior project. I'm going to write a lesbian pulp fiction novel."

Mom stopped short and raised her eyebrows. "What exactly is that?"

"Oh, I thought you'd know. They were big in the fifties."

"Believe it or not, I wasn't alive in the fifties." Mom laughed again.

"Well, all I'm saying is, they're old." Abby rolled her eyes. "Plus it turns out some of them are pretty awesome. I kind of can't stop thinking about this one that I read. Here, this is what they looked like."

She pulled up *Satan Was a Lesbian* and held out her phone. Mom peered at the screen, a crease forming between her eyebrows.

"I know that one looks ridiculous, but if you can believe it, some of the books are really good." Abby knew she was prattling on, but at least her mom wasn't awkwardly trying to relate to her anymore. "I just read one about these women living in New York, and they're both fascinating. Especially this one, Paula. She might be my new favorite fictional character of all time."

Mom was still gazing down at *Satan Was a Lesbian*, looking lost, so Abby switched to the *Women of the Twilight Realm* cover instead. "That's Paula there."

"All right…" Mom zoomed in on the screen so she could read the text. "Is this an author who's written other books you like, too? What does that say her name is—Marian Love?"

"No, that's what's weird, she never wrote another book. That's not even her real name—all these books were written under pen names because everybody was closeted back then. People have figured out who most of the writers really were, but Marian Love disappeared without a trace. And since it was the olden days, she didn't leave a digital footprint, either. It's as if she vanished into nothing."

It sounded glamorous when she put it that way. Although come to think of it, Marian Love probably *was* pretty glamorous.

She must've been a lot like Paula. Abby could picture her perfectly—an older version of the women on those book covers, standing in a shadowed doorway in a chic vintage suit with one eyebrow cocked, holding a cocktail in one hand and a cigarette in the other.

"Are you trying to find out what happened to this author for your project, then?" Mom asked, finally looking up from the phone.

"Well, I don't have to look into that specifically, but—" Although now that Mom had mentioned it, that *did* sound interesting.

Maybe Ms. Sloane's historian friend could help Abby do some extra research and track down the real Marian Love. It couldn't be *that* hard to find her now that the internet existed. If she were still alive, maybe Abby could even email her. She could ask her about Paula and Elaine and what had happened to them after the book ended.

Or maybe they could even meet. Marian Love probably lived in New York, and that was an easy train ride from DC. Abby imagined walking into some trendy coffee shop in Brooklyn where Marian Love was waiting. She'd be so impressed Abby had found her.

"I bet I'd even get extra credit," Abby mused, picturing herself shaking Marian Love's perfectly manicured hand. "I could definitely use some extra credit."

"You could?" Mom cocked her head to the side. "Are you having trouble in your classes?"

"Oh, uh…" Abby looked away, trying not to think about that paper on Danica Roem she still hadn't turned in, or how close she was to missing Ms. Sloane's deadline. "No, it's just—extra credit's always good."

"Of course." Mom seemed satisfied with that answer. "Well, I definitely want to hear more about this project of yours. First, though, honey, there's something I need to tell you."

Abby's stomach jerked violently. She didn't know what Mom was going to say, but she knew she didn't want to hear it.

She stood up. "I have to go to the bathroom."

"Sure." Mom got up, too. "I only wanted you to know that Dad's trip is running longer than he expected. He'll be back Friday instead of tomorrow."

"Oh." That was all? "Okay."

Mom was watching her closely. "He'll hate to miss coming with us to services, but he's trying to get a ticket to one out in California."

"Oh. *Oh*…okay." Now Abby understood why Mom was making a big deal about this.

Thursday was Rosh Hashanah. Their family wasn't particularly religious, but Mom, Dad, Ethan and Abby always
went to the High Holiday services at the temple up on 16th
Street, the one where Abby and her brother had gone for
preschool. Even with all of Mom's and Dad's travel schedules, the whole family was always supposed to be together on
holidays. "If he's going to services there, why can't he come
back here instead?"

"He has a very important meeting, sweetie, and it's a five-
hour flight. Don't worry, you'll see him Friday. He'll be home
by the time school lets out."

Right in time for Mom to leave on *her* next trip.

Usually they were slightly less obvious about it. This week,
though, they each kept going away and staying only one or
two nights at a time. Did they seriously expect their kids not
to notice when they pulled this kind of crap? Suddenly Abby
was in the mood to hurl some water bottles of her own.

She reached for the doorknob. "I really do need to go to
the bathroom."

"All right." Mom followed her, brushing invisible lint from
her pants. "Then I want to hear all about this new book you're
writing."

"I don't have time to talk about it. I have to email my first
set of pages to Ms. Sloane tonight or I'll get points taken off.
Plus I have to do research on Marian Love."

Mom looked as though she wanted to argue, but she nodded. Abby walked down the hall as fast as she could and closed
the bathroom door behind her. She leaned against it, staring
at the ceiling.

So Dad wouldn't be home for Rosh Hashanah. Whatever.
It wasn't as if their family was especially into the holidays.

Maybe Abby wouldn't go to services, either. She could go

to school instead. If doing stuff together didn't matter to her parents anymore, she didn't see why it should matter to her.

She turned on her phone screen and ran a search for Marian Love. The first few results were stuff she'd already seen—articles about *Women of the Twilight Realm* and the mystery of how its author had disappeared—but farther down on the page was one she hadn't spotted before called "Marian Love Changed My Life."

It turned out to be a blog. Each entry was a letter someone had sent to Marian Love, care of her publisher, since *Women of the Twilight Realm* first came out in 1956. The blogger must have gotten the letters from Marian Love's publisher and scanned them, blocking out the identifying details.

They were mostly scans of old handwritten pages, some with lines crossed out and notes scribbled in the margins. A few had been written on old typewriters and still had ink smudges. Some had dates in the corners—December 4, 1957; February 2, 1959; May 7, 1964. Abby had to squint to make out what the letters said.

Dear Miss Love,

I'm sure you're very busy and probably don't have the time to read my letter, but I simply had to write to you. I've just finished your novel, Women of the Twilight Realm.

I thought I was the only one in the world who felt the way I did. When I read about the girls in your book, I realized I'm not alone. I would like to come to Greenwich Village the way Elaine did, but my children are so young and my husband is no help with them at all. How did you first learn there were other girls who felt the way you did? Was it from a book, too? If so, would you be able to mail it to me? I will of course pay the postage. My address is [blacked out square]

Dear Mrs. Love,

I read Women of the Twilight Realm. I want to say that you are a very good writer. I didn't know there were books like this. I live in Iowa and it is very different here. There are no other girls who are like me. My father says if I stay this way I can't live here anymore but I don't know where else to live because I don't have much money. I want to ask you to please write another book about girls who live in Iowa.

Dear Miss Love,

I came across your book, Women of the Twilight Realm, in a shop, and to say I was surprised would be a tremendous understatement. I admire your bravery in writing about such an unusual subject.

I wondered if it would be too much of an imposition if I were to visit you in New York to discuss these topics further. It would be no trouble for me to travel there, as my husband allows me full use of the car most weekends. I would be very happy to take you for dinner one evening. Or drinks, perhaps. I stay at the Waldorf Astoria when I'm in the city, and you would be welcome to join me for a cocktail in my usual suite.

There were dozens more.

Some of the blog posts had comments, too, that people had

submitted over the past couple of years since the site had been active. A lot of the comments mocked the letter writers for their spelling mistakes or blatant come-ons, but most of them were from women reminiscing about their own first readings of *Women of the Twilight Realm* and other books like it.

Abby couldn't believe how many women seemed to have realized they were gay from reading Marian Love's book. Even more had read it and discovered, for the first time, that they weren't the only non-straight people in the world. That there was a whole community out there.

It was weird to think that being gay used to mean being that isolated, but it was exciting to think a book could be so important. Maybe someday, someone out there would read a story Abby had written and be as affected by it as these women had been by *Women of the Twilight Realm.*

A lot of the letter-writers talked about how they were afraid of being outed to their families. Abby wondered if Marian Love had ever come out to hers. All parents back in the fifties were anti-gay by default. If Marian Love *had* come out, her parents probably disowned her, like Paula's had.

Some parents were the same way even now. They talked about that in a lot of their GSA meetings. Homelessness was still scarily high for queer kids, and especially for trans kids, because so many families still kicked them out. Even some of Abby's friends had problems with their parents, though nowhere near that level. Vanessa's parents still refused to use "they" pronouns, even though Vanessa must've explained the non-binary thing to them a hundred times already. And last year when Ben told his mom he was going to prom with a guy she gave him this whole speech about how prom was something you remembered your whole life, and how as long as he thought he was bi he might as well go with a girl so the memory of prom night wouldn't be ruined forever.

When Abby had come out to *her* parents, though, it was a total nonevent. This was back in ninth grade when they still had family dinners, and one night Abby had reached for the platter of grilled salmon and nonchalantly announced that she was going to the winter dance with Linh. Mom and Dad had immediately started negotiating with each other about who was going to give them a ride, so Abby had jumped in to add, "By the way, you do know I like girls, right?"

Dad had looked up, paused a moment, cleared his throat and said, "Of course, honey, and that's perfectly fine with us," and Mom had said, "Yes, sweetheart, and we love you, but do make sure you're careful," and Ethan, who'd been eight at the time but still old enough to know what "careful" meant, had yelled, "Ew! Ew! Ew!" And that was the end of the conversation.

Abby wished talking to her parents was still that easy.

She clicked back into *Women of the Twilight Realm*. There was another scene she wanted to reread.

Elaine's palm was slick with perspiration as she held the phone to her ear.

"I'm terribly sorry." She hoped Wayne couldn't hear the tremble in her voice. "But I've decided I can't accept the ring. I'm not the right girl for you, Wayne. You deserve someone who makes you happy, and I know now that I'll never be that girl."

Wayne didn't respond. Not at first. All Elaine could hear was his breathing, slow and heavy on the other end of the line.

She wished she could've talked to him in person. Instead, the long-distance call ticked on as Paula clattered pans in the kitchen behind her, the smell of steaks wafting into the corner of the living room where Elaine crouched over the phone.

When Wayne finally spoke, there was fury in his voice. "It's that girl, isn't it? That one with the short hair who was in your apartment when I came to New York. I knew she was a queer as soon as I laid eyes on her. I could kill her for doing this to my girl."

Elaine's breath caught.

At home, Wayne was always smiling. In school, he had always been the first to crack a joke, and the first to laugh at someone else's.

Elaine had never heard him sound this way. She'd never had reason to fear him.

"It isn't like that at all, Wayne, you must know that."

"The hell it isn't. I saw the way she looked at you. Listen to me, sugar, you're just a kid. You don't know the first thing about what you want. We've got to get you away from that— that damn bull dyke, so you can get back to being yourself again. Look, go to Grand Central and get on the first train headed north. I'll meet you at the station and we'll sort this all out."

"Is everything all right, Elaine?" Suddenly Paula was standing in the doorway, her lean figure outlined against the low light from the bedroom.

"Is that her?" Wayne's voice rose. "Are you with her right now?"

"No." Elaine wasn't sure who she was answering.

"Hang up," Paula said. Elaine shook her head.

"Put her on the phone," Wayne ordered. "I want to tell that queer what's coming to her."

Paula strode forward, her hand outstretched, as though she'd heard what Wayne had said.

"No!" Elaine jerked the receiver away. Paula stopped halfway across the room, holding up her hands.

"You get on that train, sugar," Wayne growled, his voice clear even as Elaine held the receiver over her head. *"I'll be waiting at the station at ten."*

The line disconnected. A moment later, the dial tone began to hum.

Elaine stared at Paula, the dead phone still in her hand. She couldn't decipher Paula's expression.

"He wants you to go back to Hanover?" Paula's tone was carefully neutral.

"Yes." Elaine set the phone back on the table. The click of the receiver settling into its cradle was impossibly loud in the silent apartment.

"He thinks I've corrupted you."

Elaine couldn't be sure how much Paula had heard, but there was no use denying it. *"Yes."*

Paula folded her arms across her chest. *"Well?"*

"What do you mean?"

"Are you going?"

Elaine stared at her. *"You can't be serious. I told you, I'll never go back to Hanover as long as I live."*

"I remember. But I didn't hear you tell him no."

It was the third time she'd read that scene, and Abby still wasn't sure how she felt about it. Wayne was being horrible, that much was clear, but Paula was almost as bad with the way she ordered Elaine around. As though *she* was the one in charge of *their* relationship.

Or was she only trying to help? Why *didn't* Elaine say, straight off, that she wasn't going back? If you loved someone, weren't you supposed to think about what they wanted before you thought about what *you* wanted?

Well. Come to think of it, Abby hadn't always thought about Linh before she thought about herself.

She wondered what Marian Love had been getting at when she wrote the scene that way. Had *she* ever loved someone like Paula, who always had to be in charge of everything? Or maybe Marian Love's girlfriend had been more like Elaine— so worried about what everyone else thought that she could never let herself move forward.

Unless one of the characters was based on Marian Love herself. If that was the case, it had to be Paula. Paula was the strong one. Marian Love must have been incredibly strong herself to have written her so well.

But even Paula wasn't perfect. She made mistakes. Like when she wrote that letter—the one that led to Elaine's parents finding out she was queer, once Wayne got his dirty hands on it. Though Elaine made plenty of mistakes of her own.

That was why Abby liked them so much. They both messed up, but they knew they'd messed up. Most of all, she loved that they tried to fix it when they did.

Fiction was so much better than reality. In real life, no one cared when they messed up, and they never bothered to do anything about it. They just pretended they hadn't done anything wrong in the first place.

A sudden knock on the door made Abby jump. It must be Mom, coming to see why she'd been in the bathroom so long.

"I'm fine," Abby called. "I'll be out in a minute."

Footsteps padded away from the door, but Abby ignored them and slid down onto the bathroom floor. She dove back into the pages, until her whole world was Paula and Elaine and Greenwich Village, and nothing else mattered.

6

Saturday, July 2, 1955

"This time next week, I can do the driving." Marie's eyes sparkled as she faced Janet across the taxi's wide leather back seat. A transit strike had gone into effect, shutting down every bus and streetcar in the city right in time for the girls' Saturday outing. "I still can't believe Dad's letting me have the Buick."

"I can't believe it, either." Janet grinned. "Is he getting a new car for himself?"

"Yes, something splashy, I'm sure. The newest Chevrolet, most likely. You know my father—he always needs to make an impression, especially now that he's gunning so hard for this promotion. The Buick's too old and worn down to help him there."

"Well, at least it means *you* get a car all your own!"

"As soon as it's back from the shop." Marie smiled and swept a hand toward the open window and the quiet suburban roads they were driving past. "Though I suppose it wouldn't have done me much good today, since you still won't tell me where we're going!"

Janet laughed and bounced in her seat. "I told you, it's a surprise."

"Well, I can see we've crossed the border into Maryland. It would only be fair to give me *some* hint as to why we're going so far out."

Janet only grinned again. "I promise, you'll love it."

Marie glanced down at her unlit cigarette and smiled. Janet couldn't recall her ever smoking before. Still, the cigarette, combined with her lovely matching gray skirt and blouse, made her look impossibly refined. Particularly next to Janet, who had to keep wiping off her sweaty fingers on her slacks.

Janet slipped a hand into her purse, tracing the fold in Dolores Wood's letter with her finger. The effect was strangely calming.

She'd asked the driver to keep their destination a secret before Marie had climbed into the taxi, but they were headed to a shopping district in Maryland. In the suburbs, they'd be far enough from home that they wouldn't risk being seen by anyone they knew. Silver Spring held several drugstores and even a bus station, and Janet couldn't wait to search them all for more books of "Lesbiana."

She tried to imagine the look on Marie's face when she found out there were other girls like them. That there were even *books* about them—and that Janet was going to write one.

She'd wanted to bring along her copy of *A Love So Strange* to show Marie, but the glue had grown so weak that pages fell out every time she touched it. It wouldn't withstand being carried in her purse. Besides, it would've been terribly embarrassing if Marie had noticed that the book automatically fell open to *those* scenes—the ones Janet had read so many times.

So Janet had brought the letters instead. Dolores Wood's, and the publisher's, too. She'd show them to Marie, and then they'd go from store to store looking for more books. Janet hoped to read as many as she could.

And later, they could celebrate once more. Marie's parents, and Janet's, too, would be dining at the club this evening. There was some sort of party to honor a new ambassador, with dancing late into the night, which meant Marie's house would be empty when the girls returned.

Janet and Marie could finally be alone, *properly* alone, for the first time since that night at Meaker's. Perhaps tonight, the two of them could pick up where they'd left off.

Of course, they couldn't discuss any of that with the taxi driver only feet away.

"Tell me more about your job," Janet asked instead.

Marie beamed. After three days at the State Department, her nervousness had vanished and she was full of stories about her amusing coworkers and her demanding-but-fair boss, Mr. Harris.

"I hope you can come and meet everyone soon." Finally seeming to notice her unlit cigarette, Marie reached into her purse and withdrew the matchbook she'd taken from Meaker's. Her fingers moved hesitantly as she struck a flame. "Everyone's so funny, and they're all so kind to me, even though I'm the new girl. The work isn't nearly as difficult as I'd expected, either. There aren't many documents for me to type yet, so I have plenty of time to organize my things. Of course, that's partly because my security clearance still hasn't been finalized. It should come soon enough, but it's a nuisance having to wait."

Marie placed the cigarette carefully between her lips. A moment later, she turned away and coughed into her hand.

"Did you start smoking in secretarial school?" Janet asked.

"Oh, I smoked once or twice there, I suppose, but I fell off after that." Marie tapped the cigarette out the cracked-open window. "I decided to take it up again. To fit in at work, you know."

"I'm sure you already fit in beautifully. You fit beautifully everywhere."

Marie blushed and looked down, and Janet had a sudden, daft compulsion to reach across the seat and take her hand. It was the kind of thing Paula might do. But this taxi certainly wasn't Penny's Corner.

"I have something to show you." Janet drew the letters from her purse before she could change her mind and passed them to Marie. She kept the envelope for herself. It still felt warm against her palm.

Marie smiled, but there was some confusion on her face as her eyes dropped to Dolores's letter. Janet watched her eyes travel along each line.

Her forehead creased. "What does this mean, about a pseudonym?"

"Oh, I think she was mistaken. I signed my real name when I wrote to her, but I suppose she thinks 'Janet Jones' is so simple I must've made it up!"

Marie glanced up toward the driver. "You wrote to her?"

"Yes. I'm sorry, I should've mentioned that. You see, I found a book she'd written—it's a marvelous book, I'll show it to you as soon as I can—and I wrote to her, and—"

"Why is she talking about *fortitude*?" Marie's forehead crease deepened. "What type of books does she write?"

"Ah—" Janet glanced up again at the driver, too. Perhaps she should've waited until they'd left the taxi to share these letters with Marie.

"What's this about bus tickets?" Marie's voice had grown

tight. Janet could see her measuring her words. "Have you met this Mrs. Wood before?"

"Well, no, but you must understand—"

Marie pushed the letter aside and reached for the typewritten page from Bannon Press. Janet had a sudden wish to pull it back before Marie could read it. She should've explained first.

"What *is* this?" Marie dropped the letter and pushed it backward across her lap after only a few seconds. Terror passed over her face. "Janet, what kind of people *are* these?"

The driver's eyes flicked toward them in the rearview mirror.

"I'm sorry." Janet hoped Marie hadn't noticed the driver's new interest. "I should've explained. You see, I—"

"Did you..." Marie pushed the letters toward Janet, then flipped them over until only the blank sides were visible. When she spoke again her cheeks were flushed, her voice a fragment of a whisper. "Did you *tell* someone about—about what happened?"

"No, no, of course not." Janet tried to match Marie's low tone. Even in her urgency to reassure her, she couldn't help but note that this was the first time the two of them had spoken about the fact that *something* had happened between them that night. "I would never, I promise."

"Then how did—why—" Marie was still staring down at the letters as though one might scoot back across the seat and bite her. Janet took the papers, folded them carefully and tucked them back into her purse.

"I wrote to Miss Wood weeks ago." Janet spoke quickly. "Her book changed everything for me. When I read it, I realized there's more to the world than I ever knew. Plus, I want to be a writer—you know that's always been my dream."

"Of course." The worry faded slightly from Marie's eyes. "You're planning to study journalism."

"Well, I was. I thought journalism was the only sort of writing I could do, until I found Miss Wood's book. When you read it, you'll see. There are other people out there, people like—"

Janet cut herself off. The driver's eyes were fixed on the road in front of him, but there was no doubt he was listening to every word they said.

"Oh?" Marie's face was crimson, her voice high. She'd begun watching the driver, too. "Why, I'm sure I don't know what you could possibly mean by that."

Janet began to feel slightly sick.

"I—" She didn't know what to say. "That is, I—oh..."

She couldn't cry. Not here. Not with Marie beside her, looking strangely calm as she tossed her cigarette butt out the window.

"All right," Marie murmured after a moment. The taxi had pulled up alongside the address Janet had given the driver, a Peoples Drug store on Georgia Avenue. Streams of shoppers filled the sidewalks, but Janet couldn't imagine going shopping after this.

Marie carefully drew out another cigarette and struck a match, keeping her eyes fixed on the flame instead of on Janet.

"All right, then," Marie said again. "All right. We're here. I'll pay the fare, sir."

"I can pay it," Janet said, fumbling in her purse, but Marie had already passed a dollar into the front of the taxi.

"Let's go inside." Marie drew in a long stream of smoke as she waited for her change. Her fingers were steady, but her voice shook. "Perhaps one of these stores will be air-conditioned. It would be nice to get away from all these crowds. Do you ever feel as if everyone in the entire world is staring right at you?"

Janet watched Marie exhale, smoke blowing through the crack in the window.

The two girls' eyes met. Marie's swift smile was so warm, so open—and it was focused solely on Janet. As though it could never be meant for anyone in the world but her.

Something passed between them. A sudden, silent understanding.

Marie wanted to get away from the driver, and the crowds. She wanted it to be just the two of them, where they could talk frankly, without worrying about everyone else.

It should be this way between Elaine and Paula in the second chapter, too, Janet realized. *I can't let myself forget this feeling. I have to write it exactly this way.*

"I understand precisely," she told Marie.

"Let's go, then."

They didn't speak again until they were safely inside Peoples. Janet wanted to describe every thought churning through her, but she wanted to enjoy the quiet anticipation between them, too.

It turned out the store wasn't air-conditioned, but the broad, bright aisles still felt cool and quiet after the taxi. Only a few customers were examining the merchandise or seated at the soda fountain at the front of the store. A pair of young children darted about near the cash registers while their parents sat at the counter sipping coffee.

Janet drifted toward the racks of paperback books and magazines that ran along the back wall, even though she didn't have much hope of finding a book like *A Love So Strange* here. She'd already checked the paperback racks at the Peoples in Georgetown, and they didn't seem to carry that sort of fiction. They'd probably have better luck at another store, but Peoples was a familiar place to start.

"Is this why we're here?" Marie stared at the racks of magazines, her arms folded across her chest. She spoke in a low whisper. "To find books full of witchcraft and murder, like your letter said?"

"No, no, they aren't all like that." Janet kept her voice low, too, as she swiveled a wire rack. All the covers here featured men, often with pretty girls in the background. None of these would be the books they wanted. "The one I read was entirely different. It's about a girl, Betty. She's a perfectly normal girl at first, until she's out on a date with her fellow one night and they go into a bar for a quick drink. They realize too late that it's one of *those* bars, and Betty catches the eye of an older girl. Then she goes back to the same bar later, without the man, and—"

"Shh." Marie looked over her shoulder, but there was no one nearby. "What do you mean, *those* bars?"

"Oh, you know." Janet tried to soften her voice even further. "They have those, in New York. Maybe other cities, too. Special bars, for girls like us."

Marie looked behind them again. *"Shhhh."*

As Janet had suspected, there was nothing to be found in Peoples, so she led Marie outside and down the block. Silver Spring wasn't nearly as crowded on this Saturday afternoon as Georgetown would've been, but even so, Marie's eyes darted anxiously from face to face as they moved down the sidewalk.

"Let's try this one next," Janet said, pointing.

"Are you sure?" Marie frowned at the small, grimy building before them. The sign over the door read Gray's Drugs in faded red paint. Its windows, so different from the crowded, colorful displays at Peoples, were nearly empty save for a few signs advertising shoe polish and blood-thinning tonics. "I've never been in a Gray's before. Aren't their stores awfully shabby?"

"Let's find out. It'll be an adventure." Janet winked. To her relief, Marie laughed.

The inside of the store was as dingy as the outside. Janet ignored the crumbs on the floor and the white-haired man staring at them from behind the cash register as she led Marie to the back. The few other customers ignored them and went on perusing shelves stocked with cough syrups and cheap perfume.

When she saw the rows of paperbacks, Janet's heart did a flip. At Peoples the books had been displayed under bright lights, like all the other merchandise, but here the tall, spinning wire racks were relegated to dusty shadows. It was exactly like the bus station in Ocean City where she'd first spotted *A Love So Strange*. Janet felt a flutter in her chest as she studied the lurid covers showing men in dark suits running down alleys, cowboys on horses waving guns over their heads, and scaly science-fiction creatures looming over screaming girls in tight-fitting space suits.

"How do you tell which books are—*that* kind?" Marie was staring at the racks as though afraid to touch them.

"Trust me, you'll know." Janet lifted one of the cowboy books. Behind it was a mystery, with a dead girl's hand reaching out from a dark grave. "We just have to look through all of these until we find them."

"Well, I suppose the benefit to coming into Gray's is that no one from work is likely to see me here." Marie reached for the nearest stack. "I can't imagine anyone from the State Department coming into *this* store."

"Probably not. If they did see you, though, you could al-

ways say you were looking for a nice Western." Janet held
up a book called *Red Moon on the Ranch*, showing a swarthy
sheriff aiming his gun at a bandit in a yellow handkerchief.
Marie smiled.

"You'd like them." Marie twirled the rack and reached for
a new book. The racks weren't as full as they had initially
appeared—the two of them had already gone through half the
books here. "The girls at the office, I mean. We all gather at
the same table in the cafeteria for lunch, unless someone's on
an important project for her boss and can't be spared. Yesterday I had to bring a sandwich back to Pat because Mr. Brown
had her working on a— Oh, look, is this one of them?"

Janet looked up excitedly, but the book Marie held was
nothing but a standard science fiction novel. A green-skinned
girl in a black dress and a leering, helmeted man stood in front
of a futuristic cityscape.

"No, no." Janet pointed at the man. "If it were, he'd be a
girl. Besides, I don't think the books we're looking for would
be science fiction. We probably ought to try another store."

Marie didn't protest as Janet led her back through the aisles
and out onto the street. Janet decided to try the bus station
next.

"I don't see how you can tell by looking at the covers,"
Marie whispered as they wove through the crowd. "They
wouldn't dare show *that* right on the front. The publishers
would go to prison!"

"No, but there are certain clues. If two girls are on the
cover, that's usually a sign." Janet tried to speak with author-
ity, even though the only lesbian book she'd ever actually
seen was *A Love So Strange*. "Someday, if my book is ever
published, that's the kind of cover it'll have."

"*Your* book?" Marie's face stayed carefully composed, but

Janet could hear the strain in her voice. "You're…you're really doing that? Like the letter said?"

"No one else knows," Janet assured her. "It's just a lark, really. I've been very careful to keep it secret."

"Still." Marie pulled another cigarette from her purse.
"What if your parents find out?"

"They won't. No one knows but you."

When they pushed through the glass doors to the bus station, the fan that blew from the ticket counter brought a
welcome relief from the heat. Marie grew quiet as she gazed
around the wide, open space. The bus station was much more
crowded than Gray's or Peoples, but none of the passengers sitting in the waiting area seemed to pay the girls any attention.

Janet plucked Marie's sleeve and pulled her toward the pe-
riodical racks that lined the back wall. The light overhead
was bright, and they could see the books much more clearly
than they had in Gray's.

There were more books here than at either of the drugstores—a full four racks—and Janet's heart leaped again. Perhaps she'd find another book by Dolores Wood, describing
what happened to Betty after the end of *A Love So Strange*.
Could she have left her boyfriend and found love again? If
that were even possible for her, with Sam gone forever.

"I'm not so sure about this, Janet," Marie whispered, glancing behind them.

"Don't worry." Janet spun through the nearest rack. "We'll
only take a quick look."

As usual, the wire racks were filled with Westerns and outer
space stories. A cover painting of a blond girl pulling her robe
open and pointing a gun caught Janet's eye, until she noticed
the man in a suit at the far edge of the frame. She spun the
rack again, blinking past painting after painting of guns, of

girls with their dresses pulled down low, of huge yellow and red letters blaring words like *Desire* and *Sin* and *Outlaw.*

A blur of orange jumped out at Janet on the second rack she checked. Her eyes darted down to a pair of breasts, then up to a smear of bright red lipstick. There was another smear beside it.

Two girls, on one cover.

"I've found one!" In her excitement, Janet forgot to lower her voice. "Look, Marie!"

"Shh!" Marie didn't look at the book in Janet's hand. "Don't call me that. Anyone could—"

"But *look!*" Janet held out the paperback. *A Deviant Woman,* it was called, by Kimberly Paul. The cover showed a beach scene with a beautiful blond girl in the foreground—it was her breasts Janet had first noticed, spilling out of a tight gold bikini—and a girl with short dark hair sitting just above her. The dark-haired girl was wearing a green bathing suit with the straps undone and hanging loose from her neck. A wave crashed to the shore behind them.

Janet could only imagine what the two girls were doing alone together on that beach.

"I don't *want* to look at it." Marie glanced behind them again, checking every angle to see who might be watching. "Let's just go."

"We came all this way." Janet gazed down at the book's cover. "I thought you wanted to see this."

"Well, I don't." Marie started walking quickly toward the ticket counter. "I'll meet you outside."

Janet stayed where she was, turning back to the book.

She remembered this moment at the bus station in Ocean City. The sudden compulsion that made her slip *A Love So Strange* under her blouse.

Janet didn't want to be a thief, but she wanted this book. She wanted to take it home and read it after everyone else had gone to bed. To stare at that cover anytime she wanted to.

Well, why shouldn't she buy it? It only cost a quarter. She had ten times that in her purse.

A surge of boldness flowed into her. It was just how she'd felt that night outside Meaker's.

Janet straightened her shoulders, walked up to the cashier and laid the book flat on the counter. "Hello. I have a purchase, please."

The man smoking behind the register didn't look at her at first. He was staring down at a magazine he'd spread out on the desk. After a moment, with an annoyed grunt, he glanced over at *A Deviant Woman*.

Only then did he raise his eyes to look at Janet.

She shifted, wishing she'd picked up a packet of gum or a newspaper or something else she could have put on top of the book. Instead, the cover of *A Deviant Woman* stared up at them both.

The cashier's face slid into a smirk.

"Will that be all, then?" He glanced down at Janet's bare left hand, then added, with a low chuckle, *"Miss?"*

"Yes." Janet's voice came out very small. She cleared her throat and tried again. "Yes, that will be all, thank you."

"Twenty-six cents."

Janet handed him a dollar and shifted again while the man took his time making her change. He didn't bother to disguise his amusement, his eyes darting back and forth from the book on the counter up to Janet's face, letting his eyes linger along the way.

"You go on and be a good little girl, now." The man

winked as he passed her the change and slipped the book into a brown paper bag.

Janet shoved the change into her purse without bothering to count it and hurried out of the store as fast as her legs would carry her. Her face burned. She didn't look back, but she could feel the cashier watching her all the same.

"Are you all right?" Marie asked as soon as she stepped outside. Janet nodded in a rush. She was glad, so glad, that Marie had waited out here for her. Then Marie noticed the paper bag. "What's that?"

"Oh, it's…" A new wave of shame crashed over Janet. The bag felt dirty, suddenly, as though it might infect her. "It's nothing."

"Please tell me you didn't buy it." Marie stared at the paper bag with revulsion in her eyes. She pressed a fist against her mouth. "Janet, *please*."

"Oh, stop that, it's only a book." Janet's shame twisted into anger. "It can't hurt you."

"What? Surely you understand that's not what worries me."

"Isn't it?" Janet turned and began to walk rapidly back toward Georgia Avenue, still clutching the bag. She wished her purse were bigger so she could shove it inside. "When we're alone you seem quite pleased with me, but here it's as though you think I'm out to get you."

"What are you talking about?" Marie's whispers were laced with indignation. "I'm only worried someone could find out. Don't you remember what happened to that boy? That senator's son, the one who was caught with another…" Marie swallowed, as though she couldn't even say the word. Janet had no idea who she was talking about, but she could grasp her meaning well enough. "It was *terrible*. I can't be seen with

that book, and neither can you. To think, of you writing one
yourself! What would the sisters at Holy Divinity say?"

"I'm not planning on discussing it with the sisters at Holy
Divinity!"

"*Please* keep your voice down!"

"Oh, I'm *so* sorry." Janet shifted to an exasperated whisper. "If you're that worried someone might see us together,
perhaps you'd better leave without me."

Marie stopped walking. She stared at Janet, as though waiting for something. When Janet didn't reply, Marie finally said,
"Perhaps I should."

"Go on, then."

"I will."

For a moment, neither of them moved. Their eyes stayed
locked as shoppers moved around them on the busy street.
Janet was reminded, cruelly, of the fixed gaze Sam and Betty
shared on the cover of *A Love So Strange.*

She knew, in some corner of her mind, that Marie was
right. That it was Janet who was unusual for having become
so enraptured by these books and this exciting new world.
Still, she didn't lower her gaze.

It was frightening to think of how different all of this was
from what she'd always known, but Janet didn't regret what
she'd done. She wouldn't let her fears dictate her choices.

Finally, Marie turned toward the street and lifted her arm.
A taxi pulled up.

Marie looked over her shoulder as she slid into the back
seat. The girls' eyes met one last time. Then, just as quickly,
she was gone, the taxi pulling away from the curb before Janet
had made up her mind to stop it.

7

Monday, September 25, 2017

"I'm sorry, Elaine, but I can't accept this. Not from my own daughter."

They were the last words she'd ever heard her father say.

Elaine had called the police station in Hanover, but they couldn't answer her questions. Mother couldn't, either—or wouldn't. Every time she'd tried to call, Mother had hung up as soon as she recognized Elaine's voice on the line.

And so no one had told Elaine precisely what happened. She'd had to piece together several disparate accounts until it began to make sense.

Father had left for work in the morning, at the same time he always did. He'd parked his car across from his office, like usual. Then he'd started to cross the street—without waiting for the light to change.

A pickup truck had been speeding down the road. Father had been directly in its path, but he hadn't tried to move.

When the ambulance arrived, his body was already cold.

Had it been intentional? An accident? Elaine would never know for certain. Yet it had happened only days after Wayne had made sure her parents found the letter and learned the truth about her, and Elaine couldn't convince herself it had been entirely a coincidence.

She'd never again hear Father's bellowing laugh, or see the way his eyes crinkled when he smiled. He was gone forever.

All because of the way she was.

Abby groaned every time she thought about that scene.

It was such a cliché for a queer character to think she'd caused her dad's suicide. As though it were *Elaine's* fault her dad was a homophobe.

She knew pulp books had to have tragedy in them to get around the censors, but Abby had already read so many books and seen so many shows and movies where the gay characters wound up dead or distraught that the last thing she wanted to do was read about it *again*. Besides, she liked the book's ending a few chapters later so much better—the scene where Elaine and Paula resolved to stay together in spite of all the tragedies they'd been through.

Still, for some reason, Abby had read the scene about Elaine trying to figure out what had happened to her dad half a dozen times. Maybe that was why it was stuck in her head now, when she was supposed to be paying attention to what her friends were talking about.

"I'm ghastly at sun salutations," Vanessa was saying. The five of them had just come from a yoga fund-raiser for hurricane relief in the middle of Dupont Circle, and they were all varying levels of sweaty. "Give me Zumba any day."

"There's no such thing as being ghastly at yoga," Ben said,

as though he was suddenly a yoga expert. "You saw us all back there. I fell over, like, three times, but it was totally fine. The teacher even said my hummingbird breathing was excellent."

"It's humming *bee* breathing, not hummingbird." Abby reached into her pocket to silence her buzzing phone. "Besides, she only said that because she thought you were cute."

"Ooh, really? Hot cute or little-kid cute?"

"What do you care?" Vanessa elbowed him.

"Ow." Ben rubbed his side, but he was grinning. Abby rolled her eyes. She liked flirting a lot more when she was one of the participants.

But Linh and Savannah were walking behind the rest of them, talking about cross-country, which meant she was too far away to flirt with. Lately, their friend group had been switching up its usual patterns. Savannah and Vanessa had gone out for most of the year before, and their relationship had overlapped with Linh and Abby's, which meant for a long time their group had consisted of two neat couples, with Ben in the mix to keep things interesting. Sometimes, if he was going out with someone they'd join the group, too, but Ben had been single so far this year, which meant their group was couple-free for the first time anyone could remember.

Everything was getting all mixed up all of a sudden. Abby hadn't realized how much she'd enjoyed the easy symmetry of the way things used to be.

She shook it off and squinted at the sign on the corner, looking for the LGBT Archive headquarters. The others were taking the long route back to the metro, but Abby was meeting with Ken Aldrich, the historian Ms. Sloane knew, before she had to go back to campus for Ethan's recital.

"What does that street number say?" she asked Ben, squinting up at the sign. "Is it 1717?"

"No, that's 1715," Linh called from behind her. Abby smiled, glad to see she was listening to them after all. "We're almost there."

Abby glanced back at her. Linh smiled in return, and Abby felt a rush of delight.

It was going to be a good afternoon. She could feel it. For one thing, Linh was smiling that gorgeous smile at her. And for another, she was only a few minutes away from knowing how to find Marian Love.

If Ken Aldrich's information was as good as she hoped it would be, Abby and Marian Love could be sitting down for coffee this very weekend. Or maybe martinis. If *Women of the Twilight Realm* really was based on her life, Marian Love drank nothing but martinis.

Abby could already picture the articles. They'd have headlines like "The Girl Who Solved the Mystery" and "Out-and-Proud Lesbian Teen Finds Long-Lost Closeted Lesbian Author" next to photos of Abby with a smiling Marian Love. They'd both look fabulous in vintage pencil skirts, and the captions would quote Marian saying something like, "This brave young woman showed me I no longer have to hide."

Abby kept imagining her first conversation with Marian Love. She already had the basics planned out. She'd start by asking a few questions about *Women of the Twilight Realm*—most of all, she wanted to know if Paula and Elaine had definitely stayed together for good after the book ended, because it was kind of implied that they did, but the last chapter wasn't totally a hundred percent clear—and then she'd transition to convincing Marian Love to reveal her true identity to the whole world, starting with Abby's social media accounts.

Marian Love, and Paula and Elaine, had been taking up a significant percentage of Abby's brain space these days, in fact.

Of course, she'd been doing her homework, too, more often than not. She'd turned in that paper for Women's and Gender Studies only a couple of days late, and she'd managed to write a few chapters of her project for Ms. Sloane. She didn't have a title yet, so she was calling her book *The Erotic Adventures of Gladys and Henrietta* (which wasn't even all that bad a title, in Abby's humble opinion). The main character, Henrietta, spent most of her time railing against the unfairness in the world around her, so she was fun to write.

"I think that's the building." Linh pointed to a row house on the next block while they waited for the traffic light to change.

"Goody." Abby bounced on her toes. Her phone hummed again with a text from her dad, but she turned it off. "This Ken Aldrich guy better have some good leads on what happened to Marian Love."

"I know that would mean a lot to you." Linh's expression shifted, her eyes going wide and her smile turning fake as she slipped her hands into the pockets of her shorts.

Linh had been gamely listening to Abby talk about Marian Love all week, but now she was making a big show of looking all patient and understanding, and that wasn't what Abby wanted at all. She wanted Linh to listen to her because what she said was interesting, not because she felt sorry for her. Abby hated being pitied more than anything.

"Hey, I wanted to ask you something." Vanessa sidled up between them and nudged Abby with their elbow. Linh stepped back to make room, her normal smile returning. "You remember that movie *Carol*, with Cate Blanchett?"

"You mean the one Abby made the whole GSA watch last year?" Savannah laughed. "Because it's the only fifties lesbian movie ever made?"

"Of course I remember it." Abby glanced over at Linh to

see if she remembered, too, but Linh was typing something on her phone.

"Well, did you read the book it was based on?" Vanessa asked. "I read it last year. It was kind of weird, but still really good. Was that one of these books you keep talking about?"

"*The Price of Salt?* Yeah, same genre. I read it last week. It's gorgeous, right?"

"Totally. I read it because of the movie, but the book was *so* different."

"I know! It's completely devastating and overwhelming in a way the movie kind of isn't, right?"

"Exactly!" Vanessa was gushing, which was delightful to see. Vanessa never gushed.

"Is the book as white as the movie?" Linh asked.

"Whiter, as far as I could tell," Abby said, glad Linh was still listening to them. "I think the book's got one reference to a black hotel porter who doesn't get any lines."

"Whereas the movie had, like, *two* nonspeaking black porters," Vanessa said, and they all cracked up.

"Yeah, that's one of the things that bothers me the most about these books," Abby said as the laughter subsided. "Everybody in them is *so* generically white. It's as though they had no idea what the world is actually like. I mean, look around us."

Abby swept her arm out. She'd meant to point out the bustling groups of office workers they kept passing on the sidewalk, but her friends glanced back and forth at each other instead. They were a pretty diverse group themselves—she and Savannah were both white, Linh was Vietnamese-American, Ben was black, and Vanessa's family was from Brazil—but that wasn't what Abby had meant. It was just bizarre, how the pulp novels all seemed to exist in an entirely all-white world.

"So, excessive whiteness aside, are you saying one of these books is *good*?" Ben asked. The walk light came on, and they started across the street. "A book that wasn't written by your long-lost soul mate, Marian Love?"

"A bunch of them were good." Abby sighed. She'd already explained this to her friends a dozen times. "*Most* of them were bad, but that's because most of them were written under pseudonyms by straight cis men who had no idea what they were talking about."

"Ha!" Vanessa said. "Predictable."

"You have to hunt to find the ones by actual lesbians." Abby tried to keep her excited gestures in check. Sometimes she got carried away when she talked about this stuff. "I read one called *The Girls in 3-B* that was great—you could tell it was written by an actual real-life gay woman—but then I tried to read this one called *Voluptuous Vixens* by Kimberly Paul, and it's so obvious that a straight guy wrote it. I'm sorry, but as someone who's actually *had* lesbian sex, I want to send these guys a memo telling them lesbians don't actually bite each other's nipples all the time. I mean, that would *hurt*. A *lot*."

Too late, Abby realized she should've stopped talking a few sentences ago.

"Speak for yourself, dude." Ben laughed, trying to make a joke of it, but he sounded high-pitched and strained, and the others didn't say anything at all.

Ugh. Abby definitely should've known better than to start talking about lesbian sex in front of her friends. All of whom knew she'd only had lesbian sex—or any kind of sex, for that matter—with one person. And that the person in question was currently walking three feet away with her face buried in her phone.

"Okay, well, anyway." This time it was Abby who sounded shrill. She jerked her head up just in time to see the number on the building above them. She was in luck. "Looks like this is the place! Anyone want to come in with me?"

"I've got a paper to write," Ben said quickly.

"Yeah, me, too," Vanessa echoed.

"I'm supposed to meet my mom." That was Savannah.

Abby glanced back hopefully, but Linh shook her head. "Sorry. Can't this time."

"Okay." Abby squared her shoulders. She'd been hoping Linh would want to come in, but she couldn't let that show. "See you guys later, I guess."

She climbed the steps warily. Abby had expected the building to look like a museum, with big columns out front and maybe a domed roof, but this was only a normal row house. A tiny sign next to the front door read LGBT Archive of DC—Dial 200.

Abby dialed. The keypad rang twice, then three times, then four. She was starting to wonder if the place was closed when a man's voice coughed into the speaker.

"Hello?" Abby pressed the button and leaned in. "I'm looking for Ken Aldrich?"

The man coughed again. "What?"

"Uh..." This meeting wasn't off to a good start. "My teacher called ahead—Neena Sloane?"

"Oh, Neena." The man's voice changed, and he let out a chuckle. "Sure, come on up. It's the second floor."

The buzzer clicked. Abby stepped through into a small entryway, followed the narrow set of stairs up and knocked on a solid wooden door.

The man was still coughing when he opened it, but he smiled into his handkerchief and beckoned her inside. He was younger than Abby had expected for a historian—in his twenties, maybe.

He ushered her into a cozy space the size of a small living room with an original, obviously never-used fireplace on the back wall, exactly like the one in Abby's house. The other walls were covered in towering bookshelves. A coffee table and a few scattered chairs took up the center of the room, and a narrow hallway led to another room in the back.

The coughing man sat down in one of the chairs and gestured for Abby to sit across from him. "Welcome. I'm Ken. Sorry, I forgot this was today. I'm under the weather, so I wasn't planning on opening up this afternoon, but I can take a few minutes if there's something you need."

"Thank you." Abby tried to smile. "I'm sorry to bother you when you're sick. I'm just trying to find Marian Love."

"Ah. I believe that name sounds familiar…"

Abby widened her eyes. She'd been sure a queer historian would know exactly who she was talking about. "She was the lesbian pulp author who wrote *Women of the Twilight Realm*. She probably published it under a pseudonym, but I want to find out who she really was. Ms. Sloane thought you might have some information."

"Ohh, I see." Ken glanced toward the bookshelf. "Well, I'm not sure how much I'll be able to help you, unfortunately. Most of our materials here are focused on local history. I hate to ask this, but did you already try Google?"

"Yes." Abby was getting annoyed, but she tried not to let it show. "I read everything I could find, but it says her identity is still a mystery."

"Huh, interesting." Ken folded his hands under his chin. "I could never get into those old pulp books, myself. Too soap opera–esque for my taste, but to each his own. *Women of the Twilight Zone*, did you say the title was?"

"*Twilight* Realm." Abby resisted the urge to roll her eyes and turned to study the nearest bookshelf. It was full of thick, serious-looking history books and files. Though some of them also had seminaked men on their covers.

"Right. Well, we might have a copy of it in the back. An early edition, if that would help you at all. One of my colleagues did some research work with one of the lesbian presses."

"Sure, that would be cool to see, but do you know where I might find any information about the actual author? What her real name was, where she lived, anything like that?"

Ken frowned. "Hmm. This would've been, what, the sixties?"

"Earlier. The book came out in 1956."

"You're sure the author was a woman? A lot of those books were written by men, weren't they?"

Abby struggled to hide her annoyance. Of *course* this guy, who was far too cool to read pulp fiction himself, thought one of the most important lesbian writers in history was a man. "I'm sure this one's a woman."

"All right." Ken seemed unfazed. "Well, she probably would've been deeply closeted if she wrote it in 1956."

"Well, not *everyone* was closeted back then." Paula wasn't, for one thing. Though of course, Paula was fictional. "I've done a bunch of research on the era already, and I saw that there were a lot more lesbian bars and stuff than there are now."

Ken's eyebrows shot up. Abby smiled. She could tell she'd gone up in his estimation.

"True." He nodded. "Which is sad, really. Bar culture was huge in the fifties, since the bars were literally the only places where a lot of people were able to find any community at all.

Even so, though, almost everyone *was* still closeted if you go as far back as the midfifties."

Abby didn't answer. She couldn't imagine Marian Love concealing any part of herself. She was too strong for that.

"I'll go see if I can track down that book for you." Ken stood. "Will you be okay out here for a few minutes?"

"Sure."

Ken disappeared through a door, blowing his nose loudly as he went. It was frustrating, how he had to go into the back to hunt for one of the most famous lesbian books in the world, but someone had apparently deemed all these naked dude books historically significant enough for prominent display.

Not that the lesbian pulp covers were any less gratuitous, Abby had to admit. She pulled up the gallery on her phone again.

Some of the covers were kind of cool, if you ignored how hilarious they were. She gazed down at the cover of a book called *The Mesh*, with two women in evening wear giving each other major side-eye. It was a beautiful image, apart from the weird title and the creepy yellow text that declared it "A novel of hidden evil…"

Was the picture on the cover a drawing? Abby squinted. It looked more like a painting. How bizarre, to think that actual painters made these incredibly detailed works of art and then slapped them onto books that sold for thirty-five cents at gas stations.

Abby opened a tab on her phone and ran a new search, this time for the cover artist who painted *Women of the Twilight Realm*. She got an immediate answer: the original cover had been painted by a man named Lawrence Hastings. He'd done a ton of paperback covers in the fifties and sixties. Most of the covers on his website weren't quite as classy looking as

The Mesh, but Abby could tell the art itself was good, even though most of it focused on scantily clad women, dead bodies or both.

Abby clicked around for more details and discovered that Lawrence Hastings had kept painting until he died back in the eighties. His son had launched this website to sell posters of his old book covers. That might be fun, come to think of it, to have the *Women of the Twilight Realm* cover blown up twenty times and hanging on her wall.

Ken coughed in the back room as Abby clicked the "Notes" tab on the Lawrence Hastings website.

Hastings kept detailed records of every cover he painted, the top of the page read. These notes were discovered last year at the bottom of an old filing cabinet. A team at the College of New York's publishing division is in the process of transcribing the handwritten notebooks. Selected scanned images appear below.

A page full of yellowed scans followed. Abby enlarged one and squinted. Each of the small notebook pages had a book title, an author, a publication year and a description of the cover painting.

"*Sin on the High Seas*," the first one read. "*Adam Kane, 1965. Blond girl in bikini smoking marijuana cigarette w/ brunette in shorty jeans watching in background on dock.*"

Whoa. Abby knew which book she wanted to read next.

"I have it!" Ken boomed from the back, startling her. "Look what I found!"

He coughed again as he strolled in and held out a plastic sleeve with a thin, tattered paperback inside. Abby reached for it cautiously.

There it was. An ancient, crumbling copy of *Women of the Twilight Realm*.

There were Paula and Elaine, crouched on the bed, just as Lawrence Hastings had painted them. The colors had faded over the decades, and a rip had been torn through the left side of Paula's face. Marian Love's name was in a small, barely legible font across the top, and the words "Never Before Published!" ran across the bottom, much larger than the author's name. The sleeve was sealed, so Abby couldn't turn the pages.

"It's a first edition," Ken said proudly.

This was it. It wasn't an ebook, or a reproduction. Some woman, decades ago, must have boldly walked up to a drugstore counter and bought this book. It might have been her only lifeline to who she really was.

Now that she was holding it in her hands, the book felt like Abby's lifeline, too.

A warm, sizzling sensation settled over her, and Abby realized she was officially obsessed.

She knew this feeling well. Falling into a new obsession was like falling in love. This story, these characters—they were *hers*.

She'd had plenty of obsessions before, but this one felt different, somehow. Maybe because the characters on a TV show or in a movie were just cute actors in goofy costumes, but Marian Love was real.

"It's in great condition, considering." Ken pointed down at the cover. "Plus, look what someone wrote on the back."

Abby turned the book over carefully, not wanting to risk damaging the flimsy paper any further. The back cover was so worn she couldn't read the text that had been printed there. Plus, someone had taped a piece of paper across the top, years ago from the look of it.

Abby peered down, trying to make out what was written there. In faded pencil, the handwriting said, "Marian Love, local author."

There was no way. Abby couldn't possibly be that lucky. "Does this say 'local'?"

"Looks like it." Ken grinned and plopped back into his seat, wiping his nose. "It's news to me."

"You're saying she lived *here*?" Abby shook her head. "The book takes place in New York."

"Well, I'm sorry that I don't have more solid information for you. I'm not even sure if *local* definitely means DC—it could be that this copy was shipped to us from somewhere else. Still, if the author *was* local, then I bet that helps you an awful lot with your school project."

Was it actually possible Marian Love was just a few blocks away *right now*?

Maybe Abby *could* meet her. Maybe she could go over to her house sometimes after school, and Marian Love could give her advice. She could definitely use some.

"How do I find out for sure?" she asked Ken. "Should I try to track down an old DC phone book or something?"

"That wouldn't help you, assuming she published under a pseudonym. She wouldn't have listed the name Marian Love on any official documents." Ken was still smiling, but his eyes were starting to water. "I'd recommend you talk to my colleague Morgan Herbert. She teaches at Montgomery College, and she'll probably know a lot more than I do. I can give you her number."

"That would be great, thank you."

"I should warn you, though..." Ken sneezed again as he scribbled down Morgan Herbert's information. "If the author you're looking for *was* local, then she'll probably be even harder to find than if she wasn't."

"What? Why?"

"Well, DC was a scary place to be gay in this era." Ken

shrugged, as though he was apologizing for it. "Frank Kameny and the other local activists didn't get their work going on a large scale until the sixties, and it was dangerous to be out even then. The city was even more dominated by the federal government than it is now, if you can believe that, and the government rooted out anyone on their rolls who was at all suspected of being gay. They kept lists."

"What, like McCarthyism?" Abby had watched a George Clooney movie about that once.

"Exactly. McCarthy himself was even a part of it for a while. It was known as the Lavender Scare, because it happened at the same time as the second Red Scare, but it actually had a much bigger impact."

"Oh, right. I've heard of the Lavender Scare, but I don't know much about it."

"Well, that puts you ahead of the game. Most people haven't heard of it at all." Ken sighed. Abby was starting to get the sense that being a historian specializing in LGBT history wasn't the world's most satisfying job. "Once you got a government job, you had to apply for a security clearance as part of the process. They'd interrogate your family, your neighbors, practically everyone you'd ever known to see if any of them had ever thought you might be gay. If they caught a single whiff, that was often the end of your career."

"What, like gay witch hunts?" Abby meant it as a joke, but Ken's look was serious.

"More like that than you might think." He nodded. "Suicides were common. Very."

Oh. Abby wasn't sure what to say.

"Of course, that's part of why the bar culture flourished." Ken smiled, and Abby sensed he was trying to lighten the mood. "There was nowhere else it was safe to be open. Though

the bars weren't especially safe, either. There weren't as many
raids and beatings in DC as there were in New York and other
cities, but the police still watched who was going in and out.
If they spotted any military or government employees, that
could pose major problems for them. Though for people of
color, and black people in particular, the bars weren't usually
an option in any case, since most of them were still segregated.
Do you know if the author you're looking for was white?"

"I—" Abby swallowed. For all the research she'd done,
there was still so much she didn't know about Marian Love.
"I have no idea."

"Well, either way, if she was here in DC her community
was in the process of being devastated during the time when
she was writing this book. Thousands of people lost their jobs,
and most of them had to leave the city, too. Getting fired from
a government job for being gay meant being blacklisted by
pretty much every other employer in the area, and not working wasn't an option for the vast majority of people. Even if the
author you're looking for never worked for the government
herself, odds are that others in her social circle did. Writing
a book like this would mean putting those people in danger.
She probably used a pseudonym because she was conscious
of how bad the consequences would be if she were found."

Okay. Maybe Marian Love *had* been closeted. No matter
how strong you were, it would've been basically impossible
to live openly if you were up against something like that.

It reminded Abby of all those statistics about queer teenagers and homelessness. Sometimes there were good reasons
not to come out.

"All right." Abby stood up. She felt bad for judging Ken before. He really had been helpful. "Listen, I appreciate all this."

"Don't mention it. Feel free to email me if there's anything else you need."

Ken held out his hand for the first edition of *Women of the Twilight Realm*, but Abby didn't let go. She wanted to study it more. Maybe even take it home and hide it somewhere, so she could start to understand what life was like for all those women who'd written letters to Marian Love.

She didn't want to seem like too much of a weirdo, though, so Abby tried to keep her face composed as she handed the book over.

As she stepped outside, Abby's phone beeped with another reminder. She glanced down at the screen and groaned. Ethan's recital started in an hour.

Both their parents were coming. Dad had been in New York that morning, but he was coming straight from Union Station to school. If his train got in on time, he'd make it with a few minutes to spare. Their mother was only coming from her office downtown, but after the recital she was heading straight to the airport to catch the red-eye to LA.

Mom had made a big deal of explaining all their travel plans that morning as Abby and Ethan grabbed their breakfast burritos. She talked as if she and Dad were making this huge sacrifice to arrange their schedules so they'd both be in town for the recital. They hadn't managed to be in the same building at one time for Rosh Hashanah, and they probably wouldn't bother for Yom Kippur, either, but hey, at least they could all sit awkwardly in the middle school auditorium and watch Ethan tap-dance. Abby just prayed they wouldn't have another embarrassing blowup where people could see them.

She took the metro back to Tenleytown and walked up to campus, then sat down on a bench to wait. She had sixteen new texts—one from Ms. Sloane asking how the visit with Ken had gone, two from her mom, and twenty-four in her never-ending group chat with Linh, Vanessa, Ben and Savannah—but Abby didn't feel like texting, so she opened *Women of the Twilight Realm*. Now that she was officially obsessed, she might as well indulge.

"I know who you are." Mr. Richard jutted his chin at Paula. "Or what *you are. I know what she* is, *too."*

"You leave Elaine out of this, Mart." Paula stood her ground, her arms folded across her chest, her eyes locked on her boss's. Elaine was amazed all over again at Paula's unyielding strength. "This is between you and me."

"That's not true. She's the reason we found out about you in the first place." Mr. Richard managed to look both sickened and amused at the same time. "Not that we couldn't have guessed, of course. Look at the way you dress yourself."

"What are you talking about?" Elaine hated herself for speaking to him, but she had to know what he meant. "I've never said a word to you before today."

Mr. Richard turned back to Elaine and let out a low, mirthless chuckle. "You didn't have to. Your fellow from the country—what was his name? Wayne? He left me a note, but I wasn't sure whether to believe it at first. Then last night my wife, Anne—she sells her cheesecakes to a little bakery down in the Village sometimes, and if the delivery boy's on another job she'll take them down herself. Well, she noticed a while back that the bakery is right across the street from one of those dirty places—a little bar called Mitch's Corner. Yesterday evening she went to pick up her check and lo and behold, who should she see walking right into that disgusting bar than our very own Paula's little friend. Elaine." He spoke her name in a high-pitched, mocking tone, and chuckled again as he looked Elaine up and down. "They say it's always the pretty ones. The ones you'd least suspect."

Yesterday evening. Of course.

That night, as she'd walked into Mitch's, she'd sensed it.

Elaine had been certain *someone was looking over her shoulder. Someone who would hurt her, if given the chance.*

She'd never dreamed it would be Paula who got hurt first.

"There's no reason to fire her." Elaine's voice shook. "She had nothing to do with it. I only went into Mitch's to drop off a letter for a friend. I promise you, Paula's not like the people in those sorts of places. You shouldn't punish her because of me."

"Elaine, I appreciate what you're trying to do, but it isn't necessary." Paula hadn't taken her eyes off Mr. Richard since they'd entered the restaurant. "I am exactly *like the people in those sorts of places, Mart. If that means I can't flip cheeseburgers here anymore, so be it. We'll show ourselves out."*

Mr. Richard held Paula's gaze for another moment. He looked disappointed. As though he'd been hoping she'd put up more of a fight.

"But your pay," Elaine protested. "Paula, he still owes you for the last two weeks."

"He can keep it." Paula straightened to her full height and moved to hold the door for Elaine. "I don't need any more cash from the likes of him."

The scene astonished Abby every time she read it, and it was even more striking now that she'd talked to Ken.

Paula didn't back down, even when something so obviously unfair was happening. She stood tall, even when it must've been the hardest thing in the world to do.

Abby wasn't sure whether she wanted to *be* Paula or be *with* Paula. All she knew was that when she read about Paula, she *wanted.*

Most of all, she wanted Paula to take care of her. To hold her, the way Linh used to.

Linh really *was* kind of like Paula. She was strong in the same way Paula was. And she was kind of too much some-times, and Paula was that, too.

But that was okay. When you loved someone, you loved all of them, even the too-much parts.

That was the whole *point* of being in love. When it was real—when it was meant to be—love could withstand anything.

This weird limbo between her and Linh had to end soon. Abby couldn't make it through this without her.

"Is that you, Abby?"

Abby shielded her eyes against the glaring sunset. Her mom was standing at the top of the hill, waving. Dad was nowhere in sight. Abby climbed to her feet with a silent groan and went to join her.

Dad arrived a minute later, and they all said as few words as possible to each other. Abby found a row of seats at the back, since Ethan always said it stressed him out to look down from the stage and see them in the front.

Dad and Mom avoided making eye contact with each other as they took seats on either side of her. Abby looked straight ahead, wishing she could shrink into a ball and disappear.

"I missed you while I was in New York, Abby." Dad smiled awkwardly.

Abby slunk down in her seat and closed her eyes. She tried to imagine she was somewhere else. *Anywhere* else. She tried to pretend the auditorium was an old-school movie theater, and Paula was by her side.

"I saw a Broadway show you'd enjoy." Her oblivious father was still talking. "It's about Carole King. She wrote a lot of the great songs back in that era you like so much. Maybe we could go up together so you can see it."

Abby opened her eyes and switched on her phone. Pretending wasn't working anyway. "Maybe. I'm incredibly busy with college applications and stuff."

"I understand. What are you doing later tonight? Will you need any help with your math homework?"

Did she have a problem set due for stats? Abby couldn't remember. "I don't think so."

"Put your phone away, Abby," Mom whispered. "They're about to start."

Abby ignored her and went back to the Lawrence Hastings website. She expected Mom to take her phone out of her hand, but her mother just sat there as the lights dimmed and the voices around them hushed.

Mr. Salem came out to welcome everyone, and the first set of dancers came out. Ethan's turn wouldn't be until later. Abby turned her phone brightness down so it wouldn't bother the people behind them and held it low between her knees. Any normal parents would've scolded her, but Mom and Dad kept looking straight ahead.

Whatever. Fine. Abby bent forward so she could see the screen and went back to the page with excerpts from Lawrence Hastings's notebooks. She clicked on the scanned pages one by one, zooming in until she could read his handwriting.

Lonely Nurses, 1956, Mickey Charlson. Nurse in open white dress, man watching from doorway.

Death of a Blonde, 1962, Lionel Michaels. Dead girl in red dress lying on back with arm over head, man kneeling over her, orange background.

Alone No Longer, 1955, Janet Jones. Blond girl in nightie crying on bed, girl with brown hair smoking w/ tie leaning over.

Night of Terror, 1959, Angelo Harvey. Girl in black bra and panties holding gun, man in brown hat watching from car in background.

Wait. Abby scrolled back up.

Blond girl in nightie crying on bed...

"Abby!" Mom whispered. She finally sounded mad. For a second Abby thought she was going to take the phone, but she only pointed at the stage.

Ethan's group was up. Abby jumped upright and put the phone away.

There were six students, three girls and three boys, wearing tap shoes, suits and ties, and green antennae. Apparently this number was alien-themed. Perfect—Ethan loved aliens. He and Abby used to climb up to their steaming-hot attic on summer nights with binoculars to look for UFOs.

Then the dance started, to the song from that old *Men in Black* movie, and it actually wound up being kind of awesome. Ethan was right in the center of the group, and he was genuinely good at the tap dancing. At least, it looked that way to Abby.

When the song ended, all the dancers bowed. Ethan pulled off his antennae and swept them out with a flourish, earning a few laughs along with the applause. Abby clapped hard, and so did her parents. Then her dad stood up and yelled, "Woo-hooo!" and the dorkiness of it almost made Abby smile a tiny bit.

When the kids left the stage, Abby turned her phone back on and pulled up the cover of *Women of the Twilight Realm*. The description in Lawrence Hastings's notes fit.

It was probably a coincidence. *Alone No Longer* was a totally different title from *Women of the Twilight Realm*. The date on

that one was 1955, but *Women of the Twilight Realm* had come
out in 1956. Plus, plenty of lesbian pulp fiction novels had
covers with similar scenes, and they'd all come out within a
few years of each other.

Still, though. That description sounded *exactly* right. And
Lawrence Hastings *had* painted the *Women of the Twilight Realm*
cover...

Her mom was clearing her throat in the next seat pointedly,
but Abby ignored her and ran a search for the title *Alone No
Longer.* Nothing useful came up, even on the bookstore sites.

Next she tried searching *Janet Jones.* There were 62 million
results. Not shocking for such a common name, but not exactly useful, either. Most of the results were about an actress
who was married to a famous male hockey player.

Was it possible Marian Love had decided she liked guys and
taken up acting? No—the actress had been born in 1961, so
she would've had to go back in time to write this book. To
be sure, Abby tried searching for Janet Jones's name alongside
the titles *Alone No Longer* and *Women of the Twilight Realm,*
but nothing came up.

Mom elbowed her—not hard enough to hurt, but hard
enough to be annoying. Abby sighed, turned off her phone
and settled back to watch a group of black-clad seventh graders perform a dance that, according to the recital program,
was a metaphor for the dangers of cyberbullying.

She wished she could write a letter to Marian Love.

"Dear Ms. Love," she'd begin.

*Thank you for writing your mind-blowing book. I only have
a few questions for you. First, I'd like to ask what happened
to Elaine's father. Did he really commit suicide? If so, was it
because of Elaine, or was it more complicated than that (be-*

cause it seems like things are usually more complicated than they seem at first)?

And speaking of things being complicated, how did you write this book when you did? Weren't you afraid of what the consequences would be? How did you keep the fear from looming over you every single moment?

Also, is it true that you live near here? If you do, could I come talk to you sometime? Because I could use someone to talk to, and from what you wrote in your book, you seem as though you'd understand.

Abby closed her eyes and ordered herself to breathe.

She shouldn't be wasting her time writing letters in her head. If she was going to sit here daydreaming, she might as well think about the next scene she needed to write. It was an unhappy scene—an awful lot of the scenes in *The Erotic Adventures of Gladys and Henrietta* were unhappy—but maybe if she tried to think of how Marian Love would write it, that would help.

It did. As soon as she started channeling Marian, the words formed quickly in Abby's mind. This scene wasn't exactly inverting any genre tropes, but she'd fix that later.

"What's this?" Mother held up the letter, and Henrietta recognized the envelope at once. It was the letter she'd put in the mailbox to send to Gladys, but the seal was broken. "Henrietta, what have you done?"

"Give me that." Henrietta's father snatched the letter. As he read, his eyes grew angry. "What's the meaning of this?"

"Mother, Father, please." Henrietta knew there was no use trying to convince them the letter had been a joke, or a mistake. They were already convinced of her guilt. Oh, why hadn't she waited until she was back in New York to send the letter

to Gladys? *"I'm still your daughter, still the same Henrietta. Please, try to understand."*

"You're disgusting." Her mother spat at Henrietta's feet. *"I don't want you in my house."*

Henrietta started to cry. *"Father, please."*

"Your mother and I don't want you anymore." Her father shook his head. *"We've never wanted you. All you've ever done is get in the way. Now get out."*

"But I have nowhere to go." Marian was desperate. She couldn't bear to lose her family. *"Please, don't do this—"*

Shit. She'd called Henrietta "Marian." Well, she could fix that later, too.

Besides, this wasn't how the story was supposed to go. It was too close to *Women of the Twilight Realm*, with incriminating letters showing up at every turn. Marian Love's writing had gotten too far into her head. Abby had meant for *her* book to focus on the fun stuff, like the lesbian commune in Vermont, and how Gladys's evil ex-boyfriend was going to turn out to be secretly gay, too, and how they'd ultimately team up to outwit a vicious serial killer before living happily ever after and opening a cat café in Bennington. She couldn't let her obsession get the better of her.

Mom was eyeing her again. Abby gave in, pulling herself up straight and trying to focus on the stage in front of them.

It was a relief, in a way. To finally think about something that wasn't collapsing in on her from every angle.

8

Sunday, July 3, 1955

"Bye, Shirley." Janet pulled off her apron and tossed it into the laundry bin. "See you tomorrow."

By the time Shirley waved back, Janet had already begun the trot up M Street toward the drugstore. She had a purchase to make on the stationery aisle.

Janet hadn't had two moments to herself since her lunch shift started, and as soon as she arrived home, Mom was bound to make her sit straight down to dinner with the family. This short walk would be her only chance to think.

She hadn't spoken to Marie since her cab had sped off from Silver Spring the day before. Janet still felt just as warmly toward her as ever, but ever since their fight outside the bus station a crumb of regret had begun to linger in her mind.

There must be a word for this. Some singular term that encompassed everything Janet felt for Marie. The fondness, the passion, the admiration—and this strange new discontent, too.

A *true* writer would've known precisely how to describe it. Janet, though, was at a loss. Just as she'd been unable to find the right words to persuade Marie to stay that day.

After she'd taken a separate taxi home and listened to Grandma complain about her parents' club over dinner (*"A dress-up shop for the bourgeoisie to forget the world's problems and drink gin dandies!"*), Janet had run straight to her sweltering bedroom. It had only taken her an hour to read the book she'd bought in the bus station, *A Deviant Woman*—which was a very different book, as it turned out, from *A Love So Strange*—and after that she'd scribbled in her notebook until her grandmother ordered her to bed.

Later that night, out on the porch and unable to sleep, Janet had waited until Grandma's snores on the next cot grew soft and even. Then she'd tiptoed back inside and down the stairs to the darkened den where her father kept his papers. Her parents were still out, and everything Marie had said that day kept running through her mind.

Janet wanted to find out what she'd meant about the senator's son. A vague memory had crept into her mind, and she now believed she'd overheard her parents talking about that senator late one night the previous summer. Her father had been describing a newspaper column by that writer he hated. The man was a troublemaker, Dad always said, part of the cadre who'd brought down McCarthy. If her father's dinner table rants were to be believed, this columnist wouldn't stop crusading until every Republican in Washington had been put out to sea.

Nevertheless, Dad saved his every column. He always said it was important to know the men who were out to get you.

So that night, after she left her grandmother sleeping upstairs, Janet had pulled open the bottom drawer of the file cabinet in the den. She carefully searched through one folder after another, making sure to mark the place where each file belonged. Dad was meticulous about his papers, and if there was any indication that she had touched them—if her parents somehow discovered what she was looking for…it didn't even bear thinking about.

The folder Janet wanted was the second one from the back of the drawer. Her hand trembled as she sorted through a thick pile of clipped-out newsprint pages. Within minutes, her fingers were gray with ink.

When she finally found it, she wished she'd never gone looking.

The column was a year old. It was about a Senator Hunt, a Democrat from Wyoming, whose son had been arrested on a "morals charge." Janet waded through long paragraphs talking about McCarthyites and Republican blackmail until she reached the section she was looking for.

The senator's son had been arrested in a park, the column said, for "soliciting" a plainclothes police officer—another man. The boy had been put on trial, and the senator had promised to "straighten him out."

After the trial, the senator's wife—the boy's mother—hadn't eaten for a week. The senator's political opponents had pressured him to resign, threatening to spread rumors about his son during his reelection campaign. Until the senator brought a rifle to his office one morning and shot himself to death.

The first reports had said he'd committed suicide because of an illness. This columnist, though, had decided people ought to learn the truth.

Janet reread the column about Senator Hunt and his son again and again, as though it might make more sense than it had the first time. It never came to be.

She supposed she'd heard that certain kinds of men did

things—terrible things—in parks at night. Her mother had always given her strict instructions never to enter a park after dark, most likely for that very reason. But Janet hadn't realized that the sorts of men who skulked around those parks could also be the sorts of men whose fathers served in the United States Senate.

The government would think of Janet and Marie no differently than they did those men. For that matter, they could be right. Perhaps men like Senator Hunt's son felt the same way toward the men they met in those parks that Janet felt toward Marie.

She'd stumbled to her feet, reaching blindly for the newsprint clippings on the floor. The pages crumpled in her hands.

Her parents could come home from the club at any minute. Even if they didn't, Dad would notice if one of these columns was missing the next time he checked his files. Janet had to put everything back neatly so he didn't find out what she'd done. Rationally, she knew that was what she should do.

Instead, Janet grabbed the column about Senator Hunt and ripped the page in half.

She tore it again, and again after that. She ripped it into smaller and smaller pieces until the column was no more than confetti scattered across the den floor.

She stood in the middle of it all, her face flushed and her breath coming in pants, as though she'd just run up the streetcar line all the way to Holy Rood and back. Then she scooped up the tattered papers into a pile, making sure she got every fragment, and stuffed the pieces into her fist.

Janet ran out of the den, through the kitchen and into the foyer, taking the stairs two at a time in her bare feet. When she reached the bathroom, Janet flung the papers into the toilet and flushed it as hard as she could. Then she flushed it again.

She moved slowly, thoughtlessly, as she went back downstairs and put the den to rights. The headlights of her parents' car trailed across the living room wall just as she was climbing the stairs once more.

There was no sense dwelling on Senator Hunt's son. Or Senator Hunt himself.

The past was already written. Only the future mattered.

Janet had to make sure there was no risk to her own family, or Marie's. She had to come up with a plan to win Marie back, too. Now that Janet understood her fears, it should be a simple matter.

Yet so far, Janet had thought of nothing that could help her. And as she darted in and out of the drugstore and started toward home, she still had no ideas.

"Janet! Good, you're here," Mom called as Janet stepped inside the foyer and laid her packages on the entry table. Behind her, she could see Grandma and Dad sitting in different rooms, reading different newspapers. "I need you to set out the silverware."

At least at the Soda Shoppe she got paid to do side work. Janet moved wearily into the kitchen and retrieved the knives and forks while her mother checked the roast.

"Has your friend started work at the State Department yet?" Mom asked as she passed her the clean glasses.

Sometimes Janet wished her mother wasn't quite so interested in Marie. "Yes. Last Wednesday."

"She already passed her security clearance?" Dad called from the den.

"There's no need to bellow across the house, George," Grandma shouted from the living room.

"Not yet, Dad," Janet answered. "She said it should come soon."

Dad started grumbling about the nitwits at State, and Grandma shushed him again as Mom called everyone to the table. Janet was still stuffed from the hamburger and onion rings she'd gobbled down at the end of her shift, but she didn't mention that.

Dad leaned in to kiss Mom before taking his seat at the head of the table, and Janet looked away. She always found it terribly embarrassing when her parents kissed.

"They're all as slow as molasses over in Foggy Bottom," Dad said as Janet's mother sliced the chicken. "If you call State on a Monday and ask for a report, you're lucky if you get it by Friday. Not that Friday, but the *next* Friday."

"Well, I'm sure Marie will fix all that." Mom always tried to make their dinner conversation pleasant. She was the only one. "You remember her, George, she was one of the very best students at St. Paul's. No doubt she'll type everything so quickly the place will soon be shipshape."

"I have no doubt Miss Eastwood will do excellent work, but she's only a girl. How old is she, Janet? She was in school with you, wasn't she?"

"She's one year older." Janet avoided meeting her father's eyes. "Nineteen."

"Yes, you see, Helen? The girl's only nineteen. Besides, State is sinking, and it'll take a lot more than one good secretary to patch that particular ship." Dad chuckled at his own joke as he struck a match against the side of the table.

"Well, you can blame your old friend McCarthy for that." Grandma pointed her knife at Dad, waving a forkful of potatoes in her other hand. "How many did he force out of State with those disgraceful inquiries?"

Dad grimaced. "Must we do this yet again, Mother?"

"I'm merely saying, George, anyone could've seen the man was only out for his own gain. He had all of you fooled but good, thinking you were fighting the Soviets every time you held a hearing. McCarthy didn't care about catching Communists any more than a nun at St. Paul's cares about catching herself a curling iron."

"May I borrow the typewriter tonight?"

Silence fell across the dining table.

Janet had thought Dad would simply agree and go back to arguing with Grandma. Instead he, Mom and Grandma all turned to stare at Janet.

She squirmed in her seat, trying not to look over at the entry table where her purchases were neatly stacked in their brown wrappers. She'd bought one hundred sheets of typing paper at Peoples—the most she could afford out of that day's tips—and a packet of carbon paper, too. It should be enough to write fifty pages total. To type an entire manuscript, she'd need to buy more paper, but at the moment she could barely imagine writing fifty entire pages of anything resembling a book.

"I mean," Janet added, since the rest of her family was still silent, "if you aren't using the typewriter yourself, Dad."

"Well, I just might need to." He lifted his chin.

Janet had never known Dad to use the typewriter that sat perched on the small square desk in the den. He often sat next to it while reading his newspaper and drinking his coffee, but she'd never heard the keys tapping. Janet wasn't entirely sure he knew *how* to type.

But she didn't try to argue. Dad was the man of the house, and no one ever argued with him. Well, except Grandma, but she said she'd earned that right since Dad had taken his sweet time being born.

Mom jumped in. "Why do you need the typewriter?"

Janet had carefully prepared a lie for this. "I'd like to write to my friend from camp last summer. Lois Bannon."

"Bannon?" Grandma raised her eyebrows. "That was the name on that letter that came for you, wasn't it? From New York?"

"Er, yes." Janet had made up the name Lois Bannon in case Mom had seen the letter when she brought in the mail. It hadn't occurred to her that Grandma might have noticed it, too. "You see, Lois's eyesight isn't very good, and she can't read handwriting. She has to type all her letters, and for me to write back I'll need to type, too."

Grandma cocked her head, but it was Mom who answered. "I don't know, Janet. Typing is noisy. The rest of us won't be able to hear ourselves think with you making a racket in the den."

It was exactly what Janet had hoped she'd say. "Then perhaps I should write in the attic. Up there I wouldn't bother anyone. I can pay for the typing paper and ribbons out of my tips from the Soda Shoppe."

"Ribbons?" Grandma's eyes were still locked on Janet's. "Just how many letters do you plan on sending this girl?"

Dad set down his drink. "When's the last time you went to the attic in the summer, honey? It's sweltering up there, even with the windows open. We don't want you getting heatstroke."

"I'll put on the fan." Aside from Grandma's questions, this was all going exactly as Janet had hoped. "It will help cover up the noise, too. Please, Dad?"

"Odd, isn't it, that this girl waited until a year after camp to start writing to you," Grandma said.

But once again, Dad ignored her. "All right, honey. I'll bring the typewriter up to the attic after dinner, but bear in mind that if I need to use it you'll have to give it back."

Janet nodded fast, glad she didn't need to add further falsehoods to her story. "Of course. Thank you, Dad, you're marvelous!"

"Oh, now I'm marvelous." Dad sawed into his chicken, smiling. "Good to know."

When they finished dinner, Janet leaped up to clear the table instead of dragging her feet the way she usually did. She washed the dishes thoroughly, too, ignoring the strange looks Grandma was still giving her.

Soon, Janet would be a real novelist. She'd have a neat stack of typed pages, and she'd wrap them in brown paper and tie them with string, the way writers did in the movies.

In truth, though, the idea was a little intimidating. What if Janet couldn't write something Bannon Press thought good enough to publish? What if Nathan Levy read her story and realized Janet was nothing but a young, naive girl who didn't know the first thing about how to write a proper book?

A rejection from Mr. Levy would devastate her. If Janet didn't have the talent to be a real writer—well, she didn't know what she'd do. Writing was the only future Janet could imagine that might bring her happiness.

She'd begun saving as much as she could from her earnings at the Soda Shoppe in a small box in her dressing table. It wasn't much yet, but if she kept working after she started college in September, perhaps eventually she'd have enough to move into her own apartment. Then her real life could begin. She'd be on her own, and she'd publish book after book.

First, though, she had to write one. Even if only to show herself she could.

When the dishes were done and Mom had drifted off toward the back porch, Janet began straightening the pile of discarded newspapers in the living room. She heard Dad lift the typewriter and carry it up the stairs behind her, but she didn't turn to watch.

She'd go up and start writing in a minute. Once she was finished with these newspapers.

"I thought you had a letter to write, girl?"

Janet spun around. Grandma leaned against the living room door, a light smile playing across her face.

"I do." Janet stood, sliding the last newspaper into place. "I'm going right up."

Grandma didn't say anything, but her smile grew as Janet backed out of the living room with an awkward wave and started toward the stairs.

She grabbed her package off the entry table and climbed up slowly. As she reached the second floor and moved toward the attic stairway, Janet sniffed and realized she really ought to clean her uniform before her shift tomorrow. She'd just wash it out in the bathroom sink before she started writing.

The detergent was downstairs, though, so first she had to go back down and get it. She should wash the blouse she'd worn to church that morning while she was at it, too, and there was underwear to wash as well. There was always underwear to wash.

She changed into her pajamas and began to scrub her pile of clothes. Janet could hear her parents and Grandma moving around in their rooms, getting ready for bed. Well, that was for the best. She'd just as soon write once everyone else was asleep. That way, she wouldn't be disturbed.

"Oh, Janet." Dad glanced into the open bathroom door. "I thought you'd gone to the attic. Are you going to write that letter after all? I set up the typewriter for you."

"Yes! Yes, I am." Janet scrubbed with renewed vigor. Her uniform would be the cleanest it had ever been. "I'm going up just as soon as I've finished this washing. Thanks for bringing the typewriter upstairs."

"All right, well, make sure you're in bed by ten."

"Yes, sir."

Dad cast a dubious look down at the sink, but Janet ignored him. She doubted Dad had ever so much as attempted to wash his own underwear.

She yawned as she wrung out her clothes and hung them on the line above the bathtub. Perhaps it was too late to start writing. Besides, she should probably read *A Love So Strange* one more time first, to make sure she was familiar with the sort of book Bannon Press expected.

It might even be useful for her to take another look at *A Deviant Woman*, though she didn't much want to. Kimberly Paul was clearly a much less skilled writer than Dolores Wood. The sentences in *A Deviant Woman* were shorter and choppier than in *A Love So Strange*, and the book's characters didn't seem to act like any people Janet had ever met. Besides, none of them seemed interested in anything but, well—sex.

It made Janet blush to think of, but it was true all the same. There was a great deal more sex in *A Deviant Woman* than in *A Love So Strange*. Even so, Janet didn't find herself longing to return to it. Kimberly Paul seemed much more interested in describing the size and shape of her characters' breasts than the feelings they aroused in each other.

The book's plot—if it could be called that—centered around a married couple who invited a young girl to board in their spare room, leading to a number of increasingly unlikely scenarios in which the girl found reasons to walk about the house without clothes. She later seduced both the husband and the wife, though neither of them had ever been tempted into such scandalous behavior before. In one memorable instance, she'd even seduced them both at once, although before they'd even finished undressing the girl had produced a gun and attempted to steal a valuable diamond that turned out to be hidden in the couple's root cellar.

No one in the book had gone to the beach a single time. The cover was certainly captivating, with its oiled, bathing suit–clad bodies, but it bore no connection to the pages within that Janet could find.

Janet had thought all the "Lesbiana" books would be similar to *A Love So Strange*, but all these two books seemed to have in common were the Bannon Press logos in the top left, the paintings on the covers and girls who enjoyed the company of other girls. Well, enjoyed it some of the time. Janet could only hope Nathan Levy was more interested in books like Dolores Wood's than Kimberly Paul's.

She hung the rest of her laundry, then hurried into her room and reached under the mattress. A moment later, Sam and Betty's lovely faces stared up at her. Tucked inside the pages of *A Love So Strange* were the sheets of paper Janet had torn from her notebook, the ones where she'd scribbled her first few paragraphs.

Though it was more than a few paragraphs, Janet realized. It seemed she'd already written a number of pages. Combined, it might be nearly an entire first chapter.

As she looked them over, Janet was surprised to realize the pages weren't half-bad. Especially the ones she'd written most recently. Janet had never sat in a Greenwich Village bar, had never exchanged flirtatious banter with a stranger, and had certainly never asked another girl to dance. Still, somehow, Paula and Elaine's story already felt familiar.

Perhaps Janet should work on her book tonight after all. She could start by simply typing up the pages she'd already written by hand. That shouldn't be *too* bad. Janet stood and stuffed the notebook pages, her copy of *A Love So Strange*, and her typing and carbon paper into her purse.

The door to the attic was right outside her parents' bedroom, but they'd already gone down to the first-floor porch to sleep. Janet shut the attic door behind her and climbed the stairs slowly, trying not to make them creak.

As soon as she entered the attic, she saw what her father had meant. The heat was much worse here than in her bedroom, and it struck her with a nearly solid force. She turned on the fan—Dad must have brought that up for her, too—and stood directly in front of its whirling air while she tugged the cord hanging from the dusty light bulb.

The dim light made it easier for Janet to see the attic, cramped, narrow and unfinished. Every surface was faded, rough brown wood. More dust filtered through the air.

Janet couldn't remember the last time she'd been up here. Her mother had kept her Christmas presents in the attic until third grade, when she'd snuck up the stairs to survey the hidden wares. Now Mom used it to store the family's winter coats and blankets, sealing them into a row of dusty wooden trunks that lined the walls. The rest of the space was empty, save for the card table and typewriter Dad had brought up for her from the den. He'd placed a chair in front of it, too.

The attic's two small windows faced out onto the street. Janet stepped over to open them, letting in some fresh air.

The typewriter was only a few feet away. It looked so... official.

She could just load in the first sheets of paper. Maybe then she'd be inspired to start typing up her handwritten pages.

It took several minutes for Janet to open the packets and line up the two sheets of paper with the carbon properly in between them. Then it took her three attempts to roll it all into the typewriter. She'd taken typing at St. Paul's, of course, but they'd only used carbon paper once or twice.

Though before she started typing, it would probably be wise to take a quick look at *A Love So Strange*. Just to remind herself of how certain scenes were composed.

Janet reached for the flimsy paperback. It fell open automatically to Betty and Sam's first night together.

> *"Are you nervous, darling?" Sam asked, running practiced fingers down my arm. She chuckled when I gasped my pleasure at the touch.*
>
> *"No," I said. Sam laughed again. "Perhaps a little."*
>
> *"Don't be nervous. I love you. I'd never hurt you."*
>
> *"Oh, I know you wouldn't, Sam, dear." I gasped once more as Sam slipped open the buttons of my blouse and reached inside, lifting the brassiere and stroking gently.*
>
> *The feeling was unlike any I had ever known. I should have been ashamed to be touched this way by another woman, yet the only sensation I knew was pure pleasure. Sam's touch was the touch of the divine.*

The touch of the divine.

Well.

It really was boiling in the attic, even with the fan on. Janet should have known better than to wear her flannel pajamas.

Of course, there was no one to see her. She might as well make herself comfortable.

Janet undid her top button. Then, before she was quite aware of what she was doing, she cupped her hand over her breast. She'd never done anything like this before, so she couldn't be sure if it was the physical sensation or the words she'd read, but something made her gasp.

Her eyes fell closed. She was Betty, being touched by Sam for that first time.

No. No, she was Elaine, and she was with Paula.

Janet could see it clearly. The image came as easily as it had when Paula and Elaine first met in that smoky bar.

She saw Elaine, lying on her back on a bed…no, no, it was a couch. The couch in her living room. It was dark, with the curtains drawn, a half-drunk martini on the table beside them. Paula was leaning over her, kissing her neck and moving down to her breasts, lips tracing skin…

Janet hurled herself at the typewriter keys.

It was only the martinis, I told myself. I wouldn't be doing this at all if it hadn't been for that last drink.

I told myself that again as Paula undid the second button.

The smooth, experienced hands were warm and soft on my skin. Still, I shivered as Paula's fingers caressed my bare flesh.

"You're beautiful, my darling," Paula whispered. "More beautiful than anyone I've ever known."

"Paula, you're divine," I whispered.

I couldn't blame the martinis for making me say that.

The words poured out in a long, uninterrupted stream.

Janet wrote, and wrote, rolling the pages into her typewriter so fast some of them ripped. Before long, she was sweating. Black smudges from the carbon paper covered her hands. Probably her face, too.

Janet didn't care. She could see it all so clearly. She could *feel* it. She didn't know exactly what would happen next in the story until she typed each line, but that didn't matter. The characters lived in her. Through her.

"I love you." The words spilled from my lips, sudden and raw and true.

Paula smiled. "And I love you, my dear."

Of course, Janet mused, as she pounded at the keys. Of *course* Paula and Elaine loved each other.

It was such a simple thing. So simple, they didn't even pause to consider it before they spoke the words.

Elaine loved Paula. Just as Janet loved Marie.

Love. That was it. That was the word she'd been seeking. The one that took everything she felt about Marie and turned it into a single, fundamental syllable.

Janet loved her.

She smiled down at the typewriter. It was so funny that it had taken putting the word into the mouth of a fictional character for Janet to feel its true weight for herself.

It was funny, too, to be writing about the *act* of love. Janet had never experienced it herself, but even so the images were warm and alive in her heart as the typewriter ink spread across each page.

Paula brushed a stray hair from my face and kissed me again, hot lips on my scorched skin. "Did you enjoy that, my darling?"

"Yes." It was the only word I remembered.

"Shall we do it once more, then?"

"Yes! Oh, please, Paula, please!"

When Janet finally typed the last line of the scene and looked up again, she had no idea what time it was, and she didn't care.

She rolled the last pages out of the typewriter and added them to the uneven piles on the table. She had pages stacked upon pages now, all filled with words. Words *she* had written.

She felt as if she'd downed a few martinis of her own.

Janet stood and collected the pages to her chest, trying not to bend any corners. She would show what she'd written to Marie. Once she'd seen all that Janet had poured out onto the page—once she saw that Janet's characters loved each other, and that Janet loved Marie, too—she'd realize how wrong she'd been. She'd realize that, more than anything, she wanted the two of them to spend their every moment together, and she'd tell Janet so.

You're divine, Janet would reply.

She shut her eyes. The pages felt heavy in her hands. The solid evidence of the future that awaited her.

She was halfway to the attic door when she heard a loud creak on the floor below.

Someone else in the house was awake.

Janet's eyes jolted open, darting toward the attic door. What if one of her parents came up to see what she was doing? What if *they* saw what she'd written?

Her smile evaporated in an instant. She scanned the dim attic for a hiding place and wrenched open the nearest trunk.

Her family could never find out. Janet could never tell them. She could never tell *anyone.*

She dropped the typewritten pages into the trunk in a heap. The sheets were damp around the edges—she must have sweated onto the paper. There was a typographical error on the top page, too. She'd put two *L*s in Elaine's name.

Janet swallowed as she lowered the lid of the trunk. As intoxicating as all this writing may have been, she couldn't let herself forget who she truly was, or what the world was really like.

What she'd been doing was far from divine. And her future was far from solid.

9

Monday, October 2, 2017

"I knew a girl who looked a little like you once." Henrietta grinned at the new girl. "We were sorority sisters."

"Sisters?" The blond girl bit her lip. The hint of breast beneath the neckline of her blouse quivered.

"Well, if you can call it that." Henrietta laughed and took a long puff on her cigar. "But I think the housemother would've called the cops if she saw what some of us so-called sisters got up to when the lights went out! So, what's your name?"

The blond girl bit her lip again. "Gladys."

"Let's dance, Gladys," Henrietta said easily, blowing a stream of smoke toward the ceiling.

"I don't believe in dancing," Gladys said haughtily, sniffing in the direction of the tiny dance floor.

"You don't what?" Henrietta had never heard of such a thing.

"That's right." Gladys tossed her permed hair. "I'd prefer

*to go back to my apartment and read avant-garde poetry. Are
you familiar with the work of E. E. Cummings?"*

*Henrietta smiled. "I can't say that I am. But if it'll get me
into your apartment, Gladys, I'm ready to familiarize myself
with just about anything you'll let me."*

*Gladys smiled back and slipped off the bar stool. Henrietta
loved the way Gladys's skirt clung to her thighs.*

Abby stared at the screen, trying yet again to figure out what
was wrong with the scene. This was the third draft she'd written of Gladys and Henrietta's meet-cute, but she still couldn't
get it to work.

She'd kept reading *Voluptuous Vixens*, thinking that might
help shake *Women of the Twilight Realm* out of her head so she
wouldn't wind up copying Marian Love as much, but she
might've gone too far in the wrong direction. Abby was trying to invert genre tropes, like with having Henrietta smoke
a cigar instead of a regular cigarette and having Gladys be
morally opposed to dancing, but as it turned out, inverting
tropes was *hard*. She had a better appreciation now for why
tropes were invented in the first place.

Plus, she was starting to regret naming one of her characters *Gladys*. It looked awful in possessive form.

The one thing Abby knew for sure was that Marian Love
wouldn't have written the story this way. *Marian's* words
flowed beautifully off the page. Abby's words sounded de-
cent enough in her head, but they looked awkward and naked
on the screen.

Some of the other scenes had been fun to write, though.
Abby had more than one hundred pages so far, most of them
thanks to her evenings at the library. It was halfway between
home and school, and it was open until 9 p.m. most days,

so Abby had been staying there every night after grabbing something to eat at the 7-Eleven across the street. She'd told Dad she was too busy to get home earlier, and Dad must've told Mom, because neither of her parents had said anything to her about it.

Ms. Sloane had said Abby's pages showed promise for a first draft, but that she should slow down and revise what she'd already written before she went any further. Abby disagreed. The more she wrote, the more she wanted to write, even if the words weren't all as good as she wanted them to be. Besides, she could always revise once she had the whole thing written. But it still bugged her that this particular scene had so many problems.

"Have you looked yet at the essay questions for Columbia?" Linh's question jerked Abby out of her train of thought. School had let out a while ago and they were in the senior lounge, killing time before Abby had to leave to go meet the professor Ken Aldrich had told her about. It was the first time she and Linh had been alone together since the day they discovered the pulp novels, but Abby had been so focused on writing she'd almost forgotten to feel weird about that.

"For the supplement to the Common App, I mean?" Linh went on. "I'm stumped on the one where I'm supposed to write three hundred words on what I value most about Columbia. I mean, my parents value that it's an Ivy, does that count?"

"You're applying to Columbia?" Abby must've gotten even better at tuning out her friends' college talk than she'd realized.

"Yeah. Didn't I tell you?" Linh polished off her banana and reached into her backpack for a bag of chips. She'd come straight from a run and she was famished, as usual. "It was my dad's idea. He thinks if I get in, *and* if they give me a good aid package, I can use it to negotiate for more at MIT. Assuming I get in there, too, of course. I told him that's *way* too many assumptions, but he never listens to me."

"Right." Abby dropped her gaze.

Of course Linh didn't actually want to go to Columbia. Abby hadn't started her applications yet—she still felt itchy and uncomfortable whenever she thought about college—but even so, it was depressing that Linh wouldn't even *consider* going to the same school Abby had talked about going to.

"Listen, I know it bothers you how competitive the whole college thing is." Linh leaned in with that earnest look she got in her eyes sometimes. Her eyes were so pretty, though, the way the dark brown irises shone in the dim light, that Abby couldn't mind *too* much. "Maybe you'll get more into it after we visit Penn next weekend. But either way, you have to start your applications soon. The early decision deadlines are in a few weeks."

"Right." Abby tried to ignore the pressure in the words and focus on the way Linh's eyes were locked on hers.

"If it's that you're worried about going away—well, don't be." Linh didn't seem to notice the can-we-please-not-be-having-this-particular-conversation vibe Abby was trying so hard to send. "We can still email and text and stuff, the way we did over the summer. We'll see each other when we come home for breaks, too."

Abby finally broke her gaze.

She didn't want to live in a different city from Linh next year. That much was true. Even if Linh was being a touch too Paula-like, with the way she kept trying to tell Abby what she should want.

Paula meant well when she got that way, and Linh did, too. Besides, Linh wasn't saying anything Abby hadn't already heard from teachers and counselors, and even her parents, before they stopped paying attention.

It was just that—well, what if Abby didn't *want* to deal with all this stuff? Had anyone ever thought of *that* possibility?

Why did everyone act as though big life changes were these huge inevitable things? What if Abby *didn't* want to think about the future every second of every day?

"Anyway, we don't need to talk about that yet." Linh shifted into that gorgeous bright smile, and Abby smiled back in relief. Linh leaned over to peer at her laptop. "So, is that the book you're writing? Can I see?"

"What? No." Abby held up her hand to shield the screen. "I mean, it's only a first draft. I want to revise it before you read it."

"Oh, come on." Linh reached for Abby's hand, trying to pull it away. Abby wanted to relish the physical contact, but she was too worried about Linh reading that badly written scene. "You always used to let me see the stuff you wrote."

"Well that was when…um." Abby flushed, not sure of how to say *That was before we broke up and I got all insecure,* or *That was when I was writing stuff just to make you laugh.*

"Come on, let me read *one* scene." Linh flounced back onto the couch dramatically, making Abby giggle. "I want to see how this whole vintage lesbian porn thing works."

"If all you want is vintage porn you don't need to read *my* story. Read Marian Love. Hers is a lot better than mine."

"But I want to read something *you* wrote." Linh made a pouty face.

Hmm. It seemed an awful lot as though Linh was flirting with her again. Abby almost wanted to give in, but she didn't want to ruin their new vibe by sharing her own clunky attempts at fictional flirting.

"Trust me, this will be a lot more fun." Abby pulled up the *Women of the Twilight Realm*, trying to match Linh's easy tone. "Here, I'll find a good scene."

She clicked through to the first time Paula and Elaine slept together and passed the computer to Linh. She'd assumed Linh would read it to herself while Abby messed around on her phone, but to her surprise Linh started reading out loud, making her voice low and fake-sexy.

"Are you nervous, darling?" Paula whispered.

"What a question." Elaine shook her head. "Were you nervous your first time?"

"Terrified." Paula smiled and kissed her again. Elaine nearly lost herself in the kiss. Paula's strong arms held her tight, and her lips were gentle and greedy all at the same time. Finally, Paula broke away. "I was younger than you are, of course. Only eighteen."

"I wish I'd known you at eighteen."

"You wouldn't have liked me. I was tall, but the rest of me hadn't grown in yet. I was awkward and gangly."

Elaine tightened her hold around Paula's back and tilted her chin up so their lips met. "Darling, you've never been awkward or gangly as long as you've lived."

Linh lowered the laptop, giggling. "I can't keep going. This is *so* cheesy."

"No it's not! It's romantic."

"Come *on*. They're seriously calling each other 'darling'?"

"People used to talk that way! Anyway, keep going. It gets better."

There was no awkwardness as they touched. As Elaine carefully unfastened the buttons of Paula's shirt, reaching beneath it

to lift the bra and stroke the firm, warm breasts. As Paula un-
tied the sash at Elaine's waist, her dressing gown falling open
under her steady, practiced hands.

"Okay, this is more what I had in mind." Linh broke character to smirk down at the screen. "But I don't get what Marian Love has against possessive pronouns. I mean, '*the* bra'?
'*The* breasts'?"

"Yeah, all the pulp novels do it that way for some reason."
Abby hoped Linh wouldn't notice she was blushing. It was
weird, hearing her read this book out loud after Abby had
gotten so attached to it.

Also, it was indescribably embarrassing to hear the only
person she'd ever hooked up with talk about breasts.

Linh turned back to the book, and Abby reached for a
couch cushion she could hide behind in case this got any
more embarrassing.

They touched each other with a tenderness, a hunger, that
Elaine had never before felt. As they fell back onto the waiting
bed, leaving their clothes in an unkempt puddle on the floor
below, it was all Elaine could do not to cry out her happiness
loud enough for the neighboring apartments to hear.

"Make love to me, Paula," Elaine murmured, just before
Paula's lips crushed hers again.

"My darling," Paula murmured, sliding down to lay wet
kisses on her throat. "That's exactly what I intend to do. I'm
going to show you just how much I love you."

Linh paused again. Abby wanted to hide behind her cushion, but she also wanted to see what Linh was thinking.

They used to say that to each other. *I love you.*

It was strange hearing Linh say those words now, and having them mean something totally different.

Or did they? Linh didn't *have* to read that part. She could've skipped it if she'd wanted to.

Was there something more going on here than Linh wanting to read vintage porn? Was this Linh's way of saying what Abby had been hoping she'd say for the past four months?

But after that pause Linh just kept reading, and Abby had no idea what to think.

As the night outside the filmy window grew darker, the two girls moved as one. As though their bodies had always been united. The beauty of it overwhelmed Elaine, sweeping her away, and she cried out her pleasure again and again.

As they lay in each other's arms, exhausted but not sated, Paula asked Elaine—

"What, that's it?" Linh stopped in the middle of the sentence.

Abby tried to focus. She loved that line—*"as though their bodies had always been united."* It took her breath away every time she read it. "That's what?"

"It didn't actually say what they did."

"Well, yeah." Abby ran her fingertips over the couch cushion, wondering idly if she could get away with running them across the smooth skin of Linh's arm instead. "They couldn't go into that much detail because of the censors. Before the sixties even the trashier books were still pretty vague about anything, you know, below the waist."

"Well, then, what's the *point*? Why did they even put out books with these scenes?"

"It's—well, it's romantic." Abby flushed. "Readers can fill in the blanks. The specifics are, um, implied."

"Oh." Linh shifted over to meet Abby's gaze. Okay, she *definitely* looked like she was flirting. "So what do you think the book *implies* happened between Paula and Elaine?"

"Um." Abby bit her lip. "Well. Probably, uh, third base."

"You think so?"

Linh was still smirking, her lips curled up adorably at the corners. Abby could only stare at her.

She wasn't imagining this. Was she?

Linh was looking at Abby with a gleam in her eyes. And they were alone, on a couch, with only a couple of inches of space between them. Talking about sex.

If Abby kissed her, would she ruin everything?

And...did she care if she did?

This felt like a moment for taking risks. That was what Paula would've done.

To hell with it.

Abby moved forward. She couldn't read everything she saw in Linh's eyes, but she knew Linh wasn't pulling away. They were close now, so close...

Abby shut her eyes and leaned toward her. Their lips brushed tentatively. The warmth Abby had been seeking for so long was finally within her grasp.

Yet something felt different—almost wrong. And a very unwelcome, very un-Paula-like thought sounded in Abby's head.

Are you sure this is still what you want?

"Abby." Linh's voice was sudden and uncertain, as though she were stumbling over her thoughts. Their lips no longer touched. "Um, we probably shouldn't."

Abby's eyes snapped open. "What?"

Linh had pulled away after all. The gleam in her eyes was gone. "I don't think—or, well, I guess I'm not sure if you totally, um—"

"Yeah. I mean, me, too." Abby cut her off and lurched to her feet.

God, how *stupid* could she have been?

Abby wasn't Paula. Neither was Linh.

You couldn't expect real life to be like a romance novel. That was why fiction existed in the first place.

Abby knew she should laugh it off, but the part of her brain that was supposed to be in charge of rational decisions was too busy thinking about how she should really put this scene in her book. There would come a point when Gladys and Henrietta were on uncertain terms, and they'd nearly kiss, but then one of them would break it off and they'd both be confused about what it all meant.

I need to remember how this feels, Abby told herself, shutting her eyes tight. *I should write this down so I don't forget.*

If I can give this feeling to someone else, maybe I won't have to feel it anymore.

"Abby, wait." Linh stood, too. "I'm sorry."

"It's fine! Don't worry about it. It's time for me to go anyway." Abby had no idea what time it actually was, but maybe if she got out of this room everything would stop hurting so much.

She shoved her computer into her backpack and pushed out the door. The hall was almost empty, but on the far end a couple of freshmen were walking toward the steps carrying heavy black instrument cases.

"For real, though." Linh was following her, speaking quietly. Abby wished she'd leave it alone. "I'm sorry. I didn't— I mean, we—"

"Don't worry about it! It's cool. Gotta go or I'll be late."

Abby's stomach churned as she thundered down the stairs. She managed to run the whole way off campus and to the metro escalator without thinking about what a fool she'd made of herself, though, so she decided that counted as a win.

The train was pulling in as Abby reached the platform. It was a long ride from Tenleytown to Takoma, where Professor Herbert's office was, but it gave her space to catch her breath. In her head, she started writing another letter to Marian Love.

Dear Ms. Love,

I've been wondering about something. How were Paula and Elaine so sure of how they felt about each other? I know they loved each other—they had the true, pure, forever kind of love, but...how did they figure that out, exactly?

Because, I mean, kissing is fun. Flirting is fun. Going out on dates is fun. Sex is fun. Holding someone is the best thing ever.

Except—what if there's this one person you've always loved doing all that stuff with, and then all of a sudden it doesn't feel the same as it used to? Does that mean you don't love the person the same way you did?

And, well, if it does mean that—if love can change—then how can you be sure it was really love to begin with? Because isn't the whole idea that love lasts forever? Isn't love supposed to be the whole reason all of us are even on this planet in the first place?

Abby's phone buzzed again. She wanted to ignore it and keep working on her letter—it was probably just one of her parents—but it could also be Professor Herbert, so she looked down.

It was Linh.

Sorry again about what happened before, the text said. **I know you're busy, but do you think we could talk later? Things got kind of weird in the lounge and I think it was my fault. I feel really bad. Are you okay?**

Ouch. Did Linh seriously think Abby was so pathetic that she had to apologize over and over to make her feel better about looking stupid?

Sure, Abby replied. **We can talk later.**

There. That should be vague enough to let Abby wriggle out of it for a while. Vagueness always worked when she used it on her parents.

She was almost at Takoma by then, so Abby pulled up the map to the professor's office. She checked her website bio, too, in case she'd missed anything important when she'd read it the other day.

Professor Herbert was older than Ken Aldrich, but she wasn't as old as Marian Love. She was middle-aged, whereas Marian Love would be ninetyish, probably, assuming she'd been in her thirties when she wrote *Women of the Twilight Realm*. That meant Professor Herbert had missed the pulp era back when it was actually happening, but she'd written a bunch of scholarly articles about it anyway. Abby had read the ones she could find. They were fascinating—all about the way the books explored gender stereotypes and internalized homophobia, and how most of them were complete fails when it came to race and class and intersectionality—but there hadn't been anything in them about the real identity of Marian Love. Still, Professor Herbert seemed to know more about these books than anyone else Abby had met, so she must have some idea.

Plus, she sounded like a fun, old-school lesbian, like Ms. Sloane. Abby hoped she had an office cat. Her dad was allergic, so they'd never been allowed to have one, and Abby had always wanted a cat to pet when she was lying on her bed watching shows.

When she got off the metro she still had a few blocks to

walk. She followed the directions on her phone, trudging past parking lots and bungalows and tree-lined apartment complexes while trains whizzed by on the tracks above. When she reached the campus, the office building her phone led her to was tall and industrial looking, but inside the halls leading off into classrooms and small offices were inviting enough. Abby climbed to the second floor.

"Excuse me?" Abby knocked on the open door with Professor Herbert's nameplate attached. Abby recognized the professor behind the wide, paper-strewn desk from the photo on her website. Even with her graying hair she didn't look as old as Abby had expected, and her smile was warmer, too. "I'm Abby Zimet."

"Of course, Abby. It's very nice to meet you." Professor Herbert had a slight Southern accent. She stood up behind her desk, shook Abby's hand and gestured for her to sit down.

There was no sign of a cat, but there was a framed poster on the wall. It was the cover of another lesbian pulp novel Abby had read about, *Women's Barracks*. It showed a group of women in a locker room, with one woman in a military uniform smoking a cigarette and leering at another in a bright pink bustier and booty shorts.

Abby tried to put the awkwardness with Linh out of her mind. Professor Herbert clearly knew a lot about this subject. Today, Abby might finally get close to finding Marian Love.

"So how's Ken doing?" Professor Herbert smiled. "I don't get down to the archive these days as much as I used to."

"He wasn't feeling well when I was there last week. I felt bad for bothering him."

"Oh, he's always coming down with something or other. A regular hypochondriac if you ask me." Professor Herbert laughed. Right away, Abby liked her. "So, how can I help you? You're working on a school project, is that right?"

"Yes." Abby told her about the book she was writing, and how she was trying to read as many of the pulp novels as she could.

"I'm impressed." Professor Herbert raised her eyebrows. "Most people your age don't seem interested in such ancient history."

"Well, the books are a lot better than I thought they'd be. Some of them anyway. But the biggest thing I want to find out is what happened to Marian Love. What her real name is, and if there's a way for me to meet her. Ken said she might have lived in the DC area, but he wasn't positive."

Professor Herbert's smile faded. "You're looking for her in particular?"

Good, Marian Love really was a *her*. After Ken had asked that question, it had bothered Abby a little. "Yes. *Women of the Twilight Realm* was the first pulp novel I read, and I got kind of obsessed." She looked down, embarrassed, even though it was the truth.

When she looked up again, though, Professor Herbert's lips were pursed.

"Well, I'm afraid you won't be able to meet her." The professor folded her hands tightly on her desk. "I wish Ken hadn't gotten your hopes up. You see, Janet Jones—that was Marian Love's real name—"

"I knew it!" Abby couldn't believe she'd gotten it right. "I *knew* she was Janet Jones! I found her name online. Wow, I can't believe I figured that out!"

"Well, yes, but I'm afraid Ms. Jones passed away." Professor Herbert nodded gently. "Some time ago."

"She—what?"

Marian Love couldn't be—*dead*. She *couldn't*.

"I don't have permission to share this for publication, so I'll have to ask you not to put it in the paper you're writing for your class. If that's all right with you, I can tell you what I know."

"Um." Abby swallowed, but her throat felt as if it were closing up. She wasn't entirely sure she was breathing. "Sure. Fine."

Professor Herbert twisted around to reach into a filing cabinet. "I can't allow you to keep this, or to copy any of it down, but you can look at it here. I'm sorry to be so difficult, but I promised to keep this information confidential. I probably shouldn't be telling you at all, but I hate to think of you going off on a wild-goose chase. Here it is."

She passed a photocopied sheet of paper to Abby. It was typed on old-fashioned letterhead that read Bannon Press across the top, and it was dated September 30, 1955.

Dear Miss Wood,

I was very sorry to hear about the accident involving Miss Jones. I am sad not to have had the opportunity to meet her. She was clearly quite a talented writer, particularly considering her youth. I hope you will convey my condolences to those with whom you have been in contact, though I understand and will respect their requests to remain anonymous.

I agree that the revised manuscript Miss Jones had entitled *Alone No Longer* is an excellent work, very worthy of publication. My secretary has received the

information regarding the bank account and will make
the arrangements for payment.

   Thank you, once again, for sharing her manuscript with
me.

   I look forward to receiving your next novel for Bannon
Press.

Yours truly,
Nathan Levy, editor

Bannon Press
54 W 23rd St., 17th floor
New York, NY 10011

Abby took off her glasses and scrubbed the back of her hand
across her eyes. "I don't get what this letter is talking about."

Professor Herbert plucked a box of tissues off her bookshelf
and pushed it to Abby. "Claire Singer gave it to me. She wrote
for the lesbian pulps herself, under the name Dolores Wood.
Have you read anything of hers? Her most popular book was
A Love So Strange. It was one of the early ones."

Abby shook her head. "What does she have to do with
Marian Love?"

"Well, I had suspected for some time that Ms. Singer might
have some information about the writer who called herself
Marian Love. There was such an air of mystery about Ms.
Love, since she only published the one hugely successful book.
I found her writing strikingly similar to Ms. Singer's—even
more so than the way writers in the same genre often tend to
sound alike. I thought that either Ms. Love had been heavily
influenced by Ms. Singer, or—and this was the theory I decided to explore—that 'Marian Love' was simply another of

Claire Singer's pseudonyms, and that she was keeping it quiet for some reason. About ten years ago I went up to Philadelphia, where Ms. Singer was living, to interview her for a paper I planned to write." Professor Herbert shook her head. "I wish my theory had been correct. The truth is simply awful."

"What *is* the truth?" Abby could barely get the words out. She felt like crying, but tears wouldn't come.

"I'm afraid Ms. Jones died very young." Professor Herbert gazed up at the poster on her wall, as if she didn't want to look at Abby while she told her this story. "She was only eighteen, and there was a car accident. The details aren't clear—her family seems to have tried to cover everything up. It appears Ms. Jones and another young woman were living somewhere near DC at the time, and Ms. Jones's family must have discovered that she was a lesbian. Ms. Jones and her friend decided to do what many young people did in those situations—run away to New York. They hoped to start a new life together in Greenwich Village. The Village was very different then, of course—very poor." Professor Herbert sighed. "The car they were driving was an older one, and cars weren't as well maintained in those days in any case. We'll never find out exactly what happened—whether they simply experienced car trouble, or whether there was alcohol involved. Or whether, perhaps, the two of them were trying to outrun someone who might have been pursuing them. All we know is that there was a very serious crash. Ms. Jones was killed, and her friend was badly injured."

Abby wished Professor Herbert would stop talking. With every word she said, it was that much harder for Abby to imagine that this story wasn't true.

"When the friend recovered," Professor Herbert went on, "she wrote to Ms. Singer and forwarded the manuscript Ms.

Jones had hidden in her suitcase. She said Ms. Jones had hoped to publish it under the pen name Marian Love."

"But…" Abby couldn't make sense of any of this. "The letter says her manuscript was called *Alone No Longer*."

"It was common for publishers to change titles in those days. It was the same with cover art. Authors didn't have much control over them, even when they weren't—well. In any case, *Alone No Longer* became *Women of the Twilight Realm*, and Janet Jones became Marian Love."

No. *No*.

Marian Love—Janet Jones—she couldn't have only lived to be eighteen. Only one year older than Abby.

"How did she know all that?" Abby was desperate to find a hole in this story. "Claire—what did you say her name was?"

"Claire Singer." Professor Herbert pulled a book off the shelf and passed it to Abby. The title on the spine read *A Love So Strange*, but it wasn't falling apart, so it couldn't be a first edition. It must be one of those lesbian press reprints Ms. Sloane had talked about. "Ms. Jones had written her a fan letter, and Ms. Singer offered to connect Ms. Jones with her publisher. After the accident, the Jones family didn't want anyone to find out about the circumstances surrounding her death, so it was only thanks to her friend that the manuscript survived at all."

Abby frowned. "So that's why no one found out what happened to her?"

"That's right. Ms. Singer agreed to tell me all this, and to let me make a copy of that letter, only if I promised never to publish anything about it. I think she only told me because she was afraid that if I dug back through the records far enough, I'd figure it out for myself and publish it without anyone being able to stop me. So I agreed to keep that part quiet. It wasn't relevant to the literature itself, and by not sharing the information, we were honoring Ms. Jones's family's wishes."

"Her family who didn't want anyone to find out she was queer," Abby muttered. "Even after she was dead."

Professor Herbert sighed again. "You have to understand— I'm not excusing what her family did, not at all, but it was a different time. Everyone truly did think staying closeted was for the best, even within the gay community. It wasn't all that different when I was growing up, even though that was years later."

But Abby couldn't get past the image of eighteen-year-old Marian Love running away to New York with her secret girlfriend and dying mysteriously by the side of some highway. It was like something straight out of one of the pulp novels.

"What was that in the letter about a bank account?" She blinked down at the paper. She wished she could cry, but numbness was setting in instead. "If Marian Love died, who was that Nathan guy sending the money to?"

"Probably her family." Professor Herbert shrugged. "Ms. Singer said she wasn't clear on that."

"Did her family even know she'd *written* this book? Maybe the money went to that friend instead—the one she was running away with. If she was Marian Love's girlfriend, that would make sense, wouldn't it?"

Professor Herbert tilted her head to one side. "I suppose it might."

"Unless…" A darker thought occurred to Abby. "Wait. What if this Nathan Levy guy was keeping the money for himself? Did you ever meet *him*?"

"No, he died several years before I began doing this work in earnest. And I've never heard anything about Nathan Levy being unethical, but I suppose you can never be sure." Professor Herbert peered down at her. "You look as though you're taking this awfully hard, Abby."

Was she that obvious? Abby looked away. "I guess."

"If you really want to get to the bottom of things, I suppose you could always reach out to Ms. Singer yourself." Professor Herbert reached for a stack of Post-its. "I'll write down her email for you."

Abby did the math in her head while Professor Herbert wrote. Sixty-two years. Marian Love had been dead more than half a century. Since before either of Abby's parents was even born.

Marian Love—Janet Jones—hadn't lived long enough to see her book in print. She hadn't even known it was going to be published at all.

She'd died trying to start a new life, the same way Elaine and Paula ran away to New York to start *their* new lives. And her own family, the very people she'd been trying to escape, had made it all into a big secret.

It was the saddest thing Abby had ever heard.

"I should probably head out." Abby took the Post-it. She still felt numb. "Thanks for all this information."

"Of course. If there's any other way I can be helpful, please don't hesitate to get in touch."

Abby could barely manage to say goodbye before she left.

On the train back home, her brain kept trying to write letters to Marian Love, asking her more questions. About families and tragedies and love and heartbreak.

But there was no point writing to her anymore. Marian Love was dead.

Abby squeezed her eyes shut and ordered herself to think about Gladys and Henrietta instead. She needed to write a new scene between them. It would take place right after Henrietta's parents sent her away to be institutionalized, but before she found out that the "mental hospital" they'd picked was in fact a secret lesbian commune.

"It'll be all right, Henrietta," Gladys said softly. "I'll stand by you, no matter what happens."

"You can't mean that." Henrietta brushed away a tear.

"Of course I mean it. I'll always be here for you."

Henrietta collapsed into her arms. Gladys held her. It was the best feeling in the world, being held.

She wanted to believe that Gladys would always be here when she needed her. But if there was one thing Henrietta had learned, it was that you could never really count on anyone but yourself.

10

Saturday, July 16, 1955

I folded the letter and tucked it into the bottom drawer of my dressing table underneath a pile of worn-out old brassieres.

It was time I told Wayne yes. It was time I put away my foolish past and became what everyone had always told me I was meant to be: some man's wife.

After all, Paula's letter had made it clear she didn't want me. There was no use fighting it any longer.

Janet flipped through the manuscript one last time before she sealed the package. All 108 pages were there. She'd carefully written the page numbers on the bottom of each sheet with a thick black pen taken from her father's desk, but it still didn't look as though she'd typed them on. She could only hope Nathan Levy wouldn't mind.

She'd rewritten most of her earliest draft. She'd been forced to change much of the girls' first love scene now that she had a better understanding of all that came before it, but Janet had made sure to copy over her favorite lines. She'd become a regular at the Peoples stationery aisle, having gone through far more typing paper than she'd ever imagined would be necessary to produce five chapters of fiction.

She wasn't certain yet what would happen in the sixth chapter, or the seventh or the eighth. She wasn't sure, either, that the events she'd written about in chapter four were entirely plausible, strictly speaking.

Nor did she have the first idea of how she'd ever bring herself to write the ending she had planned. She wasn't sure she had the fortitude to write about such terrible things happening to the characters she loved. And she had no idea how she'd convey the truth of what Paula was thinking in the dark scenes ahead, as she was writing the entire book from Elaine's point of view.

Well, she'd figure all that out later. First, she had to concentrate on getting these five chapters onto Nathan Levy's desk.

Anticipation and terror battled in Janet's mind as she hurried down 31st Street. Her manuscript, carefully wrapped in brown paper cut from her mother's leftover grocery bags, was heavy in her arms, and she could barely summon the energy to smile for Mrs. Martin when they passed on the sidewalk.

Janet had a lie prepared, of course, in case one of the neighbors stopped her on the way to the post office. She'd say she was sending old magazines to her friend Lois Bannon, whose parents wouldn't allow her to buy magazines of her own. It was a bit of a flimsy excuse, and as she pushed open the door to the low gray building, Janet was glad she hadn't had to use it.

When she reached the front of the line and handed the package to the man behind the desk, though, her hands trembled.

The postman smiled and took the coins she offered, but as he fixed the stamp to the corner of the parcel, Janet longed to snatch it back.

Those were *her* words. Janet had created people out of nothing. She'd put sentences into their mouths, ideas into their heads. She'd given them lives, relationships. She'd devised their jobs and families and pasts and futures.

Now she was giving it all to someone else.

She had the carbon copy at home, of course, safely tucked away into one of the attic trunks. Still, it hurt to think she was sending off the original manuscript to some editor in New York she'd never even seen. A man who had the power to decide whether she ever became a real, published writer.

Mr. Levy may not understand what Janet had created. He may think her childish or untalented, or both.

The sight of the postman tucking her pages into a mailbag with a hundred other indistinguishable brown-paper packages made Janet want to cry. Yet moments later, as she stepped outside, a slow feeling of triumph began to simmer inside her.

Janet had done it. She'd really done it.

She'd written enough to show her work to a real publisher. Even if he didn't think it was good, *she* did, and that counted for something.

She only wished she could tell Marie.

It had been two weeks since they'd seen each other last. Fourteen long, lonely days since Janet had watched her climb into that taxi in Silver Spring.

Marie hadn't stopped by. She hadn't called. But then, neither had Janet.

Still, there was no time to linger over her thoughts. Janet

was working the dinner shift. She had to hurry home, change into her uniform and go straight to the Soda Shoppe.

When she reached the house, Janet unlocked the front door and dashed up the stairs. She waved down an apology as Grandma tried to ask her something and she was in her room, pulling on her uniform jacket and shoving pins into her hair when her father shouted "Janet!" from the foyer.

"Just a minute, Dad!"

"But, Janet, your friend is here! The one who's going to single-handedly save the State Department from itself!"

Janet paused. Was it possible?

"Coming!" She shook the pins out of her hair and grabbed her cap.

Janet took the stairs two at a time. Sure enough, Marie was standing in the foyer with Grandma. "Marie? Is that you?"

What a stupid question. It was entirely and thoroughly Marie. She was wearing one of her nicest dresses, a blue one with a scalloped neckline and crinoline puffing out the skirt. Behind her glasses she'd done up her eyes with mascara. Janet had only ever known Marie to wear mascara for dances.

"You're so funny, Janet." Marie smiled at her and then at Grandma, whose head was swiveling back and forth between them. Dad, it seemed, had already wandered back to the den and his newspaper. "Of course it's me. I've come to fetch you for the evening. We'll have to take a taxi, I'm afraid—the Buick is back in the shop. Something about the brakes acting up."

"You've come to *fetch* me?" Janet hated the way she kept asking these ridiculous questions, as though she were too dumbfounded by Marie's very presence to speak properly. Though she supposed that was the truth of the matter. "I'm supposed to work tonight."

"Oh, dear, I should've thought of that." Marie's face crumpled as she seemed to notice Janet's uniform for the first time. "I'm so sorry for the late notice, but I only just received the invitation. I'd never ask you to change your plans under ordinary circumstances, but this visit is with some very special coworkers of mine. Is there any way you can miss your shift tonight?"

Janet hesitated.

After two weeks of silence Marie was suddenly in her foyer, wearing a fancy dress and asking Janet to miss a night of work. All to visit Marie's *coworkers*.

Yet when Marie gave her that smile again—the warm, quiet look Janet knew was meant for her alone—Janet nodded. She didn't have the slightest notion what this was about, but she'd have to trust it was important. "I'll need to make some phone calls."

After Janet requested, and received, her father's permission to go out for the evening, the first phone call she made was to Shirley. Shirley always complained that she wanted more Saturday shifts, since that was when the best tips came in, and Janet made the sign of the cross as she dialed the number, praying Shirley didn't already have plans for the evening.

She didn't. In fact, she squealed with delight when Janet proposed they switch shifts. With that settled, Janet only had to make one more call.

Mr. Pritchard did not take as kindly to Janet's request.

"Shift changes must be approved at least five days in advance," he shouted over the sounds of pans clanking, carhops shouting and cooks bellowing back. "You know the rules."

"Of course, sir, but—it's an emergency." Janet tried desperately to think of what an appropriate emergency might be.

She wished she'd prepared a lie before picking up the phone. "I'm very sick, you see."

"Sick with what?" he shouted.

Janet was scheduled to work again the following night. She didn't want to miss out on those tips, too, not if she hoped to afford an apartment someday. "It's a headache, but I'm sure it will pass by tomorrow. Please, sir, Shirley can cover for me. She'll be there at the start of shift, I promise."

"Shirley's the worst girl I've got. Why do you think I never put her on Saturdays?"

Marie, standing next to Janet in the kitchen, smiled apologetically. Janet turned away. "I'm very sorry, sir."

"You do this again, it'll be the last time," Mr. Pritchard shouted. "Your headache had better be long gone by tomorrow."

"Yes, sir. Thank you, sir."

When Janet hung up, Marie clapped her hands, but Janet didn't feel like celebrating. "What's this all about?"

"You'll see," Marie promised. "First you need to change clothes, and quickly."

Janet eyed Marie's dress. "I'm not sure I have anything that nice."

"The dress you wore to the graduation banquet would be perfect."

"You remember what I wore to the graduation banquet?"

Marie raised her eyebrows.

Oh. Janet blushed. The thought that Marie had been noticing how Janet looked even then wiped away her annoyance at being shouted at by Mr. Pritchard.

She ached to touch Marie's hand, but that was too great a risk here in the kitchen. Instead Janet ran upstairs to change, calling over her shoulder, "Could you tell my father we're leaving, please?"

Moments later she'd put on a quick coat of lipstick, powder and her itchy white dress, and was dashing out the door after Marie. To make the dress fit she'd had to wear a tighter girdle than usual, plus a petticoat, and with her undergarments and high heels, walking was difficult. Marie steadied her as they made their way toward the taxis on Wisconsin.

"*Now* can you tell me what this is about?" Janet whispered once they were a safe distance from the house.

Marie answered her so quietly Janet had to ask her to repeat it twice.

"We're visiting two women who live near Shepherd Park," Marie finally murmured clearly enough for Janet to understand. "Two women like *us*."

Janet stopped walking so fast she nearly tripped. "Like *us*? Not really?"

"Yes, really! Well, that is, they're Negroes, but yes."

Janet's mind was spinning. "And they work with you?"

"One of them does. Miss Carol Barrett." Marie waved her arm at a taxi, and it slowed in their direction. "She works in the cafeteria. She came up to me at lunch yesterday and whispered that she had a *friend*, just as I did, and that I should bring *my* friend over so we could all talk. Then, this afternoon, there was a note in the mailbox inviting us to come tonight."

"You're certain she meant—*that* sort of friend?" It worried Janet a little to think that this Miss Barrett had found them out somehow. Still, she quite enjoyed the idea of being Marie's "friend."

"I believe so, but I can't be certain." Marie opened the taxi door, and Janet climbed inside. "That's part of why it's so urgent that we talk with them, and in private."

Marie gave the driver the address, and Janet tried to calm herself as the cab rolled north. Before she'd managed it, they were already pulling onto 16th Street.

Janet longed to hold Marie's hand, from nerves as much as tenderness. She'd never met anyone else who was like them. Unless she counted Dolores Wood, but a letter wasn't truly a meeting.

Would Marie's coworker and her friend be like Sam and Betty? Would they expect Janet to be fashionable and worldly?

She wondered how their home would look. If it was an apartment, like the one in Greenwich Village that Sam and Betty shared, Janet didn't feel nearly sophisticated enough to enter such a place.

Too soon, their taxi was pulling up to the curb. The house Miss Barrett and her friend shared was bigger than Janet's or Marie's, with a real lawn out front, and on either side, too. In Georgetown, the houses shared walls with the houses on either side with no more than a sidewalk in front, but here each residence stood alone.

The house was bright and clean, with a wide, covered porch and pretty, flowered curtains drawn across the windows. Marie paid the driver while Janet climbed out with apprehension.

The front door opened as the girls started up the porch steps. The tallest woman Janet had ever seen stepped onto the porch. Her short hair was styled in curls, and she wore brown slacks with a white blouse. She didn't smile, but when she beckoned to Janet and Marie, the gesture was friendly enough. "Come in, you two, come right on in."

"Hello again." Another Negro woman stepped into the door frame, smiling at Marie. She was shorter, with longer hair, and she wore a simple pink dress. "This must be your friend."

"Yes, ma'am." Marie nodded nervously. "It was so kind of you to invite us here. May I present—"

"Let's go inside for the introductions, shall we?" The taller woman smiled this time, but her lips looked stiff. The other woman ushered them inside and closed the door firmly in their wake.

The house was as lovely inside as outside, with polished knickknacks, many in the shape of cats, arrayed on spotless furniture. Janet couldn't help but notice, though, that the drawn curtains that had looked so pretty from the street lent a dark, harsh feel to the room. She wondered why the two of them didn't let in more light.

"I'm ever so pleased for you to meet my friend, Janet Jones." Marie finished her introduction with a short bob. Janet beamed—she loved Marie's perfectly proper manners. Marie glanced up and shared her smile. All at once, their argument by the bus station seemed a distant memory.

"How do you do, Miss Jones." The shorter woman's manners were as smooth as Marie's. "You can call me Carol. And this is Dr. Valerie Mitchell."

"Please, call me Mitch," the tall woman said, pumping Janet's arm in a firm handshake.

Janet turned to Marie to see if she'd known, but she looked just as surprised as she shook Mitch's hand.

"You're a doctor?" The words were out of Janet's mouth before she could remember to be polite. If only she'd paid as much attention in etiquette class as Marie.

"Yes! The only colored woman doctor in America!" Mitch let out a short laugh, but she didn't look amused. "That's what you'd probably think anyway. Have a seat, girls. Carol, shall we get them something to drink? Do you two like martinis?"

Marie answered for them both while Janet blushed. "That would be lovely, thank you, ma'am."

Carol disappeared into the kitchen, leaving Janet and Marie alone with Mitch. The doctor settled into a large armchair opposite the sofa where the two younger girls perched awkwardly. They were overdressed, Janet realized, both in their very best clothes while Mitch and Carol were dressed more like they might on any casual summer afternoon.

Carol returned with a drink-laden tray and set each glass on the coffee table. As she sat down, she laid a hand on Mitch's shoulder and squeezed it, holding it there a moment too long to be a friendly touch.

So it was true.

Janet watched them, mesmerized. Two women, together. Acting as any other couple might.

Then she realized Mitch was watching her just as closely. "So, Miss Jones."

"Please, ma'am, call me Janet."

"Janet, then." Mitch sat forward in her chair, resting her elbows on her knees. "We know a bit about your friend Marie, but not much about you. Are you a student?"

"Yes, ma'am." Something stuck in Janet's throat. She cleared it with an awkward cough. "That is, I start college in September."

"Which college?" Mitch asked her. "One around here?"

"Yes, ma'am. Holy Divinity."

Mitch raised her eyebrows. "Are you working this summer?"

"Yes, at the Soda Shoppe on M Street. I'm a carhop."

Mitch smiled. An orange cat slunk across the floor between her ankles, purring. She leaned down to pet it without taking her eyes off Janet. "Do you plan to work for the government after you finish school?"

Janet shifted. She hadn't expected all these questions. She wanted to look at Marie, but she didn't want Mitch to think she was nervous. "I suppose I'm not sure yet. I'd meant to study journalism."

"Journalism?" Mitch's eyebrows shot up even higher. "Is your father in that field? Does he write for the *Post*?"

"Oh, no." Janet laughed at the idea of her long-winded father working as a beat reporter. "He works on Capitol Hill. He's a lawyer for one of the Senate committees."

Mitch sat back, glancing at Carol and drawing her hands into her lap. Carol withdrew into her chair, too. Janet didn't understand the look that passed between them.

"Internal Security?" Carol asked after a moment.

"No, Government Operations."

"He's a Democrat?"

"A Republican."

Mitch stood up.

Janet didn't understand what was happening. She reached for Marie's hand and found that Marie was reaching out for her, too. Reassurance flowed through Janet at her touch.

Mitch and Carol looked down, their eyes zeroing in on the girls' clasped hands.

Janet sprang away from Marie in an instant. She didn't know what to make of these two.

Mitch turned back to Carol. "I think you were right."

"Well, now I'm not so sure myself." Carol eyed Janet. "Miss Jones, if you've come here with instructions from your father, or anyone else, we ask only that you tell us. It's the polite thing to do, given that we've invited you into our home."

"I—I don't understand." Janet turned helplessly to Marie.

"Janet didn't know about this invitation until a few minutes ago." Marie looked anxiously from Carol to Mitch and back again. "We didn't tell her father where we were going. I didn't even tell Janet herself until we were already in the taxi, so there's no way she could've— Carol, please, I don't understand what this is all about."

Carol nodded, slowly.

"You must understand our caution." Mitch's eyes lingered on Janet. "We don't let many strangers into our home. You can't be too careful these days."

The curtains, drawn across every window. Janet was beginning to understand.

"I want to trust you girls, though," Mitch continued. "You're quite the picture of innocence."

Carol laughed, and Janet felt herself flush.

"I think it's all right." Mitch looked at Carol. "What do you think?"

Carol nodded again, but her eyes were still wary.

Mitch settled back into her chair. "As soon as Carol told me about you two, I wanted to meet you. I imagine you're curious about us, too. Would you like to hear how we came to be here, together?"

"Of course!" Janet's eagerness bubbled into her voice, even though she couldn't tell whether it was her curiosity talking or her relief that Mitch was no longer asking her all those questions.

Carol smiled, her eyes softening a little. "I'll start, then. I'm twenty-eight years old. My family used to live in Shaw—it's not terribly far from here, though it feels farther. I went to Dunbar for high school, and all through that time I thought I was perfectly normal. I dated boys and went to dances, wearing dresses much like yours."

Janet blushed again and smoothed out her itchy petticoat.

"After the war ended, I went to Howard for college," Carol went on. "That was where I first started to realize how I was. I fell for my roommate sophomore year. Things were very exciting for a few months, but then another girl on our hall told the dean. My roommate and I were both expelled, and I went back to live with my family. Though they didn't want much to do with me after that."

Carol told the story with a half smile on her face, as though any pain she might've felt was long in the past. Janet wondered how it must feel to go through something so terrible and still come out of it able to smile.

"I still had the friends I'd made at Dunbar, though," Carol continued. "They didn't know about me—they'd only heard I'd left Howard and was looking for work. One of our former teachers knew the man who managed the cafeteria at State, and he got me a job. Soon I was making enough money that I could afford to move out of my family's house and in with roommates. Not the girl I'd been with at Howard—I heard her parents sent her to a hospital somewhere up north—but a group of Dunbar girls. I was nervous, but in the end we got along fine. The girls went out with their fellows, and through my job, I met a few fellows of my own. Fellows like us, that is. They'd go out to parties, and often they'd bring girls along for protection. That's how Mitch and I met, two years ago now, at one of those parties. We've been very fortunate."

Beside her, Marie made a startled noise. Janet squeezed her hand, but she was stunned, too.

Carol had been made to leave college, and her parents wanted nothing to do with her. It was the worst thing Janet could imagine.

"You've been fortunate?" Janet finally asked. "What do you mean?"

"She means we haven't gotten caught." Mitch's firm voice was startling after she'd been quiet for so long. "Not since we've been together, that is."

"Do the neighbors know?" This time, it was Marie who asked.

Mitch shook her head. "We moved in a year ago, and it's possible some of them suspect, but they've never spoken to us about it. We've told everyone we're roommates. Many of the folks up here are still adjusting to having colored folks on the block in the first place. It used to be all white up here, but then the covenants started letting in Jewish folks, and now here we are. Things are changing fast. Do you girls live in Georgetown?"

It had never occurred to Janet that there might be anything shameful about living in Georgetown, but suddenly she didn't want to answer. She was quite certain no Negroes lived in her neighborhood. Some worked there, like the woman who cleaned the movie theater and the men who sometimes came to install a neighbor's windows or lay shingles on their roofs, but they always left before the sun set. Everyone who lived there was as white as Janet and Marie.

Janet had never thought about that before.

She stared down at her hands. Marie answered affirmatively for them both.

"Thought so." Mitch nodded. "As for me, I grew up around here, but I went to New York for college and medical school. Schools around here weren't about to let a Negro woman become a doctor. Not that it was easy in New York, either, mind."

Carol chuckled. Janet tried to fathom Mitch's life, and found she couldn't.

"My family had just enough money to send me through school," Mitch explained. "Which was a lucky thing in the Depression. All I wanted in the whole world was to be a doctor, but that meant I had to abide by the rules. I worked and took classes during the day, but my college didn't allow girls to go out after dark or ride in cars with men, or anything else that might corrupt our virtue. So I spent every night cooped up with my books, learning all I could about biology and chemistry. I never so much as looked at any boy. Of course, now I see why that was."

Mitch and Carol both laughed. After a moment, Janet and Marie laughed, too.

"It was one of my professors who set me up with a job at a hospital down here." Mitch smiled. "He was fond of me, and he knew I longed to come back home. It hasn't been easy, of course—Washington is still the South—but when I was starting to think it wasn't worth it, that I should go back to New York and try to find work there, well, that's when I found Carol and my world got flipped upside down."

Janet's heart melted. Next to her, Marie let out a contented sound.

Carol reached across the gap between their chairs and took Mitch's hand. Janet felt Marie squeeze hers at the same time.

"As Carol mentioned, we met at a friend's party." Mitch was still smiling. "We're going over to that same friend's house tonight, in fact, so we'll need to get ready soon. Everyone in our circle takes turns hosting, you see."

"Your circle?" Now that the tension between them had waned, Janet wanted to learn everything she could about Carol and Mitch's life together.

"Other people like us," Carol said. Janet must have looked confused, because she added, "Negroes who feel the same way we do. It's safest to go to each other's houses rather than trying to go out to the bars."

"Of course," Janet said. "At a bar, you might be seen together."

"Well, yes, and then there's Jim Crow." Mitch's words were clipped but firm. "That's how it is in this city. I could save your father's life at my hospital tonight, but that doesn't mean I'm entitled to sit down beside him for breakfast tomorrow at a Georgetown café."

Janet nodded, but she cringed, too. How had she never thought about any of this before?

"Now, we need to talk about you." Mitch swung toward Marie, her lips forming into a tight line.

"Well, we don't have much of a story," Marie began. "Janet and I have known each other since we were children, and—"

"That's not what I mean," Mitch interrupted. "Of course you don't have a story yet. You're children still. All we need to talk about is what you'll say when the time comes. We invited you here so we could come to an agreement."

Marie shrunk back. Janet squeezed her hand once more. "What kind of agreement?"

"For if you're called in." Carol's eyes slid over to Marie, too. It was as though Janet had vanished from the room. "It's always better to go into that room with a plan."

Marie looked as confused as Janet. "What room?"

"Marie—both you girls, really..." Carol hesitated. "It's important for you to understand that you need to be *much* more careful from now on."

"Careful?" Marie bit her lip. "What do you mean?"

"I mean," Mitch cut in, "do you realize that Carol saw you looking at those awful books in the bus station? And if *she* saw you, *anyone* could have seen you. When you act so brazen out in public, you might as well send a memo straight to Secretary Dulles himself!"

Janet wanted to ask what Mitch meant about "those awful books," but Marie spoke first. "You *saw* us?"

"Of course I did! How did you think I knew to ask you over? It was a great risk to us, bringing you here. Even greater than I knew." Carol shot a look at Janet. "I wouldn't have said anything if I'd known your friend's father worked on the Hill."

Janet hung her head, but Marie had gone pale.

"Marie." Carol sighed. "Honey. Haven't you heard what's been *happening* these past few years?"

Marie looked ready to cry. Janet longed to help her somehow.

"Of course it would be bad if we were caught," she said, trying to keep Marie from having to speak while she was so upset. "Our parents would be terribly angry, and—"

"Your parents would be the least of your problems." Mitch sighed. "Your friend works at the Department of State, Janet, just like mine. Have you even *thought* about what that means? Does the name Joseph McCarthy ring a bell?"

Janet's jaw dropped. Had they somehow walked into an ambush? "We aren't Communists!"

"Of course you aren't." Mitch met Janet's eyes. "But Congress isn't only after Communists."

"Queers are just as bad." Carol's eyes were steely. "Maybe worse."

The word *queers* made Janet flinch. "We aren't—we don't—"

Mitch began to soften. "Carol. Look at them. They're so young."

"That's no excuse. It's been in the papers. You need to read up on your own people, girls."

"They're barely out of high school. How many papers did you read in high school?"

"Times were different then." Carol lifted her chin. Janet tightened her hold on Marie's hand, remembering the column about Senator Hunt's son. "Well, you should know it's been going on for years. We thought it might stop when they censured McCarthy, but if anything it's gotten worse. They're out to prove they're serious about this business. They have their lists, and the lists are always growing. If the administration gets the slightest whiff that someone working at the department might be a homosexual, or even might *know* a homosexual, they bring them in for questioning, and from the stories I've heard our interrogators could give the Germans a run for their money. Before they bring you in, they'll talk to everyone you've ever met, every school you've ever gone to, every place you've ever worked. They ask them if anyone ever thought you might be just a little odd. They ask if you ever wore pants, or cut your hair short, or if you ever had a girlfriend who seemed a bit too close. If anyone says yes, if anyone even says *maybe*, that's the end of it for you."

Janet shrank back. *She* liked to wear pants. She cut her hair as short as her mother allowed. And as for having a close girlfriend...

"But—*why*?" Janet regretted the question as soon as she'd asked it. Mitch and Carol looked at her as if she were an ignorant child.

"Homosexuals are security risks," Mitch said patiently. "They think we're all Communists—or if we aren't yet, the Communists will find us and blackmail us into becoming one of them."

"Not to mention that plain old *immorality* is enough to get you fired from a government job," Carol added. "Always has been."

"That's ridiculous!" Janet felt ready to explode.

"Welcome to Washington, honey." Mitch tilted her head in sympathy.

"As soon as they think they've got you, they bring you in." Carol turned back to Marie as she spoke. "They ask their questions, they humiliate you and then they fire you. A black mark goes on your file so no one will ever hire you again—in the government or out of it. They've mostly gone after men so far, but they've gotten plenty of girls, too. No one is safe. Your pretty dresses won't be enough to protect you then, honey."

Marie let go of her hand. Janet turned to her, trembling, trying to understand, but Marie's watery eyes were fixed on Carol's.

"How do you know all this?" Marie asked her.

"Everyone knows." Carol didn't break her gaze. "It happened to the man who used to work next to me on the line. Gerald. One day we were making jokes while we slung the hash browns, and the next he was gone. As though he'd disappeared into nothing. Everybody knew what happened, though. Word always gets around."

Marie turned to face the window. Janet wondered if she was thinking of climbing out of it.

"The only reason you haven't heard about this yet, Marie, is because you're brand-new." Carol's words were clipped. "That's why we invited you here—so we could come to an agreement. My pay isn't much, and I imagine yours isn't, either, but Mitch and I need my salary to pay our mortgage. I suppose you'll be wanting to put yours toward an apartment one day." She glanced over at Janet. "We both need to keep our jobs. So if they call me in, I promise I won't say one word to them about you and your friend here, not even if they ask me directly. I'll tell them whatever you'd like me to tell them. And I want you to promise the same about me."

"Of course." Marie swallowed.

"Good. If they ask, you say you've heard I've got a fellow named Tom who's away with the Navy. That's what I've told the girls who work the line with me. Now, what do you want me to say if they ask about you?"

"Tell them I have a boyfriend named Harold Smith. He goes to Dartmouth, in Hanover. New Hampshire."

Janet turned to Marie, surprised at how quickly she'd produced this story. Across from them, Carol nodded. "All right. Harold in New Hampshire. Make sure you tell the girls you sit with at lunch about old Harold, too, because you'd better believe they'll compare our stories."

"I don't understand…" Marie hadn't taken her eyes off Carol once. "Would they really call me in? Or you? Why would they ever think I had anything to do with—with—"

Carol and Mitch both fell quiet. But Janet couldn't stop thinking about the other day.

They'd fought in the middle of the sidewalk, in front of the whole world. While Janet held that incriminating novel right in her hands.

Surely there hadn't been anyone watching them, but—what if there *had*? What if someone had gone in to question the cashier who'd sold Janet that book?

And—and that night, outside Meaker's. They'd kissed. Right there on the street.

Janet hadn't thought anyone was close enough to see them, but how could she be sure?

She'd acted without considering the consequences. She'd been a fool, and she'd put Marie in grave danger.

"The good news is, you've probably already passed your clearance." Carol's tone had grown smooth, as though she was trying to be comforting. "That means they haven't found anything on you yet, but you've got to be careful. No more going out and about acting precisely as you please. It only takes one witness to start the process."

"I didn't—I don't have my security clearance yet." Marie stumbled over the words. "I still can't handle the classified documents. They said it might still be another week or two."

"Oh." Carol's lips pursed.

After another long, quiet moment, Mitch leaned forward again. "We aren't telling you any of this to scare you girls."

"Yes, we are." Carol's voice was still smooth and even. "They *should* be scared."

A tear rolled down Marie's cheek.

Janet put her arm around her shoulders. Marie began to sob, quietly, demurely, against Janet's white dress.

After a long, quiet moment, Janet felt a hand on her arm. When she looked up, Mitch was standing over them.

"This is still a harsh world we live in, but you're lucky you've already found each other." Mitch's smile was small, but it was genuine. "This isn't the end of your lives, girls. It's only the beginning. I hope you'll be very happy, as we've been."

It was strange, after hearing so much about everything Carol and Mitch had endured, to think about them being happy. Yet it seemed that was exactly what they were.

"Thank you so much, ma'am." Janet stood, letting Marie lean on her as she climbed to her feet. Her sobs had slackened. Janet tried to think of what polite words her mother might say in such a moment. "We ought to leave you to your evening."

Carol's calm, perfect manners reappeared instantly. Her etiquette was much more polished than Janet's. "It was lovely to meet you, Miss Jones. I'm so glad the two of you were able to come by."

Mitch ordered them a taxi, and as she and Marie said good-bye and went outside to wait, Janet knew something between them had changed that evening. Something that would never change back again.

The two of them stood on the porch, staring silently into the sunset. Janet ached to hold Marie's hand again, but she dismissed the thought before it had time to take root.

She'd made so many mistakes already. She had to do whatever she could to set things right. She could never again touch Marie where others might see.

The taxi pulled to the curb. Janet opened the door, then stepped back so Marie could slide across the seat.

Wait. Could the driver tell what they were to each other by the fact that Janet had opened the door? Was that the sort of thing men did for their girls? Janet couldn't remember. Did taxi drivers make reports to the government in any case? She supposed anyone might if the price was right.

Janet understood perfectly why Carol and Mitch had hesitated to welcome her. Her father never worked for Senator McCarthy, not directly, but they'd been friendly enough. They'd met at cocktail parties, and Dad had praised the senator around the dinner table many a night.

Was Janet's father aware the government was keeping lists of people like Carol and Marie? Did he approve of it?

He must. Everyone approved of rooting out potential threats to the country, Republicans and Democrats alike. That was why he was working so hard on the In God We Trust bill—to stop subversive elements from gaining power.

Now Janet *was* one of those subversive elements.

Her parents—if they knew...

What would they do? That Senator Hunt, the one whose son was caught with a man—surely nothing like that could ever happen in *her* family...

Janet couldn't bear to think about it.

Marie gave her address to the driver, her even tone concealing any nerves she may have felt. Janet was astonished at Marie's gift for pretending.

She looked beautiful, even with unshed tears lingering in her eyes. The color in her cheeks made her look young and fresh, and her dark brown hair framed her glasses in perfect loose curls. Her lipstick was uneven, with bare patches that had rubbed off when she'd bitten her lower lip, but somehow it only enhanced her loveliness.

Janet was still studying her when the taxi turned, far too quickly, onto Marie's street.

"Thank you, sir." Marie pulled a crisp dollar bill from her handbag and passed it across the seat without waiting for her change. She barely looked at Janet when she said, "Come in for a moment, please."

"Sorry?" Janet had thought to have the driver take her to her own house next, but when Marie gave her a tiny wave toward the front door, Janet didn't hesitate to follow.

Marie's hands shook as she turned the key in the lock. The narrow row house was dark and quiet, but Marie's eyes darted up the stairs and toward the windows, as though someone might be lurking in the shadows.

"Get the dining room windows," Marie said quietly. "I'll do the living room."

They moved swiftly, pulling each shade and drawing each curtain, until the first floor was even darker than it had been

before. They met in the kitchen, where half a casserole sat on
the counter under a towel. A note beside it on cream-colored
stationery read, "M—for dinner."

Marie didn't look at the note or the casserole. She only
looked at Janet.

"You haven't told anyone, have you?" Marie spoke quickly,
as though afraid to let the words linger. "You haven't said anything to—to your friends at work or your grandmother or—"

"No! Of course not."

"Your book." Marie fumbled in her purse and pulled out
a cigarette packet. "The one you've been writing. Have you
shown it to anyone?"

An image floated in Janet's mind. The postman dropping
her carefully wrapped manuscript into his bag.

"I…" Janet could lie to everyone else, but not to Marie. "I
don't—that is, I wouldn't—"

"Let's…" Marie trailed off and held a finger to her lips.
"Let's not talk anymore."

She motioned for Janet to follow her up the stairs.

On the second floor they again moved about the house
in silence, making sure no light peeked in through a single
door or window. When they were finished they met in Marie's room. It looked so grown-up compared to Janet's, with
its simple furniture and pressed white linens. No pink bedspread, no photos taped around the mirror, no schoolbooks
stacked on the desk. Even the darkened windows lent an air
of maturity to the place. Only the edge of Marie's old pink
frilled bathrobe, just visible behind the open closet door, gave
any indication that she had ever been the same girl who made
up silly cheers with Janet on the football field.

Marie reached into her dressing table for a match. Her
hands were shaking violently.

"I'm so sorry." Janet felt shaky, too. "If it weren't for me, you wouldn't have to worry about any of this. I never should have—I mean, it isn't fair that—I still don't even understand what all of this means, but, Marie, I'm *so* sorry. I should've thought about the future instead of—"

Then Marie kissed her, and she was the only future Janet needed.

They kissed, and kissed, and it was enough. They kissed again, and it was everything.

It was just as it had been in the street outside Meaker's—both of them rushed and eager, their bodies restless and uncertain even as their lips moved hungrily. Though it was different, too, here in this dark room with the curtains drawn. It was all so much *more* than it had been before.

Janet was conscious of all that. Yet somehow she was conscious of nothing at all, too, as they began to move toward Marie's bed.

Janet was fairly certain it was she who stumbled first, but it might have been Marie. In either case, the result was the same. The girls found themselves lying on their sides on the thin gray carpet, Marie's glasses tossed off somewhere, forgotten. Lips and tongues tangled while eager hands roamed. Janet's breath came in short sudden bursts, her heart pounding faster than Janet had ever realized a heart could pound.

Emboldened, or perhaps delirious, Janet reached for Marie's waist and pressed her back into the carpet, rolling onto her. Marie responded with a low sound in the back of her throat. Janet, terrified of her own actions but powerless to stop them, slid her palm over the thin fabric of Marie's dress and up, up, along the curve of her breast.

Marie didn't make a sound. Janet withdrew her hand and rolled onto her side, apologies spilling to her lips.

She didn't have a chance to speak them aloud, because all at once Marie was on her. Soon Janet lost track of whose hands were where, of who was giggling and who was groaning. She forgot to worry about whether she sounded foolish as she let out the strange sounds that matched the wave of feelings inside her. Feelings that only grew as Janet and Marie moved together.

Some time later, as the two of them lay atop the pale rug, watching the headlights from the street peer through the curtains and pass across the ceiling, Janet wrapped her arm around Marie's waist and nuzzled against her neck. She was surprised to notice that her dress was half-unbuttoned. In the books she'd read, and in Janet's own writing, too, the undoing of buttons was always a moment of heightened awareness. Life, it seemed, was more slipshod than fiction.

"Your lipstick is smudged." Marie passed her a tissue.

Janet took it silently and patted at her lips. "Thank you."

"Do I look all right?"

Janet sat up and stared down at her. "You look beautiful. And I love you."

It wasn't what she'd meant to say at all. The words had simply slipped out. Just as they had when Elaine had said them.

And like Elaine, Janet was glad for it. Especially when she saw the flush rise in Marie's cheeks.

"I love you, too," Marie said, her voice soft but clear as water.

When they kissed again, Janet felt like water too. Liquid. Malleable. She would take any form, she would do whatever was necessary, to keep feeling this way forever.

They kissed again, and again, and Janet would have kept kissing until the sun came up had Marie not broken away to check the time. Janet had to be safely gone when Mr. and Mrs. Eastwood returned from the club.

Janet agreed that it was a very sensible point. Still, as she stumbled the few blocks home, she didn't feel particularly interested in doing sensible things.

She wanted to be back in Marie's room. She wanted them to fall asleep in each other's arms. To wake up together in the morning and lie in bed together, staring at the ceiling, with no worries or fears. She wanted to kiss Marie's sleepy face awake, borrow her pink frilled bathrobe and wander lazily downstairs to make them a pot of coffee.

There was a time when Janet would've felt ashamed at such thoughts, but that night, no shame appeared. Indeed, as she walked on under the streetlamps, Janet's body felt alive in a way it never had before. Every inch of her skin was pleasantly aflame.

Janet knew she should be thinking about the future. Planning ways to be more careful, in light of all that Carol and Mitch had said. That night, though, Janet could not force herself to consider any future beyond the next time she'd hold Marie in her arms.

Nothing would ever be the same for Janet after this. And that was exactly how she wanted it.

Wednesday, October 4, 2017

"No." Paula took Elaine's face in her hands. Her touch was gentle but firm. "No. I love you, Elaine. If this is really what you want—if you never want to see me again, if you think it's too dangerous for us to be together—then I'll accept that, but I don't think that's the case. The Elaine I know, the one I love—that girl isn't afraid of anything."

Abby squinted down at her phone screen, but it didn't help. She still couldn't focus.

She was in the hall outside Ms. Sloane's classroom, trying to reread the last scene of *Women of the Twilight Realm*, but her eyes still kept drifting off the screen.

She couldn't stop thinking about the real Marian Love. Janet Jones. She'd written a happy ending for her characters, but she hadn't gotten one herself. She'd made a desperate attempt for one—she'd tried to run away with the woman she loved—but the trying alone had been enough to kill her.

"Did you already glue your sign, Abby?" Savannah called from the other end of the hall, waving a poster over her head.

Abby glanced up, blinking through dazed eyes. Shit. "Um, not yet."

The school day had ended ten minutes ago, and the hall had mostly emptied out except for Abby and her friends. The others were clustered around one of the hall outlets with a hot-glue gun, sticking handles onto the posters they'd made the afternoon before. They were leaving soon for an immigration protest outside the State Department, and they'd had to make new signs since the immigration posters they'd made back in January had been used so many times they were falling apart. Abby had meant to get her sign from the art room and come back down with everyone else, but she'd gotten distracted, again. She could hardly keep track of anything lately.

"I've got to get mine from upstairs," Abby called. "Save me some glue."

"There's a dirty joke to be made with that, except I can't think of it," Ben called back. "So pretend I said something really funny about glue."

"Ew," Vanessa said, but they were laughing. "Can I not, actually?"

Linh stayed quiet, which wasn't like her. Abby avoided meeting her eyes. Things had been weird between them since that awkward moment in the senior lounge. As eager as Linh had seemed to talk about their almost-kiss at first, neither of them had brought it up in the two days since, which was more than fine with Abby.

"Oh, hello there." Ms. Sloane poked her head through her

classroom door. "I thought I heard you out here, Abby. Could we talk for a few minutes?"

"I have to go soon." Abby caught Linh watching them and tried to pretend she didn't notice. "We're going to the immigration rally at Foggy Bottom."

"That's great." Ms. Sloane smiled. "I'll be joining you there shortly myself. This will only take a few minutes—there's something we should discuss."

It didn't seem to be up for debate. Abby grabbed her backpack, signaled to her friends to wait and followed Ms. Sloane inside.

"Have a seat." Ms. Sloane shut the door behind them.

Abby sat down and fixed her eyes on the wedding photo on Ms. Sloane's desk. She and her wife were staring happily into each other's eyes, both of them looking as though they were about to burst out laughing.

Was that the future that awaited Abby someday? A life of cheerfully settled lesbian bliss?

She used to think so, when she and Linh were still together. Now she wasn't so sure.

"Ms. Taylor spoke to your parents on the phone today."

Abby's head jerked up. "What? Both of them?"

"I believe she spoke to your mother—and told her you're behind in three of your classes. Did you realize that? Not to mention that you've missed two editorial meetings for the literary magazine."

Abby exhaled. *That* was why the principal had talked to her mom? That was nothing. She'd thought—it didn't matter what she'd thought. "It isn't three classes. I got an extension on that paper for French. Plus the lit mag meetings are no big deal, I—"

"I'm not the one you need to explain this to." Ms. Sloane

held up a hand and looked straight at Abby without blinking. It was unnerving. "I volunteered to talk with you about it because Ms. Taylor had another meeting this afternoon, but I'm not in a position to bargain with you, and I wouldn't even if I was. You've been working diligently on this senior project with me, and you've taken on additional work even beyond the writing itself in trying to track down this author, but it can't be at the expense of your other classwork. College applications will be due very soon, and you can't allow yourself to slip further behind in courses that will appear on your first-semester transcripts. Not to mention, these are courses you need to *graduate*, Abby."

When Ms. Sloane finally stopped talking, Abby asked the only question she really cared about. "Do you know what my mom said to Ms. Taylor when she called? Did she say anything about talking to my dad?"

Ms. Sloane didn't blink. "I didn't get all the details. Why do you ask?"

"No reason." Abby shrugged.

Her mom would've *had* to tell Dad about this. Right? He was in New York, but Mom had probably called him there as soon as she got off the phone with Ms. Taylor.

Maybe he'd take the train home that night to help figure out how to punish her. At least then both her parents would be on the same side for once.

Maybe, in a weird way, Abby screwing up her homework would make things better.

"I can give you extra time on your senior project if that would help you get caught up." Ms. Sloane still hadn't blinked. "You could take a break for a while and let the story rest. That can help the creative process, believe it or not. You could go

back to it in a month or two with fresh eyes, and it'll be easier to see what revisions you need to make."

"Oh, no, I don't want to stop writing. I'll figure something
out about the other classes, don't worry."

Ms. Sloane sighed. "Frankly, Abby, I think you could produce a better result if you did take a break. The pages you've
sent me so far have a lot of strong elements, but your characters are too static. Your protagonist needs to have an arc over
the course of the story, to learn and grow. Your main characters both seem to be stuck in a rut, Henrietta in particular.
It's fine that she starts the story angry, but she also needs to
develop, to change."

Abby tried to keep the hurt from showing on her face. Ms.
Sloane didn't know what she was talking about. Henrietta
was the best thing about her book, and she had every reason
to be angry. *She* wasn't the one who needed to change—it
was the world around her that sucked. "Um. I'll try to work
on that, I guess."

Ms. Sloane nodded slowly. Something on her laptop beeped,
but she ignored it. "Abby—I have to ask again. What's going
on? I've gotten a very strong sense that something's been
bothering you this year."

Abby's fingers itched to take out her phone and turn back
to Paula and Elaine. "It's nothing."

"If there's something you're bottling up, you'd be surprised
how helpful it can be to talk about it out loud."

Abby felt her lower lip tremble. Stupid worthless emotions.

"I'd like to help if I can, Abby." Ms. Sloane was looking
right at her. Abby darted her eyes into every corner of the
room to avoid her gaze. "I can be a lot more helpful if you're
open with me."

She wasn't going to back down until Abby said something. That much was clear.

Abby exhaled. "Marian's dead."

Ms. Sloane blinked at last. "Marian?"

"Marian Love. The author who wrote *Women of the Twilight Realm*."

"Oh." Ms. Sloane frowned. "How did you determine that? I thought no one knew her identity?"

Abby explained about the meetings with Ken and Professor Herbert. Ms. Sloane's eyes widened, and they widened even further when Abby told her about the car crash.

"That's terrible." Ms. Sloane's shoulders drooped. "She was so young."

"Almost the same age as me."

"That's true. Do you think that's why it's affecting you so much?"

"No." Abby shifted in her seat. "It'd be affecting me anyway. It's an incredibly sad story, even apart from her being young."

"Well, but this all happened a very long time ago. You must have realized there was a good chance she was no longer living, even if she'd died of natural causes." Ms. Sloane frowned again.

Abby didn't like where this was going. She decided to change the subject. "I've been wondering if Marian Love might've left more writings behind. They found the manuscript of *Women of the Twilight Realm* in the car when she died, but there could've been other papers with it. Letters, or something. I think I'm going to email that other author, Claire something, and ask her."

Ms. Sloane tapped her chin. "That *would* be interesting, but I wonder if continuing to look into all this is the best use of your time. After all, you're behind in your classes, and this isn't class work."

"Okay, but—" Abby clenched her hands into fists, the nails digging satisfyingly into her palms. "I only—I need to know what else Marian Love thought about aside from what she put in the book. I need to—" *talk to her*, she didn't say.

"You need to know what she *thought* about?" Ms. Sloane tilted her head to one side. "Abby, I'll try one more time. Is there something going on with your friends—or your family, maybe—that's bothering you?"

What *wasn't* bothering Abby? Ugh, why would no one ever leave her alone? "Can I please just go? Everybody's waiting for me. We'll be late for the protest."

Ms. Sloane watched her for another moment. "Sure, go on, but I meant what I said. You need to get a better handle on your assignments. You won't be happy if the principal has to call your parents a second time."

"Understood."

A knock on the classroom door made them both jump. It was Linh.

"Sorry." She glanced from Abby to Ms. Sloane and back, her eyebrows furrowed. "We're supposed to leave."

"That's fine." Ms. Sloane stood up. "Excellent protest-wear, by the way. Both of you."

Linh was wearing jeans and a hand-stenciled T-shirt that said My Parents Didn't Come Here from Vietnam to Help You Build a Wall, You Racist Jackass Cheeto-Face. Abby didn't have an immigration-themed shirt so she was wearing her #RESIST tank top with a pair of high-waist navy blue shorts, since it was still weirdly warm for October.

"Thanks," Linh said. "It's a big one today."

Ms. Sloane smiled. "Stay safe and raise hell, you guys."

Abby ran upstairs to get her poster and met the others outside. Linh looked as though she was going to ask Abby something, but then Savannah came running over with Ben and Vanessa close behind and Linh shut her mouth.

"Oh, there you guys are." Savannah smiled. "You both disappeared. Ben was about to send a search party up to the fourth floor."

"I was not!" Ben protested. "What my friends get up to in the privacy of the senior lounge is absolutely none of my business."

Abby could already feel the blood rushing to her face. She didn't dare look at Linh's reaction.

She couldn't have told them about the other day, could she? That would be so utterly unlike Linh that Abby wouldn't know how to handle it.

"Oh, relax, you two." Vanessa put a light hand on Abby's arm. "Seriously, it's fine. You'll tell us what we need to know when we need to know it."

"Hush," Savannah said. "Look, they're all embarrassed. Somebody change the subject."

"Okay, but come on, it was bound to come up sooner or later." Ben waved his Dreamers Make America Great sign for emphasis. "The elephant in this room's the size of a woolly mammoth."

"Actually, woolly mammoths weren't any bigger than modern elephants," Vanessa said. "That's a common misconception."

"Okay, well you just messed up a joke I'd been working on for a while, so thanks. What's bigger than an elephant, since you're a walking Wikipedia?"

"I don't know, a blue whale?"

"Well *that* doesn't work for my joke at all."

"It's not my fault the animal kingdom's failing you, dude."

Ben and Vanessa could clearly keep running down that conversational rabbit hole for a while, but at least they were off the subject of Abby and Linh.

Abby tried to breathe normally. It sounded as if Linh hadn't told them about the other day after all. Still, she studiously avoided Linh's gaze for the rest of the walk to the metro.

They met up with the other twenty-odd Fawcett students heading to Foggy Bottom and boarded the train in a big bunch, passing around signs and water bottles and posing for pre-protest selfies. At Metro Center they got out to transfer to the Orange Line, and their group made so much noise as they paraded through the station that they got dirty looks from the commuters with their power suits and briefcases, which only made them wave their posters higher. Abby tried to forget everything else and get her head into protest mode.

"Hey, so…" Linh caught Abby's elbow while they were waiting on the platform. "We should probably talk about that thing the other day. I still feel bad."

Abby shook her head so fast she stumbled and bumped into someone's backpack. "It's no big deal. We don't need to talk about it."

Linh's pretty brown eyes were wrinkled in concern. It was exactly the way she'd looked at her back in May after the thing with her parents. The pitying expression that made Abby want to throw up.

"It's *seriously fine*." Abby would say it as many times as necessary to get Linh to stop making that face at her. "We're supposed to be moving on, right?"

"I mean—look, things are probably hard for you now what with your parents and everything, and I don't know if we should…" Linh sounded as though she was going to say more, but when Savannah waved at them from a few feet away she dropped her voice to a whisper. "I guess—yeah."

The train slowed to a stop, and the crowd on the platform surged toward the doors. Abby plunged straight into the melee without waiting for Linh, ignoring the annoyed looks of the other passengers until she was on the far side of the train car. Only when three lobbyist-types in suits and clipped-on name badges stood between her and Linh did Abby let herself breathe.

But it was too late. The memory had already started playing in her mind.

It had happened on a Friday afternoon, a few weeks before the end of the school year. Dad had just gotten back from another trip to New York. It was the first time he and Mom had both been in the house in months. It would be the last, too.

Linh and Abby were upstairs watching a show when they heard Mom and Ethan come through the front door. They went downstairs, because that was the rule—they could hang out together as much as they wanted, as long as they didn't do it in Abby's room. It was an unbelievably stupid rule, since they'd already been having sex on the regular for six months by then, so they only bothered following it when one of Abby's parents was home.

The main door of the house was right at the bottom of the staircase, so they saw Mom and Ethan right away. Ethan was in his dance clothes, as usual, and Mom was glaring down into her purse.

Abby had assumed she was frustrated because Ethan had kept her waiting while he took his sweet time leaving class. He always did that, hanging back to talk to Mr. Salem or do extra stretches at the barre or awkwardly attempt to flirt with the girls in their leotards. When she looked closer at her mother's face, though, Abby knew this was about more than Ethan being annoying.

Then Dad came in behind them, his nostrils flaring, and Abby understood.

"The decision was already made." Mom wasn't looking at Dad, but it was clear from the tension in her voice she could only be talking to him. "There's no use discussing it."

Behind her on the stairs, Linh caught her breath. Abby did, too.

This wasn't a normal fight. There was an edge to Mom's tone she'd never heard before.

"You mean *you* already decided." Dad's eyes were tight. "I thought we agreed we'd both have a say in these decisions."

Ethan climbed up the stairs past Abby, but instead of going all the way up to his room he turned around and stood behind her, watching.

"*You* already had your say." That weird new tone in Mom's voice made Abby want to cry. "Remember? When you said *no*, absolutely not, under any circumstances, without bothering to ask what *I* thought?"

Abby expected Dad to start apologizing after that. Whenever her parents used to fight, Dad was always the one to stop and apologize first. Especially if he could tell Mom was really upset, like she clearly was now.

Dad didn't stop and apologize this time, though. Neither did Mom.

"Because I already knew very well what you thought." He sounded as if he was *mocking* her. Abby shivered. "You weren't exactly subtle about it. And you obviously aren't interested in being reasonable now."

"Oh, sure. *Reasonable*." The volume on Mom's voice had been creeping higher with each word, and by that point, she was shouting. "Because you're always so *reasonable* about everything. You're the one who gets to decide what's *reasonable* in the first place, right?"

Dad's face was tomato red. He started shouting, too. "At least I try to think things through instead of throwing money I don't have at every problem that comes my way!"

"Stop it," Ethan murmured behind Abby.

"Oh, that's *hilarious*, coming from you! Tell me again how much we spent retiling all the bathrooms because the *grout* was offending your delicate sensibilities?"

"God, would you please *listen* to yourself, Natalie?"

"Would *you* please shut *up*, Bob?"

"Stop it!" Ethan screamed.

Mom and Dad looked up. Mom's face went pale, as if she was seeing the three of them on the stairs for the first time.

Dad's face stayed red, though. As though he was still too angry to care.

"Kids—" Mom started toward them.

Ethan turned and started running up the stairs. Dad lifted his hand to cover his mouth, finally looking stricken. Mom looked back and forth uncertainly from Ethan's retreating back to Abby, glancing at Linh a few times, too.

Abby stood up and reached back blindly. "We've gotta go." She found Linh's wrist and wrapped her fingers around it tightly. "We've got to, um—"

She didn't bother trying to think up a reason. Instead she pulled Linh down the stairs behind her, brushing past Dad and dashing out the still-open front door.

She started running when they were halfway down the wide set of steps to the sidewalk. They were almost at the end of the block when Linh pulled back. "Hold on! Abby, slow down!"

Only then did Abby begin to understand what had just happened.

Linh had seen everything. Her parents, screaming at each other. Abby, running away like a little kid, dragging Linh behind her like her favorite teddy bear. And the neighbors and nannies and dog-walkers out on the street had seen her running, too.

Had they heard her parents shouting from inside the house? It seemed impossible that the whole world hadn't heard that.

"Are—um. Are you okay?" Linh tugged on her ear without meeting Abby's eyes. "That was—I mean, it was—"

"That was no big deal." Abby could hear how hysterical she sounded, but maybe Linh wouldn't notice. "I mean—sorry, I know I was dramatic with the running, but it isn't anything important."

"Abby…"

Abby hated that worried note in Linh's voice. She didn't want Linh to say anything else. She didn't want to say anything more herself, either.

So Abby kissed her instead, right in the middle of the sidewalk.

She didn't stop to worry about who might be watching. She just…needed someone to hold her.

And so they went to Linh's house, and they slept together for the last time. And a few weeks after that, they broke up, and Abby lost the one person she could go to when she needed to be close.

Now they were friends. Not girlfriends. Not friends-with-benefits who could occasionally kiss in the senior lounge without it being weird. Just plain *friends*.

Abby hated that word.

They got off the train at Foggy Bottom and started walking

down 23rd. Linh didn't look Abby's way again. She'd sped up to walk with Ben and Savannah, and soon they were talking about college applications, *again.*

Abby hung back with Vanessa, who was silently looking up something on their phone. Up ahead, Abby could hear chanting. She tried to focus on that. Maybe she could lose herself in it.

"Love! Not hate!" The chanting reached their block, and she and Vanessa joined in with the crowd. *"Makes America great!"*

The crowd stopped moving forward when they reached the rally site. Abby and Vanessa claimed a spot by a concrete barricade and Abby lifted the sign with the slogan she'd carefully lettered the day before ("Education, Not Deportation!"). She tilted her head back and joined in the latest chant. *"No ban! No wall! No ban! No wall!"*

There were hundreds of people around her, and they were all there for the same reason. All ages, all races, all genders, chanting as one. All on the same side of a fight that shouldn't have sides in the first place.

"Vanessa! Abby! Hold your signs higher!" Ben darted through the crowd in front of them, holding up his phone to take a photo. Abby tried to smile and let the chants fill her ears.

"Say it loud! Say it clear! Immigrants are welcome here!"

A woman wearing a hijab and carrying a megaphone climbed up onto a statue and took over leading the chants. Abby closed her eyes and let the shouting sink in, trying desperately to shut down every other part of her brain.

"Undocumented people are under attack! What do we do? Stand up! Fight back!"

Linh and Savannah were ahead of them, chanting with all

the others. More than anything, Abby wanted to go up there, reach for Linh's hand and squeeze it.

Nothing major. Just a touch. Just enough to make the rest of the world recede for a while.

She closed her eyes and let the chant fill her ears instead.

"The people! United! Will never be defeated!"

If Paula were here, Abby could squeeze her hand instead. But Paula had never seen anything like this. She wouldn't have lived long enough, even if she'd ever really lived.

Marian Love *had* lived, but she'd never seen anything like this, either. She'd died before the big protest movements in the sixties. She hadn't lived to see marriage equality or the first black president. She hadn't even seen women's lib. Or the Civil Rights Act, or Black Lives Matter. Life in 2017 was far from perfect—kind of the opposite, actually—but it was so unlike 1955 that Marian Love might as well have inhabited a different planet.

Even if Abby couldn't have what she wanted, she had so much more than Marian Love had ever had.

You would've loved this, Janet, Abby thought, gazing out into the sea of shouting faces, the passion plain on every one of them.

I wish you were here. I wish I could talk to you.

I wish you could tell me what the hell I'm supposed to do.

12

Saturday, July 30, 1955

College of the Holy Divinity Freshmen Dress Code

Only dresses or skirts and blouses are permitted. No slacks, shorts or culottes. Skirts should be of sufficient length that no portion of a girl's knees are visible when kneeling (staff will conduct measurements as needed). Shirttails must be tucked in and buttons must be appropriately fastened at all times. All girls' clothing must be clean, pressed and mended where necessary.

Makeup, nail polish, bracelets and necklaces are not permitted. Earrings may be small studs only. Cross necklaces are permitted but must be worn under clothing. Fingernails may not extend past fingertips.

Hair must be kept tidy and off the face. Any ribbons must be small and nondisruptive. Hair scarves, curlers, clips or other devices for setting are not permitted outside dormitories.

Janet stared into her closet, trying to remember why she'd once been eager to start college.

Only a few weeks remained until her first day as a Holy Divinity freshman, and a lifetime of school uniforms hadn't left her with many clothes that met the college's requirements. All she had were church dresses, mostly, with lines of buttons running up to her neck and hems that stopped halfway down her calves. The wide skirts were meant to make her waist look narrow, but instead they made her resemble a spinning top turned upside down. They'd be fine for chapel, Janet supposed, but she'd feel awkward wearing them to classes. She could probably use some of her tip money to buy clothes for school, but the idea of trading those hard-earned fistfuls of dimes for a set of plain white blouses and nondisruptive hair ribbons made her want to curl up into a ball on her bedroom floor.

Paula and Elaine got to wear whatever they wanted. They strolled easily around Greenwich Village in slacks and tight-fitting skirts. Sometimes they even wore men's-style button-downs.

Janet's lips turned upward in a small smile. She wondered what the nuns at Holy Divinity would do if she showed up for class in one of *those*.

Marie would fit in perfectly at Holy Divinity, if she'd chosen to go there instead of secretarial school. Of course, Marie did wear makeup most days. And though she always looked proper, some of her skirts may not be quite long enough to pass the kneeling rule.

Janet smiled again at the thought.

Two weeks had passed since they'd visited Carol and Mitch, and in that time the two girls had barely seen each other. Marie had been terribly busy at the office, and at home, too, thanks to her father's continued efforts to earn that promotion. Janet had asked to be assigned more lunch shifts at the Soda Shoppe so she'd be free to stroll through Foggy Bottom in the late afternoons and meet Marie as she was finishing work, but most days they could talk for no more than a few minutes before Marie needed to hurry off to some engagement with her parents.

So Janet returned each evening for dinner with her family, where she nodded along as Mom tried to keep the peace between Dad and Grandma. Most recently, Dad had taken to complaining about a lobbyist with the National Association of Pig Farmers who spent hours in his office talking about something to do with pork regulations. Inevitably, every evening Grandma wound up shouting at him to stand up for the rights of the farmworkers. Dad would shout back, saying that was exactly what he was trying to do, and that farm owners were workers, too. Then Mom would beg everyone to be quiet while Janet wondered if anyone in this dispute was the slightest bit concerned about the pigs. Janet had always liked pigs.

Each night, as soon as she'd finished the dishes, Janet went straight to the attic typewriter and pounded away on the stiff keys until she could no longer keep her eyes open. It was the best part of her day. She'd fallen asleep in the attic more than once, only to wake up covered in sweat and drowning in fresh dreams of Paula and Elaine.

Their story was becoming clearer with every passing night.

The characters had grown sharper and realer, and the plot was taking on a firmer shape, too. Some parts of the story had shifted slightly from the pages Janet had already put in the mail, but she would worry about that later. Besides, she'd still heard nothing from Bannon Press, so it might not matter what had been in those first hundred pages anyway.

Mr. Levy must have received the package at his office in New York at least a week ago—more than enough time for him to read Janet's first few chapters—but there had been no telegrams or scratchy long-distance phone calls from him yet. Janet had expected that he'd at the very least request that she send the rest of the manuscript as soon as possible, but she might as well have mailed her pages off into outer space.

Unless the reason she hadn't heard anything was that Mr. Levy had found her pages unfit for publication. She was trying not to think about *that* possibility.

She tried not to think about Carol and Mitch's warning, either. She hadn't been able to speak to Marie about it since that night. During their brief conversations outside Marie's office, they had to be very cautious about what they said in case any of the nearby men in flannel suits overheard. And, of course, they were careful never to touch. It pained Janet, having to pull her hand away every time it neared Marie's.

"Janet?" Grandma's voice carried through the closed bedroom door. It always surprised Janet how loud her slight, frail grandmother could be. "Are you going to heat up that casserole for our dinner, or do you want me to go hungry?"

"Sorry." Janet opened the door, forcing a sunny smile onto her face. Mom and Dad were once again out at the club for the night, and Marie had been instructed to accompany her own parents there as well, so it was just Janet and her grandmother for the evening. "I'll go put it in the oven."

"What's all this?" Grandma stepped into the room, peering at the open closet door. "We haven't decided to start dressing for dinner in this house, have we?"

"No, Grandma." Janet's smile was genuine this time. "I was only looking to see if I have enough clothes for school."

"Oh, don't you worry about that, girl. You'll look just fine. If you need anything extra I'll see if I can whip something up, but you've already got far more clothes than I had at your age." Grandma fingered the blue slacks Janet had worn in Silver Spring and frowned, sniffing the fabric. "Why—girl, is this what you've been hiding lately? Have you been smoking?"

"What? No!" Janet sputtered. Grandma had noticed that she was hiding something? "I've never!"

"This dress reeks of it, girl." Grandma sniffed the slacks again. "Now, I'm far too old to stop myself, but I've always told every one of my children and grandchildren, if you don't start you'll never have to—"

"I haven't!" Janet thought fast. "I wore them to a movie last week, and everyone in the theater was smoking. That's all."

"Oh. Well, you should give these a good wash nonetheless." Grandma reached for the dress on the next hanger, and Janet began to relax.

Would it truly be such a terrible thing if Grandma knew the truth? Out of everyone in the household, she'd probably be the least concerned. She'd been a progressive in her day, after all, and she'd lived in New York, where all the books seemed to take place. Perhaps Grandma had known other people like Janet once upon a time.

"Now, this may need to be let out a bit." Grandma pulled a green flannel skirt from the closet. "I believe you've grown since your mother last hemmed it. Why don't you try it on and we can see if— Why, girl, what's the matter?"

To her embarrassment, Janet realized her lip was trembling. "It's nothing, Grandma. I'm—I'm nervous about starting college, that's all."

"Are you?" Grandma's shrewd eyes ran Janet up and down, the green skirt still dangling from her hand. "Well, I haven't often known you to be nervous over a thing like that. If there were some *other* problem bothering you, though, even if it's something you might not want to tell your parents about yet, you can always talk to your old grandma."

"It's nothing. Really."

"Well, just in case it was." Grandma raised her eyebrows. "I've been on this earth a lot more years than you have. There's nothing you can say that could shock me."

Perhaps that was true. Still, Janet had never imagined telling anyone. Anyone who wasn't like her, at least.

Then Grandma smiled. It was the same smile she'd worn when Janet was ten years old and had just shattered the vase she was supposed to be washing in the church sink. It was the smile that said that whatever Janet might have done, her grandmother would make sure everything turned out all right.

"Grandma." Janet swallowed. Could she really say it? "I don't—that is, I... I have a question."

"Well, go on, then." Grandma sat down on the desk chair and gestured for Janet to sit opposite her on the bed. As she sank down onto the mattress, Grandma patted her knee. Janet had never been so grateful to be patted on the knee. "Whatever it is, we'll take care of it. There's a solution to every problem."

"I was only wondering, if..." Janet fixed her eyes on the thin gray carpet. "Did you ever—when you and Grandpa lived in New York, I mean—did you ever meet anyone who...any girls who wanted to go around with other girls? The way they're meant to go around with boys, that is?"

Grandma's face didn't change at first. She watched Janet closely, just as she'd been doing before.

Then she stood up.

"Oh." Grandma's smile faded. "Oh, my dear."

Janet caught her breath. Had she made a mistake?

"That is—I don't—" Janet had no idea what to say. Should she pretend she'd only been joking? "Grandma, I—"

Grandma turned away.

"Wait, I didn't mean—" She tried desperately to think. "It isn't as though—"

Then her grandmother turned back around. A fresh, soft smile was spread across her lips.

"Well, my girl." Grandma rubbed her hands together slowly. "You nearly did manage to shock your old grandma this time, but not quite. The answer to your question, as a matter of fact, is yes. I once knew a fine lady, a Miss Elizabeth Flynn. She lived with her friend Miss Equi for quite some years."

"Really?" Janet couldn't believe it. It was exactly what she'd hoped to hear. "You knew someone who was—like that?"

"Well." She'd never seen Grandma at a loss for words. "I suppose I did. Of a sort."

"Oh, I— I'm so pleased to hear that!"

"Of course, Miss Flynn is off in prison now." Grandma fixed her gaze out the window.

"Oh." *Prison?* Janet flinched, thinking again about that senator's son. "Because of—of Miss Equi?"

"No, no, it's just the standard rubbish about Communists. But never you mind Miss Flynn and Miss Equi. I want to talk about *you*, girl." Grandma turned back to Janet. Her smile had begun to creep, slowly, into her eyes. "You're far too young to worry about these things."

"But—is Miss Flynn *truly* a Communist?" Janet flinched again. Nothing in the books she'd read had said anything about lesbians being Communists, but even Bannon Press probably wouldn't allow any discussion of *that* topic. What if there was truth to the government's worries about homosexuals and Communism?

"You don't realize you're young, of course." Grandma ignored her question. "I was eighteen once myself, and I remember feeling as though I'd already lived three lifetimes. Still, you've got to keep your future in mind, and with something like this… I'm afraid many people simply won't understand. It's probably best to keep any questions you may have to yourself, lest you run into trouble."

"Well, but I wasn't—" Janet certainly hadn't planned on discussing this with anyone else. "I didn't mean to—"

"May I tell you something, girl?" Grandma's face had turned solemn. "There's a story you may find interesting."

"Of course."

"You know that I was arrested once," Grandma began. Janet nodded. "Well, that was during the Great War, when I was part of the IWW. Your father may not appreciate my telling folks I was a Wobbly, but I can talk to my own granddaughter about anything I choose. My friends and I—we called each other *comrades* then—we demonstrated against the draft. I didn't want your grandfather, or your father, or any other man to have to fight a war and kill others for a government that didn't believe in him."

Janet nodded again, though she was struggling to understand what any of this had to do with her and Marie.

"When the police caught up with us, they hauled us straight

to jail." Grandma's wrinkled face was grave. "We were there three days, but it felt like three hundred. They locked me in a tiny, stinking cell with a dozen other girls and fed us rotting meat and bread that was full of worms. That was nothing compared to seeing the others have their heads cracked by the coppers' nightsticks, though. I held one of my dearest friends, bleeding and knocked out on the floor, while the guards above us laughed."

Janet drew in her breath. She knew her grandmother had been political when she was younger, but she'd never heard any stories like this one. She couldn't imagine how the same Grandma who made her sweaters and told Dad to hush at the dinner table could have once lived such a life.

"Even that wasn't the worst part." Grandma's hand tightened on Janet's arm. "The worst was the fear. I thought I'd die in that place. Or that we'd all be put on a boat and shipped off to Moscow or someplace to live out the rest of our days. They were doing that kind of thing back then, you know. Anyone who spoke out about what they believed was called *disloyal* and *radical*. Today they call it *subversive*. They make lists of names, and if you're on their list—or if someone so much as *thinks* you're on it—that's the end of you, one way or another."

Janet nodded, remembering what Carol had said about lists. She wondered if Marie's name, or her own, was already on one.

"I knew I'd very likely thrown away my future." Grandma's voice softened. "All I could think about while we huddled in that cell was what would happen to my family when I was gone. My husband, and my children—they were so young then, your father and his sisters. Being apart from them for those three days was the greatest torment I've ever known. I was terrified I'd thrown away everything I cared about."

"Oh, Grandma."

"There, in that jail cell, I realized the most precious gift any of us have are our futures." Grandma's eyes locked on Janet's. "And that isn't something to be trifled with."

"I didn't think—" Janet pressed her hand against her temple. She understood, at last, why Grandma was telling her this. "I would never—"

"I know you'd never harm a fly." Grandma patted her arm again, smiling gently. "You're a good girl, Janet. All I'm saying is that a young person like you needs to concentrate on what's ahead. Why, women these days can have real careers and families, too. Once you're a world-famous reporter you won't have time to dwell on questions from your childhood. In fact, you'll most likely forget all about this. Someday, when you're off in the wilds of who-knows-where covering a big exciting news story, you'll probably meet a nice young fellow, and then you'll be mighty glad you put your focus on what mattered, eh?"

Janet opened her mouth. She closed it when she realized she had no idea what to say.

Grandma didn't seem to notice.

"You work hard at your writing." Grandma released Janet's arm and gave her a slight push toward the door. "The rest will work itself out. When you're all grown-up you'll be a girl we can all be proud of."

Janet felt a new wave of tears forming.

She *had* been working hard at her writing, but it wasn't the sort of writing that would make anyone proud.

She pasted on her Soda Shoppe smile. "Thank you, Grandma."

"You're welcome, girl." Her grandmother smiled, too. Janet wondered if the gesture was any sincerer than her own. "Now you run on downstairs and put dinner in the oven. You need a good meal. You're still growing after all."

Janet nodded and stood. She couldn't believe how foolish she'd been.

She'd have to pray Grandma kept this conversation secret. She might not tell Janet's parents—not with the way she ranted about Dad's opinions every night—but what about her friends from the bridge club? Or Janet's aunts, who Grandma wrote to every week?

What about their priest at Holy Trinity? Grandma went to confession every Saturday. What if she told Father O'Brien, and he thought Janet a grievous sinner?

Was Janet a grievous sinner?

Grandma lifted the flannel skirt she was still holding, bending back the hem to examine the stitching. "Wait, Janet, let's hold off on dinner for a moment. Go ahead and try on that skirt and I'll take a quick measure before we go downstairs." She passed the mound of drab green fabric to Janet and shifted over to sit on the bed. "Hope you don't mind if I take a quick rest in the meantime, your chair is awfully stiff and all that chatting's worn me out, and—why, girl, what's this? You've got a lump the size of the Great Pyramid of Egypt in your bed."

"What?" Janet's panic was instant. She knew she'd need a lie, any lie, but she couldn't think fast enough. "There's no lump, Grandma!"

Janet wanted to jump down, to yank her grandmother away from the bed, but it was already too late. Grandma was on her knees, reaching under the mattress.

"What's this?" It was clear from the worry in Grandma's

voice that she'd found something. "Janet? Are you keeping things hidden under here?"

She shouldn't have let Grandma sit on her bed. She shouldn't have even let her come into her *room*.

Should she say she'd never seen the books before? No, no, Grandma would never believe her.

"It—it isn't mine. It belongs to another girl—" Janet cursed herself for saying that. What girl would she possibly blame for this? Not Marie! "A girl from work, I—she asked me to—I was doing her a favor, keeping it for her—"

It was obvious Grandma wasn't listening. She rose to her feet, gingerly dangling Janet's worn copy of *A Love So Strange* out in front of her by two fingers. As though it were a bomb, or a mud-covered shoe at the playground.

The glue that had bound the book was almost gone, and the cover was barely attached to the pages, but her grandmother could see the picture on it well enough. That much was clear by the way the color had drained from Grandma's face.

A moment later Grandma shook her head, a thought seeming to take shape in her mind. She flung the book to the floor. The cover broke off entirely and drifted down after the pages, landing featherlight on the gray carpet above them.

"What is *this*?" Grandma's voice was lower than a whisper. Her hands shook as she reached out to grasp Janet's chin. "Why would you bring this—this *filth* into our home?"

Janet blinked back tears. She was all out of lies. "It isn't like that," she mumbled.

Grandma released her and jerked away, facing the window and pressing a hand to her forehead, as though she couldn't bear to look at Janet any longer.

"Those questions you were asking." Grandma's shoulders hunched. "I told myself you were still a child—just a curious child, but this…" She whipped around to face Janet again, her eyes alight with a strange new animation as she waved her hand toward where the broken book lay on the rug. "You have to put a stop to this. Promise me, girl."

Put a stop to what? Janet stared at the pillar of icy fury her grandmother had become.

She forced herself to take a long breath, then another, before she spoke.

Grandma didn't mean for her to stop seeing Marie, surely. She couldn't possibly know about Janet and Marie.

Did she mean for her to stop reading the lesbian novels, then? Or for her to stop being who she was?

It didn't matter. Janet couldn't have stopped any of it, even if she'd wanted to.

"Promise me," Grandma said again. Her blazing eyes were locked on Janet's.

"I promise." This lie was harder than the ones that had come before it. Janet couldn't prevent her gaze from wavering, and she knew her grandmother wasn't fooled.

"You're young." Grandma looked away, as though muttering to herself more than Janet. She kicked at the torn cover of *A Love So Strange* with her slipper. "Young people are drawn to dangerous literature. That's been true since even before my time. But reading rubbish can lead to practicing rubbish, so one can never be too careful. I can't let this go any further, Janet."

"What?" A cold ball of fear began to unfurl in Janet's stomach. "What do you mean?"

Without another word, Grandma bent and scooped up the tattered pages and the torn-off cover of *A Love So Strange*, crushing them in her fists as she pushed past Janet to the door.

"Wait!" Janet had never seen her grandmother move so

rapidly. She was already on the stairs, her slippers moving so fast Janet had a flash of worry that she might fall. "Where are you going?"

She rushed down the stairs after her just as Grandma strode into the living room. When she bent down to fumble on the end table where she kept her cigarettes, Janet almost relaxed—Grandma simply wanted a smoke, that was normal enough—until she saw her grandmother moving toward the fireplace with a matchbook in her hand.

"No!" Janet forgot caution entirely and shouted the word, but it was too late. Grandma had always had a deft hand with matches, and the pages were already alight in the cold stone fireplace by the time Janet reached her. The blaze bloomed fast and bright, the cheap gray paper turning red, then black, as the flames crept in.

"It's for the best, girl." Grandma's hands crept onto her shoulders from behind as Janet stared into the fire. She stifled a cry at the touch. "Children need guidance. It's far too easy to stray onto sin's path if there's no one looking out for you."

The flames rose higher. Most of the pages had already blackened and crumbled, but the cover took longer, the fire still licking at the edges of Sam and Betty's portrait. Janet watched as a small hole formed in the middle of Betty's nightgown and rapidly grew, until the fire had consumed both girls. A moment later they were no more than ash.

"There." Grandma retrieved a poker from the rack and thrust it into the dying embers. "Now you go and get a glass of water to douse it, and bring the broom back with you. A grocery bag, too. We'll need to sweep all this up and throw it in the garbage before your parents get home. This would be the death of them both."

Janet didn't move. She stared into the fireplace. A small

black lump was all that remained of the book that had changed her world.

"Did you hear me, girl?" Grandma reached for Janet as though to grab her chin again. Janet pulled away first.

"Yes, ma'am." Her voice croaked on the word, but her grandmother didn't seem to notice.

"Then go and do as I said." Grandma reached into her pocket and pulled out her rosary, methodically fingering the thin, clear beads as though each one told her something new. "It will be all right, Janet. You'll see. You'll forget any of this ever happened."

Janet forced herself to nod.

"You'll see." Grandma pressed a hand onto her shoulder again. Janet closed her eyes to force back the tears. "Soon, everything will be back to normal, and you'll feel good as new."

13

Monday, October 9, 2017

A pickup truck had been speeding down the road. Father had
been directly in its path, but he hadn't tried to move.
*   When the ambulance arrived, his body was already cold.*

Abby had read the scene where Elaine's father died more times
than she could count. There was something weirdly fascinating about it. She kept changing her mind about whether Marian Love had left it intentionally vague or if it was supposed
to be obvious what had happened.

But she couldn't stop thinking about that pickup truck.
Marian Love had written about Elaine's father being killed
in what might have been an accident or might have been a
suicide, and Marian herself had died in a car crash not long
after. It was such an eerie coincidence.

Obviously, it *was* a coincidence, though. There was no way

Marian Love had been *trying* to kill herself when she and her friend got into that wreck. Her friend had survived after all. If it had been some kind of—of *suicide pact*—the friend wouldn't have gotten out of that crash alive.

Besides, she'd had the manuscript for *Women of the Twilight Realm* in the car with her when she died. Marian Love wouldn't have killed herself with her unpublished manuscript by her side, would she?

There were so many questions. Abby hated unanswered questions. They made her feel unqualified to even read this book, let alone write one of her own.

Not that it mattered anymore. She'd hardly written anything in days. She kept waiting for inspiration, but all Abby had managed to do since her meeting with Professor Herbert was change her title. She'd decided to call her book *Totally Normal Women in the Daytime*, since *The Erotic Adventures of Gladys and Henrietta* might not be allowed on the shelf at Barnes & Noble.

She stayed late at the library every night now. Sometimes she tried to catch up on homework, hoping that would make Ms. Sloane leave her alone. Her parents had barely said anything about that call from the principal in the end. Dad hadn't come back into town after all, and Mom had threatened to take Abby's phone away but she hadn't actually done it.

Most nights, though, she spent hours online, searching for information about Marian Love. She was still working up the courage to contact Claire Singer, the writer who'd known Marian, but in the meantime she was hoping to stumble across a helpful post on an obscure blog, or a set of scanned documents like the one on Lawrence Hastings's website.

Then there were nights when Abby just read her favorite scenes over and over. By this point she could recite entire pages' worth of Paula/Elaine banter from memory.

But today was a holiday—Columbus Day if you were the official DC calendar, or Indigenous Peoples' Day if you were one of Abby's teachers—and the library was closed. Fawcett followed its own calendar, so Abby had gone to school that day, and afterward she'd gone to her lit mag meeting just in case Ms. Taylor was paying attention, but now she had no choice but to go home. It was the last place she wanted to be, but at least Mom was in California again. And this early in the afternoon, Dad would still be at the office.

As she walked, Abby tried to think about the scene she was supposed to be writing. What would Gladys do after Henrietta's best friend was murdered coming home from a gay bar? She knew Henrietta would bypass all the usual stages of grief and go straight to being absolutely livid, but she had no idea how Gladys would react, so she couldn't figure out how to start the scene.

Maybe this was a sign that she shouldn't write the scene at all. If the words had stopped flowing, that could mean she was on the wrong track.

Or maybe it just meant Abby was a complete failure.

The house was quiet when she unlocked the front door. She shrugged out of her favorite cardigan—white with pink flamingos—and hung it up, glancing at the pile of mail on the entry table. More college brochures had arrived. She flipped past a heavy envelope from Washington University and yet another postcard from NYU, then tossed them into the recycling and started up the stairs.

"Abby?" Footsteps above her. Shit.

Abby glanced back toward the front door, but it was too late. He'd seen her. "Hi, Dad."

Her father climbed down slowly, dressed in an old U2 T-shirt and jeans instead of his usual suit. He rubbed his hand across the back of his neck when he reached the bottom step. "Good, you're here."

"Aren't you supposed to be at work?"

"Your brother's in his room." Dad glanced toward the top of the stairs, as though that answered Abby's question.

"Okay…" Abby stepped past him. "Well, I should start my homework."

"One second." Dad kept looking up the stairs. It was making her nervous. "I need to talk to you about something first."

No!

"I've gotta go." Abby's heart thundered in her chest. She tried again to push past him. "Let's talk later."

"Abby, your brother was suspended from school today." His voice cracked on the last word.

For a second she thought she'd heard wrong. "He—*what?*"

Dad nodded. "He got into a fight with another boy."

"No, he didn't." There had to be some kind of mistake. Ethan had never fought anyone in his life. He cried when they watched *Bridge to Terabithia*, for God's sake. "There's no way. He couldn't have."

"That's what I thought, too, before I spoke to the principal. Apparently the other boy said something about your brother's dance recital, and then he— I'm not sure exactly. Mr. Geis wasn't fully clear on the details, and Ethan won't talk to me about it." Dad exhaled slowly. "He won't talk to me at all."

Abby's head spun. Whenever one of her parents said they needed to talk, her mind sped to the worst possible conclusion. The one that seemed inevitable some days. On other days, it seemed as though if she could just keep her head down—if she could just make it through this day, this week, this year, without anything changing...

Nothing in the future was inevitable. There was always a way to hit Pause.

Now, though, something *was* changing. Her brother was changing, and Abby didn't know how to stop it.

"I..." Abby swallowed. "I don't understand."

"Neither do I." Dad twisted his hands in front of him. "He's in his room. Would you please go talk to him? He may not be ready to tell us what happened, but if you could just get him to come downstairs that would be a big help. I already tried to tempt him with going out for ice cream, but he wouldn't even look up."

"You were going to take him out for ice cream for getting suspended?"

Once again, Dad ignored her question. "Actually, why don't you offer to take him instead? It would do him good to get outside. The two of you could walk down to that deli on Connecticut. Here." He fished in his wallet and held out a twenty-dollar bill.

Abby stared at the money in her father's hand.

Her parents already seemed to have forgotten about that phone call from Ms. Taylor. Now Dad wanted to give her money to buy her brother ice cream because he'd *fought* with some other kid?

Nothing in the entire world made sense anymore.

"I—I can't." Abby tried desperately to think of some reason, *any* reason, why she couldn't go upstairs. "I'm supposed to go meet Linh. I'm already late."

Dad glanced at her cardigan still hanging on the peg. "I thought you were going to your room. Something about homework."

"Yeah, um…" Abby thought fast. "This *is* homework. Linh and I are working on a project together, and we're meeting at the library. I'd totally forgotten we made this plan, but I just remembered, so I've got to go."

She started to panic before the words were out of her mouth. What if Dad remembered the library was closed?

"All right, well—all right." Dad shook his head. "We'll need to talk soon, though. This week—wait, it can't be this week, since your mom has the gala in Chicago, but once she gets back into town next Wednesday we'll all sit down and talk as a family."

"I can't." Abby's words were coming so fast she barely knew what she was saying. All she knew was that she would *not* be participating in any talking-as-a-family-related activities. "Next week I've got to work on my college applications. I'm totally behind, and I won't have time for anything else. So, well, anyway, I've gotta go." She tugged her cardigan off the peg.

Dad watched her without arguing. He didn't even seem annoyed. "Text me if you need a ride home, Abby."

She didn't answer. Instead she let the front door slam behind her, took the steps down to the sidewalk two at a time and started up toward Wisconsin.

Dad wouldn't be able to see where she went once she turned the corner. She could go to the Starbucks across from the library and find a quiet place to write. She didn't know what she'd write about, since she still wasn't sure what should happen next in Gladys and Henrietta's story, but that was fine. She could go back to one of those exercises they'd done last year in her creative writing seminar. What was that trick Ms. Sloane was always saying to use if you were stumped on a story?

Write what you know. That was it. Start with real life, and expand from there.

But Abby didn't want to write about her real life. She didn't want to write about her dorky kid brother getting into fights at school, and she didn't want to write about ex-girlfriends who randomly almost-kissed you, then fell all over themselves apologizing for it. She didn't want to write about how it felt when it seemed as though there could've been someone, somewhere, who might understand, but who turned out to have been dead for decades.

She wanted to write about something that would take her mind off all that stuff. Something happy.

Then she turned onto Wisconsin, her eyes latching on to the burger place across the street, and she knew exactly what to use for happy inspiration.

It had been—when? The beginning of sophomore year? Two years ago, now. Right after she and Linh had officially become a thing. Abby had spent years daydreaming about the relationship she'd have with an actual, real-life significant other someday, and there were so many things she'd always wanted to do with her someday-fantasy-girlfriend.

Making out in a dark movie theater. Shopping together for prom dresses. Holding hands on the metro. They were simple, silly things, so Abby had kept her daydreams to herself, but she went over and over them in her mind almost every night before she fell asleep anyway.

That afternoon, they'd all gone to the burger place right after school let out. It was a Friday, and by some miracle no one in their friend group had a meeting or a practice. They'd gone for milk shakes and grabbed one of the big tables outside, where they had a front-row view of the people walking up and down Wisconsin. Ben had started giving them a play-

by-play on the latest episode of *The Walking Dead*, complete
with his famous imitation zombie shuffle and lots of gross
hissing noises. Vanessa kept covering their ears and laughing,
and Savannah had gone back to the counter to complain because her banana-pineapple smoothie had too much banana
and not enough pineapple.

Abby and Linh had barely heard any of it. They'd snagged a
bench a short distance apart from the others, where they could
giggle together in semiprivate and share one milk shake with
two straws. (That had been one of Abby's someday-when-I-
have-a-girlfriend fantasies, but Linh had gone along with it
with such a big grin that Abby wondered if it might've been
one of *her* someday-fantasies, too.)

When Ben came over to wave his zombie arms in their
faces, Linh laughed, lifted his arm up out of her way and
leaned in to kiss Abby right over their milk shake cup.

Abby was so absorbed in the sensation of Linh's lips on hers,
on the perfect shape of how they fit together, on the softness
of Linh's hair under her fingers, that she forgot to notice it
was the first time they'd kissed in front of their friends until
the whooping and cheering started. Two minutes later, when
they'd stopped kissing but were still all flushed and giggly and
kind-of-not-really embarrassed, a college student in a paper
hat had stepped up to their table and put down a small order
of fries on Abby and Linh's tray. "We're not supposed to do
this," she'd said, biting her lip to keep from laughing, "but
the assistant manager asked me to say you two are really cute
together. Oh, and here's a coupon for twenty percent off."

There was more whooping and cheering after she went
back inside, followed by some grumbling from Savannah
about how *she'd* never gotten twenty percent off a milk shake
for being cute in her entire life. Ben and Linh immediately

started assuring Savannah they'd give her twenty percent off in their hearts, while Vanessa rolled their eyes, but all Abby could do was blush and hide behind her hand. Having a girl-friend was turning out to be even better than all her someday-fantasies put together.

Now she hid her face behind her cardigan as she sped past the burger place to keep from looking at the empty tables out front. She couldn't write about that memory. It hurt too much.

Two years ago, things had been easy. No one had expected her to apply to colleges yet. Her parents still consented to be in the same house on the same day, at least some of the time. And Linh… Linh was still Linh.

Abby took out her phone and sent a text asking what Linh was doing without pausing to think it through. A few minutes passed before she got a reply. **Homework? Why, what's up?**

I don't know, Abby wrote. She meant to leave it at that, but something made her type out another message. **My dad was home and he kept trying to talk to me and something's wrong, something big I think…**

She couldn't come up with anything more to say, so she gave up and hit Send.

Linh's reply came faster this time. **Are you okay? Where are you?**

I'm fine, Abby typed automatically. **Going to the Starbucks in Tenley.**

Linh answered even faster than before. **Meet you there.**

Abby read the text twice to make sure she hadn't misun-derstood. Hmm. Maybe things between her and Linh hadn't changed as much as she'd thought.

She climbed the hill fast and reached the Starbucks in five minutes flat, only panting a little. She didn't see Linh, so she found an empty couch in the back and opened her computer, flipping straight to the last chapter of *Women of the Twilight Realm*.

"No." Paula took Elaine's face in her hands. Her touch was gentle but firm. "No. I love you, Elaine. If this is really what you want—if you never want to see me again, if you think it's too dangerous for us to be together—then I'll accept that, but I don't think that's the case. The Elaine I know, the one I love—that girl isn't afraid of anything."

Elaine's eyes swam with tears. "I love you, too. Still, after everything that's happened, how can we do this any longer? No one will ever understand."

"You just said you loved me." Paula slipped a hand behind Elaine's neck and pulled her closer, their eyes still locked on one another's. "I've spent so many nights lately lying awake, alone in my cold bed, thinking about how much I need to be with you. If you love me and I love you, then I don't care whether anybody else understands it. You're the only one who matters."

Paula made it sound so simple. It couldn't be that simple.

Elaine tried the words for herself. "You're the only one who matters."

"That's right, darling."

"All this time." Elaine felt something warm in her chest. She couldn't put a name to it. "I've been worrying about what everyone else must think of me."

"I have, too. Believe me, I have, too."

"What's the point of all that worrying, though?" The warmth within her had begun to spread. Elaine felt herself succumbing to the astonishing idea that what she and Paula had was truly worth something. "You know what? To hell with everybody else. To hell with their opinions and their pontificating. You're everything, Paula. You're everything to me."

God, Abby loved that ending so much. It was like a freaking lesbian Disney movie.

"Hey." Linh was suddenly standing by her couch, looking worried. She slid tentatively into the empty seat next to Abby, her eyes wide, her voice gentle. "Is everything all right? Did something—happen?"

"What? Oh, no." Abby blinked up at her. Linh was staring at Abby with her lower lip held tightly between her teeth, as though she thought Abby was about to break into pieces. "I mean, there's something weird going on with my brother, but it's no big deal. Mostly I just wanted to get out of the house for a while."

"Oh." Linh held Abby's gaze for another moment, then sank backward in her seat. "You're sure?"

"Yeah."

"Oh. Okay." Linh shoved a lock of hair behind her ear and tugged on her gold stud earring. "You made it sound like an emergency."

"Oh. Sorry." Abby dropped her head. She should've realized she'd done something wrong. She'd made so many mistakes she probably never deserved to get the perfect feeling from that milk shake afternoon back. "I—I'm sorry."

"It's okay." Linh kept trying to meet her eyes, but Abby looked away. She didn't want to see pity there again. "If you ever wanted to talk—"

"Yeah, um…" Abby cut her off before Linh could start sounding like Ms. Sloane. "I did—uh. Yeah. I wanted your perspective on something."

"Sure, what's up?"

"Well." Abby tried to think. "I'm looking into other ways to get info about Marian Love."

"What?" Linh's eyebrows furrowed. "I thought there was nothing more to find."

"Well, but there's got to be *something*. I bet I could find other stuff she wrote. Letters or something."

"Didn't you say Marian Love was only eighteen when she died?" It was amazing how easily Linh could use the words *Marian Love* and *died* so close together without even flinching, when just the sound of it made Abby want to scream until her lungs gave out.

"Sure, but she still could've written stuff." Abby shrugged, trying to match Linh's easy tone. "I mean, I'm not eighteen yet and I've already written a lot of stuff. Remember all those emails we sent over the summer? And before computers, people wrote to each other a lot more. Actual letters, in handwriting even."

Linh looked doubtful. "I guess..."

"Actually, you know what I should do? I should go ahead and email that other author, Claire Singer, and see if she knows anything. I don't know why I keep putting that off." Abby was opening a blank email when a new idea occurred to her. A truly excellent idea. "Actually...hmm. *She's* in Philly."

"Who is?" Linh was typing something into her phone.

"Claire Singer. She lives in Philly. Professor Herbert mentioned that when I was in her office."

"Okay..." Linh glanced up. "So what?"

"So, we're *going* to Philly." Abby couldn't believe she hadn't thought of this before. "The fourteenth, right? That's this Saturday!"

"Yes, but—" Linh hesitated. How did she not see how obvious this was? "We're going to visit Penn."

"Oh, come on, it's perfect! Your parents already got us the

tickets, right? We can go meet Claire Singer and ask her to tell us everything she knows about Marian Love!"

"We're supposed to be checking out the campus. That's the only reason my parents are letting me go."

"Oh, it'll be fine. We'll pick up a brochure in the train station and you can tell your parents we got it on a campus tour. I mean, do you even want to *go* to Penn?"

"Not necessarily, but—" Linh was staring at Abby as though she'd grown three heads. "You haven't talked about anything except this Marian Love person for weeks, and now you're saying you want to go all the way to Philadelphia to meet some *other* author?"

"Come on, we're going anyway." If she wheedled enough, Abby was positive she could get Linh to agree. "If you really want to see Penn, there'll probably be time to do both in one trip."

"You can't be serious." Linh turned toward the counter, where two baristas were arguing over who was responsible for a spill on the floor. "Does this Claire person even want to see you? How old is she? She probably lives in, like, a nursing home."

"I'll email her and ask." Abby turned to the blank email and started typing. "Anyway, if you don't want to come meet her with me, that's fine. We can still take the train together and you can go see Penn, but if Claire's up for it, I'm going to visit her instead."

"Is that okay with *your* parents?"

"Oh, as if they care." Abby tried to shake off Linh's question and focus on her email. She hadn't actually told her parents that she and Linh were going to Philly, but she doubted they'd notice anyway. Mom would be in Chicago, and when

Dad was in town on a weekend he usually spent all day at the office anyway.

"Right. Um, well... I should probably get back home." Linh was still watching her, but Abby didn't meet her eyes again. At this point, she could guess when Linh was pitying her without having to see it spelled out on her face.

"Okay. See you tomorrow." Abby didn't turn to watch her go.

She couldn't believe it had taken her until now to come up with this plan. Claire Singer had *known* Marian Love. Talking to her would be almost as good as talking to Marian herself. If she knew anything about why Marian Love had written the book the way she did, or if she turned out to have copies of anything else she'd written, it would be the closest Abby would ever come to meeting the real Marian.

If that was the best Abby was going to get—well, then she'd take it.

14

Thursday, August 4, 1955

"So that'll be two Summer Freezes, a Big Dog, a Double-Decker Delight and a plate of onion rings—is that right?" Janet's smile never faded, but she barely glanced up from her notepad as she repeated the order back to the blue Oldsmobile in space nineteen.

"That's right, sweetheart." The college boy in the driver's seat didn't look at Janet, either. His eyes were locked on the pretty blond girl sitting next to him. Locked on the front of her blouse, at least.

"Righty-o. I'll be back in a jiff with your shakes."

It was the beginning of August. Congress was in recess, and half the city had gone up north to escape the heat until Labor Day. It was the sort of night where there was absolutely nothing to do in Washington but drive around with the windows down, trying to catch a bit of breeze.

And everyone who drove around, it seemed, drove into the

Soda Shoppe sooner or later. Janet's break had been overdue for half an hour, but she hadn't been able to take a moment's rest since her shift began.

She trotted to the counter window and called back the college boy's order, then filled her tray with burgers for the station wagon with the four screaming kids in the way back. By the time she was done passing the burgers through the wagon's rolled-down window, car nineteen's Summer Freezes were bound to be ready so Janet trotted back to the counter, eager to get the shakes passed out so the college boy would have something to do with his hands.

Janet used to look forward to busy nights. Her tips were always good, and there was so much going on it wasn't possible to think very much about anything except when her orders would be up and whether a new car had pulled into space eleven.

Tonight, though, her thoughts raced even as she trotted from car to car. She missed Marie, who was still too busy to talk, always deflecting Janet with an apologetic smile and a few quiet words when she caught her on her way out of the office.

And she was worried about Grandma. It had been nearly a week since that horrible night in the living room. Janet still couldn't look at the fireplace without remembering the thick smell of burning paper.

Grandma hadn't said a word to her about it since. Most days, she barely even looked at her. Janet could only pray she truly believed what she'd said about forgetting, and that they could both go on with their lives pretending it had never happened.

Janet would have to be more careful at home, though. For one thing, she could no longer hide anything under her mattress. She'd carefully arranged the copy of *A Deviant Woman* that Grandma hadn't managed to find, along with the carbon copy of her manuscript, her notebook, the pages she'd typed up in the last few weeks, and the letters from Dolores Wood and Bannon Press, in a musty old attic trunk, burying it all deep under a pile of winter underwear.

She was still writing, though. Or trying to. But the words weren't coming as easily as they had before.

She'd already begun the ending of *Alone No Longer*. Paula, mistakenly believing that Elaine didn't love her, had sent her a letter ending their relationship. Next Janet needed to write the scene where Elaine accepted Wayne's proposal, and the scene that came after it, where Wayne discovered the truth and came after Paula with his brother's hunting rifle. Elaine would intervene at the last moment, throwing herself between them, but Paula would tell Wayne he was wrong, and that Elaine had never loved her. Then Paula would leap to her death off the twelfth-story fire escape, sacrificing herself for the sake of Elaine's future.

So far, Janet hadn't been able to bring herself to write those last few scenes. Her characters had already gone through so much. There were so many changes happening, in the world around them and within Paula and Elaine themselves. This last set of changes was more than Janet could bear.

Her control over her own characters seemed to be slipping. She'd tried and tried again, but she simply couldn't think of a way to make Elaine realize that marriage was her best option. Even though marriage was the only proper option for any normal girl. And whenever Janet tried to write that down, it made her want to cry.

The biggest problem, though, was that despite Bannon Press's mandate that the characters face "appropriate resolutions," the idea of killing Paula made Janet's stomach twist into knots. Paula was *hers*. She was Janet's creation. Even though it was silly—Paula was only fictional after all—the idea of killing her felt like killing a piece of herself.

Maybe that was why she couldn't stop thinking about Senator Hunt and his son. Janet knew she'd have to take whatever steps necessary to make sure her own parents never discovered her secret. The senator's story had already inspired her to add a new scene to *Alone No Longer*'s ending, about Elaine's father dying in mysterious circumstances.

Between all the lying, the worrying and the struggles with her writing, there were simply too many things happening at once. Janet's life felt constantly on the brink of tipping over.

"Hey, honey!" A car horn shrieked behind her. Janet whipped around to see the college boy from space nineteen leaning out the Oldsmobile window. She'd been standing in the middle of the parking lot, halfway to the milk shake counter, all this time.

She ran, neglecting the rules altogether, and grabbed the Summer Freezes, carrying them swiftly across the lot. The boy frowned when she set the glasses down on the car-side stand. "Not really a jiff, then, was it?"

Janet didn't let her smile waver as she recited her line. "Hope you enjoy your Summer Freeze! The way to beat the August heat is with a nice orange breeze."

When she trotted back to the kitchen counter, she was dismayed to find Mr. Pritchard standing behind it.

"I saw you running, Janet." He shook his head. "You know the rules. Keep it to a trot."

"Yes, sir."

"The Soda Shoppe is where our customers come to relax,

to get away from the fast pace of modern life. They don't want to see a carhop girl running all over the place."

"Yes, sir. I'm sorry, sir."

"Well, hurry up. A car pulled into space sixteen and they're waiting for you."

They wouldn't have had to wait if Mr. Pritchard hadn't taken up so much time scolding her, but Janet knew better than to talk back.

She trotted over to space sixteen. Yet another college boy on a date with yet another pretty girl. "Welcome to the Soda Shoppe, your top spot for a refreshing drink and a bite to—"

Janet stopped.

The college boy in the green Ford looked no different from any other college boy who came through the Soda Shoppe on a summer night. But this time, the pretty girl in the passenger seat was Marie.

She stared straight at Janet, biting her lip, a pleading look in her eyes. She wasn't wearing her glasses. She looked so different without them. More vulnerable.

Janet's gaze flicked back and forth from Marie to the boy in the driver's seat. She could feel her heart slipping down. Shattering into pieces around her feet.

She'd barely seen Marie in weeks. They'd rarely even managed to talk on the phone for more than a minute or two. Marie was always too busy whenever Janet tried to make plans.

Now here she was, with some boy Janet had never seen before.

Marie was everything to her. That hadn't changed, regardless of Carol's warning or Grandma's order or Senator Hunt's son.

Yet perhaps what was happening right now *would* change things.

"Yes?" the boy asked, startling Janet. He had a crew cut and a thin, pale scar on his chin, and he was wearing a Dartmouth letter jacket despite the heat.

Dartmouth. Of course. The college man Marie's mother had tried to fix her up with. The one Marie had told Carol to call her "boyfriend."

"You look as though you've seen a ghost, miss," the boy joked. Janet swallowed.

"Ah, yes. Welcome to—ah." The script flew from Janet's head. She'd suddenly remembered the boy's name. It was Harold. Harold Smith. "May I take your order?"

"Sure." Harold turned to Marie and laid a careless hand on her arm. As though Marie was as much his property as the shiny green car. "You know what you want, sugar?"

Sugar?

Janet couldn't do this.

She backed away. At first she tried to keep her chin up in case Mr. Pritchard was watching, but she gave up when she felt the tears rushing to her eyes. When she was far enough from the car that she couldn't be heard, she trotted up to Shirley and grabbed her arm tightly. "Could you take car sixteen for me? I'm in the weeds, and that fellow looks like a big tipper."

"Of course." Shirley beamed, adjusted her blue cap and trotted over to the confused-looking Harold Smith.

Janet jerked back. She couldn't look at Marie again, sitting silent in the passenger seat as though she were any girl out on a date at the Soda Shoppe.

She rushed back to the counter to collect herself, only to find Mr. Pritchard still there.

"Janet!" He sounded genuinely angry now. "You were running again!"

She rubbed her face with her hand. The most she could do was mumble. "Sorry."

"*Excuse* me?"

She tried to raise her voice. "I'm very sorry, sir."

"Don't give me sorry. Your Double Decker and Big Dog are up. Hop to it!"

He clapped his hands twice. Janet wanted to rip off his blue vinyl apron. Instead, she loaded her tray. "Yes, sir."

She shoveled the food onto the stand for the couple in the Oldsmobile, not bothering to ask if they needed extra ketchup, and trotted straight over to the car that had pulled into space thirteen. This time she managed to get the script right, but she couldn't muster even a hint of a smile as she jotted down their order for Cokes, fried shrimp and grilled cheese.

For the next hour she trotted at top speed from car to car, all her attentions focused on *not* looking at car sixteen. Only when she caught a glimpse of a black Buick in the space did she realize Marie and the Dartmouth man who'd called her "sugar" were gone.

It didn't help her nerves. She barely smiled at any cars for the rest of the night, and she forgot to put in one family's steak sandwich order for a full ten minutes. Mr. Pritchard had her bring them free shakes to make up for it, but when Janet was halfway to the car with her tray full of Summer Freezes, her foot caught on an old root beer bottle and she toppled backward. The shakes soared off her tray and into the air, soaking the Buick's tires.

"Janet!" Footsteps came running up. Shirley's voice was almost a shriek. "Are you all right? Are you hurt?"

"No." Janet sat up. "I mean, yes. I mean, no, I'm not hurt."

"There's a new truck in space seven, Shirley. Hop to it."

Janet didn't have to look up to know that the new shadow looming over her was Mr. Pritchard's.

"Whatever's the matter with you today better be fixed, and fast." He snapped his fingers as Janet climbed slowly to her feet. Her left shin felt wet. "Take your break. I'll have Joe clean up this mess and cover your cars, and when your five minutes is up you'd better be back to normal."

Janet brushed the parking lot dust off her slacks. Blood seeped through the fabric at the knee. "Yes, sir."

She didn't look at Mr. Pritchard again. She didn't want to give him a chance to change his mind.

Ignoring the pain in her leg, Janet trotted straight to the telephone booth and reached into her tip pocket for a dime. She'd plugged it into the slot and started dialing the number before she'd even pulled the door closed behind her. Her heart raced as she listened to the phone ring on the other end.

Marie may not be home yet. She and that Harold might be at a late movie, or simply driving around. Or they might've driven somewhere and parked, and—

Janet closed her eyes and listened to the dull ringing sound until the click came. "Hello?"

It was Marie.

"Oh, thank heavens it's you." Janet turned her back to the Soda Shoppe and shut her eyes tightly. She wanted to imagine she was alone with Marie's voice. *This* Marie, the girl she'd always known, not the stranger she'd seen tonight. "I was afraid—"

"Yes?" Marie's voice was high, and exceedingly polite. As though she wasn't entirely sure she recognized Janet's voice on the line. "What is it?"

"How could you do that?" Janet's words flooded out. "*Why* would you? That boy—that—"

"One moment, please." Marie's words came quickly, too. There was a pause, and Janet could hear Marie opening doors and closing them again. When her voice returned, the excessive politeness was gone and she was speaking more rapidly than Janet had ever heard her speak before. "I'm *so* sorry. It was all Harold's idea. He was hungry, and it was the closest spot. I wanted to tell him not to go to the Soda Shoppe but I couldn't think of a reason that wouldn't be suspicious, and besides, I was sure we wouldn't wind up parked in your section, or perhaps you wouldn't be working tonight at all, but then the next thing I knew—"

"Is that what matters?" Janet covered her face with her hand. If she started to cry, she didn't want Mr. Pritchard to see. "Making him suspicious? What about *me*, Marie? Don't you even care what *I* think?"

Marie must've heard how upset she was, but Janet didn't care. She felt raw, open, exposed. Apart from that moment on Marie's bedroom floor, almost three weeks ago now, this was the most either of them had said aloud about their feelings for one another.

"I don't—" Marie seemed lost. "I can't—"

"You can't *what*?"

"Of course I care." Marie's words were quiet. "Surely you must understand, none of this was my idea. My mother arranged everything. Last week, at the club, and then tonight—"

"Last *week*?" Janet caught her breath. "You never said anything about seeing him last week."

"I'm so sorry." The pain was audible in Marie's voice. "I hate this. I hate everything about this. I want to be with *you*, but I can't tell my parents that, or Harold, either, and—oh, but we don't have much time. You're on your break now, aren't you? How long do you have?"

Janet looked at her watch. How many minutes had already passed since Mr. Pritchard had sent her away? "Not much. Why?"

"There won't be time for me to tell you properly, but I don't know how else to do it." Marie's voice shook. "Something happened at work today."

Janet was lost. Was Marie simply trying to change the subject? "What happened?"

"They're looking for me." Marie let out a choking sound. "That is, they're looking for a typist in my department. Someone they think is—" She whispered the next word, so low Janet could barely understand her. *"Subversive."*

"Janet!" Mr. Pritchard was shouting her name, somewhere beyond the glass booth. Janet turned away.

"What do you mean?" she whispered into the phone. "How do you know, Marie?"

"I shouldn't say anything more over the phone. Though if they've tapped this line I suppose it's already too late, but even so—"

"If they've *what*? What are you talking about?"

"Janet!" Mr. Pritchard's voice again. "Back to your station, now!"

"Come to my house. We can talk there." Janet was desperate. "My shift ends in two hours, and everyone will be inside listening to the radio when I get home. I'll come in through the back. You can meet me in the yard behind the house."

Marie didn't answer. A second later, Janet heard a click and then an empty dial tone.

Janet leaned forward, tipping her head against the cool glass of the booth wall.

"Janet!" Mr. Pritchard's voice was shriller than it had ever been. "Girl, get back here!"

Janet wanted to take off her cap and throw it in the man's face. Instead, she stepped sluggishly out of the booth. "Coming, sir."

The rest of her shift was a dazed dream, but she didn't drop a single tray or forget a single order. She rolled her napkins and completed the rest of her side work faster than she'd ever done it before, and when Mr. Pritchard paused in his inspection to shout reprimands at her again, she nodded without hearing a word.

Janet found, all at once, that she didn't care what Mr. Pritchard thought of her. Or what anyone else did, either. The only one whose opinion truly mattered was Marie's.

The thought was strangely liberating.

As soon as Mr. Pritchard dismissed her, Janet tore off her cap and ran the entire six blocks home, no longer caring whether anyone saw her in partial uniform. She was panting when she reached her block, but she didn't pause to catch her breath as she cut through the alley and navigated the dark, narrow path to her own gate.

When she opened it, Marie was already waiting for her.

She was sitting on the wide, wooden swing behind the storage shed with her back to Janet, gazing up at the darkened house. The shed blocked the ground floor from view, so all they could see from here was the screened-in porch at the back of the second floor where Janet and her grandmother slept. It was dark and empty now. The radio music drifting out from the den was the only sound other than the chirping crickets and the streetcar rumbling from two blocks away.

Marie no longer looked as neat and proper as she had when she was sitting in Harold's front seat. She'd washed off her makeup and changed out of her ruffled date-dress into jeans and a worn blouse.

She didn't look like a State Department typist anymore. She looked like the old Marie. The girl Janet had gone to school with for eleven years. The one she'd giggled with over the comic books they'd pilfered from her brother's bookshelves and blushed with during Sister Josephine's human reproduction lecture in junior high.

Yet what Janet saw in Marie's eyes, gleaming sharp in the distant light of the streetlamp, was a very grown-up fear.

"Can anyone hear us?" Marie whispered.

"No." Janet shook her head as she moved toward the swing. "They're all inside. And the shed would block the sound anyway, as long as we stay quiet. Please, tell me, what happened?"

"Mr. Harris is gone." Marie cut her eyes down to stare at her hands. "Another man, too."

Janet sat down lightly beside her on the swing, but Marie didn't look up. "Mr. Harris? Your boss?"

"Yes. He was there yesterday, but this morning he'd simply disappeared." Marie stuffed her hands into her armpits. "His office was completely empty when I arrived."

"What do you mean, disappeared?" It sounded like something out of a science fiction story.

"They'd gone through my desk as well." Marie's voice had grown smaller, even though there was no one in the yard but the two of them. "All his correspondence was missing, and they'd even rifled through my personal things. They'd tried to cover it up, but my comb was in the wrong place, and my pens, too. At first I didn't understand what had happened, but then Mr. Brown stopped by and told me I reported to *him* now. He said I didn't need to answer Mr. Harris's phone anymore. That was all there was to it. It was as if he'd never even existed!"

A heavy weight took root in Janet's stomach. "I don't understand. What happened to Mr. Harris?"

"He was a nice man." Marie kept talking as though she hadn't heard Janet's question. "Always telling silly jokes to make the girls laugh. Do you remember, I told you his favorite one, about the alligator and the ham sandwich?"

"Yes," Janet said, although she wasn't sure she did remember.

"The other man was one of the accountants. I'd only ever said hello to him a few times. He didn't have an office, just a desk, but by the time we got in it had been completely cleaned, as though no one had ever sat there at all. Mr. Thomas was his name. Listen to me, saying *was*, as though he's dead. Though for all I know, he might be."

"Where did they go? Your boss and Mr. Thomas?"

"It happened exactly how she said it would." Marie lifted her hand to her mouth and bit down on her thumbnail. Janet hadn't seen her bite her nails since junior high. "All anyone would talk about today was Mr. Harris and Mr. Thomas. Except at the same time, they *wouldn't* talk about them. No one used their names, and no one would really say what they meant, but it was clear everyone in the place—everyone except me—knew exactly what had happened."

"What do you mean?" Janet felt chilly, despite the heat. The more Marie said, the more it all sounded like something from a movie.

"At the end of the day, some of the other men were leaving to get a drink. I was in the elevator with them, and I overheard one of them whispering about how they had to go to a bar where there was plenty of whiskey and plenty of girls.

They all laughed, and one man said, 'We've got to make sure everyone knows the men at State aren't all a bunch of pansies.'"

Janet shuddered. "Surely no one thinks Mr. Harris and the other man—"

"They seemed perfectly normal." Marie spoke so quietly Janet had to lean in close to understand her. "Mr. Harris was the sweetest man. I knew he wasn't married, of course—the girls used to joke about who'd be lucky enough to land him—but even so, I never thought he was like *that*."

The way she spoke made Janet shiver. "Were they arrested, or simply fired?"

"I don't know, but—Janet, have you noticed anyone watching you?"

The words crawled up the back of Janet's neck. She looked over her shoulder, but they were as alone as ever. "Why?"

"We've got to start being more careful. Both of us. The FBI investigates everyone who might be a suspect, even if they don't have hard evidence. And I still don't have my clearance."

Janet tried to keep her voice steady. "They'd have nothing to investigate. You and I—we're friends. Everyone knows that. We've been friends since we were children."

"They could've been following me, though. What if they saw us go to Carol and Mitch's house? Or to Silver Spring? Or—oh, Janet, what about that night outside Meaker's? We should have been more careful!"

She was right.

That first night, out on the darkened street, Janet's thoughts had been centered solely on their kisses. It would've been easy for a man in a trench coat to sneak around the corner and snap a photo. Janet had been so consumed with Marie she wouldn't have noticed if he'd stood on her head and done a tap dance.

"They'd have no reason to follow you in the first place."
Janet squeezed her eyes shut. If she kept saying these things,
perhaps she'd begin to believe them herself. "Mr. Harris was
your boss, so he must have had an important job, but you're
only a typist. You don't know any government secrets."

"That doesn't matter. It's true, everything Carol told us. I
found a brief about it in the archives. People have been fired
all over the country for moral perversion. It's not just the
State Department, either, it's the whole government. They're
weeding out sympathizers. You know..." Marie lowered her
voice again. *"Subversives."*

"That's preposterous!" Janet slammed her fist into her hand.
"They can't really believe that just because of how we are,
we're all secretly working for the Soviets!"

"It doesn't matter if it's preposterous." Marie's voice had
grown so low and patient she sounded almost like Mitch.
"This is how things are, whether we agree with them or not."

Janet let out a short, frustrated breath, but Marie ignored
her.

"No one who's immoral can have anything to do with the
government," she went on. "Why, if the post office so much
as finds an obscene letter in the mail, they hand it over to
the FBI."

Janet felt weak suddenly. "The post office?"

"Of course. If a mailman delivered a letter like that, he
could be arrested himself." As Marie spoke, Janet's chill returned. "No, no, the government only wants to keep everyone safe."

"Of course," Janet echoed. She rubbed her arms.

If the post office so much as finds an obscene letter in the mail...

What about 108 pages of fiction, laden with obscenity
from start to finish?

Her manuscript should have arrived in New York ages ago, but Janet still hadn't heard from Mr. Levy. What if her package had never reached Bannon Press?

What if it had been intercepted? What if it was being read, right now, by the FBI?

What if there *was* a man in a trench coat following them, listening to every word they said?

Janet turned in a slow, careful circle, surveying the yard and the alley from every angle. She saw no one.

But this was absurd. The government couldn't be investigating her. She was an eighteen-year-old schoolgirl.

And Marie was a State Department typist. Whose boss had just been fired for *immorality*.

If the FBI read what Janet had put in the mail—if they realized what she and Marie had been doing...

Marie would be fired. She'd never be able to get another job, and her parents would cast her out. It would be the same for Janet, too.

Everyone would know. Just as they'd all known about Mr. Harris and Mr. Thomas.

"The worst part's the rumor I heard as I was leaving." Marie took a deep breath. "They're stepping up the questioning, and a typist is being investigated."

Janet heard her own voice grow low and thin. "Did they say who it was?"

"No, but I'm terrified that it's me. You still haven't told anyone, have you?"

"I..." Janet swallowed. She couldn't keep this secret. "I'm so sorry, Marie."

Silence stretched between them for a moment. Then Marie leaped to her feet and let out a short, strangled sound, as though she'd run out of air. *"What?"*

"It isn't what you think." Janet tried desperately to explain. "It was before I knew about all this, and—"

"*Who* did you tell? The FBI?" Marie began to pace in sharp circles around the narrow yard.

"I didn't tell the FBI!" Janet fought to get the words out. "I didn't tell anyone about you, I swear! I only—I put something in the mail, that's all."

Marie didn't speak for a long, dark moment. Janet had never hated silence more.

"What was it?" she finally whispered.

"My manuscript." Janet bent forward and picked at a loose thread on her uniform pants. Marie started pacing faster, her circles widening past the storage shed and toward the rickety wooden steps by the back porch. "The first half of the book I'm writing. I mailed it to New York, to the publisher who asked for it. It only has my name on it, not yours, but—well, I haven't heard back from the editor yet and it's been weeks, so I don't—"

"*Weeks?*"

"I'm so sorry." Janet wished she could race to the FBI office that very night and snatch the pages back from whatever pile they'd wound up sitting on. "I had no idea it would put you in danger!"

"Well, at least now I know for sure which typist they're investigating." Marie let out a bark of a laugh. "It's me."

"You can't be certain."

"Come to think of it, it's too great a risk for us to be discussing this. Even here." Marie's words grew cold. "We shouldn't see each other again."

"What?" Janet shook her head, dazed. "You mean—at *all*?"

"It's not what I want, either, but—"

"What about after your clearance comes in?" Janet's voice

broke. "It shouldn't be long, should it? A few more days? Then
we can go back to the way things were."

Marie didn't answer.

Janet's heart felt fragile. As though it were about to shat-
ter all over again.

"They'll have found your book by now." Marie sighed.
"They'll have traced the line back from you to me. It wouldn't
have been difficult if they checked the school records. The
photos of us together in the yearbook, and that time our award
at the science fair was mentioned in the *Evening Star*..." She
pressed both hands into her forehead and exhaled heavily.
"I'll be called in any day."

"No. No, they wouldn't—"

"They will. They're doing a review of our division in
any case, to see if any of us knew about Mr. Harris and Mr.
Thomas and kept it quiet. At least now I'll know what to
expect."

"But—you didn't know anything about Mr. Harris and Mr.
Thomas." Janet fought to keep her voice low. "You were as
surprised as anyone."

"That doesn't matter." Marie resumed her pacing. "Don't
you see? Everybody's desperate to make Congress think
they're rooting out security risks, and nobody cares who it
hurts. They want us all to snitch on each other. If one person
suspects even a hint of—they call it *unconventionality*—in anyone else, the investigators will want to hear about it. Everyone
who holds a grudge will get their chance to take revenge."

"Oh." Janet found she couldn't argue any further. If the
FBI and Congress and the security staff at the State Department were all so ready to ferret out homosexuals that they'd
be willing to take the word of a single spiteful coworker,

then an *actual* homosexual barely stood a chance at making it through any inquiry. "I see."

"You understand, then. It's too risky for us to keep seeing each other."

"But we can't be sure of anything yet." Janet rose from the swing and closed the short distance between her and Marie, grabbing her arm as she reached the porch steps. "I'm so sorry. I made a terrible mistake, but there's got to be something we can do to keep you out of danger. We can't let them fire you just for being—different!"

"I don't want to be *different*, Janet."

It took a moment for the words to sink in.

Janet stepped backward, releasing her arm. "You—what?"

Marie looked up at her. Their eyes locked in the dim light, and Janet understood.

"I can't do this anymore." Marie's words were low but clear in the still, humid night air. "I can't live this way. It's awful. I mean, it's wonderful, too, but—"

"You said you loved me." Janet swallowed and stepped forward, until their faces were only inches apart. Janet studied every inch of Marie, memorizing her, in case she never got another chance.

"I do love you." Marie bit her lip. "That only makes it harder."

"Then don't do this."

"I can't take any risks that might cause my family to find out." Marie looked away. "You must understand, this would *kill* them."

There was a time when Janet might have shaken her head at such talk. Now, though, she didn't argue.

She stared at Marie's bare face. The tears in the corners of her eyes. The soft tremble of her lower lip.

It would be so easy for them to kiss here in the dark, empty yard. Suddenly, foolishly, Janet was frantic for it.

"My mother thinks Harold will offer me his pin on our next date." Marie's voice was flat. Empty of any feeling. "She's anxious for me to tell him yes. She says it will help with Dad's chances at this promotion. If I accept, she says it'll mean we're—we'll be engaged to be engaged."

It felt as though Marie had slapped her.

She kept talking after that, offering further explanations about pins and plans and Harold, but Janet shut her eyes. She wished she could shut her ears, too.

I've got to remember how this feels, Janet told herself. *Every moment. Every memory. I can use this in my writing.*

She'd thought that idea might lessen the pain. It didn't.

"Please don't do this." Janet wanted to cry, but her eyes felt dry and empty. Like the rest of her. "I'm so sorry. I made a terrible mistake, putting those pages in the mail. Perhaps I could talk to someone at your office, tell them you and I are innocent—"

"That would only make it worse."

"But there's got to be *some* way I can fix this!"

"There's nothing you can do." Marie cast her eyes down, staring at a tiny patch of grass illuminated by the streetlight behind them. "You've done enough already."

It was another slap. Sharper than the first. And when Marie turned and walked slowly out the gate, disappearing into the dark alley, Janet didn't try to stop her.

Marie was right. Janet had ruined everything.

She'd put those chapters in the mail, and they had vanished into a dark, threatening void. Thanks to her, the whole world could soon find out about Janet and Marie.

All because of a stupid book she'd spotted in a bus station.

A book that was now no more than ash. Janet wished she'd walked away the moment she first spotted that garish red cover on the wire rack.

She exhaled, long and slow, as she climbed the stairs to the darkened porch. She'd had no business reading those books. No one could live this way, not without sacrificing everything that mattered. The books' own contents made that clear enough.

Janet unlatched the screen door and felt around for the light switch. She wondered if she ought to go around the front of the house—would her parents be alarmed to hear her coming in from the back?—but found she didn't care.

It didn't turn out to matter in any case. When she turned on the porch light and saw Grandma sitting there in the dark, her cold eyes locked on Janet, she realized just how right Marie had been to tell her to stay away.

All Janet had ever done was make things much, much worse.

15

Saturday, October 14, 2017

The feeling was unlike any I had ever known. I should have been ashamed to be touched this way by another woman, yet the only sensation I knew was pure pleasure. Sam's touch was the touch of the divine.

"Do you remember what Mr. Radclyffe said about how to do this permutation?" Linh squinted at her laptop screen. Their train kept hitting bumps, making their computers bounce on the tiny tray tables. "Was there something about a factorial function?"

"No clue." Abby scrolled to the next page to see how much longer the sex scene was going to last. She was sitting in the window seat, trying to read *A Love So Strange*.

Claire Singer's book had its moments, but it was no *Women of the Twilight Realm*. Abby had already skipped ahead to the ending, so she knew one of the women decided to marry a dude and the other one got flattened by a taxi. It was as if this book had invented the gay-tragedy trope all by itself.

"What do you mean, no clue? He just talked about it yesterday." Linh glanced over and pursed her lips when she saw Abby's screen. "Reading again?"

"I'm only being polite. Claire Singer is ninety-something years old and I'm about to troop into her retirement home and ask her about a bunch of painful memories. The least I can do is read her book before I go in there."

"Well, are you planning to also do your homework at some point? For your classes that aren't creative writing?"

Abby sighed. She was glad she hadn't told Linh about Ms. Taylor's phone call. "It's not a big deal. I'm not majoring in math or anything."

"But what about getting *into* college in the first place?"

"Ugh, you sound like my parents." She didn't, really—Abby couldn't remember the last time they'd brought up college—but maybe that line would get Linh off her back.

"I guess I just don't get why you're going to see this lady today." Linh clicked out of the stats assignment and opened the Common Application. Abby looked away. "I bet she wouldn't mind if you canceled. Then you could come with me to check out Penn like we planned."

"What? Of course I'm not going to cancel! Besides, I don't want to go to Penn."

"It isn't about whether you want to go *there*, specifically." Linh's tone was so patient it bordered on patronizing. "It's October of your senior year, and it's way past time to start visiting schools. For real, you've got to start thinking seriously about college, Abby."

God, Linh really *was* like Paula. Not always in a good way, either.

"How does visiting a school I don't want to go to mean I'm thinking *seriously* about college?" Abby tried not to let her annoyance creep into her voice. "It sounds like the opposite to me."

"I mean, Penn's not at the top of my list either or anything, but…" Linh shrugged as the Amtrak conductor said something over the speakers above them. His words were impossible to decipher, but from the screeching train wheels, Abby deduced that they were pulling into the station at Philly. Linh closed her laptop and bent to grab the bag at her feet as people started getting up around them, reaching into the overhead racks for their suitcases. "Going to check out a college makes a lot more sense than going to some random retirement home."

"It isn't random. Claire Singer is the one living person who actually *knew* Marian Love!"

"Look." Linh had to raise her voice for Abby to hear her over the train's lurching. "I'm only saying…don't take this the wrong way, but it's as if this whole saga of some dead author has become your entire life, even though there's other stuff that's way more important that you aren't paying enough attention to. Like school and college and—" Linh looked down. "And, you know. Your friends."

Abby had cringed so hard at "some dead author" that she barely heard the rest of what Linh said. She slumped down in her seat, folding her arms across her chest. "A *real* friend wouldn't put this much pressure on me."

Linh's eyes cut away as the train rolled to a stop. "I'm only trying to help."

"Okay, well, if you want to help, then *help*. Come with me to meet Claire. If she has any material I can look at, I could use another pair of hands to go through everything. Or you could help me parse through what she says for clues, or—"

"Clues?" A crease grew between Linh's eyebrows. Behind them, people were hurrying down the aisle to line up by the doors. "There's no mystery to solve. We already know what happened. Marian Love died."

"God, could you please not say—" Abby cut herself off.

"Not say what?"

"That she—you know."

"What, that she died?" Linh shook her head and looked around in alarm, as though finally noticing the train had stopped. "Crap, we have to go."

"I'm serious." Abby was starting to feel shaky. "For real, please don't say it again."

"What?" Linh stood up, her head swiveling toward the exits. The doors to the car were open, and the aisles were starting to empty. The only other people still in their seats were the passengers staying on until the next stop. "Come on, Abby, you've got to face reality. Marian Love is dead, and obsessing about her won't change that."

"Oh, okay." Abby jerked her backpack out from under the seat in front of her. "Sure, *I'm* obsessed. At least I'm not going to visit a college I don't even want to apply to just so I can look special."

Linh's eyes widened. "What?"

"I'm only saying." Abby turned away. Linh's voice kept echoing in her mind, saying "died" and "dead" and "Marian Love" over and over, taunting her. "All you think about anymore is this college shit."

"It isn't *shit*. It's my *future*, and yours, too. And I'm not doing this just to look *special*!"

"Right, of course." New passengers were boarding the

train heading north from Philly, but Abby barely noticed. Her thoughts were moving too fast to keep track of what was happening around her, or the words spewing from her mouth. "The future is all that's worth caring about, right?"

"Well…kind of! That's how this whole thing works." Linh swept a hand around, as though looking for a gesture that encompassed the entire universe. "I know the past is a lot easier to think about, but you can't fixate on all this random stuff just because you don't want to deal with your *actual* life. I know you've somehow got it in your head that you don't have to worry about college or anything else, because you think time will stop or something until your parents get back together, but real life isn't a cheesy romantic comedy! You have to move on, Abby!"

The announcer came on again. With the engines stopped, they could hear him clearly. "Philadelphia 30th Street Station. Train 251 to New York Penn Station, all aboard!"

Linh stood up, shrugging her backpack onto her shoulders.

Abby didn't move. She wasn't sure she *could* move.

"Okay." Linh looked down, scrubbing a hand over her face. "I'm sorry. I shouldn't have said that, but we have to go. The train's leaving."

Abby still didn't answer. She swallowed, trying to go over Linh's words in her head.

"I didn't mean to act like it isn't a big deal, what you're going through with your family." Linh glanced behind them. The new passengers were settling into their seats. "We seriously have to go, Abby."

"Train ready to embark!" the conductor shouted from the next car.

"Come on." Linh stepped out into the aisle, earning a glare

from a businessman trying to maneuver a suitcase into the overhead. "We'll talk in the station."

Abby shook her head. Nothing in the world could stop her from seeing Claire Singer, but she wasn't going anywhere with Linh. "You first."

"Fine." Linh sighed. "If we get separated, I'll meet you back at the station at five. Look, I'm sorry again, okay?"

Abby didn't answer. She waited until Linh turned to go, moving fast with a curtain of dark hair hiding her face. Only then did Abby grab her backpack and shuffle into the aisle, heading for the opposite exit. The train doors slid closed seconds after she'd jumped onto the platform.

She kept her head down and moved slowly through the station, trying to lose Linh in the crowd. It worked. A few minutes later Abby was climbing into a blue-and-white taxi, alone, and giving the driver Claire Singer's address.

She needed to push Linh's words out of her head, so she pulled up the ending of *Women of the Twilight Realm* as the cab sped over a wide bridge.

"If you love me and I love you, then I don't care whether anybody else understands it. You're the only one who matters."

Abby read Paula's words again and again until they swam in front of her eyes.

That was how it was supposed to work. You fell in love with someone, and they loved you back, and that made everything okay. As long as you had love, it didn't matter what else the world threw at you. You had something that mattered more.

Once you had love, it wasn't supposed to go away. Not ever.

But if it *did*...what the hell did that leave you with?

Abby was still reading when the taxi rolled to a stop in

front of the retirement home. She had no idea what to think anymore, but maybe someone who'd lived as long as Claire Singer would.

Abby swiped the credit card she'd taken from Dad's wallet to pay for the cab and climbed out onto the sidewalk, a huge brick building looming up before her. It suddenly occurred to Abby that she was in an unfamiliar city, alone, going to see a complete stranger.

But that stranger had known Marian Love. Which meant she wasn't a stranger, not really.

Abby squared her shoulders and pushed open the glass front door.

The receptionist sent her up to the tenth floor, where another receptionist told her to sit in a small waiting area. Abby sat, trying not to think about Linh and hoping she didn't look visibly flustered.

A few minutes later, a woman who definitely wasn't old enough to be Claire Singer walked toward her. She looked younger than Mom, even—in her twenties or thirties.

"Are you Abby Zimet?" The woman held out her hand, but she didn't smile. "I'm Julie. Claire's my great-aunt."

"Hi." Abby shook her hand. Ms. Singer's email hadn't mentioned Julie. "Is this still a good time for me to interview her?"

"Well, she already told you she'd do it, so I guess so." Julie glanced at Abby's notebook, her embroidered vintage skirt, the backpack over her shoulder. "You're in high school down in DC?"

"Yeah, I'm a senior at Fawcett. It's a magnet school. You have to apply to get in."

Abby had no idea why she was reciting her credentials, but it seemed to be what Julie wanted to hear, because she nodded. "You're working on a project for class?"

"Yep. I'm writing my very own lesbian pulp novel."

"All right." Julie nodded again. Abby got the impression Julie had come out here to make sure she wasn't some sort of fangirl stalker. Maybe that had been a problem in the past. "Claire won't be able to talk long. She's very frail, and she falls asleep a lot. Lung cancer. It's a miracle she's lived as long as she has, what with smoking two packs a day for thirty years. Not to mention all the drinking, but..." Julie shrugged a what-can-you-do shrug. "Come on back."

Abby had only been in retirement homes a few times before, visiting great-aunts of her own, but the hallways here seemed narrower. Still, the quiet rooms, shadowy doorways and antiseptic smells were exactly the same. Julie led her down winding corridors, then knocked on one of the closed doors. She didn't wait for a reply before turning the knob.

"Aunt Claire?" Julie spoke softly. "The girl is here. The one doing the school project."

Abby followed her, expecting to see a tiny, shriveled old lady lying on a bed. Instead she found a white-haired woman sitting up in an armchair with a shrewd smile and a pair of cat-eye glasses not unlike Abby's.

"Abby Zimet?" The woman spoke clearly, and her smile was sincere. She held out her hand. "Forgive me for not getting up. It's a pleasure to meet you."

Abby shook the older woman's hand. Her grip was surprisingly strong. "It's an honor to meet you, Ms. Singer—wait, I'm sorry, should I call you Ms. Wood?"

The woman laughed, a warm, full sound. Abby felt instantly at ease. "Please, call me Claire. It's been years since anyone's called me Ms. Wood."

Julie pointed Abby to an upholstered bench, and she sat down gingerly. Julie sat in the wooden chair across from her.

"Thank you so much for taking the time to see me." Abby couldn't quite believe she was in a room with someone who'd known Marian Love. She was already blinking back the threat of tears, and they'd barely spoken yet.

"You came all the way up from DC, isn't that right?" On Abby's nod, Claire grinned. Her face was deeply wrinkled, but her eyes shone behind her glasses. "I always enjoyed that city."

"I read your book on the train," Abby told her. "*A Love So Strange*. I really enjoyed it."

Claire laughed. "Except for the ending, right?"

"Well..." Abby smiled. "I know there were rules about that kind of thing."

"Rules, yes. Especially in those early years. I hated having to write it that way, though. That girl throwing herself in front of a taxi—it pained me, typing those words, but we all did what we had to do. Back then those stories were all we had, and you know what they say about beggars and choosers. There weren't a lot of happy endings for us anyway, in fiction or otherwise." Claire shook her head. "Someday I'm going to write a brand-new ending to that book and put it on that internet you all have."

"I already said I'd help, Aunt Claire," Julie piped in. "Just tell me what you want it to say and I'll type it up for you."

"One of these days." Claire smiled again. "Now, did you say you're doing a project about Marian Love?"

"Yes." Abby sat forward eagerly. "I was hoping you could tell me anything more about her. What she was like, and if she left behind any other writing besides *Women of the Twilight Realm*. Any letters, maybe, or any other stories? Or did she ever tell you anything about what happened to Paula and Elaine after the end of the book? And what about—"

"Whoa, there." Claire raised a hand. "I have to tell you, honey, that I never met Marian."

"What do you mean, you never met her?" Abby frowned. "Professor Herbert said you were the one who set her up with your publisher."

"Morgan Herbert, she's the one you talked to?" Claire frowned, too. "Well, she should've told you, then. I gave her the whole story when she came up a few years ago. Marian Love was on her way to New York, or so we assumed, when the accident happened. I'd sent her a bus ticket, but she and her friend drove up instead. I suppose they wanted to travel together."

"Was her friend a—" Abby struggled to think of how to say it. "Were they—together?"

"I thought so, but there's no way to be sure." Claire reached for a cup of water on the table in front of her and took an agonizingly slow sip. "Her friend was injured, too, but I guess she was all right in the end. I never met her, either, but she wrote to me, telling me about what happened and enclosing the manuscript. She said her friend had always dreamed of being a published writer and she wanted to make that dream come true, even if she hadn't lived to see it. So I sent everything on to Nathan."

"Do you know the friend's name? Or what happened to her after that?" Maybe Abby could track down the "friend" next. Maybe that would get her closer to the truth.

"I'm afraid I don't. In her letters she called herself Mrs. Smith, but I suspect that wasn't her real name. No more so than 'Janet Jones'—that was the pseudonym Marian Love used when she first wrote to me."

"Oh." So even "Janet Jones" wasn't her real name.

Maybe Abby was destined never to learn anything about the real Marian Love.

"Do you still have that letter Marian sent you?" Abby knew she sounded desperate, but there was nothing she could do about that. "Or anything else she wrote? Or—or do you know how I could get in touch with Mrs. Smith, if *she's* still alive?"

Claire waved at Julie. "Give her a tissue," she whispered.

Abby's tears were on the verge of breaking through. As though she hadn't already embarrassed herself in front of enough people this year.

Julie passed her a tissue from the box on Claire's dresser. Abby pulled off her glasses and turned away to blow her nose.

"I suspect you enjoyed her book more than you did mine," Claire said. When Abby glanced up through watery eyes, Claire was still smiling, though she looked tired. "Don't worry, I'm used to it. Her book would've meant a lot to me, too, even if I hadn't known her at all."

Abby blew her nose again. She'd managed to refrain from shedding any actual tears yet, but when she opened her mouth, her voice came out in an embarrassing squeak. "Marian Love's writing is kind of everything to me right now. The way she seems to—to just *get* it—"

"I understand." Claire tilted her head, but her eyes had begun to droop. "Mind you, I'll have to ask you not to put any of this in your paper for school. I'm positive you're trustworthy, but in honor of Marian's memory we need to keep her story secret."

"I understand." Abby did her best to sound professional, but all she wanted was to be alone so she could fall apart. "Thank you so much for talking to me."

"It's time for you to rest, Aunt Claire." Julie stood up. "I'll walk Abby to the elevator."

"Get her number before she goes," Claire mumbled. "It was very nice to meet you, Abby. Good luck with your project."

"Thank you so much," Abby tried to tell her, but Claire was already asleep.

Julie touched her shoulder and led her out into the hall.

"I could tell she had a good time talking to you," Julie whispered when the door was shut behind them. "Thanks for coming up."

Abby nodded. She couldn't say anything more. If she spoke, she was positive she'd lose it entirely. She wrote her number down for Julie and hurried into the elevator, praying the doors would close quickly.

Even Claire Singer hadn't really known her. It was as if Marian Love had never existed. As if she'd written one book, one perfect book, and vanished into nothing.

Abby wanted to cry. She was *desperate* to cry. But now that she was finally alone, the tears wouldn't come.

God, she couldn't even fall apart correctly anymore.

What the hell was she even *doing* here? Was Linh right? Was Abby obsessing over the past because she didn't want to deal with the real world?

If so, it wasn't working. Her present reality was painful, but history hurt, too.

And apparently she didn't have the option of losing herself anymore.

Friday, August 5, 1955

"See you tomorrow, Janet," Joe called from his spot behind the fryer. Janet forced a smile and waved as she trotted toward the sidewalk, too exhausted to speak.

It was late. The dinner shift had finally ended, and all Janet wanted to do was go home, wash the smell of boiled hot dogs out of her hair and call Marie.

But there was no use. She'd hang up as soon as she heard Janet's voice on the line.

It was her own doing, too. Janet had made so many terrible mistakes. Now she'd lost the best thing that had ever happened to her.

And things could get worse yet. Janet couldn't be sure how much Grandma had overheard the night before—when Janet reached the porch, her grandmother had stood without a word and turned to go join Mom and Dad in the living room, and

Janet hadn't seen her since—but if Grandma *had* heard what she and Marie were saying...

Janet couldn't begin to imagine what might happen. All day, she'd felt ready to faint from nerves.

"Excuse me, miss," a voice called from Janet's right.

It was a woman's voice, but it was too far away from the parking area for it to be coming from a customer. Still, Janet put on her carhop smile. "Sorry, I didn't catch that?"

"Over here."

She glanced back at the counter, where Joe was dabbing cleaner on the grill, before following the voice around the corner. She passed the main building and saw a Negro woman standing alone in the shadows toward the back of the lot, waving to her.

"Deliveries go to the kitchen door," Janet called.

"I said excuse me, miss," the woman said again, a tad pointedly.

It took Janet another moment to realize the woman was Carol.

"Oh!" Shame flushed Janet's cheeks. She'd assumed Carol was a delivery worker because she was a Negro.

Janet cast one more glance at the counter to make sure Joe wasn't watching and trotted into a dark area under the kitchen roof's overhang.

"I'm so sorry, ma'am," Janet rushed to say. "I mistook you for—"

"We only have a minute." Carol interrupted her smoothly. "I thought this would be the safest place to talk."

Janet nodded, though she didn't understand.

"Forgive me for being so direct." Carol spoke quietly, her voice thin but firm. "I need you to tell your friend they brought me in."

"I'm sorry, ma'am—I don't understand."

"Yes you do." Carol didn't smile.

She was right. Janet understood. She wished she didn't.

"Surely they wouldn't..." Janet didn't know what to say. "You've been so careful..."

"Someone gave them my name." Carol's lips were fixed in a straight line. "Probably that fool Gerald. I heard he's trying to get a new job at Interior, and he must think if he hands over names they'll take him back. Like I said, he's a fool." Carol shook her head. "In any case, it doesn't seem they have much on me. They spent an hour trying to get me to confess, but I held my own. I may be able to stay on, God willing, but you need to tell your friend I didn't give her over. They pressed me for names, and they pressed me hard, but I didn't give up a single one. Now if your friend gets brought in she'll need to protect me, as I protected her."

"Of course." Janet nodded again. Her head was spinning.

Carol was nothing like the men who lurked in parks at night. She was polite and well mannered. She was feminine. She was—

She was exactly like Marie.

If Carol wasn't safe, Marie wasn't, either.

"All right." Janet tried to stay calm, but blood was pounding in her ears. She could hear Joe shouting to the carhops just behind them. "Thank you. I'll tell M—"

"No!" Carol jumped in quickly. "No names. But you tell her she's been smiling at me when she comes through the line, and that's got to stop. We can't risk being associated, neither one of us. You tell her from now on when she's in the cafeteria, she keeps her eyes on her sauerkraut."

"Yes, ma'am."

"Good." Carol glanced over her shoulder. Janet did the

same. She didn't see anyone, but that didn't mean they were alone. "I've got to go. I've already been here too long."

"Wait." This might be the only chance Janet got. "Could I come to see you, and—your friend, again? I just… I feel so alone. There's no one else I can talk to about this, and you were so kind to us—"

"No." Carol answered immediately. "Whatever you do, *don't* come to our home. It was a mistake to have you over that first time. Promise me you'll forget our address. In fact, you really ought to forget you ever met either one of us."

Carol gave her a half smile, a gentle one, but her gaze was heavy. Janet felt her throat closing up. Still, she nodded.

Carol acknowledged her with a tiny incline of her head. Then she stepped back, melting into the shadows.

Frustration and terror bubbled inside Janet. She wanted to walk as far as her legs would carry her, until she'd sorted out all the thoughts churning through her mind, but her parents would be angry if she didn't come straight home from work.

As she walked briskly up Wisconsin, Janet tried to think. She had to reach Marie, somehow, to pass on Carol's message. She'd have to call her—to dial that number and pray she could convince Marie to listen to what she said.

Then she'd have to tell her all their fears were coming true. That Marie needed to prepare for the worst. She'd have to be even more careful than she already had been. A simple smile in the lunch line could cause all their lies to unravel.

It was too late to call tonight, though. Besides, there was something else Janet had to do first. For Marie, and for herself, too.

The house was quiet and empty when Janet unlocked the door. The Soda Shoppe closed late on Fridays, and this time of night everyone in the house would already be asleep out on the screened porches.

Good.

Janet crept up the stairs toward the attic, stopping by her bedroom only long enough to reach into her desk drawer and pull out the matchbook she'd taken from Meaker's. The house was silent as she ascended the rickety stairs.

As the sweltering, musty attic air swirled around her, Janet gazed out into the dark room, overwhelmed with the memory of nights spent in her imagined Greenwich Village. Paula and Elaine's world, where girls did exactly as they chose, without regard for consequences.

Janet turned on the fan and flung open the windows, then knelt on the floor to rummage through the trunk where she'd hidden her things. Beneath the tattered copy of *A Deviant Woman*, Janet found what she was looking for. She pulled out the rumpled carbon copy pages and the freshly typed sheets she'd tucked beneath them.

Alone No Longer, the title page read. *By Janet Jones.*

Stupid. She'd been so stupid, putting her real name down. Dolores Wood may have mistaken "Janet Jones" for a pseudonym, but that wouldn't fool the FBI.

She wanted to cry, but there was no time to get caught up in useless sentiment. Instead, Janet crouched by the window and struck a match.

The first piece of typing paper took a few seconds to catch flame, but after that it was easy to feed in the next page, and the next. Soon she was striking more matches, burning entire chapters at a time.

The words vanished quickly, the pages blackening into tiny crumbs, until they turned to dust. Fragments drifted out the window and floated away on the soft, warm breeze.

The sight of it was mesmerizing. As she watched the blackened pieces of her manuscript drift toward the river, Janet said a silent farewell to Paula and Elaine and everything that made up their world.

None of it had been real anyway. Janet had been living out a childish fantasy, writing about imaginary girls. It was no different from playing with paper dolls.

Except that this time, Janet's play had put those she cared about at risk. It may have already destroyed the one she cared about the most.

Tears flowed down Janet's cheeks as she watched the last chapter start to smolder.

The handwritten pages she'd written in those first few days were still in the trunk. Janet would need to burn those next. If the FBI searched the house, they'd be just as incriminating as the typed manuscript. She had to get rid of the letters from Bannon Press and from Miss Wood, too.

And she really ought to burn *A Deviant Woman*. It would serve as evidence of her immorality as easily as her own writing, and anyway, it shouldn't be hard to part with it. After all, she'd already lost *A Love So Strange*, and she'd read that one so many times she'd nearly memorized it.

Last year she'd read a book of Dad's—not one of his usual classics, but a science fiction paperback, one she'd had to sneak off the bottom shelf and read in secret in her bedroom. It took place in a strange, futuristic world. At the end, one character said that everyone who read a book even once would always carry that book inside them.

That story had been all about book burning, now that Janet thought about it. *Fahrenheit 451,* it was called. It was named after the temperature where paper caught fire.

Janet had lost *A Love So Strange*, but it lived on inside her.

She would remember it, and all of this, forever. Even without the actual printed words and thin, bent pages.

Janet brushed the ashes from her hands and knelt, reaching back into the trunk and withdrawing the rest of her things. The gold bikini on the cover of *A Deviant Woman* was as eye-catching as ever. Even though the novel's characters had never made it to the beach, Janet could imagine them playing in the surf together.

Maybe Paula and Elaine could take a beach trip in some future chapter of *Alone No Longer*. Elaine might wear a bikini, though not as skimpy as the one on the *Deviant Woman* cover, and Paula would wear something more conservative. Even so, the sight of her in it would make Elaine—

No. Janet had to stop herself from thinking this way. Elaine and Paula were no more than dust. Janet could forget them just as easily as she'd made them up.

A door opened and closed on the floor below, distant under the sound of the fan. One of her parents must have woken up. There was no reason they'd come up to the attic—most likely they were simply headed to the bathroom on the second floor—but all the same, Janet ought to move quickly.

As she scooped up the book and papers, the envelope from Bannon Press toppled off the stack, spilling its contents over the floor. Janet sighed and set everything else back down.

First was the letter from Nathan Levy's office. Janet wanted to rip it up, but she knew now that it would be easier to burn if she left the paper whole. Behind it was the letter from Miss Wood—that one would be more difficult to destroy. Beneath it, she spotted two smaller slips of paper.

The bus tickets. Janet had forgotten.

Miss Wood had thought well enough of Janet's letter to

buy these for her. It was such a kind gesture. What a shame they'd go unused.

Well, perhaps Janet should take the tickets down to the bus station and try to sell them. At least then she'd have a few extra dollars to buy school clothes. But no—she shouldn't do anything that might attract the attention of the police.

The footsteps came again. Closer this time.

Too close.

Janet sprang up from the floor, scrambling to grab the scattered papers and fling them back into the trunk, but the door opened behind her before she could finish.

"I thought I heard you up here, girl." Grandma stood in the doorway in her dressing gown, her silhouette barely visible in the dim light. She glanced around the room, taking in the fan, the matches, the papers piled in the trunk and scattered over the floor. Her only reaction was a slight shake of her head. Her lips set into a grim line, and her eyes locked on Janet.

Grandma shut the door behind her. "I'm not going to beat around the bush with you. I've prayed about this, all night and all day I've prayed, and the Lord has shown me what I have to do. It's what's right for this family, and it's what's right for you, even if you don't see that now. Your parents need to know, girl."

Janet blinked up at her. Some strange, useless corner of her mind had taken possession of her senses, it seemed, and told her that if she didn't say anything—if she didn't acknowledge her grandmother's words—this wouldn't be real.

Grandma would vanish from the doorway. The past minute would be erased from their lives.

But as Janet climbed to her feet, still blinking, still waiting, the grim line of Grandma's lips somehow turned even grimmer.

There would be no erasing this.

"You've got nothing to say?" Grandma pursed her lips.

Only one question mattered. "When?"

"Tomorrow morning. Before breakfast." Grandma gave another slight shake of her head. "This has already waited too long. It's clear you won't listen to me, so your father's going to have to be the one to put a stop to it before things get even worse. I only hope it doesn't break George's heart forever when I tell him the truth."

Janet swallowed. Maybe they'd send her to St. Elizabeths. Or maybe it would be someplace worse.

"I considered not coming up here to tell you, but you've always been a good girl." Grandma folded her arms across her chest. "I thought it best you have some time to ready yourself, so you'd know better than to deny it. And there's no use in that, of course. I heard what I heard last night."

"Thank you," Janet heard herself say, over the ringing in her ears.

Grandma nodded. Gratitude accepted.

She left the attic without another word, leaving Janet alone with her ashes and her papers and her trembling hands.

She probably still ought to burn the rest. If the FBI found her to be a security risk, Janet's family knowing wouldn't change that.

She gazed down into the trunk. The bus tickets were on top of the pile, fluttering in the breeze from the fan.

A thought slowly crept into Janet's mind.

What time did her parents wake up, usually, on Saturdays? Seven or so?

Surely there would be a bus leaving earlier than that.

She pictured it. Climbing those steps by herself with a small brown case in her hand. Watching Washington pass by her window, and then the countryside, as she traveled north through Maryland and into New Jersey.

In a few short hours, the Manhattan skyline would be spread out before her.

Her parents would have no idea where she'd gone. Even the FBI wouldn't think to look for her there.

She glanced at Miss Wood's letter again. *"You'll find me most evenings at the Sheldon Lounge on West Fourth and Charles Streets."*

Janet could see it all so clearly. A dark, smoky bar, with Dolores Wood sitting right up front with some equally glamorous girl. The Sam to her Betty.

They were probably there right now. Spending their Friday night in that exotic, foreign land. While Janet sat in her lonely home, with nothing that was truly hers but a closetful of high-necked dresses and a handful of matches, ready to destroy all the evidence of who she really was.

If Janet were at the Sheldon Lounge, she could walk up to Miss Wood and her friends and shake their hands. They'd be drinking something glamorous—champagne cocktails, perhaps—and Janet could sit at the bar, sip a drink of her own and be surrounded by girls just like her.

Well, what was stopping her?

Young people moved to New York every day. The books were full of their stories. Girls who left behind everything they'd known and found new jobs and new friends. Who started new lives, all their own.

There was nothing for Janet here. Marie wouldn't speak to her. Her family would never want to see her again once they knew the truth. The nickels and dimes she made shuttling burgers at the Soda Shoppe could just as easily be dimes and quarters made flipping pancakes at a Midtown diner.

In New York, Janet wouldn't have to lie. She'd keep to

herself at her job, of course, but when she went out at night, she'd be with other lesbians. They'd all be social deviants, but perhaps together they could form a team of sorts. Maybe they could even fight back against the rules that cast them out.

She'd pack all the money she'd saved that summer. Miss Wood might know a place where Janet could stay for a few nights, or maybe she could find a cheap hotel until she'd earned enough to afford an apartment. Writing was a foolish dream—it had brought her nothing but heartache, and it was obvious Janet didn't have the fortitude for it, whatever Miss Wood had said—but surely she could find some reliable income. Maybe she could even work in an office instead of a restaurant. She'd gotten a lot of typing practice in that summer, and she was skilled at making carbon copies now.

Her parents might be troubled at first by her disappearance, but there was no use writing them a note. Grandma would deliver the news once Janet was safely gone, and after that Mom and Dad wouldn't question why she'd left. In fact, they'd be relieved to have her gone. She was sparing them the pain of having to look at her now that they knew the truth. Plus, a daughter who'd left home would certainly look better to any of her father's enemies than a daughter who was known to be immoral.

She would still be on the rolls for college, she supposed, but her parents would withdraw her soon enough. Besides, did Janet really need more theology classes with Sister Josephine, or essays about the fall of Constantinople? No, the time had come to live her real life, far from home, where there would be no more risk of hurting anyone she loved.

She still needed to pass on Carol's message to Marie, but she could do that tomorrow morning. She'd write a note, seal it carefully and slip it into the Eastwoods' mailbox on her way to the bus station.

Then she'd forget about Marie. That was what Marie wanted, after all. Janet would banish her from her mind and disappear into the wilds of Greenwich Village.

For the first time in days, Janet smiled without being forced. She brushed the sweaty hair out of her face, gathered up the scraps from her trunk and went downstairs to pack.

17

Wednesday, October 18, 2017

Abby turned up the sound on her headphones until Nicki Minaj was shouting in her ears. It had been the coldest day of the school year so far, and she shivered in her cotton shift dress as she slumped against the car door. Wisconsin Avenue rolled past, a blur of fast-casual restaurants, expensive grocery stores and trendy furniture boutiques. Only the occasional siren or shouting pedestrian broke up the monotony.

She drank in the sights and sounds as though she'd never encountered them before. Whatever it took to avoid making eye contact with Dad. He kept glancing in her direction as he drove, one hand resting on the steering wheel and the other tapping out an anxious rhythm on his knee.

Abby was determined to think about something that wasn't this car ride. Linh, she should think about Linh. They'd barely spoken to each other since Saturday, when they'd met up in the Philly train station to come home. The train didn't have any empty seats together, so they'd sat separately, only speaking when Linh stopped to ask if Abby wanted anything from the café car. Abby shook her head, Linh nodded, and that was as close as they'd come to a conversation.

Which was fine. Not talking was easier than talking, most of the time. Even so, Abby hadn't counted on how lonely school would be this week without Linh.

None of their other friends knew what was going on, which was both good and bad. Vanessa had asked once after chemistry if she and Linh were avoiding each other, but Abby had only shrugged, and Vanessa took the hint and backed off. Vanessa was good about stuff like that.

But something had shifted between Linh and Abby on the train Saturday morning. Or maybe it had already shifted, and it took until the train ride for Abby to notice.

Either way, she knew she had to do something. She cared about Linh too much to let this weirdness go on between them forever. But thinking about anything clearly enough to make an actual plan was basically impossible. Especially today.

It was Wednesday. The day Mom was coming back into town. The day Dad had said they'd all need to "talk."

Abby had tried desperately to avoid this moment. Dad had told her he'd pick her up as soon as her after-school lit mag meeting ended, so she'd left the meeting twenty minutes early, thinking she could walk to the library and hide there for the rest of the afternoon. When she reached the school parking lot, though, Dad's car was already idling by the curb, as though he'd known exactly what she had in mind.

For a microsecond Abby thought about going back into the school and hiding in a janitor's closet or something—eventually Dad would give up and drive away, right?—but by the time she'd thought it through he'd already spotted her and started waving.

So Abby had squared her shoulders and marched toward the car. She fought to keep her expression neutral as she climbed in. She wasn't a kid anymore. Her parents didn't need to know they were getting to her.

So when Dad tried to say something to her, Abby put on her headphones and ordered her brain to shut down.

It didn't obey.

She shouldn't have been surprised. It had been impossible to focus all day. They'd had a pop quiz in French, but she'd dashed off a quick paragraph about *Madame Bovary*'s place in the history of Romanticism instead of the full page Monsieur De Jourlet had requested, then spent the rest of the period trying to brainstorm ideas for what should happen next to Gladys and Henrietta. She was ready to write the novel's climax, setting the characters' futures into motion. The problem was, she still had no idea how to actually do that.

Dad turned onto their street. Abby's stomach lurched. She needed to dive back into her blessedly fictional world, whether or not her brain was functioning.

She was determined to give Henrietta and Gladys their happy ending. It was just that so many terrible things had happened. Gladys had lost her job, and Henrietta's parents had disowned her, and their best friend had been murdered. Even knowing there was a secret lesbian paradise waiting for them in Vermont, Abby couldn't imagine Gladys and Henrietta living happily ever after the way Paula and Elaine had.

Of course—Paula and Elaine. *That* was her answer. *They* were who she should be thinking about. Paula and Elaine were a much better distraction than her stupid first draft.

So Abby shut her eyes tight and thought about *Women of*

the Twilight Realm as their car pulled up in front of the house. She summoned her mental image of the two women on that painted cover. She imagined them kissing, whispering sweet words, holding each other close. Promising each other that no matter what happened, everything would always be all right.

The car door swung open beside her. Abby kept her eyes shut, but she could sense her father's presence on the sidewalk.

She wished he'd yell at her. Tell her she was being difficult. She *was* being difficult, and the fact that he wouldn't acknowledge it made her want to be that much *more* difficult. She wanted to keep pushing and pushing until this spell that had been cast over their house finally dissolved and life could go back to normal.

"All right, sweetie," Dad said, his fingers still beating out that nervous rhythm against his hip. "Time to go in."

What would he do if she didn't get out of the car? He'd never *pull* her out, would he? Or would he bring Mom and Ethan out here so they could have this conversation on the sidewalk for all their neighbors to watch?

That thought was enough to make Abby pull out her headphones, grab her backpack and climb onto the curb. Dad shut the car door and pressed the button on his keys to lock it. The abbreviated beep of the car alarm was so sharp and sudden it brought tears to Abby's eyes.

God, hold it together. She took in a long, uneven breath.

Dad unlocked the front door while Abby trudged up the stairs behind him. She could see Mom coming toward them through the glass.

So it was true. Both her parents were in the same house, at the same time. It could only mean the world was about to end.

Abby clenched her fists around her backpack straps, stepped inside and stared up at the high ceiling. Maybe Gladys and

Henrietta could have one last sex scene before the end of the book. It would need to be dramatic, of course—endings of books were always dramatic. Gladys and Henrietta would need to have a major fight about something, then rise above their disagreements and get back together. Abby just had to think of something good for them to fight over.

She followed Dad through the foyer, her heart pounding so hard she could barely hear anything else.

"Hello, Abby." Mom came forward, her arms outstretched for a hug. Behind her, Ethan lay facedown on the couch, his face hidden in a pillow.

Abby didn't say anything, and she didn't hug her mother back. After a few seconds, Mom released her grip. She smiled, even though Abby stayed stone-faced. Just like Dad, though, Mom didn't seem bothered by it.

Act normal! Abby thought at them. *Act like parents! Regular parents!*

"I missed you," Mom said, after a silence that went on a few seconds too long. "You, too, Ethan. It's so good to see you both."

Her parents were talking as if this was any other day. God, this family was so messed up.

Maybe Abby could use the homework excuse again. Or college applications. She would start her college applications right this minute and submit them all by dinnertime if that would stop this from happening.

"Please, Abby, sit down." Dad gestured toward the empty armchair next to where Ethan lay on the couch. Mom and Dad had already perched on the chairs facing him.

And with that, it was too late. The escape window had officially closed.

Instead of taking the empty chair, Abby went to the couch

and picked up Ethan's ankles. He lifted them into the air and Abby sat next to his still-prone form, settling his feet into her lap and crossing her arms over her chest. They used to sit this way when they were kids, only then it had been Abby who stuck her feet in Ethan's lap.

He was her little brother. He was a brat a lot of the time, but they were a team. If this was going to happen, at least it would happen to the two of them together.

"Ethan, could you sit up, please?" Mom asked, fingering the gold chain around her neck. Ethan grumbled but slowly climbed up, swinging his feet to the floor. His face was red where it had been pressed against the couch cushions, and he turned to stare down at the rug.

Maybe Gladys and Henrietta could have a misunderstanding. Gladys could get a letter from home, and Henrietta could find it. She could think the letter meant Gladys had cheated when she was visiting her best friend in Michigan earlier that summer, and Henrietta could try to—

"You know your father and I have been having some problems," Mom said.

Abby slumped down until she was almost lying on her back.

What would Henrietta do if she thought Gladys had hooked up with someone else? How would she react? Would she feel betrayed first, or would the anger take hold right away?

"We've both been trying," Dad said, "and we've realized—"

"Are you getting divorced?" Ethan interrupted.

Henrietta would probably be angry at first. Henrietta was really a pretty angry person, now that Abby thought about it.

"We've tried to fix the situation, but we're afraid it isn't working out." Dad was obviously reciting some script he must've found on the internet. "We love you both so much, and we'll always be here for you, but—"

Ethan slapped his hands over his ears and started screeching "LA LA LA!" so loud Abby wanted to cover her own ears, too.

It occurred to her dimly that covering her ears and humming was basically what she'd been doing anyway. Only she'd been doing it for months. Maybe years.

"Ethan, please," Mom said. Abby could barely hear her over Ethan's screeching. "We need you to listen to us."

"So this is why you don't give a shit what we do anymore, right?"

Ethan fell silent, and every face in the room swiveled toward Abby. Dad's eyes grew wide, and Mom's mouth fell open. Ethan didn't take his hands off his ears, but Abby knew he'd heard her.

"The principal told you I'm barely doing my homework." Abby's voice sounded bizarrely calm even in her own ears. "Ethan got into a *fight*. He threw a water bottle at a *teacher*. I went to Philadelphia by myself last weekend and I didn't tell you. Dad, I took your credit card out of your wallet. Neither of you even noticed I was gone!"

"We noticed." Dad barely glanced at her. "The credit card company called me. Fortunately, you were already home safe by then."

"You didn't say anything." Abby stared from him to Mom. "You didn't *punish* me?"

"Well, it *was* pretty disappointing." Dad sighed. "To be honest, Abby, we'd thought you were mature enough by now that we wouldn't need to—"

"Bob." Mom cut him off, and he fell quiet.

Why wasn't Mom mad at her? Didn't she *understand*?

"We knew the two of you might—act out on occasion."

Mom bit her lip, still running her fingers over the clasp of her necklace. It was the beaded one Ethan had given her for Mother's Day a couple of years before. Abby had helped him pick it out at the National Gallery gift shop. "It's only to be expected. We didn't want to be hard on you during a tough time."

"You're *supposed* to be hard on us." Abby's voice was rising. It felt bizarrely good to be loud. "You're our *parents*."

"Well, the good news is we're finally winding down with all the legal work," Mom said, as though she hadn't heard her.

They both sounded so calm. So *reasonable*.

None of this could possibly be real.

"We're grateful for that," Mom went on, "because it means we'll have time to focus on being parents again. I'm sorry we've been somewhat distracted recently."

Distracted? Abby wanted to laugh, but found she couldn't.

"It's important for you to understand that this isn't anyone's fault." Apparently it was Dad's turn in the script. "Our marriage simply isn't working."

Abby's phone vibrated in her pocket. She reached for it automatically.

"We'll always be your parents." Dad wasn't even bothering to put feeling in his voice. Had he practiced this in front of a mirror in some generic hotel room somewhere? "But we won't be married to each other once we've finished the divorce process."

Abby should try to remember what this felt like. She could use it in her writing someday.

Except she wasn't sure there was a word for what she was feeling. It was as if she was hovering over the room from above, watching this happen. She could see herself sitting on this couch, hearing these words, and feeling—whatever it was you were supposed to feel when terrible things happened.

It was just that Abby wasn't sure she actually felt anything at all.

She slipped her still-vibrating phone out of her pocket. The caller ID on the screen said Smith.

Something stirred in Abby's chest.

"Abby, please put your phone away while we're talking." Mom finally sounded impatient. "This is important."

"But, Mom, it's—"

"I've gotten an apartment in Bethesda." Dad cut her off, looking back and forth from Abby to Ethan. "It has a room for each of you. You can set them up however you want. We're still working out the details but for now, we'll plan for you to stay here during the week and come out to my new place every other weekend. We can adjust that when we need to, since, Abby, we'll be going on college visits pretty soon, and, Ethan, we—"

"You aren't *here* every other weekend," Ethan interrupted. "You're in New York all the time."

"Well, I won't be traveling as much moving forward," Dad said, as though that should've been obvious.

"Neither of us will," Mom added.

"You have to." Ethan frowned. "For work. That's what you always said. That you wouldn't be away so much if your jobs didn't make you."

Their parents exchanged a glance.

"Well, I'll make sure not to schedule any trips when the two of you are staying over." Dad tilted his head to one side, as though the kids should've known that already. Even though he'd ignored Ethan's actual question.

Abby's phone stopped vibrating. She watched the screen to see if a voice mail alert would pop up.

The "friend" of Marian Love's. Hadn't Claire said her name was Mrs. Smith?

That would be an impossibly big coincidence, though. Half the country had that last name.

Marian Love's ex-girlfriend from sixty years ago couldn't actually be trying to call Abby on the phone during the worst afternoon of her life. Could she?

"It's normal to feel upset when you hear something like this." Mom brushed a light finger across her cheek. As though she were scratching an itch. "A lot of kids in your position might feel sad or angry or scared—"

Ethan hurled himself down onto the couch again, burying his face into the pillows.

"I have to go." Abby stood up. "I might have an important voice mail."

"Abby," Dad said, "you can't—"

Mom interrupted him. At least *that* was closer to how things normally worked. "We need both of you to listen to us. Abby, please sit down. Ethan, please get up."

Abby didn't sit, but she didn't leave the room, either. She turned away instead, staring at the empty foyer. At the world on the other side of the glass front door. And, opposite it, at the creaking wooden steps that led up to the empty quiet of her room.

It didn't matter where she went. This would be happening there, too.

"You have to understand." Dad was back to his trusty script. "This is our fault, not yours. We're still your parents, and we'll always be a family."

"Will you still come to my winter recital?" Ethan lifted his head. He'd started shaking.

Maybe Gladys and Henrietta could have a sex scene that turned *into* a fight. Or maybe Gladys was the one who suspected *Henrietta* of cheating, but it turned out she was wrong.

"Yes, of course we'll both come to all of your shows," Dad said.

"Your events, too, Abby," Mom added. "We're not so far from your graduation, of course, and—"

"May I please go to the library?" Abby interrupted.

Dad was watching Ethan, but Mom said, "Honey, we're still talking."

"We've talked. I get it. I understand. I don't want to hear any more. Can I please just go? I just *really* want to be—not here. Please, Mom, Dad, I'm *begging*."

Ethan's shaking was getting worse. Abby looked away.

"Abby, I understand that you may like the idea of being alone right now, but—" Mom began.

Dad stepped forward and bent over Ethan. "I think it's all right. She needs space to process everything, right, Abby?"

"Right." She would've agreed to anything Dad said if it meant she was allowed to get out of that house. "Space to process."

"I'll drive you to the library, honey." Mom started to get up. The idea of getting back into that car made Abby instantly nauseous.

"No, I want to walk." She started to reach for her jacket on the peg, then realized she'd never taken it off. "Okay, um, thanks. Bye."

She yanked the front door open and stumbled down the steps. She was already breathing hard by the time she reached the sidewalk. She turned around to see if her parents were watching her through the front window, but they were both kneeling over Ethan.

She pulled her phone from her pocket. There was a missed call alert, but no voice mail. Abby slid her phone back into her pocket and started walking, slowly, up the hill to Wisconsin.

As she passed the burger place, Abby's stomach growled. She hadn't eaten lunch that day, and she didn't remember if she'd had breakfast. Oh, well. She didn't have her backpack or her wallet, so buying food wasn't an option. Besides, she'd probably just throw it back up.

She'd known this was coming. Obviously. It was only—a thing. It wasn't even a big deal. It happened to a lot of people.

Abby climbed the hill, staring up at the library's glass walls. She should try to write. She didn't have her laptop, but that was okay. She could write on a public computer. She could use the feelings she was experiencing to draft a new scene and figure out what to do with it later.

Pain was good for creativity. Most of the poetry submissions they read every week for lit mag were all about pain.

The problem was, Abby *didn't* feel pain. She still didn't feel anything at all.

The sun shone bright on the library's glass exterior. It hurt Abby's eyes, but it was strangely mesmerizing, too.

She climbed higher up the hill, until she reached the library's front doors. Then she passed them and kept walking.

She sped up, until she was practically running. She ran for another five minutes. Then another ten, and another after that.

Her calves burned. It felt good. She reached the house and rang the doorbell.

What time was it? Abby had forgotten to check. Was it late enough in the day that other people's parents would be home? Normal parents, who kept regular schedules and did other normal-parent stuff?

The curtain behind the window in the front door rustled. A pair of wide brown eyes peeked out. A moment later the door swung open.

"Abby?" Linh's mouth was already forming a small, worried O. "What's wrong? Did something happen?"

"I…" Abby heard the tremor in her voice. She was shaking, she realized, just like Ethan. "I'm sorry I've been weird lately. It's just that everything is terrible."

"Hey, no, *I'm* sorry. It was asinine of me to say what I did on the train. Here, come in."

Abby blinked, trying to remember what Linh had said on the train, as she followed her toward the living room.

The cat was purring in front of the fireplace, but Abby didn't want to go any farther. She didn't want to step into that wide-open space where they'd spent countless hours watching corny shows on the big-screen TV and frantically trying to scrub crumbs off the spotless linen sofa before Linh's mom got home.

She'd loved Linh then. She was sure of it.

When you loved someone, *really* loved them, that feeling lasted forever, didn't it? Because otherwise…what the hell was the *point*?

Abby didn't want to think about that. She didn't want to think at all. She only wanted to matter to someone.

So she closed her eyes, leaned in and kissed her.

Linh kissed her back, the exact same way she always used to, and Abby tried to lose herself in it. She focused on the physical sensations. The smoothness of Linh's hair as it threaded through her splayed fingers. The softness of Linh's palm resting, light as air, on the back of her neck. The weight of her own breathing, growing heavier as the kiss went on.

She tried, frantically, not to think. Still, she couldn't stop the idea from swimming into her head.

This isn't what you want. Not anymore.

Abby hated that idea. She wanted to purge it from her mind, but it wouldn't go.

She pulled away.

"I'm sorry," Linh whispered. That pitying expression was back on her face. The one Abby hated more than anything. "I'm sorry. I'm so, so sorry."

She couldn't tell if Linh was sorry for kissing her back or for something else. She didn't care, as long as that pitying look went away.

"Don't." Abby swallowed, fighting back tears. "Please, don't."

Linh nodded and didn't say anything more. She stepped out, her arms outstretched, as though to hug her.

But Abby shrank back, covering her face with her hand. She turned and stumbled blindly through the front door and out into the cold afternoon, ignoring Linh's voice calling out behind her.

18

Saturday, August 6, 1955

Everything moved faster in New York.

Janet had come to the city before, but never alone. She'd never had to read the street signs, or figure out which direction was downtown and which was up. As she stepped out of the crowded bus depot and tried to determine which way to start walking, two men in suits with umbrellas tucked under their arms nearly knocked her down, but it would take more than a few impatient businessmen to dim Janet's excitement.

She'd made it all the way here, leaving before dawn on her rickety bus with blurry scenery flashing past her eyes. She'd tried not to think about Marie, or her family, or anything else from the world she was leaving behind, and focused instead on the mix of anticipation and dread bubbling in her stomach.

Now, surrounded by the towering buildings and honking taxis of 34th Street, she was determined to start her new life.

"Pardon me." Janet stepped up to a well-dressed lady pushing a baby carriage. "Could you please tell me, which direction is Greenwich Village? I'm looking for West Fourth and Charles Streets?"

The lady glanced up from her handbag, eyeing Janet without a smile. "Now, why would a nice girl like you be looking for that sort of place?"

Janet began to sweat. Surely this prim-and-proper mother wasn't familiar with the Sheldon Lounge.

But a moment later the lady pointed south, and Janet thanked her.

It was a perfect day for a walk through the city. It felt good to stretch out after all those hours cramped on the bus, with no one but the fictional characters in her head to occupy her. Janet's luggage wasn't heavy—she'd only packed a few things in her overnight bag, since she'd need new clothes for her new life anyway—and it was a beautiful, sunny afternoon. It wasn't quite as hot here as it was back home, though she couldn't quite see the bright blue sky here with all the tall buildings blocking her view.

Janet followed the crowd on the sidewalk for a few blocks, breathing in the smells of car exhaust and cigarette smoke and greasy food that made up New York City, before ducking into a Walgreens. There she bought a map of Manhattan, sat at the counter and ordered a hamburger and Coke. Her express bus hadn't stopped for lunch, and she was famished.

She studied the map while she ate, memorizing the route. West Fourth and Charles, it seemed, was only a mile or so down Seventh Avenue. New York was less complicated than Washington. At least when it came to navigation.

Yet as she pushed back her plate, paid her bill and left the drugstore, the lady who'd called her a "nice girl" lingered in her mind. Janet hadn't come to New York to be a "nice girl." So when, three blocks later, she spotted a fitted skirt and men's-style shirt on the mannequin in a secondhand clothing store window, she paused and went inside.

The store was bustling with shoppers and salesgirls, and no one paid Janet any particular attention. She brushed her fingers over a display of slacks hanging near the entrance, but didn't linger. It was a Saturday evening. The Sheldon Lounge might not allow her inside if she showed up in slacks.

The next rack held skirts. Janet lifted one hanger, then another, until she found one like the skirt in the window. It was straight and fitted, with a hemline several inches shorter than her church clothes. It looked far more grown-up than anything else she owned.

The dressing room was at the back. Janet took a deep breath, lifted the hanger and started walking.

A quarter hour later, she left the store feeling like a new person. She studied her reflection in the store windows as she walked south, her heels clicking on the cracked New York cement. Her new straight blue skirt was an inch or so too short to pass Holy Divinity's rule-book, and it made her stand taller, her eyes shine brighter. She hadn't been able to find a blouse that properly matched it so she'd bought a simple, short-sleeved brown jacket that had looked very sophisticated in the dressing room. The store hadn't sold shoes, leaving Janet with nothing but the plain brown heels she wore to church most Sundays, but she imagined it would be so dark in the Sheldon Lounge that no one would be able to see her feet anyway.

She wished Marie could see her looking this way. Janet felt nearly as grown-up as she always seemed.

Before she'd had time to grow fully accustomed to the feel of her new clothes, Janet was turning onto Charles Street.

The buildings had grown shabbier as she'd walked, and the passersby had changed, too. There were fewer well-groomed ladies and businessmen. Instead, she saw a greater number of young men with beards and serious expressions, as well as older men and women who sat on benches, staring silently off into the city as they smoked narrow gray cigarettes or thick brown cigars.

The sun was lower in the sky than it had been when she climbed off the bus, but in the late summer heat it would be up for a good time yet. Janet had relished her walk, allowing the city to slowly hypnotize her, and so she wasn't fully prepared when she spotted the small white sign in a dark, drab window. The words *Sheldon Lounge* had been scrawled with a thick pen over a flickering *OPEN* sign.

Janet stopped in the middle of the block.

She'd come all this way. It was time to go inside.

But what if she'd made a mistake? What if the Sheldon Lounge wasn't the sort of place she'd thought?

Or what if it *was* the sort of place she'd thought, and Janet didn't fit in at all? What if everyone inside took one look at her and knew she didn't belong?

Perhaps she ought to walk around the block once or twice first. Just to steady herself.

"Whoa, there!" a woman called behind her. Janet stepped to the side, realizing she was blocking the path. She prepared an apology and a downward glance.

But the woman who'd spoken wasn't looking at her. She was walking with another girl. Their eyes were locked on each other's faces, their lips curved up in laughter.

Both of them were wearing slacks.

Janet watched, transfixed, as the woman who'd called out— she was taller than her friend, with shorter hair and a masculine look about her that made Janet think of Sam in *A Love So Strange*—walked right up to the blinking sign of the Sheldon Lounge and pushed open the door. The other girl, the one with longer hair and dark red lipstick, followed without a moment's self-consciousness, still laughing at whatever private joke they'd shared. Janet stared as the door closed behind them.

Those girls were like her.

They were like Marie and Carol and Mitch. And Dolores Wood, and Sam and Betty, and Paula and Elaine, and who knew how many others.

Janet was really here.

She didn't want to walk around the block anymore. She had to resist the urge to run.

Then she pushed the door open and forgot everything but the sight before her.

The narrow room was even darker and smokier than Janet had imagined. None of the day's lingering sunlight seemed to reach the interior, but a jukebox on the back wall played a jazzy tune. As her eyes adjusted to the dimness, Janet could barely make out a bar running along the left side of the room, with ten or so stools alongside it.

Most of the stools were occupied. The girls Janet had seen enter had perched on two of them, leaving just three vacant seats beside the girl who'd reminded her of Sam.

A few small tables stood clustered on the opposite wall. Girls sat talking with cigarettes in their hands and dusty glasses in front of them. A small, empty space in the back looked as though it might occasionally serve as a dance floor, though there couldn't have been enough room for more than two or three couples to dance at a time unless they climbed onto the tabletops.

The scent of smoke grew stronger as she stood in the doorway. Janet waved a hand in front of her face, not wanting to cough. Thus far, no one seemed to have noticed her presence, which suited her. She'd prefer to attract as little attention as possible in this strange new land.

She peered more closely at the seated couples, trying to see if any of them might be Miss Wood, but none of the girls quite fit the mental image Janet had developed of her: tall, and fashionable, with sleekly styled hair and a tailored suit paired with matching high heels. She'd probably wear a matching hat and gloves, too.

"Hey. I don't know you." The man's voice rasped suddenly in her ear. Janet stumbled backward, and the girls at the nearest table turned to look.

She whipped her head around to see a doughy-faced, dark-haired man in a double-breasted suit, standing an inch shorter than Janet in her heels. He held a fat, stinking cigar and wore gold rings with wide, clear stones on both hands.

"Who are you?" the man asked, his eyes locked on Janet.

She froze. Surely he didn't mean for her to tell him her name? She may not have been as cautious as she should've back in Washington, but even so Janet knew better than to share her real name with some strange man in the Sheldon Lounge. "I— Pardon me. What do you mean?"

The man tipped his cigar into an ashtray perched on a ledge by the front door. "What do you mean, what do I mean? Who do you know here?"

"Oh." The man must be some kind of guard. "I'm here to see Dolores Wood."

"Aw, you mean Claire?" The man softened slightly and puffed on his cigar. "She ain't here yet, but I'll tell her to look for you when she gets in. Sorry about all the questions, but when a new girl shows up out of nowhere, I've gotta make sure she ain't a copper in disguise."

Janet couldn't tell if he was joking. She decided to play it safe. "I'm not with the police, I promise."

The man nodded slowly. To Janet's relief, the girls at the table nearby had turned back to their own conversation.

"All right, well, since you're a first-timer, here's the ground rules." The man took another long puff on his cigar. "We're a respectable establishment. We don't allow any men or any funny business in the ladies' room. Whores and johns meet outside the premises only. Got all that? Good. Have a lovely evening. Hey, Frankie?" An older woman behind the bar paused in wiping down a glass to glance up at him, then looked right back down again. "Get this girl a drink, will you? Put it on my tab."

The bartender, Frankie, kept her eyes on her dishrag. "You got it, Louie."

"Go on, then." Louie gave Janet a not-entirely-gentle push toward the empty bar stools.

Janet moved slowly, stunned from the encounter and keeping out an anxious eye for any of those "whores and johns" Louie had mentioned. Her fear had returned in full force, but there was no way she could leave after all that. She climbed onto an empty stool and focused all her attention on not falling off it.

"Whatcha after?" Frankie was still looking down at the glass in her hands. Her hair was cropped around her ears, and her men's shirt was unbuttoned far enough to hint at a swell of deeply tanned, wrinkled breasts beneath. It took Janet a moment to realize Frankie was talking to her.

"I, ah." Janet felt entirely foolish. Frankie, and every other woman in this place, might as well have climbed straight out of the pages of a Bannon Press novel.

Janet didn't fit in here at all. She wished Marie were with her. She'd have known exactly how to act and what to say.

"I'm sorry." Janet almost sputtered. "I don't—I, ah—"

Then Frankie looked up. A smile played behind her eyes, not quite reaching her lips. "It's all right, kid. You can relax. Louie scared you, huh?"

Janet bent her head, ashamed, but Frankie was still smiling. Janet decided to trust her. "Is he always that way?"

"Every night." Frankie rested both her elbows on the bar, leaning in as though for a conspiratorial whisper. "Don't worry, he's a nobody. His family, they own this place, but they only send him to do this job because they don't want him anywhere he could cause real trouble. He thinks he's the boss, but the rest of us know better. Isn't that the truth, Nancy?"

"That's right, Frankie," said the short-haired girl in the next seat. She cast Janet a shrewd smile. Janet forced herself not to giggle.

"So what are you drinking, kid?" Frankie tapped her fingers on the bar.

"Oh, uh." In that moment, there was only one drink Janet could remember. "A martini, please."

Frankie raised her eyebrows. For a moment Janet feared she'd ask her for ID, but then Frankie reached for another glass. "Sure thing, sweetheart. So, you just get here from someplace?"

"You can tell, huh?" Janet leaned forward, trying to smile the same way Nancy had.

Frankie nodded toward the overnight bag on the floor. Janet blushed. Of course. "Right off the bus, are ya?"

"Yep."

"Got a job lined up?" Frankie set down a glass of clear liquid in front of her. A drab gray olive perched on its rim.

"No, I need to look for one. I was thinking I could work in an office, or as a waitress. I've got experience at that, at least."

"Good for you. Well, I'd offer you a job here, except we don't bring in enough to pay anybody but me. Old Louie at the door keeps telling every girl who comes in to get a drink on his tab, except he hasn't paid his tab in, what, two years?"

"You on about that again, Frankie?" A new voice boomed in Janet's left ear. She hadn't noticed another girl climbing onto the vacant stool beside her. "You're gonna talk this poor kid's ear off."

Frankie's expression soured. "What's it to you, Claire?"

"Nothing at all, baby, nothing at all." Claire rolled her eyes and whispered something to the girl on her other side.

The girl beside Claire was a Negro, young and pretty, with long eyelashes and short dark hair. Janet hadn't realized there were so many Negro lesbians. In the books she'd read, she hadn't seen mention of any at all. This girl didn't look much older than Janet herself, but Claire was older—in her thirties or forties, perhaps. She was shorter than Janet, even sitting there on the bar stools, and she had cropped red hair and a smile that made Janet like her immediately.

Then, to Janet's astonishment, Claire turned to her and held out her hand. "So, old Louie said you were looking for me. To what do I owe the pleasure?"

Only then did Janet remember what Louie had said. *Oh, you mean Claire?*

"Are you Miss Wood?" Janet was so overwhelmed she only remembered at the last moment to shake the offered hand.

"I am she." Dolores Wood grinned. "You can call me Claire. I only publish as Dolores sometimes. And this is Flo."

"Hi." The younger girl gave Janet a quick wave.

"I'm Janet," she said, waiting for Miss Wood—Claire—to remember her.

Claire smiled again, but there was no sign of recognition in her eyes.

"I wrote to you." Janet stumbled over the words. "I read your book, and I wrote you a letter and you wrote back, and, the bus ticket, and—"

"Oh!" Claire clapped a hand over her mouth. She'd spoken so loudly Nancy and her friend had turned to watch them with amused smiles. "I remember you. You're the writer!"

Janet blushed. "Yes, I—"

"Flo, this is the girl I told you about. Remember? I got that letter and I said, I'm going to send this poor kid a bus ticket. I said, that's a kid who *needs* to get herself to New York. Frankie!" Claire pounded on the bar, jostling Janet's martini glass. "Get this girl another drink, on me."

"She could make it all night without ever paying a cent," Frankie muttered, but she picked up the gin bottle.

"Here." Claire stood up as their drinks arrived. After a moment, so did Flo. "Come on, Janet, let's take our drinks and get us a table. I want to hear all about you."

Janet's smile was so wide she forgot to be embarrassed as she wound through the tight maze of tables, her fresh glass clutched in her hand. She already felt a bit woozy, and she didn't know what the second drink would do, but she didn't want to seem ungrateful.

"Thank you, so much, for the book you wrote." Janet's words spilled out clumsily as they took seats near the jukebox. Claire and Flo sat with their backs to the wall, and Janet took the seat across from Claire. "It's the only book that ever really meant something to me. Well, I mean, it isn't as though I'd never enjoyed a book before—I loved *Jane Eyre*—but your book, well…it felt as though you'd written it just for me."

Claire smiled at her. "That's so kind of you to say. Thank

you, Janet. So tell me, how's *your* writing going? Did you bring your book for me to read?"

"Ah—no." Janet sipped her fresh martini. She didn't want to admit she'd burned the pages. Or that she'd given up writing forever. "I don't have it with me."

Flo pulled a cigarette from her purse and held it to her lips, and Claire leaned over and lit it for her. Then she pulled out two more cigarettes, passing one to Claire and holding the other out to Janet.

Well, maybe it would help her fit in. "Thank you."

Claire leaned across the table with her lighter, and Janet held the cigarette between her lips the way she'd seen Marie do.

It made her wish, again, that Marie were here. Janet would love to hear what she thought of Claire and Flo. Not to mention Frankie and Louie.

It was hard not to flinch when Claire struck the flame, and much harder not to cough when Janet drew her first breath. In the end, she couldn't contain it. She turned away, trying to keep her coughs small and ladylike until her eyes stopped watering.

When she glanced back, Flo and Claire were both studiously looking away, color rising in their cheeks. Flo reached out and took Claire's hand, puffing on her cigarette as though to prove she could.

Janet gazed down at their clasped hands. Here, in the Sheldon Lounge, this was a thing girls could do. Hold hands on top of a table, out in public, with no one saying a word.

"Is it your first time in the city?" Flo asked, following Janet's gaze.

"No." Janet flushed and set her cigarette on the ashtray. "But it's my first time, ah—"

"In a place like the Sheldon." Flo nodded. Janet was glad she'd been the one to say it.

"So how far have you gotten in the book?" Claire interrupted. "How many pages?"

Janet didn't want to lie. She'd have to admit what had happened. Part of it, at least.

"A hundred and fifty or so. I wrote maybe three-quarters of a manuscript, but then I—I stopped." Janet folded her hands carefully on the table in front of her, remembering the sulphur smell of the matches burning at the attic window. "I guess I was afraid. I'm not sure writing is for me after all."

"Well, I certainly can understand being afraid." Claire smiled and squeezed Flo's hand. Flo sipped her cocktail. "It's petrifying, isn't it?"

Janet bobbed her head. "I was frightened all the time. My—my friend back home, she's terrified."

"It's so hard." Claire sighed. "Putting words down on paper, and having to show them to someone else. Knowing people out there in the world, people you've never even met, are going to read them, and have an opinion on whether they're any good. Plus, what if your *mother* reads it someday?" Claire leaned in and whispered, "What if your mom finds out you wrote a book with *sex* in it?"

"Yes!" That wasn't precisely what Janet had meant about being frightened, but it was true all the same. "Yes, exactly."

"It's utterly horrifying." Claire drained her glass and waved to Frankie for another round. "Well, guess what, kid. I've got news for you. *Living* is horrifying. The good news is, writers need pain. So it all works out in the end, because being one of us is scary as hell."

Janet flushed at the curse word, but did her best to hide it. She didn't want them to think she was a child.

Frankie set three fresh glasses on the table and collected the empty ones. Janet was surprised to see that her second martini was already gone. She couldn't imagine touching another, but there it was, sitting in front of her with yet another pale gray olive floating on top.

"Claire, darling!" a voice boomed behind them. "Why, if it isn't!"

"Hazel!" Claire jumped up and greeted a short, blond girl in a tight black dress with a kiss on both cheeks. "It's been ages."

"Hasn't it? It's all Ed's fault. She's domesticating me. I've gotten to making steak dinners every night."

"If I remember correctly, you *offered* to cook last night," said the girl standing beside her. She was tall, very tall, with dark eyes and a pompadour.

Janet stared up at Ed, wondering if perhaps she ought to learn to make steak dinners herself.

She banished the thought quickly. It was far too close to a betrayal of Marie.

Though she'd been determined to forget all about Marie when she came up here. Hadn't she?

"Hazel and Ed, meet Flo and Janet." Claire waved to indicate the girls at her table, and everyone shook hands. Janet was surprised Hazel and Ed didn't already know Flo. She'd assumed Claire and Flo had been together forever. "Join us, won't you?"

Janet moved over to make room. Ed pulled out the chair beside her for Hazel, moving with a showy swagger to her hips. Ed was wearing jeans, Janet noticed. She'd never seen a girl wear jeans to a restaurant. She wouldn't have thought it was allowed.

Claire and Flo went over to the jukebox, and Hazel studied Janet while Ed went to the bar for more drinks. "Are you visiting New York?"

Janet dropped her gaze. She must look so naive. "Miss Wood

sent me a bus ticket," she mumbled, though she hadn't planned to reveal that detail to anyone else. "I mean, Claire did."

"How interesting." Hazel lit a cigarette, holding out the packet. Janet shook her head, and Hazel tucked it back into her purse. "How did you meet Claire?"

"I read her book." Janet smiled, flushing once more. Somehow, she noticed, her martini glass had nearly grown empty again. "I loved it, so I wrote her a letter, and she wrote me back. She encouraged me to try writing a book, too, but it was harder than I expected."

"Oh really?" Hazel raised her eyebrows. "I'm a fan of Claire's writing myself. I've tried to get her to write for us, but she feels locked in at Bannon. Oh, I should've mentioned, I edit paperbacks for Grier Publishers."

"Are you serious?" Did *everyone* in New York work in publishing? "Do you ever work on—*those* sorts of books?"

"Lesbian books, you mean?" Hazel puffed on her cigarette, amusement twinkling in her eyes. "Some. What's your book about?"

"Yes, tell us." Claire slid back into her seat across the table with Flo at her heels. Janet hadn't realized they'd been listening. "I want to hear all about it."

"I—ah." Janet didn't know what to say. Her book was gone forever. She'd come here to start a new life, with no looking back.

"Here we go, girls." Ed and Frankie returned to the table, carrying five drinks between them. Claire and Flo smiled up at them, and Hazel planted a soft kiss on Ed's cheek.

Janet looked away as a fresh martini was placed in front of her, the old glass whisked away again.

It hurt more than she'd ever imagined to be surrounded

by couples. If she closed her eyes, perhaps she could almost believe Marie was here with her.

"Take a sip and tell us about your book, Janet," Claire boomed from across the table. "It's always easier to talk with a drink in you."

Janet already had three drinks in her. Plus, she was suddenly very aware that she needed to use the ladies' room. The one where she wasn't to get up to any funny business. "I'm not sure I can."

"Of course you can! She can, can't she?" Claire turned to the others at the table, who held up their drinks and began to talk all at once.

"Tell us! Tell us, you've got to tell us!"

With so many voices clamoring to hear about her writing, and the martinis churning through her, Janet didn't see the harm. She lifted her drink, took a sip, and began to tell the story of Paula and Elaine.

At first she meant to give no more than a sentence or two of description, but as the others leaned in to listen, it also seemed important to describe each of the girls and their backgrounds. She told the others how Paula and Elaine met, how they fell in love, and the obstacles they faced. Soon, Claire and Hazel and the others were asking questions, and Janet was describing in even more detail how her characters looked, where they'd lived before coming to New York, where they worked, and—this in response to a question from Flo, who, Janet noticed, kept stealing sips from the other side of Janet's martini glass—how they made love. Before long, everyone at the table was howling with laughter, Janet included.

When she'd told all she could think to tell, she admitted, "But I'm still not sure about it, honestly. There are some things in it that won't work. I've learned so much just in the time since I started writing it, and there's so much I still don't know."

"Like what?" Ed swigged her beer.

"Well, I'd never even been in this kind of a place until tonight." Janet cast a hand around to indicate the dark, smoky bar. "I wasn't expecting there to be a man stationed at the front door, for one thing."

"Oh, don't you worry about Louie." Claire laughed. "I told you, he's harmless."

"He only spoke to you because you're new," Flo added. "If someone shows up at a gay bar who nobody's seen before, they could be getting ready for a bust."

Janet sat back in her seat, alarmed. Was that what Louie had meant, asking if she was a "copper"?

As the others turned back to their conversation, Ed leaned in toward Janet with kind eyes. "The trouble is, these places can be wary about anything, or anybody, who's different. A girl nobody's seen before, a girl who doesn't know the rules— well, she could be a plant working for the FBI. Do you see what we mean?"

The FBI. Even in Greenwich Village, they worried about the FBI.

Perhaps it was for the best that Marie wasn't here after all.

"I understand." Janet stood. "Where's the ladies' room?"

"Straight back there." Hazel pointed, and as she followed her gaze, Janet realized just how unsteady she felt. "Don't worry, a few more nights at the Sheldon and you'll be able to hold your liquor."

Janet laughed and made her way slowly to the sign marked Ladies. The stench of far too many cigarettes and not nearly enough bleach hit her before she'd even opened the door.

This place was nothing like the Soda Shoppe, with its rules

and scripts and perfect order. Still, she felt a keen affection for the Sheldon Lounge. Janet had never been anywhere like it, but it already felt like home. Perhaps even more so than the little Georgetown house where she'd spent all her life.

The girls here had accepted her as one of their own. She felt like one of them, too, even though they were so different from her. Hazel and Ed's impossible sophistication. Claire's warmth. Flo's quiet thoughtfulness. Even Frankie's casual regard.

None of them had to hide who they were. Not here.

This was Janet's life now. This was her future—the one she'd chosen for herself.

Perhaps Paula and Elaine's own path needn't be so bleak as Janet had first imagined. Perhaps, despite the publisher's instructions, there was a way to show the "dangers" of lesbianism while still allowing her characters to survive. Maybe she could even allow them some modicum of happiness.

Yet how could they ever have true happiness when they couldn't have each other?

Janet stared into the bathroom mirror, lost in her imaginings.

Then she spotted a black mark in the corner of the frame, a long-ago burn from a long-ago cigarette. And she remembered the burned scraps of paper, blowing in the breeze.

Paula and Elaine were gone. Janet had given up writing, forever. She'd been foolish to talk about her story to the women in the bar. She had to push it far from her mind.

When she came back out again, having washed her hands three times but with that gruesome bathroom scent still lingering in her nostrils, Janet settled into her seat and interrupted the conversation Ed and Claire had been having—something about a friend of theirs who'd moved to California to chase a girl—to announce, "I have a question."

Everyone stopped talking at once and turned toward her.

Janet ignored the hints of laughter on their faces and took a sip of the fresh martini Ed had placed in front of her.

"Do any of you know a girl named Kimberly Paul?" Janet asked. "Does she come here, too?"

For a moment, no one answered her. Then Hazel snickered, and Claire and Flo broke into flat-out laughter. Ed glanced back and forth between them, seeming not to get the joke.

"I'm sorry to have to tell you this, kid," Claire said when her laughter had started to subside, "but there's no such girl as Kimberly Paul."

"There must be. I read her book." Janet frowned. Had the martinis caused her to say the wrong name? "She wrote *A Deviant Woman*, didn't she?"

"That's one of Kimberly's, all right." Flo dunked her cigarette in the ashtray and lit another. "Except *Kimberly Paul* is a made-up name. Just like *Dolores Wood*." She laughed.

"No, it's not like mine. Not at all." Claire signaled to Frankie for more drinks, frowning. "I write every single book that says *Dolores Wood* on the cover. Even the ones I want to take back."

Hazel laughed. "You're not still on about *A Love So Strange*, are you?"

"What?" Janet blinked, hoping she'd misunderstood. "Surely you don't want to take that book *back*? *A Love So Strange* is marvelous. It changed my whole life!"

Hazel's laughter turned into a kind smile.

"You're lovely." Claire's frown faded away. "Thank you. It isn't that I want to take the whole book back, but I'd rewrite it if I could. That ending, for one." She pursed her lips. "Nathan made me tack that on. I'd rewrite it to be in third person, too, if I could. It was a huge mistake, writing it in first. I'd been reading another book that was in first, and it got in my head, and I was on a tight deadline, so there it was." She sighed.

Janet's head spun. Was that the only reason she'd written Paula and Elaine's story in first person, too? Because Claire had used it for *her* book? And all because some *other* author had done the same thing?

"No writer is ever completely happy with their book," Hazel chimed in, taking a swig of her drink. "That's what editors are for. We tell you when to stop changing your words so they can start making us all some money."

Claire held out her drink, laughing, and she and Hazel clinked glasses before turning back to Janet.

"The Paul books, though," Claire explained, "those are written by a whole set of different guys. Whoever wants Nathan's check the most that month."

"Guys?" Janet didn't understand. "But the books are—that is, the one I read was about girls."

"Oh, they're *about* girls, sure, but that doesn't mean the writers know the first thing about girls themselves." Claire scoffed.

"So that's why the book was so bad," Janet marveled. The others laughed.

"Stay away from the Paul books, that's the best advice I can give you." Claire gave Janet a somber look. "Come meet me for lunch tomorrow and I'll bring you some good ones. I've got plenty. You read *The Price of Salt* yet? Or *Spring Fire*?"

As Janet shook her head, it dawned on her that she still didn't know where she was staying tonight. It was all well and good to make plans for lunch, but she didn't especially want to camp out on a park bench between now and then, and it was probably too late to check in to a hotel.

The group ordered another round of drinks, and another after that. Frankie sat down with them to join in the conversation when things were slow at the bar. Janet had finally asked her to stop bringing martinis, and she sipped water while she listened to the others.

They talked about friends they all knew, in New York and other cities. Friends who'd gotten together, and friends who'd broken up. Friends who'd left to start over in other places—and a few who'd gone off to marry men, leaving their pasts behind.

"Do girls really do that?" Janet whispered to Ed. "I'd hoped that was only in books."

"It happens more often than you'd guess." It was Claire who answered. Janet must not have spoken as quietly as she'd thought.

"How do they stand being married, though? If they know how they really are." Janet wasn't sure if it was the drinks or the idea of marriage that had her so flustered. She was trying not to think about Marie, but it wasn't working. Her efforts on that front had been failing her all night long.

"They want to be normal." Claire shrugged as Hazel nodded sagely. "Let's face it, the world doesn't like us very much. There's nothing we can do about that, but at least we have each other."

Marie's voice echoed in her mind. *I don't want to be different, Janet.*

Ed held up her drink to toast, and the whole table joined in, stretching forward with their mostly empty glasses.

Flo was the only one who didn't smile. Janet didn't feel much like smiling, either.

Could the world truly despise every single one of them, forever? Would they always be hiding in tiny, shadowy bars, constantly on the alert for anyone who might find them out? Or hiding from the truth altogether, the way Marie wanted so desperately to do?

"Hey, kid," Flo said in a low voice as the others moved on, discussing more friends Janet had never heard of. "You got a place to stay for the night?"

"I... No." Janet's embarrassment flared again.

"Well, my apartment's nothing special, but the couch is yours if you want it. I'm working the early shift at the diner in the morning. If you want, you can come with me there and get some breakfast."

Janet's relief nearly took physical form. "That's so kind of you to offer. Thank you."

"Hey, I was a new kid in New York once. We all were."

Janet smiled.

"I think there may be an apartment coming free soon in my building, in fact." Flo drained her glass. "Could you manage fifty a month for rent?"

"Fifty?" Janet tried to think of how the nickels and dimes the Soda Shoppe customers left on their trays might add up. Fifty dollars, every single month. Tips in New York must be higher than they were in Washington.

"Yeah, it's steep. Especially when you don't have a job yet. Did you really leave your parents' house this morning and come straight to the Sheldon?"

Janet cracked a smile. "It seems I did."

Flo laughed. "I can ask around tomorrow, see if anybody knows about a job."

"That would be wonderful. Thank you."

Flo turned back to join in the others' conversation, and Janet did her best to absorb every word. She could sit here for hours, for years, and still never learn everything there was to know about this life. There were so many difficulties— keeping things quiet at work, turning down men who thought the absence of a wedding ring meant you must be hunting for a husband, lying to your family.

Not to mention the constant worries about police raids. Frankie mentioned those a number of times, always with a glance toward Louie. All night long, he hadn't moved from his post. He still sat gazing out the front door, his hand draped over a tall glass of light brown liquid at his side.

Through it all, Janet couldn't stop thinking about Marie.

If she could only see this, it would change everything. She'd see that their choices were bigger than a life full of lying. She'd see that there were other girls like them. Girls who'd been through the same things they had, but who were still themselves. She'd see that there were people who understood.

Janet had to show her.

As soon as the idea entered her mind, it took root and flowered fast. Janet needed to bring Marie here, to the Sheldon Lounge.

It was so simple, now that she'd thought of it. She had the return bus ticket Claire had given her. She could use it to go back to Washington, where she'd find Marie and say whatever it took to make her understand. Then together, they would come back to New York. They could drive up in Marie's hand-me-down Buick—it should be out of the shop by now. Perhaps they could sell it once they'd made it to New York. That would give them enough money to live on until they both found jobs. Marie should be able to find something easily with her high marks from secretarial school, and once they were settled they could share an apartment. Surely the two of them could manage fifty a month together.

Janet flushed, imagining a shared life with Marie. She'd see her all day long. All night, too.

Nothing they'd left behind would matter anymore. They'd

be on their own, but they'd be together. It would be just like in the books.

Janet stood so abruptly she pushed the table toward Claire and Flo across the way. Claire laughed and pushed it back, but Flo eyed Janet. "How many of those martinis have you had, kid?"

"I'm not sure. Do you know if there's a phone out front?"

"Yeah, there's one right by Louie's chair." Ed pointed. "You calling long-distance? Need any quarters?"

"I think I have enough." Janet patted her skirt pocket absently and walked on unsteady legs toward the pay phone.

Louie glanced at her but didn't say anything as Janet perched on the narrow seat and pulled the booth door closed behind her. The numbers on the grease-caked dial swam before her eyes. She pushed change through the slot, taking a guess as to how much a call from New York to Washington would cost, and dialed, her thoughts a dizzy swarm.

In a moment, she'd be speaking to Marie. She'd tell her... Janet didn't know exactly what she wanted to say just now. She simply wanted to hear her voice.

And she wanted to tell her she still loved her. That she wasn't ready to give up on all they meant to each other, no matter what the world threw at them.

But the voice who picked up wasn't Marie's. It wasn't Mrs. Eastwood's, either.

"Hello?" It was Janet's mother.

"Hello? Mom?" Janet was so confused, she didn't realize until it was too late that she should've simply hung up.

She must've dialed her own number by accident. How many martinis *did* she have?

"Janet? Is that you? What time is it? No, never mind that." Mom didn't sound like herself at all. In fact, she sounded almost frantic. "You need to come home. We've been so worried."

"Oh. Mom, I…" Janet's throat caught, but she forced herself to think through the fog. Her parents wanted her to come home, even now that Grandma must've told them the truth about her. Was that a good thing or a bad thing? "I—I suppose we should talk, or—"

"Never mind that." Mom rushed on, and it occurred to Janet that it was the middle of the night, and Mom had nonetheless answered on the first ring. "You need to come home. We can go to the hospital first thing in the morning, as soon as visiting hours open."

"Visiting hours?" Janet frowned into the phone dial, as though the still-spinning numbers would explain what this was about.

"Oh, of course, you haven't heard. Janet, I'm so sorry, but Grandma had another heart episode, early this morning. We've been trying to find you. The doctors said to have everyone come to the hospital right away." Mom had been speaking in a rush, but she stopped suddenly with a choking sound.

"What? Is—is she going to be all right?" Janet pushed her thumb into her forehead, trying to make herself understand.

"They aren't sure. She's been growing weaker for some time, you know that—ever since she had that episode a few years ago. She always refused to take precautions, but the doctors say what happened to her heart is worse this time." Mom paused, and Janet heard her take in a deep breath before she spoke again. "She didn't get out of bed this morning, and she—she hasn't woken up since."

Then she won't have told them. Janet hated herself for having the thought, but she couldn't help it. Any more than she could help the thought that followed.

If Grandma dies, it'll be me who killed her.

19

Thursday, October 19, 2017

It was the first morning they'd woken up together in Elaine's apartment, and as she watched Paula shrug on her old pink bathrobe, a warm thrill of delight ran down Elaine's spine.

Whenever Wayne had come to visit, Elaine had always scurried around the house first, hiding the laundry baskets and dog food bowls. She'd hung fresh hand towels in the washroom and potholders in the kitchen. She'd felt obligated to conceal anything less than pristine.

With Paula, Elaine harbored no such desires. She was willing, even eager, for Paula to know her as she truly was, with all her imperfections. Perhaps that was why the sight of Paula's broad shoulders stretching out Elaine's threadbare robe made her feel so warm and loved and happy.

And when Paula shuffled toward the hall to start the coffee, tossing a sleepy smile over her shoulder as she closed the bedroom door behind her, Elaine knew she wanted this feeling to last forever. She wanted to spend the rest of her life in Paula's embrace.

"Hey, Abby."

At the sound of Linh's voice, Abby slowly lifted her eyes from her phone and turned around.

School had finally ended for the day and she'd just drifted out the side doors, thinking about Paula and Elaine. All day, they'd been all she wanted to think about.

But she owed Linh an explanation. Abby still wasn't feeling much of anything, but she *did* know it had been shitty of her to run out of Linh's house with no explanation the day before.

Abby had mostly managed to avoid interacting with anyone all day. She'd snuck into Ms. Sloane's empty classroom for lunch, meaning to write, but she'd wound up playing solitaire on her laptop instead. Ms. Sloane had come in halfway through the period and asked if she wanted to talk, but Abby just shook her head and clicked her king into place. For the rest of the period Ms. Sloane sat silently at her desk marking papers while Abby shifted more cards around.

None of her teachers had called on her all day. Not even in stats, where Mr. Radclyffe called on everybody once a period on principle. It was convenient not to have to know the answers, since Abby hadn't done the homework, but it still annoyed her that the teachers did that. The same way it annoyed her that Ethan hadn't gotten punished for getting in that fight. Mom had said the two of them didn't even have to go to school at all that day if they didn't want to, which Ethan took full advantage of, but when Abby said she was going anyway, one of her parents must've called the office and told them to take it easy on her. It was exactly the kind of obnoxious, over-the-top pity Abby had been dreading for months.

"Hi." She stared at her feet as Linh caught up with her.

The one thing Abby had going for her was that she hadn't totally fallen apart yet. She hadn't cried, not once. But if she let herself get drawn into Linh's warm, sympathetic eyes, she was positive it would all be over in seconds.

"You heading home? Can I walk with you?"

Abby shrugged. "I guess."

They walked in silence for the first three blocks. Cars trundled quietly past as they turned off Wisconsin and started down the hill.

Abby shivered in her cardigan as she watched a squirrel dart across the sidewalk and skitter up the trunk of a nearly bare cherry tree. She hadn't had the energy to dig her winter coat out from under her bed that morning, but Linh was wearing the jacket she always wore when it turned even a tiny bit chilly—a cute, fitted navy blue thing that Abby used to mock for being too preppy to be real. Today it was weirdly comforting to see Linh in the same old jacket again, and when she reached up daintily to push the hood out of her face, the exact same way she always did, Abby remembered how striking she used to find that gesture. Linh, she remembered thinking this time last year, when Linh broke out that navy jacket for the first brisk day of the season, was the prettiest, most captivating human being who'd ever lived.

As of today, the lingering summer heat finally seemed to be gone for good. And if the seasons were still changing, that meant the rest of the world outside Abby's head must still be turning, too. Next week it would be colder than it was now, and in a month or so, actual winter would start. Before long they'd be breaking out the menorah. Abby was mostly over holidays, but this year she found herself longing to light some candles and chant some prayers and fight with Ethan over who got the last piece of gelt.

She hadn't seen her little brother since she'd gotten back from Linh's house the day before. As far as Abby could tell, he'd barely moved. In their old, creaky house Abby could hear every sound through the wall that divided their rooms, but for hours the night before, as she'd curled up in bed with *Women of the Twilight Realm*, Ethan's side of the wall had been silent.

He hadn't spoken to anyone. And he hadn't cried, not once.

Every so often one of their parents had knocked on each of their doors and asked to come in. Abby hadn't bothered to respond, and neither had Ethan. She didn't blame him. There was nothing to say.

Once, Mom had called from the hallway that she was leaving food outside their doors. Abby had waited until her footsteps thumped back down the stairs before she cracked her door. Her mom had brought her a turkey sandwich, chips, an apple and a Diet Coke. The chips were Abby's favorite kind, but Mom never bought them because they were full of sodium or sugar or whatever it was that was bad for you this year. Which meant that at some point since she'd gotten home from Chicago, Mom had gone to the store and specifically bought Abby unhealthy snacks and artificially sweetened soda.

It pissed her off. The same way Mr. Radclyffe not calling on her in stats had pissed her off. She still ate every one of those chips, though.

"I didn't think you'd be in school today." Linh spoke quietly. As if Abby was a horse she was afraid of spooking.

"I felt like getting out of the house." Abby shrugged.

Linh didn't ask anything more. Abby hadn't told her what had happened—she hadn't told anyone—but clearly, Linh knew.

Maybe she had a mole in the principal's office. But more likely, she'd just put the pieces together.

It wasn't as if she hadn't known what was going on. She'd known since that day in May. Maybe even before that.

"Sorry about—about yesterday." Abby had no idea how to say this part, but she had to try regardless. "I shouldn't have run away like that. I only— I mean, I don't— Ugh. I'm sorry."

"It's okay. We don't need to talk about it."

"No, it's not okay." Abby sighed. "Just give me a second to figure out the right words, all right?"

Linh nodded. Abby turned away so she could think.

Something hadn't felt right about kissing Linh the day before. But it hadn't been until many hours later, when she was rereading Marian Love's book again, that Abby had finally figured out what it was.

She wasn't in love with Linh. At least, not anymore.

She wasn't sure exactly when things had changed. Maybe the morning they'd fought on the train, or the afternoon of their awkward almost-kiss in the senior lounge. Maybe it was when they broke up back in the spring. Or even before that.

All she knew was that she didn't lay awake at night thinking about Linh anymore, the way Paula thought about Elaine. She couldn't remember a single time, even when they'd been together, when she'd felt that huge wave of happiness Elaine described at the sight of Paula wearing her borrowed bathrobe. She was positive she'd never felt anything like that sense of absolute certainty that she wanted to spend the rest of her life in Linh's arms.

Did that mean they'd fallen out of love, or that they'd never really been in love to begin with? Or did it just mean love felt different for different people?

Abby was pretty sure her parents had been in love, once.

She'd seen them gazing happily into each other's eyes in their wedding photos. And she remembered how they used to act when she was little, too—the way they smiled at each other in the kitchen when they were fixing Abby's and Ethan's lunches, and kissed when they got home from work in the evenings, and laughed at each other's jokes during family dinners. Now, years later, they couldn't even stand being in the same house unless there was some grand pronouncement to make.

If Abby was right—if Mom and Dad *had* been in love, years ago—that meant real love didn't last forever after all.

So what was the point of falling in love in the first place? What was the point of *any* of this?

"It's okay if you want to be alone." Linh tucked her fists under her arms. "I can go."

"No, don't." They were only a block from home. Abby slowed her pace. "I wanted to tell you I'm sorry about how I've been acting. Not just yesterday, I mean, but for a long time. I shouldn't have said what I did on the train, about you going to visit Penn."

"It was fine in the end." Linh's eyes were fixed on her shoes. "I actually realized I might want to go there after all. I'm definitely applying, at least. There's a lot to be said for staying closer to home. Is Columbia still your first choice?"

"I have no idea." Abby could only vaguely remember why she'd once wanted to go to Columbia. "Anyway, I was only going to say…you probably already knew this, but I'd kind of been hoping we'd get back together all year."

Linh's eyes brightened for a second, but then she looked down again.

"I thought we'd get back together as soon as school started," Abby went on. Now that the feelings were gone, it wasn't actually hard to talk about this anymore. "I obsessed over it for months."

Linh didn't meet her eyes. "You're using past tense."

Abby looked down. "Yeah."

"I… I used to think you and me—we'd…" Linh trailed off. "I guess I wanted to get back together, too. But I didn't know if that was what *you* wanted."

"You *didn't*?" Abby was sure she'd been so obvious. Their friends had even commented on it. More than once.

"Yeah. You're just so quiet. About the real stuff, I mean. It's as though you've been living totally inside your own head. Which, I mean, I completely get. After that—that day, last spring…" Linh trailed off again, but Abby nodded. She knew which day Linh meant. "You seemed so distant. As though you didn't want anything to do with me. I knew you'd been having a hard time, and I thought you didn't want to hurt my feelings. I wanted to make it easier for you, so I decided to bring it up first."

"You thought *I* wanted to break up?" Abby's mouth dropped open. That was the one possibility she'd never considered.

"I guess I was wrong." Linh bit her knuckle. "I'm sorry."

There was so much they'd never said to each other. So many things Abby had wondered about, without having the nerve to voice them.

She decided to voice one now.

"Is there anything happening between you and Savannah?" She finally raised her eyes to meet Linh's. "I know you guys hang out a lot, at cross-country and everything."

"What? No." Linh went pale. Abby believed her—Linh would never lie to her, not about something that mattered—but she could tell Linh wasn't surprised she'd asked, either.

Which meant that even if there wasn't anything between her and Savannah yet, it wasn't because Linh hadn't thought about it.

"Sorry." Abby cleared her throat. "I didn't mean it to sound like an accusation. I was only curious."

"Well, there isn't anything with me and her." Linh scrubbed her eyes with her fist. "I wouldn't do that without talking to you."

"It would be okay if you did." Abby would never have said this a week ago, but today it felt oddly normal. "You're allowed to like someone. We've been broken up a long time. It's okay to, you know, move on."

"Really?" Linh raised her eyebrows.

"It's like…" Abby tried to think of how to explain this. "You've been my favorite person for years. As long as I can remember, practically. I think… I'm just starting to figure out that I'll probably have another favorite person someday. And you will, too."

Linh was watching her closely. Abby nodded, and slowly, Linh nodded back.

Abby used to think what she and Linh had was everything. But it wasn't, and it didn't have to be. Her future was stretched out ahead of her, with a thousand unknowns waiting to be discovered.

Abby wasn't Marian Love. Her story would keep going long past seventeen.

She didn't have to have everything figured out yet. She could keep searching, for years if she needed to. Maybe forever.

Maybe that was how it was for her parents, too. Maybe all of them were still searching.

"Well, anyway." Abby drew a long breath. "I'm still sorry

for yesterday. I shouldn't have just shown up that way, and I definitely shouldn't have run away without telling you why."

"You can always show up, however you need to. Even if we don't... Look." Linh bit her knuckle again. "I hope we'll always be friends."

Abby nodded. "I could use a friend, I think."

She stepped forward for a hug. As Linh hugged her back, Abby began to feel something at last.

Their hug was warm and real. It was different from the kind of hugs they used to share, but that was all right. It was *good*, in fact, even as the tears started to prick at the backs of Abby's eyes.

It felt as though a piece of her was breaking off inside. But it was a part that needed to be gone.

The broken feeling lingered as they said goodbye at the corner. Abby walked on slowly, waiting until Linh reached the end of the block and turned south. When she was positive Linh wouldn't see her if she looked back, Abby sat down on the curb and finally let herself fall apart.

Abby didn't know how late it was when she won her sixth game of solitaire that afternoon. It had started getting dark earlier in the day, and she was losing track of time.

She doubted she was alone in the house, but it was unnaturally quiet. She hadn't seen anyone when she'd trudged inside earlier. She knew she probably looked like shit after crying on the curb for so long—and it had been an ugly cry, too; every tear she'd been holding back for months had apparently decided to burst through all in one go—so she was even less eager to see her family than usual.

Abby started a new game, the pixelated cards fanning out neatly on her laptop screen. A throbbing ache had formed behind her eyes, but she hadn't wanted to risk going out to the hall closet for Tylenol. Better to suffer than to risk seeing anyone.

She got two aces in the first hand. Score. She'd just clicked again when a sharp ring tore through the silence.

Abby grabbed the phone off her desk, and she was about to hit Decline—the last thing she wanted to do was talk to anyone—when she saw that the caller ID said Smith.

The missed call from yesterday. She'd totally forgotten.

She picked up. "Hello?"

"Hello." The woman's voice on the other end was warm and friendly, familiar and completely foreign all at the same time. As though Abby had spoken to her before, but on another planet, or in another life. "I'm trying to reach Abby Zimet?"

"That's me." Abby swallowed. "Is this—Mrs. Smith?"

"Not *Mrs.* anything, no." The woman chuckled. "Please, call me Janet. Though it seems you know me as Marian Love."

Abby held the phone away from her ear, staring at it. The counter on her screen ticked the seconds as they passed in silence.

This couldn't be happening. She must have *actually* lost it.

"Abby?" the warm, familiar voice said, sounding tinny with the phone so far away. "Are you there?"

Abby dove into the blankets on her bed, stifling a scream.

Marian Love was *alive*. Marian Love was *on her phone right now*.

The muffled voice said something she couldn't make out. Abby scrambled to pick up the phone. Her heart felt ready to explode.

"I'm here!" Abby said into the phone, too loud.

"Oh, good, I'm glad. Claire gave me your number, since

I'm back to living in DC these days, though I'm afraid I'm out of town at the moment," the voice on the other end of the phone—Abby still couldn't accept the idea that it was *Marian Love's* voice—said. "You made quite an impression on her. I apologize for all the subterfuge about the rumors of my passing, but, well, it's a long story, and I want to be honest with you. Plus, since you're a writer and I got a lot of help from another writer myself when I was about your age, I'd like to do the same for you if you're interested—"

Someone knocked on Abby's bedroom door.

"Not now!" Abby barked, holding the phone to her chest.

"Sorry, what was that?" the voice in the phone said into Abby's white cotton blouse.

"Sorry!" Abby shoved the phone back up to her ear. "Sorry! I didn't mean you!"

"Is everything all right, Abby?" Marian Love said.

The knocking came again. Why the hell were her parents *seriously* pushing this right now?

Abby stumbled across the room and yanked the door open. "Mom, Dad, whoever, I can't *talk* to you right—"

Ethan was standing in the hallway, biting his lip, his fist raised.

"Abby? Can I come in?"

"Look, I—"

Before she could say anything more her little brother burst into tears. Fierce, shuddering sobs, the same kind Abby had just poured out all over the curb.

For a second all she could do was freeze, watching him. Then, slowly, she raised the phone to her ear.

"I—I'm so sorry." She took a breath, trying to sound measured, and not as though she was freaking out to the depths

of her soul. "I swear, I wouldn't do this if it weren't important, but could I call you back in a few minutes?"

The voice paused, sounding taken aback. "Certainly, Abby.
You can reach me anytime at this number."

"I will. Thank you, so much."

She clicked off, staring down at Ethan.

She wanted to hate him for taking Marian Love away from
her, but she didn't. She couldn't.

He was her kid brother, and he needed her. Just like he'd
needed her on the playground the day he busted his nose.

Abby needed him, too. The two of them hadn't made this
mess, but they were still stuck in it together.

She pulled him into her room, closed the door behind him
and hugged him tight.

"Hey, hey, I know." She steered him toward the bed without letting go. "I know. I know."

Abby couldn't be sure how long she held him while he
cried. It felt like going back in time—but it also felt like she
finally had a purpose. At last, there was someone she truly
mattered to.

When Ethan finally pulled back, his sobs fading into regular tears with a few hiccups mixed in, he looked younger
than Abby remembered. His eyes were red and puffy, and his
left cheek was imprinted with the crease from the sheets he
must've been lying on in his room.

He didn't look anything like a soon-to-be teenager. He
looked like the bratty little brother who'd made a huge mess
of all the glitter glue Abby had carefully laid out for her ninth
birthday party.

How long had he been lying in his room by himself? All
day? All night, too? With no school to break up the time, it
must've been even worse for him than it was for Abby.

She scooted over on her rumpled comforter. Ethan leaned back against the wall next to her, pulling his knees up to his chin. He was still wearing his old, rumpled pajamas, the black-and-green-plaid ones with a skull and crossbones printed across the chest. The shirtsleeves only came down halfway past his elbows.

Ethan wiped his eyes and leaned forward, tracing a wide circle with his finger on the bedspread. When he finally spoke, she had to lean in close to hear him.

"When did you first know?" he asked.

Abby closed her eyes. Hugging was one thing, but if she had to think about the actual details, she'd probably start bawling again herself. "I—look, I don't want to talk about this."

Her brother nodded without looking at her. He straightened out his legs and started to scoot off the bed, wiping his nose on his shirtsleeve.

"Here." Abby handed him a tissue from the box on her desk, but he ignored her and went on using his shirtsleeve. Ugh. He was so gross.

"Thanks," Ethan mumbled, taking the tissue and blowing his nose in that over-the-top way little kids always did.

"Don't mention it," Abby muttered. But at the same time, his gross nose-blowing triggered something in her mind.

Ethan really *was* a little kid.

A year from now, Abby was supposed to be someplace far away, starting a whole new life. Ethan, though…he still had years and years ahead of him. The better part of a decade, stuck in a family that was only now getting around to admitting it had been screwed up for a long time.

Abby and Ethan were the only two people in this house who didn't want anything to change. They were also the only ones who didn't have a say.

"I think I knew last year," she finally said. "When Mom started going out of town just as often as Dad did. What about you? Was it when he didn't come for Rosh Hashanah?"

Ethan shook his head and wiped his nose again. "It was when we stopped having Tuesday dinners."

"Oh, wow. When was that? Last year?"

"The year before."

Abby had forgotten all about Tuesday dinners.

When she was younger—elementary school, probably—the rule had been that the whole family always had dinner together at least Monday to Wednesday. "We only have to make it to Wednesday," Mom used to say. What with work and school and rehearsals, it was too hard to make sure everyone could be there every single night of the week, but if Monday to Wednesday were covered, Mom counted it as a family-bonding win.

But the older Abby got, the harder it was to stick to the three-nights-a-week plan. She wasn't sure exactly when things changed, but by the time she started middle school, Mom had stopped talking about making it to Wednesday. Family dinners were on Mondays and Tuesdays, end of story.

It didn't seem like a big deal. They had those two days to eat together, and the rest of the week they played it by ear. Some nights everyone was home, some nights they weren't. Either way, everybody ate, and everything was fine as far as Abby could tell.

Now that Ethan had brought it up, though, Abby remembered how things had changed after that. Around the start of her sophomore year, Tuesdays had mostly fallen off the calendar, too. By then, Mom had been promoted to president of the organization where she worked and Dad had started going to New York more often. By the year after that, either Mom or Dad was gone pretty much all the time, which meant Monday dinners were off the table, too.

These days, whoever happened to be home on any given night might eat together, but they also might not. There was always food in the fridge, and Abby had stopped thinking about actually sitting down to dinner a while ago.

What was in New York—or Chicago or Los Angeles or any of the other places her parents were always disappearing to—that was so much better than being here with them, having family dinners?

Was there such a thing as love that made you want to stay with someone forever, outside of all those old-fashioned romantic comedies?

There had to be. Paula and Elaine were nothing like the characters in the cheesy movies, but they'd still lasted, and they'd been up against a lot more than Linh and Abby or Mom and Dad.

"Do you think they were really working on all those trips?" Ethan's words echoed Abby's own thoughts.

"I don't know."

She wished she'd talked more at those family dinners. Instead, most of the time, she'd shrugged and snuck looks at her phone under the table when Mom or Dad asked how her day had been.

Maybe if she'd talked more, they'd have wanted to spend more time at home. Maybe then none of this would be happening.

"Do you think it's because I didn't make the senior tap company?" Ethan's voice broke. "I thought I would, but they took Paul instead, and I know Mom was upset. Maybe next year—"

"No." Abby heard her dad's words, his stupid script, coming out of her mouth. "This isn't our fault, it's theirs. It isn't about anything we did."

That was what people said when something like this happened. It was supposed to make you feel better.

But Ethan still hung his head. Abby knew exactly how hard it was to believe that line.

Maybe with all this finally out in the open, they could all stop lying so much.

She tried to think of what Marian Love would do if she were the one in this position. She certainly wrote about tragedy often enough.

She wrote about what happened after the tragedy, too. She wrote about moving on.

No. Abby rubbed her eyes. It wouldn't help, trying to think of how Marian Love would have done things.

Besides, Abby had been thinking about her all wrong anyway. Marian Love wasn't some divine, all-knowing entity. She was a woman, with a real voice and a real name.

And even Marian couldn't have told her how to make this hurt less for Ethan. Abby was on her own for that. If she could figure out the words that would help him, maybe she could use them on herself, too.

"I've been trying so hard." Ethan sniffed and wiped his nose again. "I thought if I was good—if I got okay grades and stuff—Mom and Dad would want to go back to normal. But I kept messing up. Like with Mr. Salem and that water bottle."

"I know." Suddenly, Abby wished she'd been talking to Ethan about this all along. Of *course* he understood how she'd felt. He was the only one who could. "I mean—I don't think you did anything, but I... I know what you mean."

They sat in silence for a moment.

"What happened anyway?" Abby had to ask. "With the fight you had at school?"

"I don't know." Ethan scrubbed at his eyes with his filthy pajama sleeve. "Michael just said the alien antennae on my recital costume looked like balls. And I said his *face* looked like balls, and then he shoved me. Or maybe… I shoved him. I can't even remember how it started, but either way I—I lost it. I don't really know what happened after that."

Abby nodded. It sounded a lot like how she'd felt on the train with Linh on Saturday. "I get it. The losing it part, I mean."

"It was like the day I threw the water bottle at Mr. Salem. I knew it was wrong, and I hated that I was even doing it, but it was weird—it didn't feel real. It felt as if I wasn't even in that room at all. Like I was watching it all from above."

Abby nodded again. That was how she'd felt the day before. Maybe other days, too.

Nothing seemed real lately. Nothing except the worlds she read about, and the ones she made up in her head.

"I think…" Abby spoke slowly. "I used to think that if nothing else changed, this wouldn't happen. That if I didn't do my college applications—maybe even if I didn't graduate at all—I wouldn't have to go away next year. Everything could stay the way it was, forever."

Ethan didn't say anything, but he'd turned to watch her. His eyes were wide, his skin blotchy.

"I thought if I didn't leave, they wouldn't, either." Abby met his gaze, even though it only made her want to cry again. "I thought—if I could just get together with Linh again—if everything could just stay exactly the same as it's always been… maybe then, things would be normal. Only it didn't work."

"I don't think anything ever *was* normal," Ethan said.

Huh. Since when did her kid brother start sounding so profound?

"Even if it was, you can't just make things stay the same as they used to be." Abby shook her head. "We're supposed to be going forward. I guess that means we get to start new lives, whether we're ready for it or not."

"I don't think I'm ready."

Ethan's eyes were still wet. He looked calmer, but Abby knew how that kind of calm really felt.

She wrapped her arm around his shoulders, meaning to reassure him. To tell him that whatever happened, it would be all right.

It didn't seem to work. A few minutes later, he started shaking in her arms, fresh tears running down his face. Abby wrapped her arms around him tightly because, sometimes, you just needed someone to hold you.

Maybe sometimes she could be the strong one.

20

Friday, August 12, 1955

Janet watched from the alley until she was sure the house was empty.

Traffic had been light, and her bus had gotten back to Washington earlier than expected. She'd been away for nearly a week, and the sight of her hometown when she first spotted it from the road had felt entirely different than it had all her life.

She couldn't help noticing how tiny the drab government buildings here looked compared to the skyscrapers she'd grown used to in New York. Only the Washington Monument stood soaring into the skyline, as though the city was self-conscious of its failures and had tried to make up for them with false grandeur.

Washington did have a better smell, though. There was no mistaking that. In New York, Janet hadn't yet found a city block that didn't carry the same odor of grime and grease.

Here, even in the damp heat of August, she could smell the open sky. It smelled like possibility.

As she'd walked down Pennsylvania Avenue, surrounded by the city smells, Janet had felt that sense of possibility on every side of her. The prickling weight of the future that beckoned.

But it was still the early afternoon, which meant Janet's future was at least a few hours away from truly starting. First, she had to wait until Marie finished work for the day. Janet intended to catch her leaving the office and take her aside to explain why they had to return to New York together right away. It would be tricky—Janet would have to make sure no one at the State Department saw her lurking outside, and she'd have to find a nearby place where she and Marie could talk without being overheard.

And that was assuming Janet could convince Marie to listen to her in the first place. Given how their last conversation had gone, Marie was just as likely to walk away from Janet before she'd even said a word.

It was the reason Janet hadn't tried to call her from New York again. By the time she'd woken up that first morning on Flo's couch, she'd realized it was no use. Her only choice was to talk to Marie, face-to-face, and pray she gave Janet a chance to explain.

Since she had to wait, though, Janet had decided to go to her family's house for a few things. It had turned out she needed more clothes than she'd realized. Flo had helped her get a job working the lunch shift at the diner, where the boss wasn't nearly as horrid as Mr. Pritchard, but the staff there didn't wear uniforms and Janet needed to save every last dime of her tip money for her first month's rent. The new clothes she'd bought her first day in New York already looked worn at the seams.

She hadn't called home again, not since that first night at

the Sheldon. Before she'd hung up with her mother, she'd mumbled something about being home soon. It shamed her to think she'd lied yet again, and it hurt, deeply, that she still didn't know what had happened to her grandmother.

If Grandma was alive, she must've told Mom and Dad the truth. In that case, Janet would no longer be welcome in their home. If she'd died, though, Janet would carry that guilt for the rest of her life.

Maybe it was better not knowing.

Her key still worked in the back door, so that gave her some encouragement. The house was as cold and empty as she'd hoped, but it looked different, somehow. The creaky wooden staircase, the chintz curtains lining every window—it all looked skewed, as though the house had been picked up and set back down again at an awkward angle. There was dust on the kitchen countertops, too, where Janet had never noticed dust before, and dishes in the sink that hadn't been washed. Almost as though no one else had been here in all the time Janet had been gone.

She walked through to the front of the house, trying to make sense of the disarray—were her parents spending all their time at the hospital with Grandma? Or had they been busy with funeral arrangements?—when she spotted it.

The pile of mail by the entry table was high and jumbled, as if someone had been taking the mail out of the box and simply tossing it onto the table without looking at it. Off to one side was a package wrapped in brown paper, with Janet's name typed across the front.

The return address read Bannon Press.

Janet blinked down at it three times in case she'd made a mistake. The package was the exact size, the exact thickness, as the brown parcel she'd carried to the post office the month before.

The FBI hadn't found her manuscript after all. Nathan Levy had.

When the rapping noise came behind her Janet whipped around, trying desperately to think of a lie, before she realized her parents wouldn't be knocking on the door. They'd have used their keys.

But who was knocking so sharply in the middle of the afternoon? All Janet could see was a heavy shadow through the curtain that covered the glass window.

Anyone could be on the other side of that door. Including the FBI. Janet hadn't seen anyone watching the house when she'd come through the alley, but what if someone had been watching *her*?

She was backing away, willing the wooden boards behind her not to creak, when she heard the voice calling softly through the glass.

"Janet? Are you home?"

It was Marie. God be praised, it was *Marie*.

Janet lunged at the door, twisting the lock and jerking it open. Her heart leaped into her throat, and she wanted to shout.

I love you! I love you, I love you, I love you! Come back to me!

But when she pulled open the door and got a look at Marie, her mouth fell closed.

Marie looked terrible. She was dressed for work in the same neat blue suit she'd worn to dinner with Janet on that first night at Meaker's, with a shiny new brooch fastened to the collar, but the jacket was damp around the armpits, and her makeup was streaked with tears behind her glasses. Her hair, usually so neatly pinned, was mussed, with loose strands blowing in the breeze. Her purse was tossed over her arm, and she was holding a small cardboard box. Janet could see a comb and a single floppy carnation poking out of the top.

"You're here," Marie whispered. "Good. I need to tell you something."

"Of course." Janet stepped back, holding the door wide. She longed to reach out a hand to touch Marie, but something made her hesitate. "Please, come in."

Marie stumbled as she stepped inside, and Janet noticed for the first time that one of her high heels had broken off, as though she'd run all the way from Foggy Bottom.

"Where can we talk?" Marie was still whispering as Janet shut the door behind her, even though it must've been obvious they were alone in the darkened house.

Janet spread out her hands. "Here. My father's at work, and I can't imagine from the look of this place that Mom will be home anytime soon."

"The neighbors, though…" Marie glanced from side to side at the thin brick walls. "Let's go to the attic."

"The attic?" Janet swallowed. The last time she'd been in the attic, she'd burned the remains of her manuscript and listened to Grandma speak what might've been her final words. "Can't we stay down here? There's something I need to tell you, too. Several things, in fact."

"No, we can't." Marie pushed past her toward the staircase, still cradling that fragile cardboard box. Janet had no choice but to follow.

When they reached the second floor, Marie wasn't certain how to reach the attic and Janet was forced to take the lead. As they climbed the rickety stairs, the clack of Marie's single high heel on the wooden steps behind her brought forth an ache of memories. It was all Janet could do not to reach back and grasp Marie's fingers with her own.

By tomorrow, if everything went as she prayed it would, they'd no longer have to think about the risk of being heard or seen, not indoors. Starting tomorrow, Janet and Marie could be their true selves. Together.

When they reached the impossibly stuffy attic room Janet went straight to the windows and threw them open, then switched on the fan to cover the sound of their voices. When she turned back, Marie was setting her little box down on the table and eyeing the dusty typewriter beside it.

All summer, this room had been about fiction. Fantasy. Now, though, at the sight of Marie—the real, live girl who'd swept Janet off her feet—all she wanted to do was close the distance between them and take Marie into her arms.

There was something else she should do first, though.

"Have you heard anything about my grandmother?" Janet had to ask, even if she didn't want to know the answer.

"You haven't heard?"

"I've been in New York until today."

Marie's damp eyes widened. "Oh, I see. Well, Mom told me your grandmother's still in the hospital. She's awake, but she's very weak. The doctors hope she'll be able to return home, in time."

Janet nodded. She was grateful, immensely grateful. But this meant she'd need to make absolutely certain she was gone before her parents returned.

She had to withdraw from this family forever. It was the only way any of them would be able to go on.

"I have good news." Janet felt around for the package, only just realizing she'd left it on the entry table. "The publisher sent back my manuscript. The FBI couldn't have seen it after all. We're safe at last."

Marie reached into her cardboard box, pulled out a cigarette packet and slit the cellophane wrapper. She didn't look as relieved as Janet had expected. "Safe," she repeated.

"Yes."

Janet longed to take Marie's hand. She longed to kiss her.

Most of all, she longed to tell Marie everything she felt for her. Yet some unspoken tension between them pulled her back.

"The men at your office will have no reason to think you're guilty of anything." Janet's hands trembled as she stared into Marie's watery brown eyes. "Even if they did, we can fight back. If they tried to fire you, we could appeal it. I went to the library in New York and read all about it. There's a process built into the government personnel system for exactly this purpose—unjust termination. All we have to do is fill out the right forms. Except..." Janet took in a long breath, steadying herself before she said the words that mattered most. "Marie, you should quit your job in any case, and come to New York with me instead."

Marie didn't answer. Instead, she walked over to gaze out the window. Her silence was unnerving.

"You'll love the city." Janet was talking faster, the words spilling out, trying to fill the emptiness between them. She hadn't thought Marie would agree right away, but she'd expected her to say *something*. "There are so many people like us. You wouldn't believe it."

Marie just went on staring out the window. "Like us?"

"You know." The memory of her nights with Claire and Flo and her other new friends surged bright and vivid in Janet's mind. "Other girls. There's a place called the Sheldon

Lounge. I hadn't even been certain such places were real, but they are, and it's glorious, Marie. I'll introduce you to the girls, and we can—"

"*No.*" Marie turned around so fast Janet flinched. "I can't go anywhere like that."

"I understand that you're worried, but no one would know us there. All you have to do is quit your job, and we can—"

"I quit." Marie thrust a careless arm behind her toward the cardboard box on the table. "Those are my things."

"You already quit? *Today?*" Janet felt a surge of joy, though it was tempered by the tears still visible in Marie's eyes. "Well—that's good, isn't it? You won't have to worry about them finding out anymore."

"They *did* find out." Marie shook her head. "Or if they haven't yet, they would've soon enough."

"I—I don't understand." Janet wrung her hands. She hated feeling so lost.

"They called me into this tiny room." Marie shifted her gaze away from Janet's to stare out the window once more. There was a fierce gleam in her eyes. "There were three men sitting across the table from me. They made me take an oath, and then they asked if I'd ever had contact with…" She stopped.

"With me?" Janet understood, now, why Marie had been crying. She suddenly wanted to cry herself.

"No." Marie turned back, an unlit cigarette clenched between her fingers. Behind her, the golden afternoon sunlight shone brilliantly through the attic window. "With any—*homosexuals.*"

"Oh, no." Janet couldn't contain her shudder.

"They said the news about Mr. Harris cast suspicion on me. Then they said another typist in our department, a girl

I'd been seen with in the cafeteria—Bertha's her name—had confessed that she'd gone to meetings. I told them I didn't know anything about that, that I'd barely even spoken to Bertha, but they didn't believe me."

"What meetings?" Janet had never heard of lesbians going to meetings.

"You know. *Meetings.*"

Marie emphasized the word until Janet understood.

She'd heard Dad talk about "meetings" in that tone before. She'd heard Senator McCarthy do it, too, on television.

Bertha wasn't a lesbian. She was a Communist.

"Is she actually..." Janet couldn't say the word out loud.

Marie threw a hand up into the air. "Oh, what does it matter?"

It matters a lot, Janet thought, but she knew what Marie meant. "Well—but then, you should be safe. Bertha must've been the typist they were after, not you."

"That wasn't all they said." Marie turned her gaze to the floor. "They also said they'd had reports that my—that my *voice* was too low. That I didn't talk like a normal girl."

"Your voice?" Janet was more lost than ever. "Your voice is beautiful. It isn't low, it's perfectly normal—"

Even as she spoke, Janet heard the absurdity of her words.

The State Department had received reports that Marie's *voice* was too low? What could that possibly have to do with *anything*? Who would have told them that, and why would the government investigate such "reports"?

Janet tried to imagine how it would have felt to sit in that narrow room, hearing those questions. How Marie must have tried so hard not to flinch. How she would've done anything to keep from crying where the men interrogating her could see.

But she'd endured it, somehow. Marie was stronger than Janet had ever realized.

"They already knew the truth. Whether because someone saw us, or because they tapped my phone, or something else—I'm certain they knew." Marie finally met her eyes. Janet could see the blame there. Or maybe it was simply sadness. "No one's safe. Carol was there, too. I saw her when I was going in, and I spoke to her later, outside, when I was leaving with my things. She was leaving with a box of her own, and she wanted to make sure I hadn't given them her name. She's worried about something happening to Mitch's job at the hospital."

Janet's hand flew to her mouth. Carol had thought she was safe. That was what she'd said.

It wasn't fair. It wasn't *fair*.

"Do you think Mitch will be all right?" she whispered.

"It seems she is for now, at least. I promised Carol I hadn't said anything about her, and she said she didn't give them my name, either. She thinks it all comes down to that fellow she used to work with in the cafeteria, but I'm not so sure. It could've been anyone. They asked me for names, again and again, of anyone I knew to be homosexual, or anyone I even suspected, until I finally told them I'd quit. After that they had no choice but to let me leave."

Janet took a half step toward her. The urge to reach out was more than she could bear. "I'm so sorry, Marie."

"I'm only praying that since I quit, rather than being fired, no one else will find out what happened." Marie jerked a stray lock of hair behind her ear. "Still, as far as I can tell it doesn't matter what you say or don't say. There's nothing they don't know."

A sob began to form in Janet's throat.

"They can't do this." Janet wished she were still a child so she could stomp her foot. "Not to you, not to Carol, not to anyone. Not even that man from the cafeteria, whether he gave them names or not. It isn't *right!*"

"Of course they can do it." Marie met Janet's eyes again. "You heard what Carol said. This has been going on for years."

"No! They can't fire *every single person* who's like us!" Janet pictured all those girls at the Sheldon. So many more than she'd ever imagined.

If they worked together, there must be some way they could fight back. Surely things couldn't go on this way *forever.*

"Yes, they can." Marie shook her head softly. "Filling out some appeal form isn't going to change anything. This has gone way too far for that."

"You have to at least *try.*" Janet shook her head, too. Giving up in the face of such horror was too awful to contemplate. "Even if they don't grant the appeal, we can look for other people in the same situation. We can start with Mitch and Carol and their friends. We can all go to the White House and take the appeal forms to the president himself. The sorts of demonstrations my grandmother used to be part of aren't really done anymore, but perhaps we could call that *Post* columnist who wrote about Senator Hunt's son, and—"

"I can't talk to a newspaper." Marie brushed at her eye, the unlit cigarette still hanging from her hand. She stepped closer, until she was so near Janet could see through her thin layer of streaked makeup to the warm, golden skin beneath. "Not if I ever want to live a normal life."

Janet stared at her. "What normal life?"

"Harold's given me his pin." Marie fingered the brooch on her collar. It was gold, with tiny stones around the edges and strange markings carved into its center. Her words were coming out more smoothly now. She was using her secretary voice. "I'd been thinking of moving to Hanover in the fall. That's where Dartmouth is, you know."

"New Hampshire."

"Yes." Marie still wouldn't look at her. "Now I suppose I'll have to go up for certain. Harold's mother—she's very kind, you'd like her—she knows of a family there who's looking for a nanny. I can live with them for the time being, until Harold and I make our plans."

"Don't do this." Janet wanted to tear the brooch from Marie's collar. To toss it out the window into the same breeze that had claimed her blackened pages. "There's another choice. You already left your job—there's nothing to tie us here any longer. If we start driving now, we'll be in New York in time to make it to the Sheldon before it closes. We can start a whole new life."

"That kind of life isn't for me, Janet."

Marie's eyes had lost their blazing look. Janet knew she was speaking the truth.

She thought again of the faceless man she'd once imagined herself marrying. She could barely envision that future anymore. She'd thought it must be the same for Marie.

She'd been wrong.

Janet's legs felt wobbly. She dropped down onto the stiff wooden trunk, in the same spot where she'd crouched when she struck her first match the week before. Marie moved toward her, her heel thumping on the splintered wood.

"Being with you was a dream." Marie knelt in front of her. Janet forced herself to breathe. In, out. In, out. "It was a perfect dream. The best I've ever had. But it could never have been more."

Marie was talking as though there was no discussion to be had. As though it had always been over and done, even before it had truly started.

Janet scrubbed at the tears in her eyes. They hadn't been careful enough. *She* hadn't been careful enough.

There had to be something she could do to help. Some way she could ensure Marie's safety.

"I can only pray that whatever they've found won't follow me to Hanover." Marie turned her gaze back to the cigarette still clutched in her hand. "If Harold's family found out, they'd want nothing to do with me. And as for *my* family, *my* parents—this might be my only chance."

"Will you be happy there?" Janet whispered, then added—perhaps more importantly—"Do you love him?"

"It isn't about that." Marie barked out a humorless laugh. "There's more to life than silly, childish notions of romance."

Janet choked. Was that all she was to Marie?

"That's just it." Janet stuttered on the words. "You and me—we make each other happy. *That* can be enough. Maybe the rest of the world doesn't understand, but if we can only get away—"

"You talk about the rest of the world as though it's some small thing." Marie's shoulders quivered. "I can't give up everything. My family, my life—my future. I don't want to spend my days lying to everyone."

Janet nodded, slowly.

She'd been lying all summer. She'd hated it, but she'd wanted to be her true self. If that meant lying, well, that was the price she'd pay until lying was no longer necessary.

If this were one of the books Claire had given her, Janet would have the perfect words for this moment. She'd know exactly how to make Marie understand what they had to do.

But this wasn't a book. This was Marie, carefully wiping the makeup stains from her face and straightening out her pretty blue suit.

The brooch on her collar caught Janet's eye. Harold had marked Marie as his property, and she'd let him. She'd welcomed it.

They all had to give up something. That was the unspoken truth of all those girls she'd met in New York. It was the truth for Elaine and Paula, too, but sacrifices were easier in fiction.

It took so much courage to do what Marie was doing. To leave everything she cared about, everything she'd dreamed of, behind. To set out on a new, entirely unfamiliar life.

"But you can't ever tell anyone about any of this." Marie's voice had grown heavy and serious. "That's why I came straight here from the office. I need you to promise me, Janet. As long as you live, you must never tell anyone."

"Never," Janet promised. A new plan began to bloom in her mind. "I'll get another bus back to New York, tonight. I should have enough money saved for a ticket. That way, if anyone comes trying to find out more about you, I'll be long gone."

Marie sucked in a breath. "For how long?"

"For good." Janet looked away. The fear in Marie's eyes was almost more than she could bear. "I never would've come back at all if it hadn't been for you. There's nothing else for me here. Even if my parents don't send me to St. Elizabeths, they'll never let me truly live."

Marie held her gaze for a long moment. She didn't try to argue, and Janet was more grateful for that than she could ever say.

Marie knew her better than anyone. And after today, they'd never see each other again.

"I can't let anyone—not you, and not my parents, either—get in trouble because of me." Janet thought quickly. "I'll tell that publisher to forget he ever heard my name. Although, come to think of it, that may not be enough—he could still write to me here again. Maybe I could find a way to make him believe I've left here forever. Or even…perhaps I could make him think I've died."

"Died?" Marie's face colored. "Janet, please, don't—"

"I think I have to—it's the safest way. Besides, it'll only be a story." A light had switched on in Janet's mind. The pieces of the plan fell together neatly as she spoke. "If Mr. Levy thinks I'm dead, he'll have his secretary record that in his files, and the investigators won't be able to trace me. There'll be nothing to connect a dead girl with a common name in some old file to you. Besides, you'll be hundreds of miles away in any case."

"You're certain this is what you want?" Marie still sounded anxious, but Janet could see she understood. This plan was the only one that made sense. Besides, it was a relief, in a way. Janet would truly be leaving her old life behind.

"I'm certain." Janet would need help, of course—but Claire, surely, could help her write letters once she'd arrived in New York. Janet trusted Claire with all her heart. The other girls she'd met at the Sheldon already knew her as Janet, but she could begin calling herself by a different surname.

Smith, perhaps. Janet Smith.

She smiled up at Marie, though she didn't dare tell her this part of the plan. *Smith* was such a common name it would go unnoticed by everyone she met, but it would also become Marie's name when she married. To call herself by the same name would be a small but powerful way of connecting her to Marie forever.

"All right." Marie nodded, once. Janet nodded back.

There was nothing more to be said.

Janet led the way down the narrow, rickety stairs. Marie stumbled on her uneven heels, and Janet reached back to steady her. It was the last time they would touch.

She didn't look back as they descended to the first floor. She didn't meet Marie's eyes as she opened the back door, either. Only when Marie was walking away into the hot summer afternoon did Janet allow her eyes to linger on her slumped shoulders in that sweaty, powder-blue suit.

I love you. Janet sent the thought out into the empty, quiet air.

When she turned back and crossed to the front door, something caught on Janet's slacks. Only then did she remember the brown package on the entry table.

Slowly, she lifted the parcel and ripped the seal. A thick stack of pages fell out. On top was a typed letter.

Dear Miss Jones,

Thank you for submitting your partial manuscript to Bannon Press. Mr. Levy has just finished reading it, and he requested that I contact you, though our office does not respond to every submission we receive from previously unpublished authors.

Mr. Levy informed me that he enjoyed your pages a great deal, and that they speak to your promise as a writer. He recommends that you take the kernel of a story you have here with Elaine and Paula and write a new version that's bolder in its approach, truly exploring the world of these

characters beyond their inner lives and physicality. Mr.
Levy recommended considering several questions as you
write, including: What is their broader community like? What
obstacles do they face in society as well as within their
budding relationship? Et cetera.

I've enclosed your pages, where Mr. Levy marked additional
notes on some passages.

We hope you'll submit your revised manuscript at your
earliest opportunity.

Yours truly,
Sally Johnson,
assistant to Nathan Levy, editor-in-chief

Bannon Press
54 W 23rd St., 17th floor
New York, NY 10011

Beneath the letter was the original manuscript Janet had put
in the mail. All hundred and eight pages, with pencil marks
in the margins. Scribbled notes that said things like "Good
description" and "Need more detail here."

Janet had set Elaine and Paula free into the world, and
they'd come right back to her.

Tears swam in Janet's eyes as she gazed down at those five
chapters. She'd have to rewrite them completely. She'd lost
all the pages she'd written since she'd put that first half in
the mail, too, but that was all right. She'd only just begun to
understand how to tell Paula and Elaine's story.

They weren't the girls she'd thought they were all those weeks ago. Paula wasn't the exalted, flawless creature she'd first imagined, and Elaine wasn't such an innocent herself, either. They'd both already survived heartbreak.

In the next draft, both of them would make mistakes, but they'd each show their true strength, too. Not a single choice either of them made would be easy. It took tremendous courage to give up the life you'd known, no matter which path you chose. Janet hadn't understood that until today.

Tears flowed down her face, but her fingers itched for her typewriter. She'd have to write in the library in New York until she'd saved up enough to buy a machine secondhand. She'd need a pen name, too—*Janet Smith* was too close to her real name.

But the novel itself was already taking shape in her mind. Paula and Elaine's story was a story about love. It was about a girl who was certain of what she wanted, until it turned out she wasn't certain at all. It was about a girl who was afraid, terribly afraid, but who still knew who she was. It was about a pair of girls, still young, with no choice but to separate from the families who could never accept them.

She'd planned for Wayne to ruin the characters' happiness, but Janet saw now that their problems weren't all about one man. Paula and Elaine were up against an entire world, but they would prevail. Because they had each other.

Their story was about two women who refused to back down. Who fought back, no matter what the world put in their path. She'd leave the conclusion open for the reader to decide where Elaine and Paula's paths led them in the end, but both girls would live to face the future—Janet would make that much clear.

The first line of the book would be different, too. Bolder. The words took shape in her mind even as the sobs still choked her throat.

Elaine had already had her heart broken once. From now on, she was keeping it wrapped up in cellophane.

Janet felt the pieces of the new story sliding into place as she climbed the stairs to pack her clothes. She could see it all so vividly Paula might as well have been standing right in front of her, a cigarette dangling from her hand and a fierce expression on her face.

And suddenly, Janet knew *her* name, too. The one she would put on the cover of her book, if she was lucky enough to have a cover someday.

Her new name would have its own power. It would reflect everything she'd learned so far, and her dreams for the future, too. It would come from the love and heartbreak she'd known and the tears that still flowed down her cheeks.

She would become Marian Love.

21

Saturday, November 4, 2017

The real Marian Love looked nothing like Paula.

Not as far as Abby could tell anyway. Marian was supposed to be somewhere in the same building she was, and though Abby had scanned the crowd at least a dozen times, there was no one who remotely resembled a glamorous 1950s lesbian. Not a single person out of the hundred or so huddled around their canvassing scripts was smoking a cigarette or wearing a pencil skirt.

"Okay, my turn." Linh hid her script behind her back and turned to Ethan, pasting on her thousand-watt smile and pantomiming knocking on a door.

Ethan pretended to open it. The campaign office around them buzzed with other practicing volunteers, so he had to raise his voice. "Hello?"

"Hi!" Linh chirped. "My name is Linh and I'm a volunteer with the Danica Roem campaign. We're talking with your neighbors today about the election for the state legislature, and we wanted to learn your thoughts and feelings about the race. Have you heard of Danica Roem, running for state delegate?"

"Yep." Ethan bobbed his head. "She's the trans lady, right?"

"Dude, no one's going to say that," Vanessa interrupted. "At least, not in those words."

"Okay, but if someone *does* say that, we just say yes, right?" Linh asked. "Then pivot to talking about Route 28?"

Savannah and Ben flipped through the handouts the campaign staff had given them. "Exactly," Ben said, reading off the page. "You say, 'Yes, that's her! You've probably heard Danica has taken a strong stance on Route 28. On a scale from zero to ten, how important is fixing the traffic here in Manassas to you?'"

"Is anyone actually going to believe we know anything about the traffic in Manassas?" Abby cut in. "Most of us can't even drive."

"True," Ben said. "Plus, no offense, Ethan, because I'm really and truly psyched to go knock on doors with you, but, well—you look about eight. You're not much of a poster boy for talking about road rage."

"I don't look *eight*!" Ethan stuck out his tongue, which didn't exactly make him look more mature. "Abby, tell him!"

"Yeah. Come on, he looks at least nine." Abby grinned down at him, and Ethan stuck his tongue out again.

She knew she was supposed to be focusing on these practice sessions along with everyone else, but the idea that Marian Love—well, Janet Smith—was somewhere in this room was making it incredibly hard. Abby had never volunteered for a political campaign before, and she needed this training badly. Virginia's election was coming up on Tuesday, and if enough Democrats won here, it would prove that change really was possible everywhere. So the GSA had driven down to Manassas to volunteer with Danica Roem's campaign, going door-to-door reminding people to vote.

"Well, that's why we're *practicing*," Savannah told them. "We need to make it sound as if we drive on Route 28 every day."

"No, we don't." Vanessa sighed. "We aren't supposed to lie to people. We can just talk about how Danica's mom got stuck in traffic trying to pick her up from school when she was a kid."

While the others went through another practice round, Abby scanned the crowd again. She didn't know how she was supposed to recognize Marian Love in this throng of excited, nervous people. There were plenty of older women in the group, and a lot of them were wearing rainbow accessories and T-shirts that said things like United Against Hate and This Is What a Queer Feminist Looks Like, but none of them also had buttons that said I Am a World-Famous Lesbian Pulp Author.

Even so, Marian Love was here, somewhere. Abby only had to find her.

She still couldn't believe she was this close. She'd been obsessing about this moment for weeks.

At first, though, Abby had been too terrified to call her back. In the end, she'd only done it because Ms. Sloane made her.

The morning after she and Ethan talked, Abby had woken up so early it was still dark out. There was no way she was going to fall back asleep, so she'd taken a long shower, gotten dressed and walked to campus as the sun was rising. When she got there, the building was deserted except for the early-morning cleaning crew, but when she got to Ms. Sloane's classroom, she found her teacher sitting with a laptop open on her desk.

"Good morning, Abby," Ms. Sloane had said, as though nothing about the moment was unusual.

"Um," Abby had said. "Hi."

She sat down at the long table and took out her own laptop. She'd meant to write, or maybe play more solitaire.

Instead she heard herself say, "Um. Is it all right if I tell you something?"

Ms. Sloane closed her laptop and looked right at her. "Of course."

And suddenly Abby was telling her *everything*.

About her parents, and her brother. About Linh. About college, and how she couldn't bear to even look at an application.

She told Ms. Sloane about her book, and how for weeks she'd been unable to focus on anything but the stories in her mind. And about Marian Love, and how desperate she'd been to track her down.

"I don't even know why." Abby's throat felt sore from talking so much. "It's as if—if I can just figure out this *one* thing, then maybe the rest of my life won't be…the way it's been. It's dumb."

"It's not dumb at all." Ms. Sloane hadn't looked away from Abby once the whole time she'd been talking. "I'm so sorry you've been going through this, Abby. You've been having an absolutely horrible year."

"It's not that—" Abby started to say. Then she stopped.

It really *had* been an absolutely horrible year.

Hearing it said out loud—hearing *another person* say it…it made something snap in her brain. Abby swallowed once, then again, to keep herself from bursting into fresh tears.

"Also, you won't believe this." Abby pushed up her glasses

on her nose and took out her phone, eager to change the subject. "She called me. Marian Love. I mean, Janet Smith—apparently that's her real name. She's alive after all, and I guess the other author I talked to must've given her my number, because she called me yesterday. But I couldn't talk then, because of all this, and now I don't know what to do."

Ms. Sloane's eyebrows shot up. "You're sure this phone call was genuine?"

"I think so." Abby explained about meeting with Claire Singer in Philadelphia.

"You're saying Marian Love is alive? And you *found* her?" Ms. Sloane's eyebrows climbed even higher. Abby couldn't remember if she'd ever seen a teacher look so genuinely thrilled. "Do you realize how significant this is?"

"I said I'd call her back, but I don't know what to say." Abby fixed her gaze on the early-morning light shining through the high, narrow classroom windows. "She's *Marian Love*. She's famous. She shouldn't be spending her time talking to someone like me. All I ever do is mess things up."

"Abby, if you don't call her back, you'll spend years regretting it." The words were stern, but Ms. Sloane's smile was tender. "I'll help you write down what to say. That sometimes makes it easier for me when I need to talk about something difficult."

So they spent the rest of the morning until the first period bell writing a script. And at lunch, Abby came back to the classroom and called Marian Love.

Her blood was pumping so loud she could hear it in her ears. Still, Abby forced herself to read the script, and Janet Smith turned out to be astonishingly nice. She didn't seem surprised that Abby was nervous, and she said thank you a bunch of times when Abby stuttered out that *Women of the*

Twilight Realm was the best book she'd ever read. Then she told Abby that she was in Alabama for the next few weeks volunteering on the Senate race, and that she was going to be working on campaigns in Virginia once she left there, but she wanted to find a time for them to meet after the election. They'd traded email addresses. Janet even said she wanted to read Abby's manuscript.

Since then, Abby had reread *Women of the Twilight Realm* three more times. She'd deleted a hundred pages from the first draft of Gladys and Henrietta's story, too, and written a hundred new ones. The new pages were nothing like the first draft she'd dashed out, but Ms. Sloane had told her this version was a huge improvement. Abby's characters, she said, had finally started growing and changing. The book had a story now, not just a plot.

Plus, she'd managed to catch up on most of the homework she'd missed. Ms. Taylor had given her until the end of the semester to finish everything, and Ms. Sloane had sat down with Abby to write out deadlines for every assignment she'd missed. They met once a week to talk it through, which was strangely helpful. Ms. Sloane must've said something to her other teachers, too, because they'd started calling on Abby in class again, though she noticed they asked her easier questions than usual.

And she'd started walking to and from school with Ethan again. Sometimes they spent the trip talking about Mom and Dad and what was going to happen next, but mostly they just talked about French class, or told each other funny stories from school that day, or made plans to binge-watch a show together.

When they got home, they sat at the kitchen table and did their homework. Sometimes Abby even helped Ethan with his algebra, which she was surprised to realize she remembered pretty well. Then when Mom got home from work she made dinner and the three of them all talked together.

It was kind of nice having family dinners again, even though the family was different now. Plus, Mom was talking about getting a kitten. Abby hadn't admitted it, but she couldn't wait.

They were already used to only one parent being home at a time. Even so, it felt different knowing Dad didn't live there anymore. They'd be going to his new apartment for the first time soon, and Abby was dreading it, but Ethan kept talking about the stuff he wanted to get for his new room. He wanted to paint a mural on the wall showing a UFO flying over the Washington Monument. Abby had told him to go for it. If there was ever a time in their lives when their parents would allow an alien mural to be painted on a bedroom wall, it was right now.

Abby didn't have any plans for *her* new room, but maybe she should make some. Pretending none of this was happening hadn't exactly worked for her so far.

Maybe she should order one of those *Women of the Twilight Realm* posters for her wall. Then next year, when she came back from college for visits, Paula and Elaine would be there waiting for her. She could gaze up at them on the wall if she ever needed a reminder that committed relationships were a real thing.

"Okay, folks," said a short guy with a red crew cut and square glasses who'd climbed onto a table at the front of the room. "Now that you've practiced, we're going to divide you into teams to go out into the precincts. Is everybody fired up?"

"Ready to go!" shouted an older woman in a rainbow scarf

at the front of the crowd. Everyone laughed, and then they all joined in, chanting.

"Fired up!"

"Ready to go!"

"Fired up!"

"Ready to go!"

"Fired up!"

The chant rolled over Abby, filling her ears. She closed her eyes and soaked it in. "Ready to go!"

It was because of Janet Smith that she was in this room. Well, her and Vanessa. Abby had told her friends about Janet's phone call and lamented that they couldn't meet in person until after Election Day. Vanessa had pointed out that they should really be volunteering in the Virginia election, too, and that Danica Roem's district was only a short drive from DC. Danica was the first openly trans candidate to run for the Virginia legislature, and she was running against a self-described homophobe who'd made his name supporting anti-trans legislation. Plus, hardly anyone in his district even seemed to like him, so Danica had a real chance to win. It was the most exciting race they could've imagined volunteering for.

The next thing Abby knew, she and Vanessa were recruiting the entire GSA to carpool down to Manassas the Saturday before Election Day, and Abby was nervously emailing Janet to ask if by any chance she'd be volunteering for the Roem campaign that weekend. To her surprise, Janet had replied right away. She said she'd been planning to canvass in that district sometime soon, and that she'd gather up some friends and meet Abby in the campaign office during the training session.

When Abby told Mom about the plan over dinner one

night, she'd half expected her to say no, given that the last time Abby had left town she'd lied and stolen a credit card, but Mom only thought about it for a few minutes before she agreed. Her sole stipulation was that Abby ride down with Ms. Sloane, who was coming along as a faculty chaperone.

That was when Ethan announced that he wanted to volunteer, too. There was a time when Abby would've groaned about her kid brother tagging along, but this time she just grinned.

After all that, she'd been sure she'd recognize Janet as soon as they entered the campaign office. But the room had been too packed to move around much, and there was so much to do between reading the scripts and filling out forms that Abby hadn't found her yet. She could only hope Janet might notice her. Abby had told her she'd be wearing her Equality Is Power shirt and a plaid skirt.

"Last round!" the campaign worker shouted. *"Fired up!"*
"Ready to go!"

"All right! See you when we break at six, everybody!"

As the chanting faded out, organizers started moving through the crowd. Abby and her friends got assigned to a group, and as they all started shuffling toward the door a familiar voice sounded over her shoulder.

"Hello there! Are you Abby Zimet?"

Abby caught her breath.

It was the older woman who'd started the chanting. She had gray hair, thick glasses and a stoop in her step, and she was dressed in comfortable-looking blue pants and a saggy flower-print shirt with a rainbow scarf tied around her neck.

She didn't look anything like the woman Abby had pictured. She didn't seem particularly glamorous, and she obviously wasn't holding a martini glass or sitting at a typewriter.

Still, Abby knew that voice. She knew that solid, steady look in her eyes, too, somehow.

"Are you Marian Love?"

Abby's voice broke. Suddenly, she wanted to cry again.

The woman's smile widened. "Yes, but please call me Janet. It's so lovely to meet you, Abby. Come on over here and let's—"

"Hey hey! Ho ho! The homophobe has got to go!"

The chanting had started again.

Abby covered her face with her hand. She'd turned bright red, she was positive. Ugh, emotions were the *worst*.

"Ms. Smith?" Ms. Sloane had appeared, suddenly, at Abby's elbow, shouting to be heard over the chant. Most of Abby's friends had been caught up in the throng pushing its way outside, but Ms. Sloane ignored all the jostling and stuck out her hand, business-style. "It's such an honor to meet you. I'm Abby's teacher, Neena Sloane. Do you think we could go somewhere and talk for a few minutes before we all start knocking on doors?"

"Of course." Janet started to say more, but her words were drowned out by the crowd around them.

Abby could still see her friends up ahead. Linh caught her eye, and when Abby nodded, she leaned in to say something to the others. They'd already decided that if Abby found Janet, she'd meet up with the rest of them later.

Being friends with Linh—*real* friends this time, not pining-to-get-back-together "just friends"—was turning out to be pretty great. It was kind of amazing how much you could care about a person even without the romantic part.

Ms. Sloane offered her arm to Janet as they left the building. Abby wished she'd thought to do that. Janet was eighty-one years old, after all. She probably appreciated the help.

"I must say, Ms. Smith," Ms. Sloane was saying as they reached the small park across the street from the campaign office, "I'm an ardent admirer of your work. I first read your book in college, and it had a huge impact on me. For so many other women I've known, too."

Janet thanked her politely, and Abby looked up with interest. She'd assumed Ms. Sloane had never actually read *Women of the Twilight Realm.* In their American lit class, she'd only ever talked about highbrow authors like Emily Dickinson and Toni Morrison and Gabriel García Márquez.

"Well, I'll leave you two to talk." Ms. Sloane glanced down at her phone. "Abby, I know you're planning to meet up with the others, but text me if you need a ride."

"Oh." Abby hadn't realized Ms. Sloane wouldn't be staying with her. "Um, all right."

"Abby, I'm so glad we'll have some time to talk." Janet smiled as Ms. Sloane left, leading Abby to an old sedan parked on the curb down the block. "I brought a few things with me that I thought you might want to see."

"Oh, you didn't have to bring anything!"

"Let's say I wanted to." Janet smiled again and passed her a set of car keys. "Would you be so kind as to get them out of the trunk, please? My back's not what it used to be."

Eager to help, Abby opened the trunk and pulled out the reusable grocery bags Janet pointed to, carrying everything to the nearest park bench. Janet settled down and beckoned for Abby to sit beside her.

"I dug out my old scrapbook." Janet's smile was astonishingly warm. Abby already felt as though she'd known her for years. "Would you like to see it?"

"You have a *scrapbook?*" It had never occurred to Abby that she might see real, physical evidence of Marian Love's life.

She was still getting used to the idea that Marian Love even *had* a life. "That would be beyond fantastic."

Janet reached into the bag and pulled out a thick, old-fashioned photo album, the kind where the pages stuck together, and passed it to Abby. She carefully opened the stiff cover, making sure not to tear anything. The pages were crowded with photos, some in black and white, most in color. There were other things tacked in between the photos, too—Post-its, napkins, even matchbooks.

"Who's in this picture?" Abby pointed to a black-and-white photo that showed a group of people laughing and walking down a city street. From their clothes—badly fitting suits on the men and unfortunate shaggy hair on the women—Abby guessed it was taken in the sixties or seventies. A man at the front of the group looked familiar, and a woman toward the back could've been a younger version of Janet.

"That's me with Harvey Milk." Janet traced her finger along the photo's faded edge. "I hope you've learned about him in school."

"Not really, but I saw the movie." Abby peered closer. "Was this in San Francisco?"

"Oh, yes. I spent a year out there, and I decided to volunteer for his campaign. That's the only photo I have of the both of us, so I treasure it." Janet pointed to another photo higher on the page. "Up there, I'm with Frank Kameny. I don't suppose you would've learned about him, though. He hasn't had a movie yet."

It was another black-and-white photo, showing a picket line. A smiling man held a sign with Gay Is Good written on it in old-fashioned block letters. Next to him, the younger Janet was carrying a sign that said Sexual Preference Is Irrelevant to ANY Employer. The look on her face was fierce.

"I think the historian I met with mentioned him. He was an activist in DC, right?"

"Yes. Frank used to work for the federal government, but they fired him for being gay. He was the first to fight back. That we knew of, anyway." Janet turned the page. "There, that's what you want to see, isn't it? That's an advertisement I saved for *Twilight Realm*. My first ever advertisement of any kind."

"Oh, my gosh." Abby bent down to study the tiny piece of newsprint. It was so old and faded it was barely legible.

"They walked together, into an evil world where no man dared venture," the thick black type read, right next to a tiny image of that gorgeous painted cover. *"The unashamed tale of two girls with twisted desires and a fierce love…for each other. A harrowing tale of modern lesbianism."*

"Why did you tell everyone you were dead?" Abby finally looked up, meeting Janet's eyes. "You could've written so many more books. Didn't you want to keep going?"

"I did keep going." Janet smiled. "Just not in the way I'd once imagined. It was worth it to convince my publisher that Janet Jones—that used to be my name, when I was a child—was no more. I had to do it, to help someone I cared about who was in jeopardy because of me. But it meant I got to start over, too, and it turns out that was exactly what I needed. I stopped being the girl I'd been and started a new life."

"A new life," Abby echoed slowly. She shook her head. "How did you keep people from finding out?"

"Well, it wasn't quite as unusual to change your name in those days. Particularly if you were a lesbian, or some other identity that wasn't the norm." Janet chuckled. "A few of the people I met in New York might have guessed there was something strange going on—I always had a feeling my editor suspected the story Claire gave him didn't quite add up—but no one asked much in the way of questions, and soon, enough time had passed that it hardly mattered. I've been Janet Smith ever since. Except when I'm publishing under another pen name, of course."

Abby turned the pages of the album carefully, studying the photos as she went. Some were so faded they were hard to see clearly, but there were things she recognized. Newspaper cutouts showing the AIDS quilt spread across a field. Black-and-white photos of smiling women marching on the mall with rainbow flags. Color photos of Janet beaming next to a gorgeous drag queen in full regalia. Digital printouts of women in nineties-style grunge gathered around a bar, with Janet right in the center of the group.

"Well, Abby Zimet." Janet smiled and closed the album. "I want to hear more about you. Tell me all about this book you're writing."

"Oh, um. There's not much to say." Now that she was talking to a real writer, Abby hated to think about how bad her first draft of *Totally Normal Women in the Daytime* had been. "I'm rewriting the whole thing."

"Well, there's nothing wrong with that. Why, I rewrote my first book completely. The original draft was utter rubbish. I'd written it in first person, for one thing, which turned out to be all wrong."

Abby leaned forward, fascinated. "You mean *Women of the Twilight Realm?*"

"Yes, though it wasn't called that when I was writing it. It was Nathan who came up with that silly title. When I wrote it, it was called—"

"Alone No Longer?"

"Yes!" Janet slammed both her hands down on her knees,

making Abby laugh. Suddenly Janet didn't seem quite so old. "How on earth did you know that?"

"Er, well." Sheepishly, Abby explained about finding Lawrence Hastings's notes.

"My goodness. The internet really is amazing, isn't it?"

"Have you seen any of the fan sites about you?" Abby reached for her phone to show her.

"Yes, I have." Janet smiled again. "It's lovely of people to do those things. Some of my friends from Strangers showed them to me a few years back."

"Strangers?"

"Yes. I suppose you haven't heard of it." Janet sighed. "It used to be very popular among young lesbians. It was a bar in southeast DC."

"Ohh, I get it. It was called *Strangers*, the same way all the pulp novels used to have *strange* or *twilight* or whatever in their titles."

"That's right. It closed a few years back, I'm sad to say. We tried to save it, but the past few years haven't been kind to lesbian bars."

"Was Strangers around in the fifties?" Abby tried to picture a DC version of those smoky Greenwich Village bars. "Was it like the bar in your book?"

"Oh, no." Janet laughed. "We started Strangers in the seventies. By then the raids were becoming less common, so we could be a bit more open about what sort of place it was."

"*You* started a bar?" It had never occurred to Abby that a writer might also want to be a bartender. Or a bar owner.

"Well, not by myself. I moved back to DC with a few friends I'd made in New York, and we joined up with some women we knew and pooled our money to get it going."

Janet smiled. "Those early years were the best. We had lines waiting down the block nearly every night."

It was surprisingly easy to picture eighty-one-year-old Janet waiting in line to get into a lesbian bar. Abby smiled.

"You said you moved *back* to DC?" she asked. "So you really are from there?"

"Oh, yes. I grew up in Georgetown." Janet gazed off into the trees that lined the park. "That neighborhood was very different then, of course. I moved to New York the summer after I finished high school, though my parents wanted me to go to college. That wasn't so unusual in those days, either, but all the same, my parents were furious when I finally spoke to them about it."

"Wow." Abby couldn't even fathom that. What would *her* parents say? "So *they* didn't think you'd died?"

"Oh, no." Janet seemed startled at the idea. "No, I only concocted that story for my publisher. For the readers, too, I suppose, though I never dreamed at the time that I'd have any. No, all my parents knew was that I'd run away to New York and left behind everything I'd ever known. Which, of course, was still rather alarming in their eyes."

"I'll bet." It all sounded simultaneously thrilling and terrifying to Abby. "Did you know people in New York when you moved there?"

"I'd made some friends." Janet's smile had taken on a faraway quality. "I lived on the tips I made waitressing at first, plus the money Nathan put in my bank account. Of course, the book sold better than I'd ever dreamed, so that changed things for me."

"It's such an incredible book. I've read it a bunch of times."

"Well, that's lovely to hear." Janet's smile softened. "When

I look back on it, though, I can only remember how foolish I was. I'd rewrite the whole thing, given the chance."

"What?" Abby's eyes widened. "But it's perfect!"

Janet laughed. "There's no such thing as a perfect book, and I was only eighteen when I wrote that one. I thought I'd already learned so much, but the truth was, I still had my whole life ahead of me. Of course, I didn't understand that at the time."

Abby wasn't sure she quite understood that, either. "Why didn't you write more books? Was it because that one sold so well?"

Janet chuckled. "Well, no. Remember, paperbacks only went for thirty-five cents in those days. Even with millions of copies in print, it wasn't exactly enough to buy myself a mansion."

"So you just kept waiting tables?" Come to think of it, waiting tables in 1950s Greenwich Village sounded pretty fabulous, too.

"Off and on. But I never stopped writing, either. I used quite a few pseudonyms with several different publishers. I wrote Westerns, science fiction, shoot-'em-ups, that kind of thing. There were dozens of books on my shelf by the time I left the city, but I never wrote another book about lesbians, and I never used the name *Marian Love* again."

"Why not? You were famous!"

"Of a sort, I suppose." Janet laughed. "But Marian Love was a name that only applied to one chapter of my life. That chapter had ended when I moved to New York and started truly living as myself."

Abby sat back, astonished. Janet's life really had been exactly like one of her books.

"Of course, it's all so different for a young woman of your

generation." Janet smiled at her. "If you don't mind my asking, do your parents know you're a lesbian?"

"Oh, yeah. I came out in ninth grade."

Janet shook her head, her smile shifting to a grin. "Hearing things like that never ceases to delight me. I'm so glad
I've lived long enough to see your generation."

Abby grinned back. "I am, too."

"Your friends at school, do they know about you, too?"

"Oh, yeah. Most of my friends are queer. I'm the treasurer
of our Genders and Sexualities Alliance."

"Of course you are." Janet laughed. "How many students
are in your group?"

"Well, if you asked, probably half the school would *say*
they're in it, but we have about twenty who come to the
meetings every week. My friend Vanessa, they're the president. Vanessa's non-binary," Abby added, figuring Janet might
not recognize the pronoun.

"It's quite a world. A wonderful world. I'm so happy for
you all. Now, should we go join our friends and knock on
some doors?"

"Right, of course." Abby switched on her phone. "I'll text
them. We can wait a few minutes first, though, if you want
to rest."

"What, do I look like an old lady to you?" Janet's eyes
flashed with amusement. "I've been pounding the pavement
for liberal politicians since long before you were born, Abby
Zimet, and I assure you, I can knock on doors with the best
of them."

So Abby texted Ms. Sloane, and a moment later she got a
text back promising that one of the drivers would come by in
a few minutes. Janet and Abby had been assigned to different
precincts, so they'd have to split up after that.

"Can I ask you a question?" Abby asked as they waited. "Did Elaine and Paula stay together at the end of the story? Or did Elaine go back to Wayne?"

"I can't believe I named him Wayne." Janet laughed. "Listen to that when you say it out loud. *Elaine* and *Wayne*. Who gives their characters names that rhyme?"

Abby laughed, too. "I never thought about that. I named one of my characters Gladys, though, and that *s* on the end is so annoying when I need to make it possessive."

"The things writers think about." Janet laughed. "Now, as for your question about Paula and Elaine, I'm afraid I don't know the answer. What do you think?"

"Why does it matter what *I* think? I'm not the one who wrote it!"

"Well, after the book ends, it's up to the reader to decide what happens next." Janet gazed toward the other side of the park. A woman knelt by a chain-link fence, trying to strap a squirming toddler into a stroller. "I ended the story the way I did because I wasn't sure what would happen next in the characters' lives, either. I wanted their world to be full of possibility."

"Okay—but did they stay together, though?"

Janet paused and turned to face Abby. "Do *you* think they did?"

"Well…yes. Or, I guess, I wanted them to." Shit, Abby was getting emotional again. "I want them both to have love in their lives."

"Oh, but they would've had love in their lives no matter what." Janet's smile faded slightly, but her eyes were as warm as ever. "There are more ways to love than the burning, passionate kind I wrote about in that book. Though I

suppose I might not have realized that when I was writing."
Janet paused. "I was young and in love then myself after all."

"You were?" Abby smiled. So Marian Love really had been
writing her own life story.

"Oh, yes. I based the character of Paula on her, at first."

Abby wanted to pump her fist—she'd *known* Paula had to
have come from somewhere—but she restrained herself.

"She didn't *look* anything like Paula, of course." Janet
was still gazing off into the park, half smiling. "She never
would've been caught dead in pants."

"Are you talking about Mrs. Smith?" Abby was already
picturing herself meeting the real-life Paula. "Does she live
with you in DC?"

"Ah, no." Janet's eyes slid over to a stone fountain at the
corner of the park. It had been shut down for the winter, and
the pool was already dry, the cracks in the cement glaring
in the sun. "That is, I suppose her name is still Mrs. Smith,
but we aren't together now. We only had that one summer,
in fact. I was heartbroken, of course, and I'm sure that bled
through into my writing. Though I can't be certain, since I
haven't read that book in years."

Abby didn't know what bothered her more—that Janet
and the real-life Paula had only been together for one summer, or that Janet hadn't read *Women of the Twilight Realm* in
years. "You *haven't*?"

"Not since it was first published, I'm afraid." Janet met
Abby's eyes, still half smiling. "You'd be surprised how fast
the memory of your own writing can fade."

"What? It's a classic!"

"You're kind to say so." Janet fingered the plastic covering
on her scrapbook. "But there were simply too many feelings
tangled up in that story for me to return to it. I suppose, at the

time, I couldn't tell my love of writing and my first true love with a girl apart. In the end, writing was the love that lasted."

Abby's mouth dropped open.

She'd been so sure Paula and Elaine were proof that real love existed. But apparently the great, true love Marian Love had written about hadn't been so great and true at all.

They'd only lasted one summer. Even Abby and Linh had lasted longer than *that*.

Did love *ever* last?

"So you just...broke up? After all that?"

"Well, it wasn't quite so simple as breaking up." Janet turned her gaze back to the fountain. "She wanted—well, she wanted to be free of all that being a lesbian entailed, and I certainly couldn't blame her. It was 1955 after all."

"What happened to her?"

Janet pursed her lips. "I didn't see her again for many, many years. Until one afternoon in New York. I was leaving my publisher's office when I spotted a woman in Bloomingdale's, shopping with her children. I wasn't certain it was her at first, and she never looked my way, but later I found a note in my bag. She must have placed it there, though I can't imagine how. She must have learned to be very secretive over the years." Janet paused. She almost looked as though she'd forgotten Abby was there. "The note was an invitation to meet her for a coffee. I thought she might want to reminisce about old times, but that wasn't the case. She only had a minute before she expected her mother-in-law to come looking for her, and she spent that min-ute begging me to promise I'd never say anything to another living soul about what had happened between us. I'd already promised that, years before, but it seemed things had grown especially delicate with her husband's family, and she wanted to be even more certain."

Janet's words trailed off, and she turned down to gaze at her scrapbook. After a quiet moment, she went on. "I suppose that's why I kept up the story about Janet Jones having died, even after all these years. I never tried to correct the record, not even after I heard, many years later, that she and her husband had divorced."

Janet smiled weakly. All Abby could do was shake her head. "Do you think she got divorced because she was gay?"

"If she did, it isn't any of my business. I'd already decided I wasn't going to trouble her again. We both gave up something, in the end." Janet paused, blinking rapidly. "She made the bigger sacrifice, though. It took tremendous strength to do what she did. I only hope she was happy in the end."

An SUV pulled up at the traffic light on the corner. It was probably their ride, but Abby didn't want to stop talking. "When did you move back to DC?"

Janet finally looked up. "Oh, that was many years later, when my father got sick."

"Were things any better by then?"

"Well." Janet paused, but she seemed to understand what Abby meant. "By that point, my parents knew about me. My grandmother had passed away some time before then—she had a health scare when I left home, but she'd recovered from that, though I never saw her again—and I was living with my lover Ed. And there's no need to pull that face, Abby, you've seen enough movies to know we called each other 'lovers' back then."

Abby tried to stop grimacing. She was glad Janet thought she was just reacting to the word, and not to the idea that Marian Love had been with someone else after the real Paula. "Sorry. How long were you and Ed together for?"

The SUV rolled past them. It must not be here for them after all.

"Eight years, give or take," Janet said. "She got married last year, if you can believe that, to another woman we were friends with at that time, Flo. A surprising number of my friends are married, in fact. Though the whole idea of marriage never felt quite right for me."

So Janet had been kind of a serial monogamist. It wasn't what Abby had expected at all.

"So, you were out by then?" Abby asked, trying not to betray her disappointment.

"Well, this was the very early seventies, so it was still a different time. Ed and I didn't hide our relationship, but we didn't talk about it with everyone, either. Certainly not our parents, though I'm quite certain mine had learned the truth much earlier than that, one way or another. Still, it was all very 'don't ask, don't tell,' as people began to say later. But Ed and I were together when we opened Strangers, and a very impressive community grew up around the bar. There was a lot of organizing in those days. Frank and the others had been picketing the White House for some time, trying to put an end to job discrimination. Though it was already too late for many." Janet trailed off, staring into the distance.

"Were you writing then, too?" Abby couldn't imagine doing all those things at the same time.

"The whole time." Janet met her eyes again, smiling for the first time since they'd started talking about all this. "I couldn't have stopped writing if I'd tried. Books, articles, stories. In that era, you had no choice but to pour yourself into a career. Women didn't earn as much as men—we still don't, of course—so if you weren't planning to get married, you had to work much harder than the men did, just to get by. I always knew I'd be writing to live."

"Well, you became a legend in the process." Abby smiled, trying to shake off the nagging feeling that this was all turning out wrong. "The internet's going to go crazy once we tell them who you are."

"Oh, that isn't necessary."

"Don't worry, it'll be easy." Abby reached for her phone. "We can take a selfie right here, and I'll send it to the people who run those fan sites about you tonight. Autostraddle and a bunch of other sites will probably want to interview you, and all the podcasts, too, but I can coordinate with everybody on the internet stuff, so don't worry—"

"Abby." Janet laid a light hand on her arm. "Your heart's in the right place, but that's not what I want. If I'd intended to be famous, I would've done a lot of things differently before now."

"But you already *are* famous!" At that, a new idea popped into Abby's head. "You know what you should do? You should write a book about your life! People will go crazy for it. You've done so much—just look at all these photos, all the books you've written—"

"Marian Love is the famous one, not me." Janet's voice was gentle, but firm. Abby felt defeat setting in. "I told you, that chapter closed a long time ago. Marian's life was over as soon as her book was published, and the rest of *my* life finally began."

Abby had never imagined she'd disagree with Marian Love about anything.

"It's been a great pleasure meeting you, my dear." Janet clasped her hand fiercely. "Please, send me your book when you have it ready. I'd love to read it."

A station wagon pulled up in front of them. There was a middle-aged woman in the driver's seat, and Linh was sitting next to her, waving. Abby stood up, holding out a hand to help Janet. "This is our ride, unfortunately."

"It's not unfortunate at all." Janet smiled. "Let's go get Danica Roem elected. If we can get this right, we'll have something major to celebrate in just a few days."

Their precincts weren't far away. Abby and Janet climbed in with Linh and their driver, who turned out to be a local volunteer, and it was only mildly embarrassing when Linh started gushing about how exciting it was to meet the author Abby had been obsessed with all year. Janet was nice about it of course, and too soon, it was time to say goodbye.

"Now, Abby..." Janet lowered her voice as she climbed out of the car, so the others wouldn't hear. "I wouldn't normally say anything about this, but since it seems important to you—it's true that when I wrote the book, I envisioned Paula and Elaine staying together for the rest of their lives."

"You *did*?" Relief flooded Abby, tears pricking behind her eyes. "That's exactly what I was hoping you'd say. Thank you so much."

"Still, if I were to rewrite it, I'm not sure I'd make that decision." Janet's lips curved up in a slight apology. "Love is wonderful, but change can be wonderful, too. There are a lot of different routes to happily-ever-after."

"Abby!" Ethan's voice was shrill behind them. "There you are! Come on, Ben won't let me do enough of the knocking!"

"That's totally not true," Ben called. "He's knocked on every single door. He's only sad I wouldn't let him tap-dance at the last house."

"That guy would've liked a tap dance! Abby, tell him. It

was this old guy, and he kept saying I reminded him of his grandson, and I asked if his grandson was a tap dancer, and—"

"I get it. Sorry, dude." Abby gestured to Janet. "This is my kid brother, Ethan. Ethan, this is Ms. Smith. She's a famous author."

"Nice to meet you, young man." Janet shook his hand just as warmly as she had Ms. Sloane's. "Now, we ought to get to work. It was lovely talking with you, Abby."

As the car pulled away, Abby tried to imagine writing a book that was good enough to show to Marian Love. She wanted to think she could do it. Someday.

Maybe that would be Abby's happily-ever-after.

The rest of the GSA wasn't far away. Ms. Sloane smiled at Abby when she joined them, but she didn't ask her any questions, which was a relief. Abby wanted to tell her everything Janet had said, but not right now. She wasn't sure she could talk about it without getting emotional again, and they had doors to knock on.

She teamed up with Ethan, and the two of them took turns going through the script at each house. Ethan did a lot better than she'd thought he would, and Abby found that asking strangers their opinions and reminding them to vote was actually kind of fun. Plus, it felt *really* good to think they might actually make a difference in the election results.

As they crossed the street to the next block, Abby's phone buzzed. Mom was asking when they'd be home. As Abby typed out a quick reply, Ms. Sloane came up alongside her.

"How are you and your brother doing so far?" Ms. Sloane glanced down at the scribbled notes on Abby's clipboard.

"Pretty well. No haters yet, and Ethan convinced two different women to sign up to volunteer."

"Nicely done." Ms. Sloane smiled at Ethan. He smiled

back and veered away to tell Ben something. "By the way, Abby, I've been meaning to ask you. Would it help if I gave you a set of deadlines for the first drafts of your college application essays?"

"Sure. How about Monday for the first one?"

Ms. Sloane raised her eyebrows. "That soon?"

"Yeah. I'm feeling kind of inspired."

And she was. Because…maybe Janet was right. Maybe change could be a good thing, sometimes. Even if it hurt.

Marian Love had written a romantic, happy ending for Paula and Elaine, but it hadn't turned out that way for her and the woman she'd loved. Still, Janet seemed satisfied with how her life had gone. She hadn't needed a permanent, fairy-tale love to make it worth living. She was strong enough to be happy on her own terms.

Maybe Abby was strong enough, too.

They knocked on doors for the rest of the morning, took a quick break for lunch at a nearby Wendy's and knocked on more doors all afternoon. They signed up a dozen more volunteers, and Abby was sure they'd convinced at least twenty people who'd been on the fence to turn out and vote for Danica on Tuesday.

By the end of the shift, Abby was happy, too. In fact, she couldn't remember the last time she'd felt this good.

When she and Ethan got home that night, the house was quiet. Ethan trudged straight upstairs to bed, but Abby took out her laptop and set it up on the kitchen table. She'd meant to start the college essay she'd told Ms. Sloane about, but as she was waiting for the blank document to open, the beginning of a new story crept into her mind. A new character, too—a girl named Hannah Love.

Abby let her fingers wander over the keys, waiting to see what came.

Hannah used to think she knew exactly what she wanted.

She used to lie in bed at night, dreaming of the day she'd fall in love. She'd been sure that once she really, truly loved someone, everything else in her life would fall into place. Love meant never being unhappy again.

She knew better now. Love was great, but it wasn't everything.

Flowers and flirting and kisses—they were fun, but they weren't what made the world go around. Sex didn't, either. Not by itself.

You didn't have to be in love for your life to matter. Maybe all you needed was to care about someone. Or even something. Caring might not make the world go around, either, but maybe it was enough to at least give it a push in the right direction.

Hannah hoped it was. Because she was done with the endless waiting to find that elusive, perfect love...but she knew she would always care.

★ ★ ★ ★ ★

WHO'S WHO AND WHAT'S WHAT

The fictional authors writing within the world of *Pulp* are:

Janet Jones, later to be known as **Janet Smith**, better known to history by the pen name **Marian Love**.
Claire Singer, also known by the pen name **Dolores Wood**.
Kimberly Paul, a pen name shared by several authors.
Abby Zimet (no pen name yet, but give her time!).

These are their books and characters (all of which are equally imaginary):

Women of the Twilight Realm, by Marian Love (working title: *Alone No Longer*), starring Paula and Elaine.
A Love So Strange, by Dolores Wood, starring Sam and Betty.
A Deviant Woman and *Voluptuous Vixens*, by Kimberly Paul, starring an array of forgettable characters.
Totally Normal Women in the Daytime, by Abby Zimet (working title: *The Erotic Adventures of Gladys and Henrietta*), starring Gladys and Henrietta.

But the other books mentioned in *Pulp* really DO exist.
The following books were real lesbian paperback novels published in the 1950s and 1960s, and they're still available in print and ebook form in the US and many other countries today. Check your library!

> *The Beebo Brinker Chronicles* (1957-1962) by Ann Bannon (five-book series); later adapted into a play by Kate Moira Ryan and Linda S. Chapman.
> *The Price of Salt* (1952) by Patricia Highsmith, originally published under the pen name Claire Morgan; later adapted into the film *Carol*.
> *Spring Fire* (1952) by Vin Packer, pen name for Marijane Meaker (who also writes as M. E. Kerr).
> *Women's Barracks* (1950) by Tereska Torrès.
> *The Girls in 3-B* (1959) by Valerie Taylor.
> *The Third Sex* (1959) by Artemis Smith.
> *Twilight Girl* (1961) by Della Martin.

The following books mentioned in *Pulp* were also real, but you may not be able to find copies of them as easily. Many of the best ones are excerpted in the terrific compilation *Lesbian Pulp Fiction: The Sexually Intrepid World of Lesbian Paperback Novels 1950-1965*, edited by Katherine V. Forrest, which is a great place to start if you're interested in exploring this genre. Also check out *Strange Sisters: The Art of Lesbian Pulp Fiction 1949-1969* by Jaye Zimet, which collects many of the best lesbian pulp covers.

> *I Prefer Girls* (1963) by Jessie Dumont.
> *Warped Women* (1956) by Janet Pritchard.
> *When Lesbians Strike* (1965) by Frank G. Harris.

My Wife the Dyke (1965) by Rick Lundeen.

Dormitory Women (1954) by R. V. Cassill.

Woman Doctor (1962) by Sloane Britain.

Strange Sisters (1962) by Robert Turner.

In the Shadows (1962) by Joan Ellis.

Edge of Twilight (1959) by Paula Christian.

The Mesh (1951) by Lucie Marchal.

Satan Was a Lesbian (1966) by Fred Haley.

ACKNOWLEDGMENTS

My first encounter with lesbian pulp fiction came when I stumbled across a magnet featuring the gorgeous cover of *I Prefer Girls* in a gay bookstore in the 1990s. I was thoroughly captivated by the image, so much so that I bought the magnet without having any idea of what it actually represented and proudly stuck it on my dorm-room fridge. It wasn't until years later that I learned lesbian paperback fiction had been an actual literary genre, and that it had been incredibly significant in the lives of many queer women in the middle of the twentieth century.

When I finally read my first lesbian pulp novel, *Spring Fire* by Marijane Meaker, I was astonished. I'd known, of course, that queer women lived in this era—we've been around since the dawn of time after all—but I'd had no sense of what life was actually like for lesbians in the early 1950s. And it wasn't until very recently that I learned much about the mass expulsion of gay, lesbian and bisexual employees from the federal government, a long-running purge that became known as the Lavender Scare.

The height of the Lavender Scare also came in the 1950s, coinciding perfectly with the rise of lesbian pulp fiction, which tells you a lot about the many contradictions of that era. It was a time when no one talked about "coming out," since for the vast majority of LGBT people, living openly simply wasn't an option. It was a matter of course that your relationships would never be legally recognized, that having children with a same-sex partner was next to impossible, and that you could be fired or evicted for your sexual orientation (you still can today, by the way, in twenty-eight states—and in twenty-nine states, you can be fired or evicted because of your gender identity). In the 1950s, being queer meant constantly looking over your shoulder and coming up with new cover stories, just in case anyone got too curious about your life.

And yet, during this same period, lesbian pulp novels sold millions of copies, and the queer bar culture thrived. The longing for community, for developing connections with people who understand you, has always been powerful. So it's no surprise that so many of the queer women who stumbled upon the scandalous covers of paperbacks like *Spring Fire* and *Odd Girl Out* in drugstores, bus stations or newsstands latched on to these books. In many cases, they were the only representation those readers had ever seen of women like them.

I learned so much in the process of writing *Pulp*, both about the tremendous challenges this era presented and about the long and vital tradition of queer authors and publishers creating stories about queer characters. It was wonderful to immerse myself in this story. But I knew from the beginning that I couldn't do it on my own.

The legendary pulp author Ann Bannon was kind enough to read an early draft of *Pulp* and offer her feedback, and I'm more grateful to her than I can express. Her notes on my draft were a true gift, and I only hope the finished book honors her work and that of the other authors who defined this genre. Thank you, Ann, for everything you've done for queer readers.

Thank you to Katherine V. Forrest, the incredible author, editor and educator whose anthology *Lesbian Pulp Fiction: The*

Sexually Intrepid World of Lesbian Paperback Novels 1950-1965 was enormously helpful to me in the writing of *Pulp*. I was also lucky enough to have Katherine as the faculty member for my genre fiction workshop at the Lambda Literary Writers Retreat for Emerging LGBTQ Voices several years ago, and her insights into the writing process were infinitely valuable. Thank you, Katherine, for connecting me with Ann, and for sharing so much wisdom with me and other newbie writers.

Thank you to my editor extraordinaire T. S. Ferguson, who's believed in my work from the beginning, and who always encourages me to push myself. And thank you to the rest of the team at Harlequin TEEN/Inkyard Press for helping to put this book out into the real world: Laura Gianino, Nicole Rokicki, Gina Macedo, Linette Kim, Bryn Collier, Evan Brown, Krista Mitchell, Kathleen Oudit, Shara Alexander and so many more. Thank you, too, to Chris Arran, the immensely talented illustrator behind that gorgeous portrait of Abby on the cover.

Thank you so much to my amazing agent Jim McCarthy (no relation to the late senator, fortunately) for saying "YES, please. Do that one!" when I first told him about my idea for *Pulp*, and for being with me every step of the way in this odd and awesome journey. I honestly have no idea how I'd do this otherwise.

Thank you to my astonishingly helpful fellow authors who read early versions of *Pulp*: Nicole Overton, Katherine Locke, C. B. Lee and Kaitlyn Sage Patterson, this book is so much better because of your savvy. Thank you so much for digging into the drafts and helping me figure out what worked and what didn't. And thank you to Lindsay Smith, who drove through a pounding rainstorm while helping me brainstorm a detailed subplot involving Russia that ultimately wound up on the cutting room floor (though someone who isn't me should totally write that book—hint, hint, Lindsay!), and to the rest of my wonderful DC writing community for commiserating over drinks and panels and movies and general awesome writerly social-ness.

Thank you so much to all the heroic librarians, teachers and booksellers I've been fortunate enough to meet and talk to over the past few years. You guys are the ones putting books into the hands of the young readers who need them, and we're all so grateful to you for it.

Thank you to the fabulous team behind Autostraddle.com, without whom this book would not exist. (Literally. The premise of *Pulp* was directly inspired by an Autostraddle post from 2013.)

Thank you to my family for always encouraging my love of literature and history, and for creating a household where reading was always the number-one leisure activity, whether it was *The Baby-Sitters Club* or Jane Austen.

Thank you to Darcy, for providing constant creative inspiration via your frequent song compositions, whimsical sentence structures and impossibly sunny smile. I hope you still love doing your penguin walk and making up lyrics about ceiling fans when you're old enough to read this book.

And finally—I set out to write a book about the joy of the writing process, but somewhere along the way it also decided to be a book about the nature of love. So thank you to my wife, Julia, for listening patiently every time I sat down at the dinner table and said, "Can you believe this bizarre thing I learned in my research today about vice squads/pomade/ the history of carbon paper?", for entertaining our toddler while I reoutlined this book for the seventieth time (and the seventy-first and the seventy-second…), and, most of all, for being the reason I know enough about love to write about it in the first place. You're my very favorite.